Assa's Eggs

Assa grew up in an enchanted land, believing she would become a teacher and perhaps marry and have children of her own. Though this was not exactly a preordained fate, it was certainly a time-honored outcome for a woman in her place and time.

Assa's parents were loving and kind to her. She was an only child and therefore susceptible to being spoiled, but her parents were also aware of the dangers inherent in Assa's circumstances and sought to mitigate them by making sure Assa had productive work during her childhood. She helped her mother and father in their mill which produced flour for the local bakeries in their small town.

They lived on the edge of the sea, on a rocky coast near a craggy bay. Townspeople went out onto the sea to catch fish and other sea creatures.

The king and queen of Assa's land were kind to their subjects and did not tax them excessively. Indeed, one could petition the royal couple to be exempted from taxation and such audiences were taken seriously. The petitioner's request was accorded solemn attention and as often as not, the burden was reduced, if not always erased. One had to have a good reason such as disability or infirmity or a large family to support, and one had to re-petition each tax year, but such burdens were not too excessive for many petitioners.

In addition, the royal couple was quick to maintain the infrastructure of the land, allocating resources to maintaining roads, keeping dragons at bay, and supporting the army and navy in their efforts to protect the land from foreign aggression.

One might say that Assa lived in an idyllic world, and that her future was bright and secure.

That is, until one morning, when Assa was sixteen and her mother informed her that word had gone forth from the royal palace that the queen had died in the night. Assa's mother delivered the news with a solemnity Assa had not witnessed before. That day a solar eclipse shadowed the land and to Assa the shadow, in its way, never left the land or her life, because, though the sun returned from behind the moon, the carefree way of living never did.

The king, so it was reported, went into seclusion. He entertained no visitors and saw no petitioners. His children, two young sons, were loosed upon the land and they were both malicious and dangerous. They vandalized at will and bullied whenever possible. The king's advisors tried to lift him out of his depression but he would have none of it. It was said he stayed in bed all day ordering elaborate meals be brought to him constantly. Some villagers with contacts to the royal court reported that he ate upwards of twenty pounds of game a day and had nearly doubled his weight.

In Assa's village by the sea, there were murmurs of discontent. The king had a right to grieve, but he had responsibilities to the land and his people. If he did not come out of this depression, the land would continue to deteriorate and people would be forced to leave it and establish their lives elsewhere. Assa knew of at least three families that were either building boats with which they could sail away, or were fixing up old boats to make them seaworthy.

A mass exodus was in the offing.

Without strong and steadfast leadership, the land began to deteriorate. Funds were not allocated. Roads were allowed to fall into disrepair. Officials charged with maintaining order took to extortion and bribery as a way of holding the people hostage and lining their own pockets. They knew no retribution would come down on them. Her parents were paid visits by some of these officials and they were forced to give up almost all of the mill's profits to them.

In the royal court, the officials charged with maintaining the health and integrity of the king were in a shambles. Nothing they tried revived the king's spirits. It was as though he had decided his land and his people no longer mattered. They presented the king with musicians and jesters to try to cheer him up. They took him outside and endeavored to get him to hunt game, one of his favorite activities, but to no avail. He would not pick up a bow, much less notch an arrow into it. They brought him counsellors, with the thought that if he talked through his troubles, things would get better. They did not. For a full year after the queen's death, the king, his heart broken, barely said ten words to anyone.

Finally, the advisors decided on a plan. They would find the king a new queen. Such a course of action involved delicate political maneuvering, since royal marriages, despite the evidence of the king's shredded heart, were not usually about love. They existed to bring two disparate lands and peoples together.

Emissaries traveled from the palace to many other lands, in search of a princess who would be suitable for the king. There were few such candidates because news of the king's depression had preceded the emissaries so that the parents of the princesses would have nothing to do with such a union. The emissaries were stymied by this fact several times.

Finally, on a small island off the coast of the king's land, an island which had maintained its independence with stubborn aplomb, they found, not a princess, but a queen who had, like the king of Assa's land, lost her mate.

It was not usually the case that a king married a queen, as custom decreed a male monarch should be wed to a princess, but the situation was unique and a unique solution seemed the best option. The emissaries made their case. If the queen agreed to meet the king, with the possible outcome being matrimony, it would be very advantageous to her little island. She would no longer be alone, as it were, a tiny dot in the ocean, but be allied with a mighty kingdom, one with resources to support her land and her people.

And what of my children? asked the queen. I have two daughters.

The emissaries nodded sagely. And the king has two sons, they said. It would be a blended family. Both parties would benefit from the support and the camaraderie.

The queen agreed that she would like to have more power. She went back with the emissaries to the king's palace.

What ensued in the following days has been the subject of much speculation. The king, it appeared, must have courted the queen and they must have taken to each other fairly soon, because less than a week later the queen sent for her daughters, who arrived with much fanfare. The king announced that he and the queen would be married in a month's time.

This caused all sorts of reactions around the king's land. People were relieved that the king seemed to have finally come out of his depressive state. The very trees and mountains seemed to brighten with the news. At least, that is how many of the land's inhabitants saw the situation.

However, as with all things, it was not completely marvelous. Many people were dismayed that the king had found a stranger to marry. No one knew anything about the queen. Her home, a small island in the middle of the ocean was so insignificant to the people of the land that no one knew where it was or anything about it.

Assa's parents talked about the situation with some caution, but mostly with a sense that here was news everyone could be happy about. They told Assa that with the king re-engaged with life, things would be different. He would again cast his benevolent influence across the land and should call off the thugs who were extorting money from them.

Assa could only hope that this was true. She continued to work at the mill. The two men who had been demanding money from them came around a week after the king's announcement, demanding from Assa's father a payment of cash. For the first time since the men began this behavior, he refused their demands. He told them they no longer had any authority and could not intimidate him any longer.

Assa was well and truly frightened by what her father said. She thought that perhaps the men would grow angry with him and attack him on the spot. Instead, startled by the reaction, they mumbled something about how next time he had better comply or there would be dire consequences, and then they left the mill.

Assa was relieved her father was not hurt, but she wondered if the men would return. That night, Assa and her mother and her father vowed they would not sleep. Instead, they planned to stay awake until dawn, guarding their mill against the possibility of the men returning, perhaps with torches to burn the place down. Assa and her parents were each armed with pitchforks. They were prepared to stab the men if they showed their faces.

I don't think they will be back, said Assa's father to Assa and her mother, but just in case, we should be prepared. We will each station ourselves on the perimeter of our property. Should we see anything of the men approaching us, we must shout to the sky as loud as possible and call the others to us. We will not allow them access to our property and we will stab them with our pitchforks as they would deserve no less from us. Do we all understand?

Assa and her mother nodded at Assa's father. Then, as the sun began to set, they took up their positions around the mill. Assa held her pitchfork in her hands. The weight of the instrument was unfamiliar to her, but it felt right in her hands. She did not know if she could use it as her father intended, but hoped that if it came down to her life or the thug's life, she would dispatch the scum with gusto.

The sun dropped in the sky and touched the ocean. It sunk out of view and darkness began to cloud her vision. She heard her father shout to the sky. Is everyone safe and ready?

Assa called back. Safe and Ready!

Her mother also shouted to the darkness: Safe and Ready!

Assa's senses were on high alert. She heard sounds she had never heard before: birds rustling in the trees, bats flicking in the air above her, the wind magnifying the sound of the leaves on the trees. The very stars above her seemed to radiate sound: they crackled slightly, like insect wings buzzing in the air. Her hands and arms began to tremble from holding the pitchfork in the air. She stuck the tines into the ground to give herself some relief. If she needed the instrument, it would be there.

Every half hour or so, her father called to his family and they answered back.

Assa heard the waves of the ocean crashing against the beach in the distance. She saw meteorites streak against the sky, leaving white gouges in the blackness that gradually dissipated and finally disappeared. She imagined taking a scythe and swinging it against the belly of one of the brutes that had been extorting her family. She pictured the blood welling up like the meteorite trail.

The image disturbed and thrilled her at the same time. It was wrong to kill, wasn't it? And yet, her family was, this night, here and now, prepared to do this wrong.

A creature, somewhere in the woods beyond the mill, snapped a branch. The sound was like an earthquake in Assa's head. Was that man or beast? She didn't know. She grabbed the pitchfork from the ground and raised it high so that the tines faced forward. She shouted to the night: I hear something! Father, Mother, come quickly.

Assa knew she should wait for her parents, but the thrill of a possible confrontation was too enticing. She took a step forward, away from the property. Her parents answered her call: We'll be right there. But Assa did not wait. She hesitated only another instant, then sprang forward, running full speed toward the edge of the woods that began just on the other side of their property.

The ground beneath her feet was uneven and several times she thought she would turn her ankle. She did not, however, and within seconds was upon the shrubs edging the mill property. However, she was so filled with adrenaline and the excitement of possibly spilling blood, that she did not stop and simply kept running. She put her pitchfork out in front of her, holding it like it was a giant fork and she was attempting to snag the biggest meal ever.

An animal growl, off to the side, made her hair stand up on end. She stopped and swung her pitchfork around to face the sound.

She took in great breaths of air. It was cold and bracing. Her lungs hurt and her limbs ached beyond anything she had ever experienced before. Her entire being was electric with dread and excitement. It was as though some being had invaded her body and pushed out her normal personality. She felt the air pressing on her skin. The very cells of the leaves and tree limbs around her fairly crackled and simmered with a sound so loud she thought her ears would split. The handle of the pitchfork, clutched in her fists, seemed heavy and the grain of the wood felt like it was carving itself into her skin.

Another snap of twigs, this time from the other side. She was supposed to call out to her parents, so that they would run to her and lend support. Three was stronger than one, after all, but a peculiar need for a solitary confrontation overcame her. She kept silent, if only to keep her ears open to the possibility of more noise from the unknown source. She half expected the intruder, whoever it was, to spring up and fall upon her at any moment.

Assa gathered her wits about her, took one deep long breath, held it, then released it slowly, and shouted to the night around her, an incoherent cry of exaltation, with a good chance that it would be the last sound she would ever utter, and ran toward where the snapping sound had been.

She stepped over cushiony moss, around branches and advanced with fierceness, brandishing her pitchfork in front of her, ready to use it on whatever was daring to invade her home.

She ran for several seconds, encountering nothing.

She stopped and spun around. The tines of her pitchfork clanged against a tree: curious sound, like the tissue of the tree was tuning up for a song.

She pricked her ears to the night. She thought she could almost hear the sizzling of the stars in the sky above her, but no more sounds from the woods.

A few seconds later she heard the footsteps of her parents, running toward her. They crashed through the woods and were upon her in no time.

Are you all right? they asked, breathless.

I'm fine, said Assa.

We heard your call, said her father. What did you see?

Nothing, said Assa, I saw nothing.

Her mother held Assa's face between her palms. Child, she said, what happened?

There was something here, said Assa. Then it was gone.

The three of them stood in the darkness for several seconds, listening. Then Assa's mother spoke. I think maybe you are attuned to the spirits, she said.

THE NEXT FEW weeks changed everything. Word spread over the land that the king was happy with his new queen. The royal couple's children all got along very well indeed. Their blended family was like a tonic of good feeling and warmth. They filled all the inhabitants of the king's land with joy and merrymaking.

Many of the extortionists were found out and publicly executed for their wickedness. Assa's parents felt uneasy about such a course of action. They thought that perhaps a lesser punishment would have been more appropriate, but Assa did not agree. They were the lowest form of life, she said, bent only on furthering their own fortunes with no regard whatsoever to the welfare of others.

Her parents could not disagree with Assa's assessment, but still favored a retribution that did not dispatch the miscreants to the realm of death.

Assa stated her support for the action once more, then fell silent on the subject. She was learning that people can love each other without agreeing on everything.

Meanwhile, as if the land itself approved of the royal household, crops grew with unprecedented fecundity. Couples across the land began making children again. A general buzz of activity and prosperity was everywhere. When the new crop of grain came in, the mill was overwhelmed. Assa and her parents worked day and night turning the grain into flour for the land. People wanted to make loaves of bread and cakes and biscuits and cookies. It was a glorious time.

Assa asked her parents a couple of times about that night with the curious sounds in the woods. She wanted to know from her mother what it meant that she had some connection with the spirits.

Some people have an affinity for ghosts, said her mother. I think you were so excited that night that you heard ghosts. You experienced a contact with the spirit world. My grandmother had the same thing. She spoke about hearing the spirits.

What about you? asked Assa. Have you ever heard the spirits?

No. And neither did my mother. It's not a common thing, but it can run in families even if it sometimes skips a generation or two.

Assa nodded. She liked that she seemed to have this power, but she wasn't sure exactly what she was going to do with it.

For the moment, she let it be and spent her days helping at the mill and taking her lessons at school. And it was at school that she first heard of a new crisis on the land. One of her schoolmates told her that the queen's children were homesick and wanted to go back to their island.

At first, Assa did not believe this. Didn't everyone know that the children were supremely, deliriously happy in their new home? Didn't everyone agree on this? Wasn't it completely true?

Other students at school corroborated the story of her classmate. They said they had heard things from their parents. The children were not of this land. They did not find contentment in the woods and fields and rocky shore here. They longed for the sandy island where they grew up.

Assa took this information back to her parents, who listened with interest.

Such things happen, said her father. They will be homesick, surely, for a while, but they will get over it.

Assa's mother looked doubtful. Some things, she said, cannot be fixed with time. They require a more drastic remedy. The children may have to return to their island.

Assa's father nodded, reluctantly. If such a thing occurs, he said, then the king will be sick at heart, and our land will be plunged into despair again.

Assa listened to her parents speak of their land descending into chaos again and she was afraid for herself and everyone else in the kingdom, but she tried to keep an optimistic outlook on her life. After all, she was still a young woman, not quite grown up yet. It was to her advantage to maintain a sunny disposition. Everyone said this was true. Everyone knew that if you kept a light heart, you would be more likely to have a good life.

Assa believed this with all her being. She saw it in her parents. They were humble people, but they often said they were the luckiest people in the world because they had their health, and meaningful work, and Assa. They really couldn't ask for anything more.

ASSA SPENT THE next year absorbed in her studies. She wanted to learn everything she could about the world, but she soon found that the facts and figures, the dates and biographies that existed in the books she studied at school were less than she could have hoped for. There was something sterile about them. She took to walking the beach near the mill. The great ocean brought the energy of the depths and the expanse of water in incessant waves that some found monotonous, but Assa found to be very comforting in its constant power. The ocean never rested, and never wavered. This was a miracle, Assa was sure of it.

When she had her fill of the beach, she climbed the rock that rose out of the coast on the edge of the bay. From there she surveyed the round inlet of water. Three rocks rose out of the center of the bay. The townspeople thought of them as people. They stood like sentries, guarding the town from the ocean, or so it seemed. On the other side of the bay, a small harbor sheltered a few fishing boats. They went out most days and returned with their holds full of fish, which the locals ate and traded with other towns. Many came to Assa's town for the dried seafood and left very happy.

As Assa stood on the point of rock at the entrance to the bay, she tried to see the world for what it was: a rock covered in some places with water, since that was plainly what was before her. Yet, she could not make herself believe the world was so simple. All kinds of creatures roamed the rock and lived in the water. Wasn't that the world, too, just as much as the physical elements?

And what of the spirits that her mother spoke about? Where were they? Did they live in people, or did they float around in the air? Or were they in the rocks? Did anyone know?

Assa had not repeated the experience she had the time she was guarding the mill, so Assa doubted her mother's belief that Assa had powers of perception regarding the spirit world, whatever that was. But then, she had not repeated the experience of terror she felt on that night. So maybe she had to be terribly frightened to contact the spirits? It seemed a strange way to arrange the world. Shouldn't people have communication with the spirits all on their own? Why would an unpleasant emotion have to be in place beforehand?

It all whirled around in Assa's head.

Sometimes she went back to the spot where she had felt the odd sensations that her mother believed to be contact with ghosts. She tried to bring back the fear as she stood on criss-crossed piles of branches and matted layers of leaves. The birds sang out in the trees above her. They made it impossible to call in the terrible fear. They were so sunny and cheerful.

Assa called back to them, then laughed. Who needed the spirit world, anyway? Not her. Not if it meant that she had to remove herself from the joy of the world as it was here and now.

As the months went on, the rumors of the royal family grew more and more dire. The children, it was said, had grown quarrelsome with each other. The king's sons wanted the queen's daughters to be more like themselves. They required them, so it was said, to eat the food of the new land, wear the clothes of their new land, and behave in manners appropriate to their new land.

The daughters refused to do so. They begged their mother to take them back to their island. They threw temper tantrums. They destroyed their rooms, throwing things about and making a general mess of everything. They screamed at night with sorrow and grief. Those living closer to the palace heard them, and said it was a terrible sound, like the dying wails of slaughtered animals.

Assa doubted that. She thought they must be exaggerating, until one night when the sea was calm and the air was still with the absence of wind, Assa heard piercing wails cut through the night. They made the hairs on her arms and neck and back stand up.

It was a terrible sound, and then it came again. There were two of them, intertwined in the night, like some horrible death song that floated above her and snaked into her ear. She immediately felt fear for herself, and the night in the forest when she protected her family's mill came back to her. She felt the spirits of the queen's daughters wrap themselves around her and squeeze her.

Assa rose from her bed and tried to run away from the sensations, but she could not. They were too closely wrapped around her. She ran from her room, through the house, and out the front door and into the night. She ran toward the edge of the mill's property and did not stop running.

The moon was full in the sky and illuminated the ground beneath her feet. She stepped here and there, sure-footed, but filled with terror. Somewhere behind her, so distant that it could have been from another world, she heard her parents call to her, but their voices were so small that they seemed no louder than mice.

She had no time for them. She could see no comfort in having them closer, so she increased her pace and soon broke out of the forest and was on the beach.

She ran across the sand and was soon splashing through the surf and wading into the waves. She had no idea why she was out in the water. It was dangerous to be on the ocean at night like this. One could lose one's footing and fall into the waves and drown. Everyone knew that. Everyone knew to stay away from the waves when it was dark. Assa knew it as well as anyone, but that didn't seem to matter.

She stood in hip deep water. The waves rolled past and around her, enveloping her in cold. It was as though the deepest and coldest part of the ocean wanted to take her down. She shivered. The wails that led her here seemed to increase in intensity. The sound was like another being under her skin, trying to drown out her true self. She fought against that, willing the sound to flee.

But the sound was agile and determined to go its own way. It seized her and tossed her on the waves so that Assa ended up face down, gulping water. She flailed wildly, until her hands and feet touched bottom and she gained a purchase on the sand and pushed herself to a standing position. But only long enough for a wave to come and knock her back down.

Confused and blind from the salt water stinging her eyes, she ended up sitting on the ocean floor and another wave tossed water on her and immersed her completely. She pushed off the floor and tried to reach for air, but the *presence* in her body twisted her around and pushed her down again.

She gathered all her strength and will and tried to run back to the beach, but was so confused that she did not know where the beach was. She screamed into the night air. The sound of her own voice mimicked the wails of the girls that had brought her to the water's edge in the first place, and now the sound seemed to have moved into her skull.

It wrapped itself around her brain and began squeezing. It felt like her head was trapped in some press bent on breaking her. She put her hands up to the sides of her head and held them there, covering her ears, but it was no good.

The wails snaked through her fingers. They slid under her palms. They kept coming and wound themselves even tighter around her brain.

She heard splashing, somewhere far off in the distance. It was as though she was recalling an old memory, though she knew that couldn't be true. She had no memory of anything like this happening to her. The splashing stopped and she felt arms holding her, supporting her, carrying her out of the water to the sand, where she was placed, gently, on the cold ground.

Shapes moved around her. Familiar shapes.

Assa! Her mother's voice. Assa! Child what happened to you?

Another shape—her father?—put a blanket around her and wrapped her up in it. Assa welcomed the rough feel of the cloth. It was something outside of her brain that she could hang onto.

Don't you hear the cries? said Assa.

We don't hear anything, said her father. Come on. We'll take you home. Warm you by the fire.

Her parents tried to get her to stand up, but Assa was too weak to move. She felt herself go limp as her mother and father tried to make her stand.

Eventually the sounds of the wails diminished enough for Assa to attempt standing up. She raised herself slowly, clutching the blanket close to her. Her teeth chattered and her skin trembled. She was so cold.

The wails were almost completely gone.

Assa's parents took her back home, but not through the woods, which they thought would be too treacherous. Instead they went north on the beach to the creek, and half dragged, half carried Assa along the banks until they reached their property. The paddles of the mill lapped at the water. Such a soothing sound. Assa welcomed it into her being as though it was the warmest of fires. She felt her whole body go soft, just listening to it, the way it seemed to whisper to her of everything she loved about living in her town.

Her parents were not inclined to slow down or relax. In fact, they seemed frantic with worry, as though they needed to get Assa inside the house and if they did not, something awful would happen.

Assa wondered, idly, what that something could be.

They deposited her, still wrapped in the blanket, on the floor in front of the fireplace. Assa's father put more wood on the fire, to get it roaring, while her mother rubbed her arms and legs vigorously, trying to get them warm, Assa supposed.

She didn't care. None of it mattered. All she wanted was sleep. She drifted into some semblance of oblivion, the world sliding off to one side, it seemed, while she held on, barely, a small case of vertigo stirring her belly and making her head dizzy. Sleep was just there on the other side of this feeling. All she had to do was reach for it.

A slap on her cheek startled her. She put her hand up to her face. Ouch, she said. Then she laughed. A small chuckle at first, then louder and more spirited, until she was laughing uncontrollably. Her mother grabbed her up from the floor and drew her close to her body and hugged her tightly.

Is she going to be okay? asked her father, still shoving wood into the fireplace. The flames were crackling now, and tall, like shimmering beings that wanted to wrap themselves around Assa, like her mother was doing. Assa wanted to put her hand out and feel the soft flames. She wanted them to consume her.

She just needs to get warm, said her mother. Once she's warm, she'll be fine.

As Assa slipped into sleep, she tried fighting the urge, but could not. She wanted to stay awake so she could listen to those screams. They felt right to her, like the universe was saying something she could understand for the first time in her life.

Assa slept for two days straight. When she thought about that time later, she always considered it a period of renewal. It was a time her body needed to be dormant so that she could build up her reserves of strength. At least, that is what she told herself it was.

Secretly, she thought what was more likely was that she needed to descend into the world where the spirits lived. That would be a time for her to find her true people. This was not something she wished to tell her parents. She was sure they wouldn't understand because she wasn't sure she understood either. How could her people be located anywhere but in her own town?

But during those two days of sleep, she had the most vivid dreams imaginable. They were of strange creatures, long and sinewy, thin and fluid. They floated in the world around her, like jellyfish in the ocean, and they seemed drawn to Assa.

In her dreams she reached out to them and felt their soft exteriors and interiors. She wanted to clothe them with flesh and skin; they seemed unfinished, like clay sculpture that needed to be fired and glazed. She tried to speak to them, and some sound came back, but not enough for her to understand.

When she woke up, her parents were hovering close to her. Their faces seemed alien and strange, at first. Then quickly slid into familiarity, as though their images had slotted into the section of Assa's brain that coded for normal.

You've been sleeping for days, said her mother. She smiled, but the smile was strained and tinged with fear.

Her father looked at her with an anxious expression, as though he thought she might explode at any minute. She saw they both had been through an ordeal and realized the ordeal was their worry about her.

I—don't know what happened, she said.

You ran out of the house like a crazy girl, said her father. Right into the ocean. We thought you were going to freeze to death.

Yes, said Assa, but I don't know *why*.

Her mother elbowed her father in the ribs. He kept his mouth shut.

All we care about now, said her mother, is that you're well. The rest did you good, I'm sure.

Assa nodded. I'm sure, too. I'm really hungry. Can I eat something?

Of course, of course, said her mother. We'll let you get dressed, then you can come have some food.

They left her room and closed the door behind them. Assa suddenly felt more alone than she thought was possible. She quickly tossed aside her covers and put on a shirt and pants and went to the table near the stove.

Her mother, busy at the counter, turned around and beamed at her. That was fast, she said. You have your energy back.

Assa went to her mother and leaned close to her and put her arm around her.

Oh, oh, said her mother. What's this? You haven't wanted to hug me like this for a long long time.

I just miss you, said Assa.

Well, said her mother, I'm right here. Don't worry.

Assa's father came in from outside, carrying a stack of wood, which he dropped next to the stove. That should be enough for breakfast, lunch, and dinner, he said, laughing.

Thanks, Dad, said Assa.

Her father looked startled. You're welcome, Assa, he said.

Assa sat at the kitchen table and her mother brought her a plate piled high with potatoes, sausage, eggs and biscuits. Assa dug in eagerly. Everything tasted better than she ever could have imagined.

Her parents ate with her, though their plates were more modestly laden.

When you're ready, said her father, I think it would be good for you to get back working. Your mother and I have talked it over. We think that whatever you went through must have been very traumatic, so we're not going to push you to work, but it would be good for you, we think. Take a day or two to get your bearings back, but then you should really think about working again.

Okay, said Assa, without elaborating.

All we're saying is it would be best for you, said her father. People are better off when they are doing something. I know I feel better with work to do. I think almost everyone does.

Okay, said Assa, again.

Her father started to say something more, but his wife put her hand on his arm and he stopped. He took a breath, then turned his attention back to his plate.

Assa felt bad for him. He didn't know what to do or how to talk to his own daughter. That must have been hard for him.

I'm okay, said Assa. Really.

Her parents both nodded at her.

Just as Assa was finishing her second helping of breakfast a knock came from the front door.

They all three looked up. Now who could that be? said Assa's mother.

Her father got up from the table and went to the door and opened it.

He returned a few seconds later. His face was pale. Behind him a large man, his belly surrounding him like a bag of flour, followed. His hair hung down to his shoulders and his feet were adorned with shiny red shoes.

Assa's mother put her hand up to her chin. Your majesty, she said. She started to get up, but the king of the land put out his hand.

No worries, he said. You don't have to bow down to me or anything. I hate that. Don't know why people think they need to do that.

It's because we're all afraid of you, said Assa.

The king laughed uproariously. Assa wasn't sure if it was a real laugh of if he was trying to appear jolly, one of the people. She had heard that the king liked to think of himself as not really a king. He was just a regular guy who happened to have complete control over all of the people of the land. Assa could hardly believe that adults could believe such a ridiculous thing, much less an adult like the king, who had grown up with his special place in society.

Your daughter is quite humorous, said the king after he had laughed his fill.

Would you like to sit down? asked Assa's mother.

Certainly, good woman, said the king.

Assa's father pulled out a chair for the king. He began to wedge himself between the chair and the table. Assa's father pulled the chair out even more, until there was a wide gap between them. The king finally plopped himself down on the chair. Everyone in the room heard it creak and and splinter, just the tiniest bit. Assa and her parents held their breaths, waiting for the chair to break. The king seemed oblivious to the possibility. His overflowing flesh hung off the edges of the chair like lava flowing out of a volcano and accumulating on the sides. The chair held. Everyone breathed a sigh of relief.

Would you like something to eat? said Assa's father. We still have some of our breakfast.

I have already eaten, said the king, but, if you insist, I could polish off your leftovers. He smiled broadly at the thought of food.

Assa's father went to the stove and began piling a plate. The king turned to Assa.

Good child, he said.

Assa felt her mother tense beside her. Assa looked at the king. Yes?

I have heard stories. You have some kind of connection with my step-daughters.

Connection, your majesty?

That's another thing, said the king. Don't call me your majesty. That's just another part of the role that I don't like. It makes me feel old and feeble.

What should I call you, then?

Try Robert, he said.

Okay, said Assa. What connection do you see between me and your step daughters? Robert.

Assa's father put down a plate heaped with food in front of Robert. The king rubbed his hands together, tucked a napkin under his chin, and began digging in. He ate with no manners whatsoever. At least, none that Assa could see.

He chewed with his mouth full, shoveling in food like he was feeding a hungry dragon, and generally made a mess of the table around his plate. Assa and her parents watched the proceedings with dumfounded shock. This was the leader of their people? A boorish everyman who plainly could not contain his appetites?

Robert cleaned his plate in less than a minute. Assa's father took the plate away, leaving an empty circle on the table in front of the king, surrounded as it was by remnants of bits of food.

The connection, said Robert to Assa, as though his ingestion of the meal had never happened, is grief. Do you understand grief?

Assa had heard the word, but never thought too much about what it meant. She understood it was a painful thing that people sometimes got when someone they loved died.

It's sadness, said Assa.

Robert slapped his hand on the table. Yes! he said. That's it. Profound sadness. Which you experienced just the other night, did you not?

Assa shifted in her chair. She wasn't sure that was sadness or grief. It felt more like craziness. Like she didn't know where she was or what she was doing. I heard your stepdaughters crying, she said. I think.

Oh, yes. They cry. They cry all the time. They are filled with grief. And do you know why?

Assa shook her head.

They miss their homeland.

Really? said Assa.

Robert nodded. Yes. It pains me to say it, but my sweet bride wants to take them away from this land and return them to their island. She says our union has not been good for them because it ripped them from their native land.

They don't know what to do on our soil. They miss the spirits of their soil. Do you understand any of this, Assa?

At the mention of spirits, Assa perked up. The step-daughters knew about spirits? That made her feel like maybe there was a connection. Perhaps she could be friends with them.

I bet, said Assa, that if they had more friends, they would forget about their island.

You *are* a clever child, said the king. But, alas, it is not so. We bring other girls to the palace all the time. They play together, but it does not assuage their grief. It is causing me all kinds of problems. I am consumed with their happiness. I want them to be happy, but I cannot make them happy. You can, possibly, understand how this makes me, a king, feel. I have taken to eating more than I should. You might not know it by looking at me, but I believe I have put on a few more pounds than I should.

Assa's mother spoke up next. Perhaps, your majest—er, Robert, you could bring the girls out of the palace and into the greater world. Maybe if they spent time on the soil of this land, they would become used to it.

Now I see where the child gets her smarts, said Robert. You are brilliant, as is your daughter, but, again alas, we have tried this, but the girls cringe from the ground as though it was poison. In truth, I have never seen or heard of such a thing as this. Don't all children love to play in the dirt? But they simply cannot bring themselves to feel comfortable on this land. My advisors have nothing for me. They speak of spirits that might help the girls, but don't how to conjure them. They have no experience in this area, you see. But you, Assa, I have heard you know of spirits. Is this not true? I come to you humbly, asking for your help. If the girls cannot be assuaged of their grief, they must return to their island, with their mother, and I will be bereft again, and the land will suffer, as before.

He looked at Assa, unblinkingly. His eyes looked watery, as though he was about to cry.

Assa had no experience with kings and queens and princesses. They were not part of her world and she never expected that they ever would be. And yet, here was the king, at her family's kitchen table, asking for her help.

She knew what was expected of her. Her parents had taught her well.

She was to stand before the king, bow slightly, or even curtsy, if that was her inclination, but in any case, offer some humble gesture toward the king, and then she was to say something like: whatever your majesty needs, I will be glad to provide it. But Assa did not want to do this.

For one thing, she didn't know exactly what the king wanted. For another, she thought the king was rather disgusting and did not want to spend time with or near him. Certainly no more time than was absolutely necessary. He smelled bad. That was the worst part. Maybe. Or it could have been how his massive body seemed to flow everywhere. Some parts of him looked like they were going to burst out of his clothing. It could also have been the breathing noises he made. They were loud gasping things, and seemed labored, like the air had to fight its way in and out of his body. And Assa did not even want to think about the other noises, the ones that seemed to come from his posterior at regular intervals. Assa thought the land must be in some kind of terrible shape if it depended upon the good graces of a man like Robert, disgusting creature that he was.

Assa did not say anything for a long time. The king had made a request of her and expected an answer. An answer in the affirmative. Assa's mother leaned close to Assa's ear. Do you need help with your reply? she asked.

Assa shook her head.

Your majesty, said Assa, I have always been taught that one must be respectful toward you, and I do not want to insult, but I do not want to help you in the way you have asked.

Robert's face registered surprise and anger. Assa thought, for one fleeting moment, that the king might strike her. His hand twitched at his side and his arm tensed up. He clearly did not know what to do with a subject who disobeyed him so firmly.

Well, he said. He looked up at Assa's parents, who were white as clouds. Your daughter is as obstinate as mine. Must be something with daughters, eh?

Assa's parents nodded.

Assa didn't see any reason to stay in the presence of the king. Robert, she said, I think I'm going to go do some of the chores that my parents would like me to do. It was very nice meeting you. I hope you and your step-daughters have a good life.

Assa got up from her chair and went outside. As soon as she was out of sight of the king, she put her hand over her mouth and ran for all she was worth along the creek. What had gotten into her? She could hardly believe she had said those things to the king. And refused his request! Wasn't that something she could go to jail for? She was sure of it. The king had the power to lock up anyone he wanted to and why wouldn't he want to now, after what Assa did?

She didn't get far with her running, though, before she ran right into a man and a woman, standing on the banks of the creek. Assa found herself flat on her bottom, with her hands behind her, stuck in the dirt. She felt more embarrassed than injured, and she scrambled to get herself up again.

The two adults in front of her were about the age of her parents. They looked quite menacing. Assa had never seen them before and by their fancy clothes, she was sure they were not from her part of the world. The woman looked really mean. Like she would as soon tear Assa in two as look at her.

Child, said the woman, I am your queen. Why do you run so quickly from your house? Did not my husband ask a task of you?

The man beside the queen did not speak. He looked tough and mean. Assa guessed he must be the queen's protection. She had heard that kings and queens needed to be protected from their people, since a lot of the people, or at least some of them, would like nothing better than to kill their majesties.

Assa did not have any thoughts in that direction, but decided that she could understand those who might.

Nothing to say? said the queen.

Um, said Assa. I—um.

Um, um, said the queen. Yes, and what does that mean, um um?

The king, said Assa.

Yes? said the queen.

He's—

What, child? What are you trying to say?

He's kind of gross, said Assa.

The queen's expression softened. She laughed. He's in mourning, don't you see?

Did someone die?

The queen shook her head. Not exactly. It's more that he is anticipating the loss of me and my step-daughters.

Loss? Assa began to feel more comfortable standing next to the queen, who reached out her hand and placed it on Assa's shoulder. Assa braced for the unpleasantness that this pressure would have on her, but it did not come. Instead, she felt quite warm toward the queen.

Her bodyguard, on the other hand, she could have done without. He kept staring at Assa, as if she might be an assassin. Did kings and queens go around all day and night afraid that they might get killed?

The king wants me help your daughters, said Assa.

Yes, and it appears you are not inclined to do so?

No, said Assa.

And why not?

The king kind of makes me sick.

The queen thought this over for a time. She appeared to be unsure of how to proceed with Assa, who was likewise in unfamiliar territory with the queen.

The thing to remember about the king, said the queen, is that he has a tender heart. He is easily broken. He eats to insulate himself from the pain of the world. Do you understand?

Assa shook her head.

You will, perhaps, when you get older. My daughters are causing him no end of grief. They must return to their own land, and me with them. That is why the king is broken-hearted.

As the queen talked, she slid her hand down Assa's back and gently guided her on a return walk to her own house. Assa hardly noticed that the queen had done this. She seemed so gentle, now, and understanding. Her whole attitude did nothing but calm Assa. She wanted to lean into the queen and feel her warmth and softness, just like she sometimes hugged her own mother. She thought that the queen's daughters must be very lucky to have such a mother as this woman next to her.

The bodyguard allowed them contact for only a few seconds, then he intervened by putting his hand between Assa and the queen.

Oh, I know, said the queen. I'm breaking the rules. But this is a child. A girl. She's no older than my daughters.

Nevertheless, your majesty, said the bodyguard.

The queen shook her head and removed her hand from Assa. I'm going to have to have a talk with my king about this, said the queen.

Very good, your majesty, said the guard, but until then I must discharge my duties according to his instructions.

Yes, yes, said the queen. I know, I know. She sighed. They continued walking in silence. A family of geese swam in the river: a mother and six goslings. The queen stopped to look at them. Assa stoped with her. They watched the geese for several minutes, neither of them talking. The body guard stood between them.

Sometimes I wish I was a bird, said the queen, finally.

I think that too, said Assa. Sometimes.

What do you think would happen if I took my daughters and left this land?

Assa knew what would happen. Exactly what happened before when the king was alone. Thugs would come to their house. Their town would be a terrible place to live again.

Are you trying to make me do something I don't want to do, so you threaten to make our land awful again? said Assa.

The queen hesitated. They told me you were a clever girl, she said. They were right.

Did they also tell you I conjure spirits? said Assa.

Of course, said the queen. My daughters know this. They sent me and my husband. They wanted to come themselves, but they are afraid to walk the land.

Assa followed the trail of the birds on the water. They left a wake behind them. The tiny waves spread out, crossed each other, and made a kind of checkerboard pattern on the surface. It made Assa think of the disruption of the land, how it had affected her family.

You could make me do anything you want me to do, said Assa.

Not anything, said the queen. I can't make you want to be the savior of your land.

The birds on the water began swimming in circles, agitated by something in the air. They spread their wings and in a frenzy of splashing water, they rose into the air and flew away.

I think we spooked them, said the queen.

They do that if you stop, said Assa. If we kept walking, they wouldn't have cared.

My daughters want to do that, said the queen. They want to fly back to their own land. I don't blame them. They are miserable here. Will you come talk to them? Will you be their friend?

Assa wished the king and the queen could find another way to make their family happy. She didn't want to be in the palace. She heard rumors about that place. It had all these dark rooms where ghosts and rats and who knew what else spent their time scaring people, especially young people like Assa. But the queen looked so upset, and she wanted so much for Assa to help her, that Assa couldn't say no.

Can my parents come with me? asked Assa.

Of course, said the queen. We'll bring you all to the palace in style.

The birds were a long way off now. They were only tiny dots against the sky and they made no sound.

Okay, said Assa. I'll do it.

THE KING AND queen went back to the palace, but they left several of their staff behind at Assa's house to assist her family in preparing for their visit. They were told what clothes they needed to wear, how to behave when they met members of the court, and even how to eat.

I think I know how to put food in my mouth, said Assa's father, who, as far as Assa could see, was thoroughly disgusted by the whole way he was being treated.

Don't make a fuss, said Assa's mother. We're doing this for Assa. And for the land.

It just seems to me, said Assa's father, that they could bring the girls here.

No, Dad, said Assa. Don't you get it? They can't leave the palace. They get sick when they walk on our land.

Assa's father just grew more grumpy whenever Assa mentioned the problem of the queen's daughters. He didn't believe such a thing was even possible.

It's ridiculous, he said. We walk on our land all the time. Wildlife walks on the land constantly. People are not going around all the time sick.

But they're *different*, said Assa. They don't come from here.

If you really can't stand all this, said Assa's mother, you don't have to come with us. Assa and I can go on our own.

Assa's father considered the possibility, but in the end decided he needed to be with his family. I'll go, he said.

Well my goodness, said Assa's mother. You are such a generous man to bless us with your presence. Can you also bless us with a minimum of grumpiness?

I'll try, said Assa's father.

The visit was to last three days and two nights. Assa was allowed to take one small suitcase. There were issues of people smuggling items into the palace, she was told by one of the representatives from the palace. Dangerous things. They had to be very careful, so they made sure visitors took in only a small amount of material.

Even though, said Assa, I'm being asked to come help the palace?

We take very precaution, said the representative.

Two of them offered to remain in the house, to keep it safe, while the family was in the palace.

Assa's father thought this might be a good idea, but Assa's mother did not. I don't want strangers in my home, she said. I don't know what kind of habits they have. I don't want them fiddling with our things.

But we should at least protect the mill, said Assa's father.

The mill will be fine, said Assa's mother.

Assa could see her father thinking this over. He wanted to object, but finally agreed with his wife. They would politely refuse the offer of help.

In the meantime they were given an itinerary and told to study it carefully. There are many formalities involved with a visit to the palace, they were told. You don't want to come across as ignorant country folk.

Assa bristled at those words, and she felt her parents' smoldering anger in the air as well. By the time they had been given their schedules, they had already been subjected to lessons on proper conduct, and proper ways of speaking. They were well and truly sick and tired of the whole enterprise.

I think, said Assa's father, that we are done with all this now. Leave our house, please, and let us get some sleep, and you all can come back in the morning and escort us to the palace. He said the word palace with a hint of disgust in his voice, as though he wanted to swear instead. In fact, the way he said palace made it seem like a swear word to Assa. She laughed as the palace staff hesitated, then bowed and retreated out the door.

Suddenly the house fell silent.

Glad to see them gone, said Assa's mother.

Do you think they are going to report us to the king and queen? asked Assa.

Report us for what? asked her father.

For kicking them out. They were only trying to help.

That kind of help we don't need, said Assa's father. Now you get to bed and get some sleep. We'll all be ready in the morning. By the end of the week all this will be over and we can get back to living our lives. Our simple country folk lives. He laughed.

Assa kissed her parents goodnight and went to her room and got into bed. She tried to sleep, but could not. She was too excited about tomorrow. For a girl to go to the palace was enough excitement. But for the queen to say that she held the fate of the land in her hands, that was almost more than she could bear. She got out of bed and went to the window and pushed the pane open so she could hear ocean, roaring in the distance.

It sounded more like a sigh or a whisper from so far away. It was a soothing sound. It made her think of how her mother sometimes told her she needed to appreciate what she had. It wasn't necessary to her happiness to always be thinking of something new and different.

Assa did not even know she was doing that, but her mother said she was. You stare at the stars, said her mother. I think maybe you think you can make a wish and the stars will grant them.

That wasn't it. Not exactly. It was more like thinking the stars knew something she didn't know. They were there for so long, they must have some wisdom that she didn't have. They must know things she would never know. And maybe they would tell these things to her. She would spend time with the stars. She liked that they were there, every night, making her feel good.

On this night, the stars were not so bright: The moon was out. Its light washed out the stars and illuminated the fields in the distance with a milky light. The creek flowed next to the house. The mill wheels turned and creaked. She liked the sound of them and she always liked being here. This was her home, after all.

Beyond the field the woods beckoned. She knew wild animals lived in those trees. She heard their calls and scampering at night. She sometimes thought the animals were the soul of the forest. They felt like the energy she sometimes felt in herself: like creatures in her body, moving around and taking up room.

Assa sometimes wished she didn't have those abilities. No one else did, after all, so it meant that she was some kind of oddity. Nothing wrong with being an oddity, but it made things difficult. Different. It meant she had thoughts and experiences that others did not.

And what about the queen's daughters? Were they oddities as well? Did they have powers from the other world?

She wondered what it would be like to be taken from the only home you ever knew and be told that you had to get used to another land. She didn't want to have to experience that. She shut her eyes and remembered the wails of the girls. How it made her run from the house.

A chill wind came through the window, raising bumps on Assa's arms. She closed the window and went back to bed. If the stars had something to say to her, it would have to wait.

In the morning, clouds had moved in and the sky was gray and menacing. There was every possibility that rain would come down on the land by the end of the day.

The palace assistants, apparently chastened by their dismissal the day before, waited until Assa and her parents had eaten their breakfasts before they came back to the house.

The journey will take a few hours, they told Assa. Are you prepared?

Yes, said Assa.

They were escorted out of the house and taken to a carriage that was waiting for them. A young man extended his arm to Assa, who at first did not know what to do, then she took it and stepped up into the carriage. She found it was much roomier inside than she had expected. There were two cushiony seats facing each other and even a small table between them, laden with bowls of almonds and figs. Her mother and father followed behind her and took the seat across from her.

Well, said Assa's father, this is ridiculous, isn't it? Do they really expect us to be comfortable in this cramped little thing?

Hush, said Assa's mother. Don't be such a grouch all the time. This is perfectly comfortable. I predict you'll be asleep five minutes after we get going.

Assa's father ignored his wife's remarks. Those horses look emaciated, he said. They'll tire out long before we get to the palace.

Shhhh, said Assa's mother. Do try to not complain so much. It's no fun to be around.

I only hope no one vandalizes our property while we're gone. Do you think it'll be all right?

It'll be fine. I said a blessing. Nothing will harm our home.

The carriage jerked forward. They all bumped themselves against the padded walls, and then they were off. The wheels of the carriage transmitted every rut and bump in the road directly into their back and posteriors. It was going to be something of a rough trip.

Dad, said Assa, did you see all the food?

Assa'a father looked at the bowls and nodded impatiently. Sure, sure, he said. Fruit and nuts. How imaginative.

Assa and her mother exchanged looks, then burst out laughing.

What? said Assa's father. What is so funny?

You are, Dad, said Assa. You are able to find the bad in anything. It's quite a gift.

Assa's father sniffed and shrugged his shoulders several times, as though he wanted to shake them loose of his arms. Yes, well, he said. It only seems to me that if the king and queen want to upset our lives, they could be more congenial about it.

Assa's mother patted her husband's back. There, there, she said, it'll all be over soon.

Assa smiled at them both, then turned her attention to the landscape passing by the carriage window. The trees seemed very close. She had never been on this road. She had never been very far from shore at all. Most of her life had been spent near the creek and the ocean. The vast territory inland was a complete mystery to her. She was ready to be dazzled by her new surroundings.

But instead she quickly grew bored with the monotonous landscape. She fought to keep her eyes open, but soon lost the battle and fell asleep with the rocking of the carriage lulling her to a state of relaxation.

In the next instant, so it seemed, the carriage bumped and skidded to a halt. Assa snapped awake. She raised her head from the seat cushion, where she had been resting, and saw her mother and father at the windows, trying to look outside the cabin.

What's going on? she asked.

Before they could answer, the door swung open and a woman poked her head inside. She looked to be about thirty or so and glanced at Assa, then turned her attention to Assa's parents. What's this? she said. I expected only her. He hooked a thumb in Assa's direction.

What are you doing? asked Assa's father.

The woman brought a knife around from behind her back and brandished it in the direction of Assa's father. I'm kidnapping your daughter, sir. It would be best for everyone involved if you did not interfere.

Assa's father and mother both moved, as one, toward the woman, springing forward and pushing her out of the carriage and onto the ground. Assa got up off the bench and went to the door where she saw the three of them sprawled next to the carriage. Assa's father had the woman's hand gripped and pressed to the ground, and Assa's mother stood up and was ready to kick the woman in the head, when others, four of them, swarmed over her mother and father and restrained them despite their struggles. Assa retreated to a corner of the carriage, but someone opened the other side and reached in and grabbed her from behind and pinned her arms to her back.

The first woman got up off the ground and made a dramatic show of dusting herself off. One side of her head displayed a line of red where blood had streaked down from a cut. Assa's parents struggled against their captors, but they were held fast. The ones restraining them were a mix of women and men. All seemed to be in their late 20s to-mid 30s. They were obviously a group that had been working as a team for some time.

Assa's captor pulled her out of the carriage and took her to stand next to her parents. Assa tried to twist around to see what happened to the driver, but she could not. She quickly determined that these men and women were not interested in harming her or her parents. If they did, she was sure they would all be dead by now.

Well, said the woman after putting her fingertip to her blood and tasting it. It seems you are full of spirit and energy. Very commendable, but it will not do you any good at all. As you can see, there are many of us and we are quite strong.

Assa, said her mother, are you okay?

I am unhurt, said Assa. She lifted one foot and brought it down on the toe of her captor, who yelped and pulled back her leg. Assa grinned.

You have inherited the rebelliousness of your parents, said the woman.

Who are you? asked Assa.

My name is Hoyal, said the woman. You may better know me as Princess Hoyal.

The king's sister, said Assa's father.

Hoyal bowed. The very one. Denied my proper place in the royal family by my corpulent sibling.

What do you want with us?

Not you, said Hoyal. Her. She pointed to Assa.

You can't take our child, said Assa's mother.

I can and I will, said Hoyal, but do not worry. I will return her to you unharmed within a week. Give or take. Now say your goodbyes and we'll be off. Be brief, please.

Their captors pushed them closer. Assa's father would not allow himself to look at Assa. His attention was still on Hoyal. Where are you taking her? he asked.

Ahh, said Hoyal. As much as I would like to oblige your request with an answer, I cannot. Her whereabouts will be secret, and then she will be at your door again.

This is ridiculous, said Assa's mother. Release us all at once.

Hoyal tapped her knife blade against her thumbnail. I have been more than patient, she said. You have twenty more seconds for any sentimental expressions you wish to execute. Then we will be off.

Assa's parents both began crying. They continued to struggle against their captors, but still to no effect.

I'll be okay, said Assa. These people don't want to hurt me. Or you.

Hoyal turned from them and looked to the trees on the side of the road, as though they held the secret of existence. Assa was not afraid, which surprised her. She kind of looked forward to being a captive of Hoyal. It would at least be less boring than being at the palace with the king and queen.

She and her parents did say goodbye to each other. Assa found herself embarrassed by the tears and the anguish. Her parents were so upset! It made no sense. Couldn't they see that she was going to be safe?

Hoyal turned around and bowed to Assa's parents. She took Assa by the arm and guided her to the door of the carriage. She didn't need to push her inside. Assa put her foot on the step and went inside. Hoyal followed and closed the door behind her.

I admire your attitude, said Hoyal.

Assa put her head to the window and looked outside just as the carriage jerked forward. She saw members of the royal party, the assistants who were supposed to get her to the palace safely, standing in a group looking lost and puzzled. Her parents were released from their captors. They ran after the carriage for a short time, then stopped running as the carriage picked up speed. They stood, red-faced, their chests heaving, and watched the carriage move away from them.

Assa felt her stomach flutter and her heart thump loudly in her chest. She was much more upset than she thought she would be. She watched her parents as long as she could. They stood in the road, hugging each other. Then they disappeared from view as the carriage rounded a corner in the road.

Assa took her seat again. She looked at Hoyal, who smiled back at her. In any other circumstance, Hoyal would have looked like a friendly woman. Here in the carriage, she just looked like what she was: a criminal.

Where are you taking me? asked Assa. Her voice cracked, which she instantly hated. She didn't want to display any weakness in front of Hoyal.

You'll find out. There's no need to cry, Assa. I won't hurt you.

You already have, said Assa as tears welled up in her eyes and she began sobbing.

Well, I suppose you'll need to get that out of your system. I know I used to cry, just thinking about how my stupid brother was king and I was nothing.

Assa curled up on the couch and kept crying. She felt so lonely. When would she ever see her parents again? When would she ever return to her home?

ASSA FOUGHT TO stay awake during the trek, but it was no good. She ended up sleeping most of the way. She didn't understand how she could be so tired just from getting kidnapped, but reasoned that it was a stressful thing to happen to someone, so it made sense that she would be weary. She was also hungry and she had a headache. She felt more depressed than she ever had in her life.

The carriage traveled on into the night and kept going through dawn and into the day. Hoyal slept sometimes as well.

A guard came in partway through the journey to keep an eye on Assa. She didn't say anything, even when Assa asked her questions about who she was and if she felt good about what she was doing. Hoyal didn't stop her from asking her questions. In fact, she smiled and looked like she was having a good time with Assa's curiosity.

You're quite a spunky girl, Assa, but I'm sure you already knew that.

And you're quite a wicked woman, said Assa in return, but I'm sure you already know *that*.

The guard was also the person who accompanied Assa off the carriage when she had to pee. They would stop by the side of the road and walk a short distance into the forest. The guard would stand near Assa while she squatted.

Assa tried running from the guard once, but it didn't work out. The guard was much bigger than her and Assa didn't get five steps away before her long strides caught up with Assa and the guard grabbed her around the collar and pulled her back, jerking Assa's neck and lifting her feet off the ground. The guard raised Assa and put Assa's ear next to her mouth.

If you don't ever try something like that again, said the guard, I won't tell Hoyal about this one time. If you do, I'll tell her you can't be trusted and things will go bad for you. Got it?

Assa nodded. The guard put her, gently, back on the ground. They returned to the carriage waiting for them.

Everything okay out there? asked Hoyal.

The guard nodded. Assa waited a beat, then nodded as well.

Good, said Hoyal. It won't be long now. Get some more rest, Assa. I want you fresh for when we get where we're going.

The guard looked at Assa. Stared at her, then turned her head slowly, like a bear might turn from a person before walking away, and she looked out the carriage window, watching, Assa supposed, the scenery going by. There was no other reason to look out the window, but Assa had long since given up that particular activity. There was no change. Mile after mile of trees with narrow trunks and green leaves. To think, she had once adored the idea of living in the forest. Not anymore. Much too boring.

Assa ate the food that Hoyal offered. Once or twice the carriage stopped and the driver got down from the top of the carriage and retrieved food supplies from a cache that had been left slightly off the road, out of sight, but readily accessible for anyone who knew it was there. They even stopped a few times and replaced the horses with fresh ones. Obviously this was not an impromptu operation. Hoyal and her cronies had planned this very well.

Approximately a full twenty-four hours after they began, the carriage came to a stop and Assa looked up from her sleeping position on the bench. Sunlight streamed in from the outside, bathing the interior of the carriage in a soft glow. Hoyal got out of the carriage and stood on the ground and leaned back in. Wait here, she said to Assa. Make sure she stays, she said to the guard, who nodded back with her customary silence intact.

Hoyal disappeared from the door and walked away from the carriage. They were no longer on the road they had been traveling. They had come to a meadow. Soft grass waved in the wind and wildflowers dotted the landscape with bits of blue, yellow, and red. Assa watched Hoyal cross the meadow and walk towards a structure on the other side of the meadow. It looked like a house built of stone. It was hard to tell how big it was, exactly, since it looked like some of it was hidden by the trees surrounding the meadow, but it certainly looked at least larger than her house. Hoyal went up to the building and opened the front door and went inside.

Assa leaned back on her bench. You are a wicked person, she said to the guard. Just like your leader, Hoyal.

The guard remained impassive.

When I'm free again, said Assa, I will find you and hurt you. I'll learn how to kill people and you'll be the first person I kill. Maybe the second, after Hoyal. You won't like the way I'll kill you, either. It'll be bloody and painful. Don't think I don't know about blood and pain. I slaughtered animals. I know how to do it. My parents taught me to be merciful, so I know what to do and what not to do. I'll make sure when I get to you and Hoyal that it won't be merciful.

The guard let a smile cross her lips. You're family are millers, aren't they.

Yes, said Assa.

Millers don't know anything about killing.

That's not true, said Assa. That's not true at all. Just last week I killed a bird. Did you?

Assa nodded vigorously. I *enjoyed* it too.

From what I heard, said the guard, you love birds. I don't think you would kill any of them.

But I don't love *you*. I *hate* you.

No you don't, said the guard. You're just tired. We haven't hurt you. You know we won't.

Assa truly did want to hurt the guard. She wished she had the strength of an adult. She would use that strength in ways she did not understand, but wanted to.

One day, she said, when I'm old enough and big enough, I will carve you up. Assa felt her voice rise. It sounded like someone else was using her mouth and vocal cords. The guard leaned toward her and went to put her hands on Assa's shoulders, but Assa scooted across the bench so that she pushed herself into the corner. She lifted her legs so the souls of her feet were pointed at the guard. She made fists and held them high enough so that the guard hesitated.

Don't be this way, said the guard. Don't be difficult. We're more than you and we're bigger than you. You're just a kid. Don't resist. You can't win.

My father says anyone can win, if they have a good strategy.

The guard chuckled. Is that why your family won against us? Because of your superior strategy?

Assa felt her legs begin to tire. Soon even holding up her fists was hard work. Her arms and legs began to tremble. The guard sprang forward and wrapped her arms around Assa.

Assa tried pushing herself away, but it didn't work. The guard was much too strong. She made a cocoon of her body, with Assa the worm inside of it. Once she stopped struggling, Assa found she was quite comfortable there. It reminded her of being hugged by her mother. She took in a great breath and let it out in a long sigh, and actually moved closer to the guard, trying to feel her softness.

Hoyal appeared at the carriage door. What was all that damned shouting? she asked.

The kid had an episode, said the guard.

Assa looked at Hoyal. She felt anger toward her, but she didn't want to hurt her anymore. At least not just then.

Hoyal studied Assa for a couple of seconds, then clapped her hands together. We don't have time for this, she said. The house is still safe. Let's get her inside.

The guard released Assa to her bench, stepped out of the carriage, then leaned back in and picked Assa up and maneuvered her out the door. Assa could have stepped out herself, but she suddenly didn't mind being carried out of the carriage and over the meadow. Hoyal and the guard walked quickly across the meadow and to the house. As they neared the door, she heard the sounds of girls shouting. Two of them.

Hoyal went first. She pushed the door open and stepped inside. The guard followed, and dropped Assa to the floor. She stood in the middle of the room and looked around. The floor was made of stone. The walls were stone as well. Above her, the ceiling was constructed of logs that had been stripped of their bark. A criss-cross of wood gave the impression of a spider web. There were some wooden furnishings: a few chairs, some tables.

At the far end of the room, a fireplace stood like a sentinel. It contained some charred wood, but had no fire in it at the moment. In front of her, a wooden staircase led to a loft. Two faces, girls about Assa's age, peered down at her.

Assa waved at them. They waved back.

Those are the queen's daughters, said Assa to Hoyal.

You're a clever one, said Hoyal. Now get upstairs. They'll show you their rooms.

What are you doing stealing kids? said Assa. And royal kids, at that. You're going to hang for this.

The king and queen don't believe in executions, said Hoyal. Besides, once they find out what I did, they'll give me a room in the castle for the rest of my life. Now get. Hoyal swatted Assa lightly on her behind. Get to know you're fellow captors. We'll bring you up some food in a minute.

Assa put her hand on the banister and slowly trudged up the stairs. Hoyal and the guard watched her. She felt their eyes on her, like they wanted to make sure she was really going up the stairs and not somewhere else. At the top, another guard stepped out of the shadows and put her hand on Assa's back and guided her around a corner. Then that guard retreated and stood at the top of the stairs. Once she turned the corner, she was in a medium-sized room that reminded her of her own room back at her own house. She felt like she wanted to cry.

She sat down on the floor and let the tears come freely. She sobbed and sobbed. The two girls who had looked down on her from above came to her and stroked her hair and hugged her and told her it was going to be all right. Don't cry, they said, it's not so bad. Our parents will come and get us. They'll save us any day now.

Assa did not believe a word they said. How could they know anything? They were children. They were the *royal* children who got kidnapped from the palace. Their *parents*, the king and queen of the land, could not prevent them from getting kidnapped by Hoyal.

But Assa did not say anything like this to the two girls. They were just as frightened as Assa was. Maybe more. Assa decided she was going to stop crying and try to be strong. After all, the two of them were not collapsed on the floor, helpless and pathetic.

She brushed her hair back from her face, wiped the tears from her eyes and put on a smile that didn't hold for long. The ends of her mouth tugged down and her lips started quivering. The girls laughed at her. Not in a nasty way, but enough for Assa to understand that she was kind of a funny thing, sitting on the floor drowning in tears. She started laughing too.

After a few minutes of this, they all three hugged each other and then sat in a small circle on the floor.

My name is Dawn, said the girl on the left, who sported blond curls and a light complexion and blue eyes. And this is my twin sister Dusk.

Our parents were so into nature when they named us, said Dusk. Her hair was dark and her eyes were black, and her face looked like she had been baking in the sun.

I had no idea the queen's daughters were twins, said Assa.

People don't believe it because we look so different, said Dawn. But it's true.

Who's older? asked Assa.

They both shrugged. We don't know. My mom won't tell us. She doesn't want one of us to think she's better than the other.

But, don't royalty have to know who's born first? asked Assa. Isn't it all about the oldest getting the throne.

Well, we're not older than the king's sons, said Dawn, so one of them will be king and then their kids will be the king or the queen, so it doesn't really matter.

Unless, said Dusk, we kill the king's sons. She made here eyes go wide and looked at Assa with a fiendish smile on her face.

Don't mind her, said Dawn, she likes to pretend she's evil sometimes.

I don't pretend, said Dusk, I *am* evil.

Oh please, said Dawn.

I'm ready to kill Hoyal, said Assa. And her guard.

Well sure, said Dawn, we all want to do things that we are never ever going to do. I'm just saying don't take any of that too seriously. When you've been princesses like us, you get to know a few things about the world. The first thing to know is that just because you want something now doesn't mean you're going to want it tomorrow. Or even in an hour.

Okay, said Assa. I'll wait a day before being absolutely *sure* I'm going to kill Hoyal.

Dawn's expression registered surprise and a little nervousness, Assa thought. How strange to think someone might be frightened of her. Especially a princess.

Dusk clapped her arm on Assa's back. There's my friend, she said. Ready and willing to get into the fight. Any fight. These people are going to die, you know. Once my parents get us back, there's no way they aren't going to be executed.

What do they want with us? asked Assa.

They think we have powers, said Dawn.

What kind of powers?

The kind that they think will help them take over the land.

What am I doing here?

They think you are connected to us. They think you can talk to ghosts. Just like us.

I don't talk to ghosts, said Assa. I hear them, but I don't talk to them.

Dawn and Dusk looked at each and smiled. Then they opened their mouths and began wailing. Assa was startled by the sound. She jerked her head back and put her hands up to her ears. What, what, she said.

Dawn and Dusk stopped. See, they said, that's what you heard the other night, isn't it?

It's exactly what I heard. You mean that sound was you?

The twins nodded.

But I thought I was hearing the sound of the land.

Not exactly, said Dawn. But sort of.

Yeah, said Dusk. See, we're completely homesick for our island. We can't stand it here. We're so sad so much of the time, that we end up crying and wailing. Those sounds go out on the land. Most people can't hear them, but some people, like you, can.

Why don't you like it here? asked Assa. I think our land is great.

And we think *our* land is great. What would you think if your parents took you from this land and put you on our island?

I don't know, said Assa. I've never been to your island. Maybe I'd like it.

But that's just it, said Dusk. You can *like* it just fine, but it doesn't mean you *belong* on it. The spirits of the island wouldn't be spirits of the land you grew up with. It's the same for us. The spirits of the island miss us. We miss them. We don't connect with the spirits here.

Dawn nodded vigorously. Without our real spirits, the ones from our own land, we're most likely going to die.

And that's why, said Dusk, we need to find a way back to the island. We've been trying to get our mother and the king to fight so she would take us back. It's been working, kind of. Then this. She spread her hands, indicating their current situation.

Assa tried to take in what the twins were saying, but it didn't make any sense to her. Spirits could not be that important. They were only strange things that hung around people. They weren't what kept you alive or anything.

So what does any of this have to do with Hoyal?

Well, said Dawn, that's something we haven't figured out. She thinks we can help her do—something. We aren't sure what.

They took me from my parents, said Assa.

Dawn rolled her eyes. That's not a big deal, she said. Parents suck.

Assa didn't know what to say to this.

You want to take a look around? asked Dusk. Assa nodded. Dusk and Dawn both stood up and Assa followed them into a room at the end of the hall.

This is where we sleep, said Dusk. Assa saw two beds on either side of the room. There were no decorations on the wall, or much of anything, really, except the two beds. A window on the wall between the beds showed the meadow. Assa looked through the window, which also had metal bars on it.

Dusk and Dawn stood beside Assa, and looked out at the world. I don't like these bars, said Assa.

We'll figure out a way to get them loose, said Dusk. Maybe tonight. Then we'll escape.

Assa stood on her tiptoes and tried to look down the house to the ground below. It's a long way down, she said.

We'll figure something out, said Dawn. Come on.

She grabbed Assa and they all ran out of the room, making as much noise as they could by slamming their feet on the floor. Assa laughed with Dawn and Dusk. They seemed to be able to have fun, even though they were trapped here. Was that something she should try to learn?

They dashed across the hall to a smaller room. It held one bed. This is your room, said Dusk. Assa looked at the bed. It wasn't a bad bed, not really. It looked like it was clean, and she didn't think it had any bugs. Not that she could tell, anyway. She had a window, as well, with bars. She felt sad just looking at the bars. She hated being trapped here.

Stamp your feet, said Dusk.

Yeah, said Dawn. They both started marching in place, making sure to drop their feet sharply with each step. Assa did the same. Soon the house began to shake with their movements.

Now run, said Dusk.

They ran from Assa's room to a bigger room across the hall. This one had a fireplace on one wall and a table with chairs. Also a bookcase with a few books. There was a deck of cards on one of the shelves, and a few rugs on the floor.

This is what they think a play room should be like, said Dusk. She rolled her eyes.

Another window, with more bars, framed the sky outside. Assa was drawn to the window. She stood in front of it and stared at the outside world. All she could think of was her own house and the creek that ran beside it, and the mill that ground the grain, and her parents. Where were they? Did the people who stopped her carriage let them go home? Did they want to go home? Were they looking for Assa right now?

Dusk and Dawn came and stood on either side of Assa.

You don't have to be so sad, said Dusk. It's not all that bad and it won't last long. Let's just have some fun, okay?

Assa opened the window by undoing the latch on the side and swinging the pane towards her. A cool breeze came into the room. She grabbed two of the bars and tried to twist them but they wouldn't turn. She pulled on them with all her might. She put her feet on the wall to gain some leverage and strained against the bars until she felt her face turn hot.

It doesn't work that way, said Dusk. We tried to pull them off when we first got here but they're stuck in the wall pretty good.

Assa heard steps outside the room.

Dawn put her finger up to her mouth. Shhhh, she said. Assa dropped down from the window and stood on the floor. Dusk swung the window shut and latched it just as Hoyal came into the room.

Could you girls be any noisier? she asked.

None of them answered.

Hoyal had her arms crossed in front of her, then she let them drop to her side. She still looked uncomfortable. Assa noticed this but made no comment. Hoyal did not like doing this. She did not want to be holding her or the twins captive.

It's okay, she said, we want you to have fun.

It's fun to be outside, said Assa.

Yes, said Hoyal. I know. But we can't allow that. It's for your own safety. There are—animals—outside. We don't want you to get hurt.

I don't believe you, said Assa.

Hoyal clapped her hands together and tried to look brighter, like she could make her face shine. It wasn't working too well. We have our cook preparing a good meal for you girls. We'll bring it up when it's ready.

We're not hungry, said Dusk and Dawn.

Assa was hungry, but she knew instantly that she should agree with her fellow prisoners. Me neither, said Assa.

I don't believe *you*, said Hoyal. You are growing girls. You need your nourishment. Of course you are hungry. You'll see. When we bring up the food you'll want to eat it. Then we'll talk about what you are doing here.

We're not doing anything here, said Dusk.

We're just princesses waiting to be rescued and looking forward to you being hung, said Dawn.

Hoyal tried to smile again, but it really wasn't working. She didn't know *how* to smile.

Hoyal left the room and went down the stairs. Assa heard her footsteps.

We're doing a hunger strike, said Dawn.

What's that?

It's to protest our treatment. We don't eat. That's supposed to make them understand that they are doing something wrong. My mother talked about it once.

The queen? asked Assa.

Yup, said Dusk.

How long are we supposed to not eat?

Forever. Until we starve to death. You have to make a point.

I don't think I could do that, said Assa.

Oh, said Dusk, we don't expect you to. You're not royalty. You aren't as strong as us.

That's not true, said Assa.

We're not trying to make you feel bad or anything, said Dusk. It's just the truth. Don't let it bother you.

But it did bother Assa. She did't like the way it made her feel. Could she be friends with people who didn't think she was worth being friends with? She might have to prove to them that she was just as good as they were.

So, she said, all you do is not eat?

Yup, said Dawn. That's it.

Hoyal came up the stairs again and entered the room. She was holding a tray with three plates. Here you are, girls, she said.

She put the tray down on the table. The plates bore potatoes, eggs, and meat. Also fruit. And a grain of some kind. There were also bowls of soup, with chunks of beef and lots of vegetables: carrots and peas and other things. Steam rose from the bowls and the plates. The smell was amazing, laced with spices and herbs. Assa's mouth watered.

None of the girls moved from their chairs. Assa wanted to jump up and dig in, but she remained sitting. She wasn't going to eat if Dawn and Dusk weren't going to eat. She could be just as strong as any princess.

What's going on? asked Hoyal. You must be hungry. Eat.

None of them said anything to Hoyal. She narrowed her eyes. You think I'm trying to poison you, is that it? Well, let me reassure you. She took a spoon and ate from each bowl. Then she took a fork and picked off bits of food from each plate and ate that. Then she put down her fork and made a show of dusting her hands off. There, she said. Perfectly safe. And very tasty. Now go on. Eat.

Assa had to swallow, her mouth was so watery. But she did not get up. Neither did the twins.

Well I don't get it, said Hoyal. I guess you're not hungry? She waited for an answer. None came.

Okay, she said. Have it your way. I'll leave the food here. You can do what you want with it. She shook her head and walked out of the room and went down the stairs.

Immediately Dawn and Dusk got up and picked up a plate and a bowl and walked out of the room. Assa grabbed the remaining plate and bowl and followed them to the bathroom, which was little more than a closet with a hole in the floor where they were to do their business. They all three crowded into the room and then they dumped the food into the hole. The soup splashed and the potatoes splatted and Assa suddenly felt a little sick.

Then the girls took the empty dishes and put them at the head of the stairs.

We dumped your food into the shit, said Dusk.

Don't use that word, said Dawn. Dusk giggled. Assa smiled. She liked hearing a princess say shit.

Yeah, said Assa loudly. Your food is shit so we gave it to shit. Ha!

Dawn shook her head at Assa. You shouldn't talk that way either, she said.

Why not? said Assa.

It doesn't help us. They'll think we're a bunch of bratty kids.

Dusk rolled here eyes. They already don't care about us, she said. They only want us for what our parents can do.

She's right, said Assa. They don't care if we curse up a storm.

Curse up a storm? said Dusk. What does that mean?

My Dad sometimes uses curse words. My Mom says he's calling up a storm. She doesn't like it. Says it's a bad influence on me.

See, said Dawn. This is a commoner and she knows curse words are bad.

Hey, said Assa. I'm not common.

Dusk sighed. Assa, she said, you have to stop worrying about your place in the world. Just because you're common doesn't mean there's anything wrong with you. It's just the way things are.

But you aren't special because you're the kids of royalty.

That's not true, said Dawn. We are special. We get special treatment. It's just how things are.

Dawn and Dusk turned from Assa and went back to the big room. They sat around the table and took out a deck of cards.

Now we'll play a game. Do you want to play too? asked Dawn.

Is it okay for a commoner to play with royalty? asked Assa.

Normally, no, said Dusk. But these are special circumstances. And I think maybe you are a special commoner or you wouldn't have been kidnapped. Plus, we like you. You're trying to do the hunger strike with us, even though you will start eating again before we ever do.

No I won't.

Dawn and Dusk looked at each other and smiled.

I'm telling you, said Assa. I won't.

Dawn dealt the cards. Assa sat down in front of her pile and picked up the cards. Each one showed a picture of a fearsome creature. Most were dragons, with fire coming out of their mouths, but there were others: basilisk, cockatrice, hellhound, and more. Assa knew she never wanted to meet any of these animals in person. Where are these monsters from? asked Assa.

From our island, said Dusk.

These things live on your island?

Dawn and Dusk both nodded.

But, said Assa, we don't have anything like this here.

No you don't, said Dusk. That's why we want to go back.

You *want* to live near these things? Aren't they dangerous?

Only if you don't know how to talk to them.

And you know how?

Well, of course, said Dawn. It's one of the things we're taught. We don't expect you to understand.

Because I'm not royalty, said Assa.

This is getting so tiresome, said Dusk. Can't you just accept that there are things we know and do which you don't know and do? It's not that hard to understand.

They stopped talking about it and Assa played a few hands of a game they called Pickup. It involved asking the other players for a card like the one in your hand and putting them together. Whoever got the most pairs won. The only part of the game that Assa cared about were the pictures. They were beautiful and scary at the same time. They made Assa think of her own dreams, the kind where she was flying or changed her shape into something that wasn't real.

Hoyal came into the room while they were playing. Hmmmm, she said. Still not hungry? Well, we'll see about that. I don't think any of you girls can go longer than two days without eating.

Hoyal stood in the doorway with a bowl of fruit and cream. She dipped a spoon into her dessert and stuck some of the fruit and cream into her mouth. Oh, my, that is good. Sure you don't want some?

She showed the bowl to the girls. They all looked up from their cards and stared at the bowl. It was all Assa could do to not spring up from her chair and grab the bowl from Hoyal and wolf down the berries, bananas, and peaches. They looked so sweet and good with the cream on them. She could imagine the taste of them, the way they felt in her mouth: velvety smooth. The tang of the berries mixed with the pulpy goodness of the peaches.

But she didn't. Hoyal didn't move from her spot until she finished the bowl, which she did slowly, enjoying every last bite. Then she licked the spoon clean and left the bowl and the spoon on the floor by the door. Assa saw that there were bits of fruit and some cream still in the bowl.

She likes to torture us, said Dusk, but it isn't going to work.

No, said Assa slowly. No it is not.

Dusk matched up the last card in her hand and put the pair down for them all to see. She won the game. They played more hands. Dusk won most of the games.

I'm getting tired of this, said Assa. I never win. What fun is that?

My mother says all the fun is in the playing, said Dusk. Not in the winning.

Mom's wrong about that, said Dawn. Plus, she doesn't even believe it herself. She said marrying the king was a way to win in life, and that's all that matters.

Dusk nodded, reluctantly. That's true, she said.

I think both are important, said Assa.

Do you? said Dusk.

Assa nodded. It's good to play, but better to win.

Dusk got up from the table and went to the window. It's getting dark, she said.

They're going to want us to go to sleep soon, said Dawn.

Tonight, said Dusk, we escape.

Oh no, said Dawn. That's what you said last night. And the night before.

How long have you been here? asked Assa.

This will be our third night. Time to flee, don't you think?

Where would you go?

Well, said Dusk, we talked about that a lot. Dawn wants to go back to our mother and the king. But she still thinks life is beautiful. I know better. Life with our mother and the king is dreadful. So I want us to get away and go back to our own land.

How will you do that? asked Assa.

We'll steal a ship, said Dusk.

Assa snorted.

What's that for? asked Dusk.

How can you steal a ship? asked Assa. And if we're going to escape, shouldn't we have eaten something? What good is a hunger strike if we're just escaping anyway?

Before Dusk could answer, Dawn stood up and went to the window. She waved over Assa and Dusk. They ran and stood beside her. I've loosened up the bars enough that we can take them out, she said.

Let me see, said Assa.

Dawn grabbed two of the bars and tightened her grip until her knuckles were white. Then she pushed the bars *up* instead of out or in. The bars moved. Assa squealed and put her hand over her mouth. Dawn and Dusk smiled at each other. Their way of doing that was going to get annoying pretty quickly, thought Assa. They were so sure of themselves that it was sickening.

Assa and Dusk then grabbed some of the other bars and gripped them as tight as they could, then pushed them up. Assa felt her two bars move up and into the window frame. When they got up far enough, she could see a gap between the end of the bar and the bottom edge of the window frame.

Look, said Assa.

Good, said Dawn. Now *pull!*

Dawn, Dusk, and Assa all pulled their bars at the same time. Assa heard the crack of wood splitting, and fell back on her behind. She kept her grip on the bars, though, and held them up in the air.

Behind the bars, she saw the window frame, not open to the outside world. Dawn was already scrambling to get through the opening, with her feet scraping the walls like windmills spinning. Assa went and gave Dawn a boost. Dawn slipped through the window and hung out on the other side with her face in the frame.

Wish me luck, she said. Then she let go and Assa heard her hit the ground. She poked her head through the frame and saw Dawn sprawled on the ground in a heap.

Are you okay? she whispered as loud as she dared.

I'm good, said Dawn. Your turn now.

Dusk pushed Assa up and through the frame and before she knew it, Assa had fallen the one story down to the ground. She knew enough to roll as soon as she felt the ground. Her legs smarted from the fall, but she was pretty sure she didn't break anything. She looked up. Dawn cupped her hands to her mouth and called out to Dusk.

Come on, sister, she said.

But she didn't come. Instead, Hoyal poked her head out the window and stared down at them. What's this foolishness? she asked.

Dawn didn't answer. She grabbed Assa by the hand, and turned and ran. Assa could do nothing but follow Dawn. They ran from the house as fast as they could, then into the forest, and kept running. They were going blind at full speed. Assa wanted to slow down, but she didn't want Dawn to get away from her.

We can't leave Dusk alone, said Assa.

She can take care of herself, said Dawn. And also, she's not alone.

What do you mean? asked Assa.

Don't you know twins can talk to each other without talking to each other?

Assa didn't know this, but also didn't want to admit it to Dawn.

Of course, she said. I just forgot.

Dawn did finally slow her pace a little. They were in a particularly dense part of the forest. The branches were thick on the ground, and the leaves and moss were cushiony and hid some of the branches. Assa was terribly afraid that she would twist her foot or trip and fall and break something.

She kept going, but she wrenched her hand free from Dawn and ran a short distance behind her. Off in the distance, she heard shouts: Hoyal and someone else.

Come back, girls, said Hoyal loudly. There's nowhere for you to go. If you come back now, I won't punish you.

What does she mean by punishing us? said Assa. What will she do?

Keep your voice down, said Dawn in a whisper. She won't do anything, because she isn't going to catch us.

I can hurt Dusk, said Hoyal.

Dawn stopped. Assa stood beside her. They were both breathing hard, taking in big gulps of air. Assa felt her lungs burning and her heart was racing much faster than normal.

If you both come back now, princess, said Hoyal, as calm as calm could be, I won't punish Dusk. We'll forget this ever happened and I might even give you some cake tonight.

She's forgetting we're on a hunger strike, whispered Assa.

But she's not forgetting my sister is alone, said Dawn. She's scared. She shouldn't be. She should know Hoyal is all talk.

Then we keep going, right? said Assa.

I can't be sure, though.

Yes you can, said Assa. Hoyal is big bag of hot air. You know it, I know it, and Dusk knows it.

We need to get to my parents and tell them where we are.

Yes, said Assa, yes. We can't let Hoyal keep us.

Assa's eyes had gotten used to the darkness. She could make out the shapes of trees, and looking up high, through the tops of the trees, she could see some stars against the black sky, which seemed to be giving some light for them to move by.

I'm just worried, said Dawn. She shouldn't be afraid. But she is.

She's probably just scared that she's alone, said Assa. That doesn't mean she's in danger.

They stood there for another five or six second. Dawn seemed, for a second or two, in another world. Her eyes were wide and she looked as though her gaze went through Assa to the forest behind her.

Then she took a deep breath and let it out in a rush of air, grabbed Assa's hand again and kept running away from Hoyal who continued to call to them, but whose voice diminished in volume as they ran, until they could no longer hear her. They had outrun their captor and left a princess as his prisoner.

Assa wondered what was going to happen to the three of them, and if she and Dawn and made the right decision.

AFTER RUNNING FOR at least a couple of hours, the two girls were tired and thirsty. And very hungry.

They slowed their pace, but not stop moving. They kept going through the night.

Their pants and shirts were torn in places where the cloth had snagged on twigs and thorns. Their legs were scarred and bloody. Assa knew they must have looked like a mess, but she felt invigorated by their run through the woods.

She was the friend of a princess now, and that felt grand, even though they were running for their lives.

The eastern sky was just beginning to lighten up a little as the woods began to thin out. Assa noticed eyes around her: deer most likely, but maybe other creatures, too. The woods cracked and swished as the animals bounded or scurried away from them, as though clearing a path for the princess and the miller's daughter.

There was something else, as well: Assa could hear the sea. Waves broke on a beach not far from where they were. They pressed on and came to the edge of the woods. Light seemed to stream in on them and cast shadows ahead of them.

Dawn and Assa both instinctively crouched down on the matted leaves and the moss at the edge of the forest. In the medium distance, over rolling hills and mounds of beach sand, they could just see the tops of waves cresting white and foamy.

Where are we? asked Assa.

Don't you know the ocean you live next to? said Dawn.

Yes, but where is my village from here? North or south?

I don't know about your village, said Dawn. I also don't care about it. What I'm interested in is out there. She pointed to the ocean. Assa followed the direction of her finger as though it was some kind of broken instrument.

You can't be serious, said Assa.

I am. That's my home and I intend to get back to it. Then I'll come back with an army and get Dusk and my mother.

But your mother doesn't want to go back.

Yes she does. She just doesn't know it yet.

Assa hardly knew what to say. Before she could formulate some kind of coherent response, Dawn slapped her on the back. Thanks for coming with me. I don't think I'll be able to do it without your help. You're a good friend.

But, said Assa.

But what?

I don't want to go to your island.

Doesn't matter, said Dawn. I'm a princess. You have to do what I tell you to.

Assa wasn't at all sure that was true. A princess had no power. She was just someone who *might* have some power in the future. When her mother or father died. Or something. Assa wasn't sure about how all that worked.

It didn't matter, though, because even if she was the queen of the world, Dawn wouldn't be able to tell Assa what to do, not if Assa didn't want to do it. She already proved that when she didn't do what the king wanted her to do.

Assa just wanted to get back home to her own parents. She just needed to know where they were. Did she go north from here or south?

You can try to fight me all you want, said Dawn. But it isn't going to work. The reason is that if you don't help me, then you'll be charged with a crime. You'll go to jail. That's just the way it is with princesses and subjects.

Dawn said this as though she was telling Assa about the weather. It was going to be warm and sunny today, with maybe a little bit of cloud decorating the blue sky. Assa tried to recall, from her carriage ride, if they crossed the creek. If they did, then they would have to be on the south side of the creek and that meant she would walk north along the beach to get home.

If they crossed the creek, than she would be north of her home and that meant she would walk south to get back to her house. But Hoyal had kept her from looking out the window of the carriage. She didn't remember them going over a bridge, or splashing through water. That meant they probably didn't cross the creek. But she couldn't be sure. It was a long carriage ride. She wasn't awake the whole time.

Dawn looked Assa directly in her eyes. I like you, she said. You're not a regular non-royal. You have some spunk. But just because I like you, doesn't mean I won't make you pay if you disobey me. It's what princesses do. You have to understand how things are.

That isn't very nice, said Assa.

I'm not trying to be nice, said Dawn. What I'm going to do, is I'm going to steal a boat and I'm going to go to my island. Then I'll get my strength up from the spirits of my island and I'll come back here and rescue my sister and my mother. The spirits will be my army.

That's sounds like a brave and wonderful thing to do, said Assa. You want to get your family back together. Well, so do I. I want to find my mother and father. So why don't you let me? Why do you need me?

I need help on the water. I don't know how to sail.

I don't either, said Assa.

Dawn stared at her. That can't be true, she said.

Of course it's true. I've never been in a boat on the ocean. I wouldn't know the first thing about sailing.

But, said Dawn. You're a *commoner*. Commoner's know these things.

Dawn looked so astonished, that Assa felt sorry for her, then stopped herself. Why should she feel sorry for a princess. She had a privileged place in the world. She was going to be a queen one day. The most Assa could hope for was to have her parents' mill when they died, which wasn't much. Not compared to what a princess would have.

But Assa also saw that Dawn was not the all-powerful person she thought she was. She didn't know the first things about people and how they lived and survived. She knew how to threaten Assa, she was very good at that. But she didn't know how to make friends. Not real friends.

Here's what I think you should do, said Assa. Find someone with a boat, then order them to take you to your island. If they have a boat, then they'll know how to sail it. You're a princess. You can do that. There. Simple. She smiled at Dawn, then she turned from her and began walking away from her in a direction, she hoped, that would take her to her family's mill.

Assa expected Dawn to bark an order at her, but she didn't. Then she expected Dawn to run after her and grab her, but she didn't do that either. In fact, Dawn didn't do anything. Assa looked back once or twice, but Dawn didn't move from her place on the beach. She just watched Assa walk away.

Assa wanted to slow her pace. In fact, she *wanted* to stop and invite Dawn to come with her, but she didn't. Dawn was a princess. She could do what she wanted to do. The beach curved into a bay. Assa kept walking until Dawn was out of sight, eclipsed by the bend in the shore.

Things got a little rocky. The sand thinned out almost completely, and Assa found herself treading carefully on rocks covered with squishy seaweed.

The tide was out, which was fortunate. Otherwise she would not be able to traverse these rocks. Gulls and cormorants scattered away from her. She heard the distant calls of—something, she wasn't sure what. At first she thought it might be another bird or birds, then possibly some other creatures, but eventually she realized it was like the cries she had heard a couple of nights ago, the cries of Dawn and Dusk, wailing after their homeland.

Assa let her ears and her heart listen to the cries. She stood on a rock, with small waves lapping around her, the smell of fish wafting up in the air, the water making sucking noises as it lapped over mussels attached to some of the rocks.

Sea stars crowded the sides of a massive rock just off to the side. The whole of existence seemed to be converging in this one place. Assa felt the dizzying power of the world. It awakened in her another being, which seemed to inhabit her, the way a hand might inhabit a glove.

All the parts of the being fit into all the parts of her. The cries increased in intensity. It was the princesses, calling to one another. Wasn't it? Didn't they do that? And didn't the calls go out into the world where people with special abilities could hear them, not just the twins with their secret language that only they could understand?

Assa's head seemed filled to capacity with thoughts and images. She saw a land she never saw before: it was high and rocky, tinged red with some kind of grass that clung to it. There were dragons, as well, great fire-breathing beasts, that lifted up into the air and wheeled around the sky just as easy as you please, their wings folding and unfolding with uncommon grace.

Where were these images coming from? Below the red rocks, waves crashed on rocky shores. They seemed like they might be made of some caustic agent, because they were eating away at the base of the rocks, causing hunks of them to be chewed off, as though some great monster had taken a liking to the rocks and bitten off pieces of it.

The dragons began crying out to the air. Their screams were high-pitched and too loud for Assa's ears. She tried to put her hands up to her ears, to protect herself, but the ghost inside her would not let her. It exerted its strength and kept her arms at her sides. Assa felt panic. How could this—*thing*—whatever it was, make her do things she did not want to do?

The images of the land being destroyed began to fade from her mind's eye. She fought the ghost inside her, but it wouldn't succumb to her will. Instead, she found herself turning back toward the way she had come. Her legs began stepping without her consent, even in spite of her determination not to let it happen. Before long she was on her way back to Dawn.

Dawn stood on the beach, in the same place she had been when Assa left her, and watched as Assa approached. She had a smile on her face, as though she was having the time of her life.

As Assa got closer to Dawn, the presence inside her began to fade. It shriveled from a dominating being to a slight phantom, almost a memory of what she had felt before. The images of dragons and strange lands also faded. Assa had the distinct feeling, however, that if she turned around and walked away from Dawn, the princess would just make sure that the ghost would come back and make Assa move in a way against her will.

How did you do that? asked Assa when she was close enough for Dawn to hear her normal speaking voice.

How do you think I did it?

Don't tell me it's because you're a princess. I don't believe that.

My sister and I can combine our thoughts and do things like that. Isn't it amazing?

Assa had to admit that it was, definitely, amazing, but that didn't mean she liked it. In fact, she hated it.

You shouldn't make people do things they don't want to do, said Assa.

I don't. I just make you see that you want to do something you didn't think you wanted to do but you really did. What does that mean? said Assa.

It means you want to help me. At least, you had this tiny thought in your brain that you should help me, at least a little. I just made it bigger. If you didn't have that tiny thought to start with, we couldn't have made it big enough for you to come back to me. Get it?

Assa wasn't sure she got it at all.

Why didn't you just make Hoyal let us go? she asked.

Because she didn't want to, not even a little. She wanted to keep us imprisoned. We can't just implant things. We can only make intentions bigger.

What about the dragons? said Assa. Did you put those there?

Dragons? Don't be silly. There's no such thing. Where did you come up with dragons?

I never would have thought of dragons on my own, said Assa. You and your sister put them there.

Dawn studied Assa's face for a few moments. Assa looked back at her. They both wondered if the other was lying.

Finally, Dawn looked away to the sea. We'll have to figure this out later, she said. For now, we need to find a boat. Come on.

She began walking down the beach, in the opposite direction from where Assa had been headed just a couple of minutes before.

What if I don't want to go with you? asked Assa.

You know what will happen, said Dawn without turning around.

Assa picked up her speed until she was walking next to Dawn. Will you always have this power? asked Assa.

I think so, said Dawn. Don't know why it would go away.

Lots of people lose some of their abilities when they get older. They can't see as good. They get deaf. They don't move around the same way. My mother and father are always talking about how they feel old and creaky.

I'm not old or creaky.

But you will be. One of these days everyone will.

That's a long time from now. Do commoners often talk about things that don't concern them?

I don't know about commoners, said Assa. But I talk about anything that I want to talk about.

Dawn laughed. You have no idea, she said. No idea at all.

No idea about what?

About anything.

Assa decided right then and there that she didn't like Dawn. Not one bit. She was just a person who happened to have a queen for a mother, and she thought she was the greatest thing in the world. But she wasn't. Not by any standard. She was just a spoiled brat who always got what she wanted. What she and her twin wanted. Well, maybe not always, but a lot of the time.

They walked on the beach in silence for several minutes. The beach narrowed to a few feet of sand with the ocean on one side and a towering cliff of rock on the other. Out on the water, Assa saw a couple of small craft, fishing boats looking for a place to put out their nets.

What about them? said Assa, pointing to the craft. Can you put the ghost in them and get them to come help you?

It doesn't work that way, said Dawn.

Why not? It worked on me.

I told you, you really wanted to stay with me. The people in those boats don't even know I'm here.

Assa stopped for a few seconds and stared, wistfully, at the fishing boats. They bobbed in the waves like toys. They made her think of fish dinners she would eat with her parents. It seemed like the best thing in the world. Any food, now, seemed like the best thing in the world.

We need to eat, she said to Dawn.

No, said Dawn. My sister isn't eating, so we aren't going to either. We're on a hunger strike, remember?

Assa remembered very well, but it seemed crazy to be on a hunger strike now. They weren't being held captive.

But we're doing physical stuff. We need our strength. Dusk is just sitting in that room.

You shouldn't be so concerned about food. Hunger makes you stronger. It keeps you alert.

That didn't sound right at all to Assa. You're making that up, she said to Dawn.

No I'm not. It's a proven fact. The royal naturalists have done experiments. They have figured out the truth. We know that if you are too full of food you can be tired and make bad decisions. You also don't even want to do anything: it makes you lazy. But. When you are hungry, everything is on high alert. You are more likely to see dim things, hear quiet sounds, and think better thoughts. They used mice. Starved them and overfed them. They figured it out.

Assa was mystified. They figured out stuff for mice?

Dawn nodded vigorously. They are very clever, the naturalists. They think up questions, then they devise ways to test the questions, and then they answer the questions.

But for mice, said Assa.

Yes, yes, said Dawn impatiently. For mice. Of course for mice. You can't very well starve people or forcibly stuff them full of food. They don't like that sort of thing.

Assa could certainly see that. I'm sure, she said, but I'll bet the mice don't like that either.

You are annoying me, said Dawn. Who cares what mice like or don't like. They're mice!

I care, said Assa. So should you. Especially you. You're a princess, you should care about *everything* because one day you'll be in charge of *everything*.

Dawn's face turned red. Assa saw it and laughed.

Don't laugh at me, said Dawn.

I can't help it, said Assa.

You shouldn't even be *talking* to me, said Dawn. You should be happy that I *let* you. I could have you killed if I wanted to.

Assa stopped and looked around. She looked at the sea, at the rocks, then at the sand at her feet. She looked up at the sky. Finally she spread her arms and her hands and called to the clouds. Dawn wants you to kill me, she said, so follow her orders and squash me like a bug.

She held her pose for several seconds.

Very funny, said Dawn.

Hmmmm, said Assa. I guess you can't order me killed after all. I'm still alive.

Dawn turned her back to Assa and kept walking. The thin bit of beach had narrowed even more. The cliff loomed even larger, if that was possible.

At the base of the cliff, where Assa and Dawn were walking, chunks of rock were littered before them and they had to step over and around them. In some places, there was no beach at all and they had to wade through water up to their knees. Assa saw that if it was high tide, they would not be able to pass here at all. She looked ahead and saw they had a long way to go and the beach did not appear to be coming back. With the water rising, they were going to be trapped in a short time.

We need to turn around, she said to Dawn.

Don't be ridiculous, said Dawn.

I'm serious, said Assa. The water's rising. We're going to drown.

We are not going to drown.

The water doesn't know you're a princess, said Assa.

This narrow beach can't last forever. It'll widen up ahead.

Assa let Dawn get ahead of her. She looked back the way they had come. It wouldn't take long to walk that short distance and get to a safe section of beach. She looked ahead to where Dawn was walking. The cliff wove in and out, like a wave itself, but she couldn't see how far it went that way. It might bend in to the shore, or it might bend out to the water. Maybe there was a bay with a wide beach ahead, and maybe there wasn't. She stood shivering in the water as waves lapped at her legs. This was crazy. They couldn't risk their lives like this.

Dawn! she called.

Dawn raised her hand and waved at Assa without turning around. She had made her decision. She was going ahead.

Dawn! Do you know how to swim?

Dawn didn't respond. She picked up her pace and kept going.

Assa wanted to leave Dawn to her own skills and weaknesses. It would serve her right if she drowned in the sea just because she didn't want to listen to a commoner. She watched as the princess scrambled over rocks, splashed through shallows, and trudged with determination through clumps of seaweed.

Assa knew what the smart thing to do was. She should abandon Dawn right here and now and go back the way she had come. She could return to the forest and find her parents. What did it matter to her how the royals dealt with their troubles? Compared to regular people like Assa and her parents, the royals didn't *have* any problems. Not real ones.

Dawn looked so thin and weak. Assa wondered if she could even stand up on her own for much longer.

It didn't matter. It didn't matter at all. Assa turned from Dawn and began clambering over the rocks she had already climbed past. The water was already noticeably higher compared to even a few minutes ago. She put more distance between herself and Dawn. The wide beach was soon within view. All she had to do was take a few steps and—

She couldn't.

She stopped and sighed heavily. She looked out to the sea. Waves advanced toward her in steady succession. They would keep coming and keep coming. Eventually, they would come and drown Dawn.

Assa didn't want Dawn to drown, which surprised her. It bothered her that she cared at all.

Assa turned around and set her sights on Dawn once again, now a tiny figure in the distance. Assa would have to quicken her pace considerable to catch up to her. She splashed through the water lapping at her feet.

Ignoring sensible precautions, she threw herself headlong into her pursuit of the royal, all the while thinking about what her dying words were going to be when the tide rose high enough to drown her.

It took a long while for her to catch up to Dawn. In some places the ground dipped and allowed the water to rise up so high that she had to swim from one rock to the other. The cliff, rising higher than she could see, gave no signs of diminishment. It soared above them and seemed to want to rise as high as the clouds.

It probably took at least an hour, maybe more, before Assa finally caught up with Dawn. When she did, Dawn was standing on a large rock, surrounded by water. She was shivering and looked like she was looking for a way out.

Only there was no way out. It was swim or stay where she was. But the water was so cold. Assa knew it was hard to make your muscles work right in that kind of cold. Assa climbed up on the rock and stood nest to Dawn. Dawn grabbed Assa and hugged her and began crying.

Assa didn't know what to say or do. She let the princess wail on and didn't try to stop her. She was cold and scared herself. Was it right that she should try to comfort a royal? Shouldn't it be the other way around?

Crying is okay, she said, but it isn't going to get us out of here. Do you have any ideas?

Dawn pulled back from Assa and wiped away her tears and tried to look strong. Assa kept from laughing only with a great effort. She was surprised by her own reaction. She was in trouble here with no obvious way out and she wanted to laugh. Crazy.

We could wait until low tide, said Dawn. Then we could get off this rock.

I don't think that'll work, said Assa. There is a high tide before the low tide. We haven't gotten to the highest part yet. The waves are going to come up over this rock.

Dawn stood up straight and tried to present as strong an outward appearance as possible. Assa could see her straining from the effort.

Then we swim for it, said Dawn.

Do you even know how to swim? asked Assa.

Well, said Dawn, how hard can it be? You float on the water and windmill your arms and kick with your legs. Right?

Assa put her hand to her mouth. Oh no, she said. You *don't* know how to swim.

Dawn shrugged. We've never had to learn, she said. You could teach me.

I can't teach you to swim in five minutes. Besides, I don't think swimming would work. The waves are going to get big and they would smash us on the rocks.

Dawn looked up at the cliff just a few feet in front of them. Then we climb, she said.

Assa followed Dawn's gaze. The rock was not exactly a sheer cliff, but it also didn't look very friendly to climbing. There were a few places she could see where they could put their hands and feet, but mostly it was just smooth rock.

Dawn pointed a short way up the face. Right there, she said, is a little ledge. We could climb up on it and wait for the tide to go out.

Assa looked at the ledge. It didn't seem big enough, but what choice did they have? Okay, she said, let's go.

They held hands and clambered down off the rock and waded into the water. They put their hands on the cliff face and grabbed pieces of rock and pushed themselves up. Their feet found indentations big enough to support them and help propel them up the face. The ledge they had seen was about fifteen feet above the water. Plenty of height to avoid the incoming tide.

They climbed slowly, making sure of their footing the whole way and before long the two of them were on the ledge. It was big enough for both of them to stretch out, which they did. They arranged themselves so their heads were next to each other and their legs were stretched out.

They panted. Assa's lungs burned. Why was it so hard just to climb?

I'm cold, said Dawn.

Me too, said Assa. And hungry.

The sun will warm us up, said Dawn.

What do you hear from your sister? asked Assa.

She's still imprisoned.

Where's Hoyal?

Dawn shook her head, bumping against Assa's head as she did so. They both laughed. I don't know where Hoyal is, said Dawn. It doesn't work that way. We can sense each other, but we don't necessarily know what each other is seeing.

We're going to be here about four or five hours, said Assa.

I know, said Dawn.

That's how long the tide takes to go out again.

I know about tides, said Dawn. I live on an island. Or used to.

What was it like? said Assa.

I loved my island, said Dawn. Dusk and I walked very inch of it. I knew the whole shore line, and where the water met the rocks. I knew where the sun came up on the horizon every day. I picked oranges off the trees on the south side and apples off the trees on the north side. When we played in the hills, we found these tiny rocks, almost like jewels, buried under other rocks, or in the dirt. We'd pull them out and collect them. We had hundreds of them. We filled bags and bags with them. Sometimes we would go to the top of the island, in the middle, where the rocks rose up to the sky and we'd look down at the water all around. It was a small island but it was our home and we loved it. My mother and father were nice to all the people on our island. They adored my parents. We would talk to them, sometimes. They would talk to us. They were commoners, but that was okay. We all lived on the island, and we made sure the island was taken care of. It's not like here. If you mess up part of the land here, you can go somewhere else. You can't do that on an island. It's like its own little world. We had people in the court, too. There were people who took care of us and other people who knew things. Like the naturalists I told you about. They knew where the island came from. They told me that a big earthquake a long time ago. It made a big rip in the ocean and a big rock on the ocean bottom rose up high and stuck out of the water. That rock is our island.

Assa was very tired. She listened to Dawn as long as she could, but after a while, her voice was so soft and soothing, that it made Assa even more tired and after a while she fell asleep.

When Assa woke up, the sun was beating down on her face. She blinked her eyes open, and put her hand up to her forehead to shield herself. Beside her, Dawn stirred and groaned. Assa's stomach felt like it was as thin as a piece of paper. She had to think about how she had got there under the sun. She heard the waves down below her, and lifted her head slightly. She remembered climbing up on the rocky ledge to get away from the rising waters, but she wasn't on hard rock. Whatever she was lying on was soft and warm under her.

She sat up and immediately felt dizzy. She was no longer outside. She was in a small cabin, and it was bucking and pitching like a cork on water. The sunlight was coming in through a small window in the wall.

She was on some kind of water-going vessel. A sailing ship, most likely. She stood up. The floor—or, she supposed, the *deck*—below her would not remain still. She weaved her way to the door of the cabin and tried to pull it open. The door moved, rattling in its frame, but the handle would not turn. She was locked inside. She made a fist and hit the door several times.

Hey, she said. Who's there? Someone let me out.

No answer.

She went back to the window—*port*—and looked outside. She saw only the ocean spreading out to the horizon. She saw no land whatsoever.

She pulled away from the port and looked around her room. Cabin. The walls were wood. Worn and old. They creaked with the movements of the ship. Except for her bed, she saw only three other objects in the room. There were two buckets in the corner. She supposed those were there for her elimination necessities.

In another corner, she saw a large bucket with a ladle in it. Must be water for drinking. She was glad whoever put her here had seen fit to keep the two buckets away from the one bucket.

And that was it. Nothing else. No desk, no chair, no lamp.

She went back to the door and called Dawn's name several times. She hit the door again and again.

Finally she heard a voice on the other side of the door. It sounded very familiar.

Now, now, it said. What's all this ruckus?

The door swung open and Hoyal stood before her. Assa groaned.

Aren't you glad to see me? said Hoyal.

Where's Dawn? said Assa. And Dusk?

All in good time, said Hoyal. We have some matters to discuss.

I have nothing to say to you, said Assa.

That's fine. I have some things to say to you.

Assa folded her hands and glared at Hoyal.

Such spunk, said Hoyal. It's very gratifying to see. I was afraid you might have been broken by your ordeal. She stepped into the cabin. Assa tried to see if she could scoot around Hoyal to the door and out the cabin, but Hoyal didn't leave her any room to do so. And even if she did, where would she go? This was obviously Hoyal's domain. The crew, if there even was a crew, would be loyal to Hoyal. Assa wouldn't be able to get anywhere.

Behind Assa a young woman, not much older than Assa, brought in a tray laden with food. Assa saw a bowl of thick bean soup, a pile of roasted potatoes, some eggs, strips of pork, and several slices of bread next to a small pot of jam. Her mouth instantly watered and her stomach growled and lurched.

The girl put the tray down on a small table next to Assa's bed, then she backed out of the cabin and was gone.

Go on, said Hoyal, waving her hand at the tray. Don't let me stop you.

Assa wanted to eat all the food on the tray, but she hesitated. Is Dawn eating?

Hoyal smiled at Assa and did not answer for several seconds. During that time, Assa's hands almost moved toward the tray on their own. She had the feeling she remembered from before, when the spirit had taken a hold of her and made her body move in a way she did not want it to move.

But that feeling soon passed. This was not the same thing at all. The spirit in her was not some ghostly thing, it was her own hunger. Or, rather, her own instinct to alleviate that hunger.

I wonder why you girls stick together so much, said Hoyal. Have you ever wondered why that would be? She reached out to the tray and picked up a strip of the broiled pork and bit off the end of it and chewed noisily.

If Dawn's still on a hunger strike, said Assa, then I'm not going to eat.

There is no hunger strike, said Hoyal. The twins are eating. They ate as much as is on this tray and more. You can too. Once you finish this, we can bring you more.

I don't believe you, said Assa.

You don't believe me? Now, why would I lie to you?

For the same reason that you have me locked up in this room. For the same reason that you kidnapped me.

Hoyal sighed. Last chance, she said.

Assa shook her head.

As you wish, said Hoyal. She picked up the plates from the tray and took them to the port hole and scraped them through the hole and into the water.

The fishes will be happy to eat your scraps, said Hoyal. She sat down next to Assa. Assa moved slightly away from her, but Hoyal slid closer to her so that they were touched.

We found you on a rock, said Hoyal. You were both so tired, you and Dawn. Weary, really. Something beyond tired. More like the world had released you from its hold. We picked you up and you did not wake. It was extraordinary. And now, we have the three of you aboard this ship.

I knew it! said Assa.

We're going to the land of Dawn and Dusk's parents.

Assa didn't say anything. She didn't tell Hoyal that this was exactly where Dawn wanted to go. Hoyal was making them go where they wanted to go anyway. Everything would be so much easier if Hoyal would stop being such a mean person. Couldn't she just ask them nicely?

Where are my parents? said Assa.

They're safe and sound. Don't worry about them. You need to think about yourself.

Let me go, said Assa. Take me back to my land.

We will, we will, but there are bigger things going on than your home. We will arrive at the twins' island by tomorrow. Then the three of you will earn your keep. Until then, enjoy your hunger.

Hoyal stood up. Assa, overcome by anger and frustration, not to say desperation, made fists and hit Hoyal on the back repeatedly. Her blows were pathetically weak, and Hoyal stood and took them without comment or retaliation until Assa stopped a short time later.

Feel better? asked Hoyal.

Assa stepped back and sat on the edge of the bed and began sobbing. Hoyal said nothing. She stepped through the door and shut it behind her. Assa heard a bolt slide into the frame. Assa wanted to break the door down, but she could not.

She went to the bucket with the ladle and drank water. It was warm, but it tasted okay. She drank a lot of it, filling her belly with as much liquid as she could stand. She thought it might assuage the hunger, at least a little, but it seemed to only make the hunger worse. Her stomach wanted food, not liquid. Her body needed solid food to digest, otherwise it was going to start digesting itself.

She sat in silence for some time, only her sobs breaking the quiet of the room. Presently she heard a voice whispering. She was sure it must be some kind of hallucination, brought on by hunger and anger, but it sounded so real that she looked up at the ceiling and around at the walls.

Who's there? she asked. Is that you, Dawn? Answer me please. Anyone.

She heard the whispering again. She couldn't make out the words but she could tell where it came from. It wasn't from outside the room or the walls or even from the sea. It came from inside herself.

Assa couldn't move. She remained as still as she possibly could and listened with all her concentration to the voice inside of her. She heard more whispers. Sentences, but the words were so dim that she couldn't make them out at all. She did get the feeling of them, though. It was some kind of warning. Something telling her to be calm and pay attention. It was like the kind of talk her parents might give her when she had hurt herself in some way: scraped her knee, maybe, or cut her hand on a rock. It was a voice of reassurance. Only, what was she being reassured about? And where was it *coming* from?

She tried to isolate the source. She closed her eyes and waited for the voice to come back. She listened so closely that when it returned, she wasn't sure that it was a voice anymore. Maybe it was just random sounds.

She remained like this for some time, perhaps the rest of the day, she wasn't sure. The voice was her only companion and she wanted to know more about it. The whole time, there were feelings that she might know the voice. It had to come from somewhere, and probably somewhere Assa knew about.

Before the day was out, she had decided the voice was her own body talking to her. What else could it be? And even though she couldn't understand the words, she thought the voice had to be some kind of hallucination. Voices don't live in people, talking to them. That's ridiculous. Most likely the voice was telling her to eat. But it was so weak from *not* eating, that it couldn't speak loud enough. None of that mattered to Assa, however. She was just glad that she had some kind of companion.

She used the smaller of the buckets, producing only a few tablespoons of liquid. Having not eaten, she had no use for the bigger bucket.

The ship settled down to a smoother course. It no longer bobbed on the water. As night came, the room dimmed and dimmed. She felt very sleepy. Soon she could see some stars through the dark clouds outside the port. The sound of the ocean became an incoherent hiss. It invaded her cabin and seemed to fill it with the promise of good things to come. But Assa didn't believe in good things anymore. All she believed in was herself and her voice.

It got cold in her cabin. The port hole had a door on it. She swung it shut. The ocean was on the other side. She was on this side. With that simple delineation of realms settled, she stretched out on the bed and fell asleep to the sound of the strange voice in her body.

HEY, YOU NINNY. Wake up.

Assa opened her eyes. The voice had snaked into her dreams. It crawled around and flowered into a tree rooted in the earth, but reaching up up up to the sky. The cabin was still pitch dark. She couldn't see anything but blackness. She blinked and tried to locate the porthole, but nothing was there where she expected to see it.

Wake up!

Those last two words weren't from her dream. They were the voice, again. The voice from her body. Deep in her bones, maybe? Or coming from her veins? Her skin? She wanted to tear at her own flesh to try to find the source. She moved her hand to do so, placing her fingertips over her chest and stealing herself to push her nails into her skin.

But she stopped before she did any damage. She left only tiny lunules of indentations over her breastbone. She felt them with the tips of her fingers. She felt sick with the pain. The hunger that she was able to tolerate for so long was now incessant, like a child clamoring for attention. It seemed to fill her up and was trying to break her in two.

Now go to the porthole.

Assa blinked. I don't remember where the porthole is, she said to the walls.

Right above you. Don't be so stupid. Keep up!

Keep up with what? Who? She stood on the bed and immediately dizziness overtook her and she fell in a heap. A sour taste invaded her mouth and burned her throat. She swallowed hard, trying to stuff the acid feeling back into her stomach.

We don't have forever. Let's go, girl!

Assa wanted to reach inside her throat, deep down in her gut, and pull up whatever was there, talking to her.

She felt miserable and was tired of feeling miserable. The weariness pulled at her spirit. She felt, in fact, that she had no spirit of her own anymore. It was all someone else. Or some*thing* else. She did not know how to decide which.

A nice long rest, without any stress, would be just the thing. She could sleep, maybe for a few days, and let the world go by her. Especially the wet world, the great ocean that surrounded her. It was beginning to feel unbearable. So large. So empty. It went on and on.

Where was this ship going? It didn't matter. She just wanted the weariness to go away. The weakness. She slumped against the wall and let herself slide down to the bed. The thin blanket felt scratchy against her cheek but she didn't care. The roughness of the cloth seemed to settle her right down. She closed her eyes and forced the world to go away. She felt like she was in a floaty reality that had nothing to do with the ship she was on.

In fact, the ship seemed to slip away, like smoke dissipating in the air. She bucked and bobbed on the ocean of air. Nothing around her at all.

But the voices were unrelenting. They called to her. She tried to bury her self in the void. Tried to push her face into the clouds. Tried to tried to tried to.

Wake up, you fool.

Leave me alone, Assa said to the world.

Take a look at where you are.

Assa had her eyes closed. She didn't want to open them. She willed her eyelids to remain tightly shut, as tightly as possible.

Okay, said the voice, *have it your way.*

Suddenly a *force* exerted itself from inside Assa's eyelids. It seemed to snake out of her brain, or maybe her heart, she wasn't sure. Couldn't tell exactly. It might just as well have been her spine or her toes, for all she could determine. Wherever it came from, it went directly for her eyes. It was as though some tiny demon in her head had found a crowbar and had wedged it into the space where her eyelids met.

Now the demon was working the crowbar, pumping it up and down and wiggling it from side to side. Assa pressed her eyelids tighter and tighter, bringing all her will to bear on the task.

Now another demon was at the other eyelid. The crowbars were pumping up and down and sideways and in a circle with alarming energy. It was as though they had found some power source from out of this world and were amping up the energy for all it was worth.

Assa put up a great fight. She wanted the comfort of darkness over the stark reality of her true situation, but she could not last forever. The demons were overpowering and after a few minutes of gallantly fighting, her eyelids finally popped open and she was staring at the sky. No deck, no ship, no nothing. She was floating above the ocean.

It was—unsettling. And yet, at the same time, it felt free. She was truly happy to have this experience.

There, now. Isn't that better?

Where am I? said Assa to the voice. Her words felt like they were snatched by the wind and sent to some other realm.

The wind was everything here. She felt that immediately.

She spread out her hands. The currents of air flowed over and under them, supporting her with a gentle lift. Her legs, streaming behind her, caught currents as well. It was like being a bird. Or what she thought a bird might be like.

Assa angled her arms and dipped down toward the ocean. Then she angled them the other way and she rose back up. That was interesting. She leaned to one side and banked a wide turn. Even more interesting. She experimented with her new found powers and was soon executing competent paths of loops and turns. She laughed. Something she had not wanted to do in days.

Having fun? asked the voice.

Yes! said Assa.

Watch out for the dragon.

Wha— said Assa, just as she looked up from admiring the waves beneath her. A dragon, no more than three feet long, was coming right at her.

Assa reacted instinctively by tilting her spread hands down as steeply as she could. She dropped like a stone and the dragon, apparently oblivious to her presence in the sky, kept going on its track.

Assa twisted in the air so that she could see the dragon receding from her.

What was that? she asked the air.

Follow her, said the voice. *She's going where we want to be.*

Assa arranged herself so that she was flat to the sea again and tweaked her hands and legs so that she picked up as much as speed as possible. She directed the flow of air over her to be as smooth as possible and before long she was gaining some air on the dragon. She was able to see it a little more clearly. It was shimmery with reds and greens, like a lizard. It had leathery wings that spread out and flapped almost lazily against the air. That was interesting. The dragon had to flap. Assa did not. She mostly glided.

The dragon's tail swished from side to side as it flew. A stabilizing strategy? Possibly.

It also had a long snout. Tendrils of smoke rose from its nostrils and melted into the air. The snout mimicked the tail, swishing slowly from side to side as it flew.

It looked back at Assa. Its big green eyes appeared to be made of jewels. This couldn't be, but it was what Assa thought. After examining Assa for a second or two, the dragon let out a fiery breath—no more than a spurt of a single flame, like the energy tipping a lit candle—and turned to face forward again, and then instantly increased its speed considerably, so that it zipped away from Assa at what seemed like an impossible velocity.

Assa could only plod along at her own pace and marvel at what the dragon had been able to do with what looked like no effort at all.

Keep following, said the voice.

I can't, said Assa.

We didn't say keep up. We said follow.

That, thought Assa, she could do. The dragon was only a dot by now, but it was a bright dot and she kept it in her view and worked to maintain lift over he arms and legs. Was she going to get tired? She was already weak from lack of food. How long could she keep this up?

She didn't know, but didn't really have any other options. Presently the dragon approached what looked like a thin wafer on the horizon.

A thrill went through Assa. That wafer had to be land of some kind. A distant shore that the dragon needed to get to.

Should I follow? she asked the air.

Of course you should follow. What do you think this has been all about?

I don't know, said Assa.

All she knew was that she liked being up in the air like this. She was part of the sky, enveloped by it. She needed nothing else but the air to sustain her.

The dragon seemed to pick up speed. Or else Assa was slowed by her thoughts. In any case, the distance between Assa and the dragon lengthened. Assa tried to pick up speed, but found she could not. She was going as fast as her abilities allowed.

The wafer thickened until she could discern some details of topography: greenery at the top of the wafer, and a pale line of beige at the bottom. On the ends, a descent into the ocean. The pinpoint of the dragon disappeared completely from her view so that she wasn't actually following the creature anymore, simply going to where she guessed it would be going, based on its flight path before then.

Before long, the wafer became an actual geographic feature. She saw rocks, crashing waterfalls, trees. A beach that varied in width from one end of the island to the other. She thought to descend to one of those beaches but instead chose to fly over the island to get a picture of its extent and topology.

From what she could determine, it appeared to be approximately five miles in length and about two miles in width. It was mostly flat, with some rocky prominences. In some places it appeared to be no more than a few feet above sea level. There was one large feature at one end of the island: a giant rock that jutted up into the air at least a hundred feet or so. Assa knew that some islands were created by volcanoes sticking up above the surface of the ocean. Their lava rose up and flowed down the sides of the mountain and created land as the lava touched the water and froze into rock.

But this did not look like that. She didn't see anything that looked like frozen lava. Instead, the big rock looked like some giant had plunked it down on the island. It gave the impression of a toy ball sitting on a table.

There were some buildings on the island, toward the other end, away from the big rock. She saw a cluster of them, suggesting some small community. Assa determined to land among those buildings and tilted her arms and legs and let air spill over them and began her descent. She had never landed before and was a little apprehensive about the dangers. She instinctively knew she could not be going so fast when she touched ground, but was not exactly sure how to accomplish this. If she grabbed air and stalled, she might simply fall. If she let air spill, she might hit the ground too fast and break a leg or worse.

In the event, she did the best she could, letting her arms slice through the air and judging her speed as best she could. She opted for a spiral landing, slowly circling her landing spot.

A fleeting thought occurred to her: how was she going to take off again? She didn't know how. Her soaring began in mid-flight.

How am I going to get off this island? she asked the air.

Don't worry about it. We'll help you.

That did not reassure her, but she had to land, she decided. She was getting too tired to go on, and where, in any case, would she go if she did not elect to stop here?

The roofs of several shacks turned and turned below her like a kaleidoscope. The surrounding greenery added a blur of life, there, so it seemed, just to make her dizzy. She tried to concentrate on the roofs: they appeared to be made of wood and were sloped to the ground. Assa widened her circle of approach so that she would be out of the center of these huts. She crashed through the tops of a couple of trees.

The branches snapped against her arms and legs making her cry out in pain. She slowed her speed to avoid getting slapped so hard and realized she couldn't land in the trees. The branches were going to hurt her.

She tightened her circle of descent and found a spot bare of huts or trees. She tilted her body as steeply as she dared. She dropped quickly. Her hand touched sand. Her foot dragged over grass and abruptly she stalled in the air and all her limbs pulled into her body so she hit the ground with a solid impact, and she rolled a few times and stopped.

Her back hurt and her arms felt bruised and tired. She stretched out on the ground. Her head still seemed to be turning. She looked up at the towering trees all around her. They made a canopy that felt good to be under, but they turned and turned, like pinwheels, and did not seem to want to stop.

She closed her eyes and the world seemed to slow down, at least a little.

I'm here, she said to the air, the trees, the huts, and the big rock. Now what?

Rest, said the voices. *You'll need your strength.*

I don't want to rest, said Assa. I want to know what I'm doing here.

Shhhh. Stop being so interested in what's next. Just be where you are now.

I'm so hungry.

That's good. It means you're alive.

Assa shook her head. That sounded like crazy wisdom to her. Like the voices didn't know a thing about her. Or where she was. She thought to open her eyes and look around, but the effort seemed overwhelming and instead she kept her eyes closed as tightly as she could manage and before long the darkness she saw spread through her world and sucked the energy out of her surroundings and she fell asleep.

WHEN SHE WOKE, she was curled into a tight ball and she was shivering. Her teeth chattered against themselves and her stomach was so empty she was sure she would feel her spine through her belly if she put her hand to her navel.

Rain was falling and collecting in pools around her. It wasn't a heavy rain, but it was enough to pull the heat from her body. She curled up tighter, wrapping her arms around her legs, but it didn't help. She was still colder than she had felt in a long time.

With great effort, she stretched out on the wet ground and tried to limber up her muscles and joints. She wanted the help of the invasive spirit now, but it was absent. Also the voice wasn't there. She rolled over on the ground and looked up at the sky, shielding her face with her hands.

No dragon in the sky. Nothing to assist her.

She sat up and looked around. She was in the midst of several huts made of wood. She heard the ping ping ping of the the raindrops falling on their roofs. The sound quickly grew annoying and she stood up and walked to one of them.

It had a door, also made of wood. There was a handle that looked like it was a piece of driftwood. She pulled it and stepped into the hut.

It was a relief to be out of the rain, but she was no warmer. She crossed her arms and hugged herself, as if trying to keep in some of her heat. The rain on the roof was even louder than it was outside, but it was not as high-pitched. The hut held some furniture: a table, a couple of chairs, and behind a wall she saw the end of a bed. This must be someone's house. Where were they?

Hello? said Assa, quietly, tentatively. She went around the wall and saw there was no one in the bedroom, if that was the proper term for that part of the hut. She went back to the area with the chairs and table and saw cabinets on the wall. She pulled a cabinet door open and found piles of dried fruit and what looked like smoked fish.

She pulled the food down and began eating. She took no time to savor or even taste. She bit off big chunks of fish and pineapple and some sweet fruit she didn't recognize, and swallowed them with barely a few chews. When she was finished she went back to the cupboard and devoured more. She didn't care how long the food had been in the cupboard, whether it was safe or not, or even if it was poison. She might have eaten it even if she had been told it would kill her. She didn't care about the hunger strike anymore. Who would know, here? Certainly not Hoyal. And not Dawn or Dusk.

Towards the back of the cupboard she found a small bag made of some plant fiber. She pulled it down and separated the top edges enough to look inside. The bag held shriveled little creatures, no bigger than Assa's thumb. She pulled one out and held it up to the meager light coming in through a window in the wall next to the table.

At first she thought the thing was an insect, but when she looked closer, she saw it didn't have six legs, only four. And it had leathery wings. A long snout. Her mind took a while before it finally saw that she was holding a tiny dragon. She held it for a long time. Such a small creature had to have been a baby. The people who lived here dried up baby dragons? For what? To eat?

Assa shuddered, this time from disgust rather than cold. She looked inside the bag and found more of the dried dragons. Perhaps a dozen. Also, at the very bottom of the bag, several small round objects. She pulled a couple of those out and put them in her palm. They weren't exactly round, more oblong. They bore lines that resembled\ lightning bolts and held a deep dark greenish color.

Dragon eggs, said Assa to the air.

Did they hatch them, then kill the babies?

The walls did not answer her question.

She put the eggs and the dinosaurs back into the bag and dropped the bag on the table. Then she went back to the bedroom and found a door to a closet.

She opened the closet and discovered a few garments, apparently made of the same material as the bag in the cupboard.

She pulled down a shirt and pants and held them in front of her. They looked like they would fit, so she took off her own wet clothes and put on the clothes from the closet. She expected the plant fibers to feel scratchy, but they weren't at all. The clothes felt nice and warm and dry. She felt her body begin to warm up a little.

The food in her stomach felt strange, like a foreign lump had invaded her. She was still hungry. She went back to the cupboard and pulled out more dried fish. She ate that, then pulled out more and ate that too. Finally, after many minutes, she stopped. There was more food, but she didn't know how long she was going to be here. She might need more.

She wondered if the rest of the huts contained food as well. It might be a good idea to look into each one and make an inventory, so she would know what she had to sustain here here.

She stepped to the door and looked outside. The rain had increased. It came down in heavy drops that splashed mud as it landed on the ground. She wanted to go outside and explore her new—what would she call it? Home? Prison? Vacation spot? She didn't know.

A thought occurred to her. She went back to the closet and looked down at the floor. Sure enough, she saw an umbrella. Well. That would be just the thing, wouldn't it?

She picked it up and held it by one end and pushed the slide along the handle. The umbrella burst into bloom, covering her head with a nice round canopy. She liked the feel of it immediately. The people who lived here didn't like getting rained on either, so it seemed.

Assa spent the next hour or so going from one hut to the other, seeing what each one held. There was not a lot of difference between them. Each had the same general layout as the first one she stopped at, and each had some food in the cupboard, and each had a bag containing dried dragons and what she supposed were dragon eggs.

The huts, numbering approximately two dozen, were arranged in a great circle. At the center of the circle a larger hut, of the same shape and general layout, but much bigger, filled the space. Assa thought it might be different from the others, but it was not, save for the size. It had larger rooms and bigger cabinets, but the contents were more or less the same.

She saw no people at all, which troubled her. Obviously people built and lived in these huts. Where were they? If there had been tracks on the ground, they were gone now, obliterated by the constant rain.

Thick foliage, green and robust, surrounded the circle of huts, but Assa saw there were trails through the forest, which must have been traversed by the inhabitants of this village. Maybe they were routes hunters took. Or maybe they led to gardens. When the rain stopped, she was going to follow one of the trails to see where it went.

Once she visited all the huts, she went back to the first one she had entered and sat on the bed, thinking. She had a good idea, now, of the total food available in the village. She also knew, approximately, how much she needed to survive each day. She put those two facts together and determined that if she was careful and did not eat too much, she could last here for about two months. Sixty days or so.

That seemed like a long time, but what if no one came to get her? After all, no one knew she was here. She would have to follow those trails and see if they led to gardens. Or she would have to see what she could eat of the local plants. Were there animals? There might be. Some she would have to catch and kill and eat.

Even if there weren't big animals, she knew that there must be bugs. Insects lived everywhere, so they must be here as well. She had never eaten bugs, but she knew they could be eaten. Some people liked them. She wasn't sure she could stomach them, but hoped that eventuality, if it ever came, was a long way off. She shouldn't worry about it yet. Anyway, before she had to resort to insect eating, she could always try her hand at fishing. The ocean was filled with fish. Surely she could catch a few every now and then to keep herself going.

She laid down on the bed. She wasn't cold anymore, but she was very tired. She could barely keep her eyes open.

Then a thought made her bolt upright in her bed. *Water.* She could have all the food she could stuff in her mouth, but it wouldn't do her any good if she didn't have water. She told herself she was a stupid girl for not thinking of that, then told herself she shouldn't be calling herself names. That didn't help anyone.

She would sleep for a while. Then look for water when she woke up.

The rain seemed to increase in intensity. The sound of the water on the roof did little to get her in a mood to fall asleep. She got up off the bed and floated to the ceiling where she put her hands out and tried to stop the rain. She squeezed her eyes tightly shut and felt the rough surface of the hut's construction against her palms.

The ceiling of the hut felt cold but solid. On the other side, she heard the rain change in pitch and intensity. Before long, it was talking to her. In voices. Voices she recognized.

Assa, said one of the voices, her mother's, are you well? Are you warm?

We're worried about you, came the other voice, her father's.

Assa put her mouth up against the ceiling and shouted to the voices on the other side. I'm fine, she said. I have everything I need to survive. I'm lonely, though. Come visit me.

She gripped the ceiling. She put her feet up to the ceiling and worked her toes into the fibers there, so that she hung onto the sloped embroidery like a bug, upside down and precarious. She angled her head back and looked down at the bed below her. She saw her own sleeping form, tucked under the blankets. Now when did that happen? She didn't remember getting under the blankets.

She pondered this fact for a time, then her attention was turned away by the sound of screeching from outside. It was a horrible sound. It pierced the flimsy material of the ceiling and seemed to snake through the air and aim for her spine, where it settled in without her permission and raised the hairs on her back, neck, and head.

Her skin was all goosebumps and she was afraid, especially when she began to feel an intense heat. It baked her skin and filled the room. Presently she saw flames erupting around her. The hut was on fire and the flames were spreading very quickly. She clung to the ceiling with even more determination, even as the hut dropped in burning pieces to the floor. The destruction of the ceiling allowed her to peak through in places. She saw a circle of dragons, at least ten of them, breathing fire onto the hut.

Assa could not move now. If she let go, she would fall and break herself for sure. If she tried flying away, she would have to fly through fire, since the dragons were showing no sign of letting up. They belched fire the way a volcano might belch lava and ash.

She blinked away the heat and the smoke. Her eyes burned. She released one hand from the ceiling, just one, so she could brush away the discomfort, and opened her eyes and saw early morning sunlight streaming through the window of the hut, onto the bed and onto her face.

The sun felt warm and cool at the same time and this puzzled her for a moment, until she saw that half her face was in shadow and half in sun. She wasn't on the ceiling, either, she was in the bed in the first hut. Her stomach churned and growled. She was hungry.

She went to the cupboard and pulled out some of the dried fruit and wolfed it down. Her salivary juices burned her mouth and throat, but it wasn't an altogether unpleasant experience. She supposed she would have to get used to eating again, after not taking in any food for so many days. How long was it, her hunger strike? She felt like it was weeks, but she knew that was wrong. She had only been at the house with Dawn and Dusk for two days. Or was it three? Maybe only one. Oh, it was getting harder and harder to keep track of what was happening to her.

Assa pulled down the bag with the dried dragons inside. She spread the top open and looked inside. There they were, jumbled up like candy in a bin. Without thinking, she reached inside, pulled one out, popped it into her mouth, and closed her jaws on it. Her teeth encountered little difficulty in pulverizing the things. She felt tiny bones crunch into dust. The leathery skin made her think of the crust on a wheel of cheese. The taste was slightly bitter with a little sweetness thrown in, almost like chocolate.

She ate another, then another, and had to stop herself from finishing off the bag. She held up one of the eggs and examined it carefully. It looked like it had to come from another world. She had never seen an egg like it, ever. It shimmered and changed colors as she turned it in her hand, catching the light from odd angles and refracting it back to her eye with a dazzling display of illumination. She felt like she was holding a sunset in her hand.

She had an urge to try the egg, but thought better of it. Raw eggs were not the best thing to be eating, she knew that. Maybe she would cook one later. If she found a way to cook things on this island.

Assa put the egg back in the bag and put the bag back in the cupboard. She went outside and stood in front of the hut. The sun was well over the horizon and flooded the hut with hot light. In front of her, the large rock looked as though it reached up to the clouds. A slight breeze rustled the leaves of the trees around her. They sounded like voices and she wanted to know why the voices that had guided her here were now missing.

Hello! she shouted into the air. Is anyone there?

No answer. She didn't expect one, but it would have been encouraging to hear *something*.

Suddenly, she felt so *lonely* that she had to sit down and cry. She plopped herself onto the ground and let the tears flow. The sobbed for a good five minutes or so. She tasted the salt on her face and her chest convulsed.

Images of her parents rose up before her. They seemed to float in the air and she reached for them, but as she did so, they receded from her. The trees and the sand blurred through her tears. Assa dabbed her face with her shirt and finally stopped crying after draining herself of any wish to die. It would be nice to just sleep and never wake up, if this was going to be her life from now on: living alone on an island in the middle of nowhere. She couldn't fly anymore. That was puzzling. How could she fly to get here, but not fly to get away?

She stood up. None of it mattered. She was here, now. It was up to her to survive long enough for someone to come get her and take her back to her parents.

She stepped away from the hut.

She had to find water.

Assa followed a trail that took her to the base of the rock. Along the way, she found pools in the woods that looked like they had been filled by the rain. She also discovered jugs, made of wood carved out of trees, that held water. That was encouraging. She dipped her hands into those jugs, cupped them together, and drank several handfuls of the water.

The water was rejuvenating and refreshing, sweeter than anything she had ever drank before. The jugs were everywhere, now that she found one. They were behind the huts, they were in the woods, along the trail, and there were several of them in the center of the circle of huts. She had thought they were some kind of ceremonial grouping when she first saw them. How could she not have seen that they served a functional purpose?

At the base of the rock, she looked for a way to climb up, but the angle was too steep and the foliage too thick. The rock was completely out of place here. It did not grow up from the island. It looked like it had been plopped onto the land.

She could see where the soil of the island came up to the rock and where it looked like it continued under the rock. The rock also had different plants growing on it, mostly a kind of iridescent moss that caught the sun and transformed it into a dream-like shimmer. It was as though an artist had taken a paint brush and dipped it into a dream, then applied it to the rock.

Assa spent a couple of hours walking the perimeter of the rock. There was no trail, so whoever lived on the island before they all disappeared had no interest in the rock. It was just there.

Assa kept her hand on the rock as she walked. The surface alternated between blankets of moss and bare rough stone. Some parts of the rock made her think of the ledge she and Dawn had been on before they were taken to the house. It had the same color and texture as that other rock. It even displayed the same sort of fissures and topography: the sort of rock you could grab onto and hold fast because of the roughness: It gave your hand something to grip.

But the way it curved around above her made it impossible to climb. Too bad. She wanted to climb it. She wanted to see what was at the top of the rock.

Assa continued to circle the rock. The foliage grew close here, and she had to bat away fronds and branches, large leaves. The trunks of some of the trees grew right up against the rock, as though they were trying to push the rock aside. Move over! they seemed to say. We want to grow here. You don't belong.

The trees hid the sun from her. She kept walking in the semi-darkness and saw light through the trees. She stepped towards the light and broke out of the forest and came to a sandy beach, just like the beaches back home. She stopped and blinked twice.

If she didn't know any better, she might have thought her house was just down the coast a bit. The thought filled her with longing. She missed her parents and her house so much. She even missed the work she had to do around the mill. She missed all of it: the sky over her head, the sound of the creek next to the house, the wind through the trees surrounding their land. All of it.

She realized she was crying and couldn't remember when she started. It felt like she should have been crying for days now. It was the only response that made sense. She was taken from her home and ended up alone, on this strange island. She collapsed on the beach, put her hands through the sand and let the grains fall through her fingers.

The sun, which had been behind some clouds, peeked out and shone on her head and face. The warmth felt soothing, like someone was hugging her. This made her cry even more. She sobbed quietly until something in her said she shouldn't be quiet. She should shout to the world.

She opened her mouth and wailed and screamed, alternating between sadness and anger. Her cries rose into the air and she hoped something, someone, would find them and follow them to their source and come and rescue her. Was such a thing even possible? Maybe there wasn't anyone left in the whole world. Maybe she was the last person alive.

By the time she sopped crying, she was completely wrung out. She felt like she had no energy left and was ready to collapse on the sand and let the tide come in and take her out to be whale food. She dropped to her knees, then curled up on her side. She closed her eyes and was just about to let herself drift into oblivion when a sharp cry pierced her ears.

She put her hands up to the sides of her head and tried to keep the sound away, but it was too loud. It penetrated her hands and went directly into her ears. It made her spine feel like it was vibrating. Her skin raised bumps. She got up on her knees and looked around. Where was the sound coming from? She heard it again, only this time it wasn't a single cry, it was many cries all at once. Some kind of bird? She looked up in the air. The sound of leather moving air descended on her. Small dots circled way up above her in a flock. The dots grew bigger. They had to be birds. The dots descended, each one flying a lazy circle, but the bunch of them—perhaps twenty or so—circling together, created a kind of whirlpool effect. She saw, finally, that they were dragons, and they were coming down precisely where she was.

Assa didn't waste any time. She rose from the sand and began running toward the forest. The sand was thick and soft, which kept her from running at full speed, but she put all her strength into it and made it to the edge of the forest before the dragons lighted on the beach.

They screeched in the air. At the shelter of the trees, she turned around and watched the beach. The sky was obscured from her view by the big leaves above her. She watched the beach and listened to the cries of the dragons. She watched and watched.

They never landed on the beach. Instead, they crashed through the canopy of leaves above Assa, descended toward her with their wings spread wide and their talons extended. As soon as Assa saw that she was, after all, not safe in the trees, she bolted from the beach again, but it was no use. There were too many of them. As she ran through the forest of tree trunks, one of the dragons grabbed her arm. Her legs, working fast, only churned against air.

She screamed as she was lifted through the trees, held only by the talons of the dragon. She reached wildly with her other arm for something to grab onto, but only managed to scratch the belly of the dragon and it did not impede the dragon's flight at all. The beach and forest dropped away from her. The island grew bigger and changed from an environment to a picture, painted on the blue ocean.

She wanted to be still. She willed her legs and arms to stop working against the dragon. If it let her go now, she would die for sure. But her limbs didn't want to cooperate. They seemed to have a life of their own, fueled, no doubt, by her terror. They waved madly in the air—

—until another dragon swooped in next to her captor and grabbed her other arm. Then the two of them, their wings flapping lazily in the air, lifted her higher and higher. She wondered where dragons build their nests. She also wondered if she was going to be food for dragon babies. The thought terrified her, briefly, but then she decided if that was how things would turn out, then that was okay. She would just have to accept her fate.

Now that two of them had a hold of her, she felt much more secure soaring above the island. It was as though the dragons wanted to take care of her. She stopped kicking her legs and let them hang loosely. She looked down, dizzied by the view. The island was tiny, now, just a green dot on the ocean. It circled as she circled, the two of them executing some kind of strange long-distance dance.

All the while, dozens of dragons circled with her. They swooped next to her, then veered away. She heard the air rip over the surface of their leathery wings. They screeched into the sky so that their shrill voices seemed to scare away everything else for miles around. The air was empty except for dragons and Assa.

A lot of them, Assa noticed, held twigs and branches in their talons. Some of the wood was so big that the dragons looked as though they were laboring just to remain in the air. Their wings flapped rapidly. The dragons breathed with a loud rasping sound, like they were laboring and maybe they weren't going to make it.

Eventually, the island began to get bigger again: they were descending. The big rock at the end of the island rose up to meet her.

The wings of the dragons holding her flapped a little more rapidly, the better, she supposed, to control the air currents swirling around them. Updrafts caught their wings. Heat seemed to rise up from the rock. Assa looked down and saw a pile of wood on fire on top of the mountain.

The last fifty feet or so of air beneath her collapsed quickly and the two dragons holding her released their talons from her arms. She dropped ten feet or so and rolled up and let herself tumble onto the ground. She felt bruised and banged up, but was sure nothing had broken. She remained on the ground.

The heat from the fire warmed her. It was only a few feet away. As she lay, unmoving and watching the sky, she saw dragons swoop in and drop their branches onto the fire. A couple of them landed on the ground beside the fire and breathed flame into the pile of wood. It was already burning well enough, so Assa didn't see the point of adding more flame, but decided it was a kind of ritual for some of the dragons.

After they dropped their cargoes, they took to the air again and descended down from the rock to, she supposed, the forest to get more wood for the fire.

Not all went down. Some of the dragons remained perched on the ground. They unfurled their wings and appeared to be warming them at the fire. One of the dragons that had been carrying her did just that. It rose up on its stubby legs as high as it could, then opened its wings as wide as they would go. Its eyes narrowed to slits and it stood in the heat for a long time. Assa sat up and rubbed her arms. They were especially sore from where the talons had held her.

So what am I doing here? she asked the dragons.

No answer came.

She stood up and faced the fire. She put her hands in front of her and warmed her palms. Then she turned and let the heat warm her back. It felt good to be near the fire. It felt like she had come home from somewhere she didn't want to be.

But that was a ridiculous feeling. This wasn't home. She didn't know *what* this place was.

Assa heard a voice coming from the other side of the fire. She turned around and tried to look through the flames. She thought she saw a human figure. Or, at least some figure without wings.

Who's there? she said.

The figure moved around the fire and came around to Assa's full view.

Welcome to my little escape from the world, said Hoyal.

Assa's eyes went wide and she turned from Hoyal and ran as fast as her condition would allow, away from the flames and away from her captor and tormentor. But the dragons would not allow it. They swooped into formation around her, enclosing her within a flock of dragons.

Assa probably should have stopped right there and seen what was going to happen next. After all, she couldn't escape so many dragons. And even if she did, she was on top of the rock. Where would she go? There was no easy way down. She could have leaped off the top of the rock and ended this strange journey once and for all. But she wasn't prepared to do that. Not yet. Maybe later.

But none of those considerations entered her mind right then. She just wanted to be away from Hoyal and the dragons. She reached out and seized one of them by the neck. The muscles throbbed and tightened against her palm, but she didn't let go. The dragon screeched into the air, but it was a muffled screech, dampened by Assa's hold on its neck.

The wings of the dragon flapped spasmodically. The sound made her think of the wheel at her parent's mill, the way it turned and turned, endlessly, the wood creaking and grinding.

She tightened her grip on the dragon. Its eyes bulged, it jerked and tried to put its talons onto Assa, but she held it far away, enough so that the feet couldn't get close to her. She would have killed it and been happy for the opportunity, if the other dragons did not, as one, sent a coordinated burst of flame in her direction.

Their combined fires singed her hair and brought a brief and unbearable pain to her skin. She cried out and released the dragon. It flopped to one side and breathed heavily into the dust. The other dragons closed an even tighter circle around Assa and kept her immobile. Her chest was heaving with the effort to breathe. She shook with fatigue and rage. The dragons maintained their configuration until Hoyal advanced on the group and began pushing them aside until she was standing directly in front of Assa.

Is that any way to thank your hosts? asked Hoyal.

Assa ran towards Hoyal and made fists and beat her on her legs and belly. Hoyal stood and took it. Assa didn't have much power behind her blows. She was drained and weak. Whatever strength she had in her had been spent on trying to choke the dragon to death.

There, there, said Hoyal. It's okay. She put her arms around Assa and hugged her tightly. Assa's blows turned to taps and finally stopped. I'm sorry it had to be this way, said Hoyal. It wasn't my doing. There are bigger things than little old you and me in this world. Now, if you will allow me, there is a nice room I can take you to. There's food and a fireplace. Comfy chairs, too. And after you eat, a nice bed to sleep in. Come on.

Hoyal pulled away from Assa and took her hand. They walked towards a cave entrance. The dragons parted for them, their shuffling noises mixing with their rasping breath. Assa saw thin curls of smoke rise from their nostrils. She smelled burning, like someone had put flame to piles of paper. In the cave, a soft light flooded everything. Assa heard sounds coming from far inside, voices engaging in conversation. She recognized some of those voices. She looked up at Hoyal, who smiled down at her.

Yes, said Hoyal, it's true. Go on.

Assa released Hoyal's hand and ran to the sounds. She found a spacious cavern at the end of a rocky hall. Dragons roosted up near the ceiling and looked down on a table. Around the table sat Dawn and Dusk. They looked up and smiled at Assa as she came close. Assa ran to them and hugged them both. Tears streamed down her face. Dawn and Dusk held her and stroked her hair and face and comforted her as best they could, but Assa could not stop crying.

I thought I heard my parents, she said.

I know, said Dusk. When we first got here we thought we heard our mother.

What does it mean? asked Assa.

The cave does weird things to sound, said Dusk. You'll get used to it.

Assa looked up at the dragons. There must have been fifty of them. They perched on ledges way up high and looked down at the three girls.

Those things give me the creeps, said Assa.

Us too, said the princesses.

But you get used to them, said Dusk. They're actually kind of fun. I wouldn't mind one as a pet.

Dawn rolled her eyes. Dusk is always wanting a pet. It's ridiculous. Dragons can't be pets.

Anything can be a pet, said Dusk. Even commoners.

Hey, said Assa.

Oops, said Dusk. Her face turned red and she put her hand over her mouth. Sorry. I didn't mean *you* Assa. We like you as a person.

Dawn's face was slightly flushed as well. She put a hand on Assa's shoulder. You'll have to excuse my lame sister, she said. She's still learning to be human. She turned to Dusk and stretched her lips into a wide fake smile.

Well, said Dusk. Whatever. You going to eat something with us?

What about the hunger strike? said Assa.

That was when we were prisoners, said Dusk.

We aren't prisoners now? asked Assa.

Dusk shook her head emphatically. We can leave anytime.

Dawn slapped her sister on the back of the head.

Hey, said Dusk. Watch that.

My sister is an idiot, said Dawn. Be glad you don't have one.

I've always wanted a sister, said Assa.

You can have mine, said Dawn.

Hey. *Again.*

Sit down, said Dawn to Assa. Assa pulled out a chair and sat in it. The table was made of heavy solid wood. She saw that parts of it were edged with black, charred. Probably from the breaths of the dragons, she thought.

Dawn put a plate in front of Assa. It was piled high with vegetables, rice, and some kind of meat in a sauce. It instantly made Assa's mouth water just to look at it.

What is it? she said.

Don't ask so many questions, said Dawn. It's good. Take a bite. She put a fork in Assa's hand.

Assa held the fork for a few seconds, then shrugged and took a mouthful. Then another. She barely had time to taste the food. She wolfed it down without another thought. It felt good to have real hot food for once.

Here's the thing, said Dawn. Dusk is mostly right, in a way. We can leave any time. There are not gates or guards. No doors to the cave. Nothing. All we have to do is walk outside and step off the rock.

Assa chewed and swallowed. If we step off the rock, we'll—

—die, said Dawn. Yes. You've found the flaw in Dusk's theory.

Dusk stuck her tongue out at Dawn. Dawn stuck her tongue out right back at her. Assa laughed. You two sure have a funny way of being sisters, she said.

Never mind that, said Dusk. Here's the thing. How did you get up here?

Dragons, said Assa.

Us too, said Dawn.

So that's how we get down again, said Dusk.

Dragons? said Assa.

It's the only way. We have to convince them to take us off the island.

Assa took another bite of her food. It was good. She couldn't identify the meat, but it hardly mattered. It felt good be satisfied. She looked up at the dragons, all in a row and staring down at them. They don't look like they want to help us, said Assa.

That's because Hoyal has some kind of spell on them, said Dawn. Dusk nodded.

Spell? said Assa. There's no such thing.

That's what we thought, said Dawn. But we were wrong.

Where are we? asked Assa. What is this place?

This is our land, said Dawn. Our home. This is where we wanted to get back to.

Well, said Assa, you're back. Are you happy yet?

This isn't the way it was supposed to happen, said Dawn.

I never knew there were actual dragons in the world, said Assa.

Hoyal came up to them. She clapped her hands together several times. Assa was growing very irritated with Hoyal. Didn't she have better things to do than confine dragons and little girls?

Getting your strength back? asked Hoyal.

Assa said nothing. Dawn and Dusk were just as quiet.

Come on, now, said Hoyal. You can't say I'm not taking good care of you. All I want is a simple thank you. Nothing more.

You won't get it from us, said Assa. She felt Dawn and Dusk stiffen, as though Assa had done something dangerous. Assa herself felt like it was maybe not such a good thing to have said what she said.

Hoyal turned her eyes to Assa and stared at her for several seconds. Assa, at first, stared back, but before long she faltered and averted her eyes.

You're a feisty one, said Hoyal. I'll give you that. She swept her arms out to indicate the expanse of the room. Just like the dragons here, she said. They were feisty, once. Now they do as I ask of them. I think eventually, that will happen with the three of you as well.

Assa is a commoner, said Dawn. You should let her go. Your quarrel is with the royals.

And what, said Hoyal, do you know of my quarrel?

We know, said Dusk, that you hate our parents. You want to be queen. You wanted to take over the island.

Well, said Hoyal, look around. Haven't I done that?

Dusk looked down at the ground. Assa had to agree with Hoyal. She was running things here.

Anyway, said Hoyal. It doesn't matter now. You're all tired. I'll show you to your rooms and you can rest up. You need rest, I can see it. You've all three had a somewhat trying few days.

Some of the dragons moved closer to the three girls, herding them in the direction that Hoyal was walking. The girls went further into the cave, leaving the rows of dragons like strung out gargoyles on the walls. Assa had decided that the dragons gave her the creeps. She was glad she ate some of the baby ones. It gave her a feeling that she had done something to hurt them, and that was a remarkably good feeling to have right then.

The cave turned and twisted and grew slightly narrower. Illumination seemed to come from some strange devices attached to the walls here and there. They flitted by as Assa walked. At first they looked like candles, but they didn't burn like candles. In fact, they didn't burn at all. They resembled twisted pieces of paper, but eventually Assa saw that they were actually hunks of dragon skin that had been twisted into irregular thin columns.

They gave off a subdued shimmering light. Not enough to read by, but enough to help show them the way down the corridor. After a few minutes the cave opened up wide and high into a chamber with a gracefully rounded ceiling. The dragon lights were arrayed near the top in a big circle. The combined glow of them all filled the chamber with dragon light.

It was a glorious feeling to be under all that light. Assa, Dawn, and Dusk, all held their breaths. None of them wanted to break the spell of this light.

Hoyal stopped and looked around with them. It's marvelous, isn't it? she said. All this sacrifice by the dragons. They give so much and ask so little in return.

Assa wanted to say how incredible the chamber was. How it made her feel like she had come to the right place, but she kept her silence. No reason to talk to Hoyal. No reason to give her any satisfaction at all. The twins seemed to agree with her. They chose not to say anything either.

Well, you girls are suddenly strangely quiet, said Hoyal. Time for some sleep, perhaps?

She showed the girls to their rooms, which were small wooden structures, almost like oversized wardrobes, arranged against one wall of the chamber. Assa stepped to her room and pulled the door open. She peered inside and saw a simple arrangement of furniture: a small bed and a small chair. That was all. She turned back to Hoyal, who had a wide smile on her face.

They are modest, said Hoyal, but comfortable. Go on, now. Get inside. Tomorrow we have work to do.

The dragons stepped forward and snorted with menacing insistence. Ass stepped through the door and into her room. A dragon threw the door shut with a slam. Assa heard it on the other side of the door, snorting every few seconds. Assa wondered how she was going to sleep through the dragon breath.

Are you two okay? she called to Dawn and Dusk.

They answered with muffled voices. Assa couldn't quite make out what they were saying, but they sounded like they were comfortable. Not panicked, at least.

What kind of work do you think we'll be doing tomorrow? she asked.

The dragon rattled Assa's door, apparently wanting her to quiet down. Assa kicked the door two or three times, just to show the dragon she wasn't afraid of some fire-breathing lizard. The dragon kicked right back, raising such a ruckus with its repeated blows that Assa stepped back from the door with her hands on her ears to block out the sound.

Well, she said to herself, I guess it wants quiet. Assa got into bed and pulled the covers up to her chin. She was getting tired of not sleeping in her own bed. And she was getting very tired indeed of having Hoyal in her life.

THE DRAGON PULLED the door open and came into Assa's room and pulled her out of bed.

Hey, said Assa. What's the idea?

She was sprawled out on the floor. The dragon gestured with a wing toward the outside of Assa's hut.

You want me out of bed, just *ask*, said Assa.

She heard giggles coming from the atrium. They did the same with us, said Dusk. Or Dawn. Assa wasn't sure. Sometimes they sounded so much alike she couldn't tell them apart. She got up off the floor and walked into the atrium of the cave. Dragons still presented a gargoyle-like tableaux in a line near the ceiling. They kind of gave Assa the creeps and she wasn't even sure why. Maybe it was the way they did Hoyal's bidding without seeming to object at all. Maybe it was how they gave up their skins—however reluctantly it may be—so that Hoyal could make torches out of them.

Dusk and Dawn ran to her and hugged her. How was your night? asked Dawn.

I slept, said Assa. I cried some, too.

So did we, said Dusk.

What do you think we're going to have to do today? asked Dawn.

Assa looked at the dragons surrounding them. They had dull eyes, as if they had been asleep and were not fully awake yet. She wanted to take a stick or a poker and push it into those eyes. It would be nice to hear the dragons squeal as they bled to death out of their eyes. Why didn't they look more alive? If she had eyes like that, she would assume that she was close to dying. Isn't that what it meant? Wasn't it crazy that a creature could walk around with dead eyes?

Hey! said Dawn. You still with us?

Assa shook her head and brought herself back to her present situation. I was just wandering, she said.

Dawn put her arm around Assa's shoulder. We understand, she said, but we need you with us. Alert and ready for anything.

Dusk nodded. We need to bide our time, she said, then we'll break out of this place.

Assa smiled at them. You need a commoner to help you? Isn't that kind of against the royal way?

Oh, commoners are important to us royals, said Dawn. Without you, we wouldn't have anyone to boss around. She grinned.

Assa laughed, but it wasn't a full on laugh, it was more of a knowing kind of fake laugh. It was a laugh to let them know that she got the joke, but she wasn't going to let that keep her from knowing her place. She looked up at the dragons again. Just like them, she had her place. Just like them, she didn't upset things too much.

Assa heard footsteps. All three girls turned around. Hoyal walked toward them from out of the darkness at the entrance to the atrium.

Let's not say anything to her, whispered Dusk.

Okay, said Dawn.

Assa didn't reply. Dawn elbowed her in the ribs. Okay, okay, said Assa. I won't say anything.

They stopped talking and waited for Hoyal to get closer. The dragons also became very still, like fluorescent statues. The light from the twisted sticks made of their skin cast a soft light that highlighted Hoyal's features. She looked like she would scare the rocks if she wanted to.

Good morning girls, said Hoyal. Did you all sleep well? I hope you did.

Assa almost answered Hoyal automatically, but held her tongue just in time.

Hoyal raised her eyebrows and looked at each of them in turn. Hard of hearing this morning? she asked. I inquired as to the quality of your sleep.

The girls kept their silence. Dragons shifted on their feet around them. The silence of the atrium was punctuated only by the raspy breathing of the dragons.

Very well, said Hoyal. I'm getting the silent treatment. That's to be expected. I'm not angry. Not a bit. On the contrary, I admire your determination and tenacity. Also that you got together and devised a plan, then saw it through. It shows such—how can I put it?—*initiative*. Bravo. Very well done.

Hoyal clapped her hands together three times, very lightly, hardly make a sound at all.

Assa felt her face turn warm. She wanted to scream at Hoyal. But she didn't. Dawn and Dusk kept their silence as well.

Well, said Hoyal, since you are so determined to fight me, I'm sure that you are not interested in any breakfast. So I won't offer you any. We'll just get right to work. Follow me.

She began walking back the way she had come in. The dragons around the girls pushed them forward to follow Hoyal. Assa reluctantly lifted her feet and shuffled after Hoyal. Dawn and Dusk followed, but took as small steps as they could. They held back as much as possible, leaning against the dragons pushing them forward. This went on for a few seconds until the dragons lost their patience and snorted a few flames in the air.

Assa felt the heat on her back. They all three picked up their pace then and followed Hoyal more closely, who held her head up high, as though making sure the dragons had a good look at her. Soon they were out of the cave.

The sky was clear and blue. Only a few fluffy clouds here and there. A slight breeze rustled the leaves of the trees and nudged strands of Assa's hair against her forehead. Early morning light gave everything a fresh look. It was a relief to be outside after spending the night in the cave.

Hoyal stopped and put her hand up to her forehead. Oh, silly me, she said and turned around. I forgot to tell you. I heard from your parents.

Assa and the twins stopped and looked up at Hoyal, who smiled at them and made her eyes go wide. She tilted her head and clasped her hands in front of her.

Yes, it's true, she said. I just got word from them. By dragon. They carry messages to me. Clutched in their talons. It's charming, really. Assa, your parents are well and wish you the best. Dawn and Dusk, your parents want you to know they have every confidence that you will behave in a manner appropriate to the royals that you are.

Assa didn't believe a word Hoyal said. She didn't think Dawn or Dusk did either.

Hoyal looked at the three of them as though she were examining piles of garbage in her way. She tried to hide it with a fake smile but it didn't fool Assa. Not for one second.

Why aren't you telling me you're glad to hear this news? asked Hoyal. What? You think I'm lying? If I'm lying, how do explain these?

She pulled two pieces of paper from her pockets and extended them to the girls. Here, she said, take a look for yourselves if you don't believe me.

The papers were turned over, so Assa couldn't see the words on them. Despite herself, she wanted to take the message and read it. Not to prove that one of them was from her parents, but just to prove that Hoyal was lying.

Neither of those papers are on royal stationary, said Dawn.

Well, said Hoyal, they probably didn't have any lying around. They wanted to get the message to you right away. Sometimes you have to compromise on niceties, don't you?

Dawn reached for the pages while Dusk and Assa glared at Hoyal.

Before Dawn could touch the paper, a dragon swooped in between them and snagged the pages in its talons and flew away.

Wha— said Hoyal, then laughed. Oh, those crazy dragons. They think this is a message. Come back, she called. Come back with those. They aren't meant for you. Come back.

Hoyal went to the edge of the rock and stood on the precipice and called out to the dragon, which was a long way away. Oh, drat, she said. That poor dragon can't hear me. Now you'll probably never see how much your parents care for you and love you. A pity.

Hoyal sighed and turned back to the girls. She stood highlighted against the sky. It almost looked like she was floating in the air.

Well, she said. No matter. There will be other messages, I'm sure. Now, let's get to the important business of why you are here.

Assa was very interested in learning the answer to that question. She wondered what lie Hoyal was about to spring upon them.

But before Hoyal could say another word, Dawn and Dusk, acting as one, ran forward with their arms extended in front of them. They ran at full speed, with the power of fury churning their legs. It only took them three or four steps to get to Hoyal, and she did not react fast enough to prevent her from being pushed off the edge of the rock.

Assa cried out. Hoyal's eyes went wide and she reached forward, trying to grab something to save her, but only grabbing air. She dropped from view.

Dawn and Dusk tried to stop themselves from going over with Hoyal, but only Dawn remained on the rock with Assa. Dusk tumbled over the edge, following Hoyal down.

Assa ran to the edge of the rock. She saw Hoyal and Dusk falling toward the island, both of them waving their ams and legs wildly. A great screeching noise rose up around her. The dragons mobilized in an instant and several of them swooped over head and dropped in a powered flight toward the falling figures.

Assa was transfixed by the sight. Two dragons, talons extended, converged on Dusk and grabbed her by the arms and swooped away from the rock and began lifting her up. Meanwhile, three or four dragons converged on Hoyal, but she was tumbling end over end, and they had a harder time grabbing her.

It didn't help that Hoyal appeared to be fighting the dragons. She kicked at them and hit them with her fists. It was as though she didn't want them to rescue her, but Assa couldn't believe that was true. Surely Hoyal wanted to live.

Finally, one dragon wrapped its talons around Hoyal's ankle and began lifting her up. But the dragon was having trouble. Hoyal was too big. As Assa watched, Hoyal pulled the dragon down until the dragon, unable to hold on, released Hoyal, who screamed out to the air and hit the ground a split second later and lay there at an odd angle, her body bent and her legs splayed. Assa made herself look for another few seconds. Hoyal didn't move.

Behind her, she heard Dusk and Dawn calling. Assa, said Dawn. Is she dead?

Assa turned and faced them. Blood streamed down Dusk's arms where the talons had broken her skin. She didn't seem to mind, though. She had a giant grin on her face. Dawn had her arm around Dusk and was grinning just as widely. The two dragons that had brought her back to the top of the rock perched nearby in gargoyle mode as though nothing spectacular had just occurred.

How about that, said Dusk. We did it.

You killed her, said Assa.

Did we? said Dusk. Did we really? Is she really dead?

I think so, said Assa. She isn't moving.

Doesn't mean she's dead, said Dawn. What are the dragons doing?

Assa looked around. The dragons all remained in their places, like statues watching over everyone. Their eyes blinked only every minute or so, just like before. Their wings remained as still as stones.

They aren't doing anything, said Assa.

Then she's not dead, said Dawn. If she was dead, all the dragons would be dead too.

What? asked Assa. What do you mean?

Hoyal has power over the dragons, said Dawn. She's their energy. Without her, they are nothing.

Dusk nodded. Yup, she said.

How do you know this? asked Assa. And don't tell me it's because you're royals.

Okay, said Dusk. We won't.

Assa went back to the cliff's edge and looked down at the bent form that was Hoyal. She still didn't move. Assa tried to see if her chest was rising, but could not tell from this distance. If she was alive she was definitely broken. They had to help her.

She turned back to Dusk and Dawn. Did you plan this? she asked them. Did you plan to push her off the edge?

The twins exchanged glances. We didn't *plan* it, no. But we did decide together, when we both saw her at the edge, that we would push her off.

We've got to get down there, said Assa.

Look, said Dawn. We don't have to worry about anything now. She can't move, right?

Assa nodded.

So she can't eat or drink. She'll soon die of starvation or dehydration or something. Then the dragons will all keel over and we'll get rescued.

The only way off this rock is with the dragons, said Assa. If they die, then we're stuck.

You are always looking at the dark side of things, said Dusk. It must be your commoner upbringing. We royals know that everything will turn out in the end.

Maybe for royals, said Assa. But for most people that isn't true.

The twins laughed and put their arms around each other. Come on, they said to Assa. Let's go find something to eat. We're starved.

They turned from Assa and went back to the atrium. It seemed to Assa like they were purposely making her feel small and ridiculous. She saw their point. Why should they try to rescue Hoyal, who did nothing but terrorize them? Still. She couldn't get out of her mind that there was someone at the bottom of the rock who needed help. Even if she was mean to them, she was still a person in trouble. Wouldn't it be better to help her live, then have her be punished for her crimes? It wasn't right to just let her die. Was it?

Her thoughts went around and around like this for some time. She wanted to help someone who didn't deserve help. What was there in Assa that yearned for this kind of mercy to someone who showed them only the very minimum of any kindness? Who, for the most part, treated them very poorly indeed?

She heard a yelp of joy coming from the atrium. The twins must have found something good. Or something interesting, at least.

She looked down at the still form of Hoyal again, then, reluctantly, walked back to the atrium. She found Dusk and Dawn sitting on the ground facing each other with wooden containers arrayed between them on the ground. They had taken off the lids of some of the containers and had pulled out food: dried fruit and meat, some fresh apples and mangoes, cheeses, and loaves and loaves of bread.

Dusk gnawed on a hunk of the bread and Dawn had a wedge of cheese in her hand. She chewed noisily and waved at Assa to come over. We're having a feast, she said. Come eat.

But I'm a commoner, said Assa. I can't eat with royals.

We'll make an exception, said Dusk, wiping crumbs from her lips.

Assa came and sat next to the twin princesses. She took some of the dried meat and bit into it. It was leathery and sweet, but hard to chew. Must be dragon meat, she said.

Dawn and Dusk nodded. Yup, said Dawn. Tasty, isn't it?

Assa could hardly taste anything. The crumbly meat was like ashes in her mouth.

She's suffering, said Assa. She must be in pain.

That'll be over soon, said Dusk. Don't think about it so much. You'll worry yourself to death.

Yeah, said Dawn. That's what our mother the queen always says. Worry will kill you faster than anything. So don't worry.

Assa took another bite of the dragon meat, then tossed it back in the box with the rest of the strips.

Hey, said Dusk. That may be the way commoners deal with food, but you don't put back something you chewed with the rest of it. That's gross.

Assa leaned over and spit into the box. There, she said. How's that for common?

Dusk's mouth fell open. What is the matter with you? she said.

Dawn sighed. Well, she said, I guess that box is yours. But that's all you're getting. Make it last, because we're not letting you have any more food. If you think acting like a brat will get us to help that criminal who got what she deserved, you're very mistaken.

Dusk and Dawn gathered up all the boxes except for the one Assa spit into, and carried them to Dawn's cabin. Assa watched them with a sense of longing and irritation. They were so used to having power and she wished she could have some of it for herself. But they were also so used to using it in a way that helped no one except themselves, that she wished they would both die.

Or better yet, spend some months working in a field, or the mill, or being forced to make things with their hands. Difficult things that involved wire and nails and knives so that their hands got cut and they were in pain.

Such disturbing thoughts did not normally occupy Assa's mind. She shook her head and tried to make them go away, but they wouldn't. She had more thoughts of causing pain to the princesses. They deserved it just as much as Hoyal did.

Dawn stood in front of her hut and called to Assa. When you can be a civilized person again, she said, then you can ask for our forgiveness and we will think about letting you be friends with us again. Assa didn't answer. Dawn retreated inside and shut the door behind her.

The air was still and the atrium was quiet, punctuated only by faint echoes reverberating off the walls as she shuffled her feet. She looked down at the box of dried meat. She picked out the two or three with her spit on them and tossed them to the ground. Even though it was her own spit, they disgusted her and she didn't want o keep or eat them.

Then she put the lid back on the box and took it to her own hut and put it in a corner. All the while, she thought of Hoyal. She stepped out of her hut and looked up at the dragons, still looking down on her.

She called to them. Hey dragons, she said. Your master is wounded. Aren't you going to help her? They blinked. All of them. They all blinked at once.

Assa put up her arm. Come on dragons, she said. Come land on my arm. Come on.

A few of the dragons shuffled their feet, as though in response to her request, but they did not leave their perches. Many turned their gaze to her and watched her with a bored indifference.

Fine, said Assa. Have it your way. I'm going to find a path down without you. Just you watch.

She returned to her hut and saw that the structure had been laced together out of logs tied with some kind of cord. She unraveled some of the cord from the logs and tested its strength by grasping it in her hands and pulling as hard as she could. She decided it was very strong.

She started pulling more of the cord. Logs came loose as she unraveled. They slipped and scraped against each other and fell to the ground, unmoored.

Assa stepped out of the hut and pulled at the cord from outside. The logs continued to find paths inward. Before long, she had bundles of cord in her hands and at her feet, and the logs that had made up her hut lay in a jumble in front of her. About this time, Dusk and Dawn came out of their huts to see what the noise was about.

What did you do? said Dawn, sounding as horrified as if she had come across a dead body.

I'm getting off this rock, said Assa.

You can't do that by yourself.

Yes I can. She lifted some of the cord for Dawn and Dusk to see. I'm going to make a rope out of this, she said. I'll use it to lower myself down.

You'll slip off and fall, said Dusk. You'll die.

We'll see, said Assa.

She began laying out lengths of the cord on the ground. She tied ends together with knots she had learned from her father. She tested each knot by stepping on the cord, holding it fast against the ground, and pulling on the knot with all her might, trying to get it to slip off. Each knot she tied went through this testing and she was happy to see that not one of them slipped.

The work was slow and tedious. She was acutely aware that the entire rope would only be as good as its weakest knot, so she made sure every knot was as strong as it could be.

Dawn and Dusk watched with only slight interest. It was the sort of attention you would give something because you had absolutely nothing else to be doing that might absorb your attention.

You're going to have sleep out here, said Dusk. We're not going to let you stay in our huts.

That's fine, said Assa, as she yanked on a length of her rope. I don't want to sleep in your huts anyway.

Out here, said Dawn, the dragons could swoop down on you in the night and gobble you up.

Dragons don't eat people, said Assa.

How do you know?

If they did, we'd be dragon poop by now.

Dusk laughed. She's got a point, she said to Dawn.

The point is on her head. Anything gets hungry enough, it'll eat whatever is handy.

Anyway, said Assa, I won't be sleeping here. This rope is coming along nicely. Almost done. It'll be finished soon and I'll be on my way.

Hmmmm, said Dawn. If you say so. Good luck with lowering yourself down.

Good luck with waiting here to die, said Assa.

Dawn and Dusk hung around a few more minutes, but soon grew bored with Assa's project and went back to their huts. An hour later, Assa had knotted all the pieces of the cords together into one long rope. She gathered up the rope and looped it repeatedly on itself so that it made a giant circle on the ground. Then she lifted the loop and dragged it onto her shoulder so that it hung down at her side. Thus encumbered, she walked out of the atrium toward the lip of the rock.

She looked down the rock, to assure herself that Hoyal was still there, but the ground at the bottom was bare. There was some sand, but no body. No Hoyal. No person of any kind.

She must be mistaken. Hoyal couldn't have simply walked off. Assa rubbed her eyes and looked down again. There was no mistake. Hoyal was gone.

Assa turned toward the atrium and the huts of Dawn and Dusk. She should tell them, shouldn't she? Hoyal was not only alive, but she was getting around.

Well, that was their problem. Not hers. Assa was getting off the rock. If Hoyal came back up, it was going to something Dawn and Dusk had to deal with. Not her.

Assa wrapped one end of her rope around a tree trunk near the lip of the rock. She secured it tightly with one of her expertly executed knots. She pulled on the rope with all her weight. The tree stood rock solid, the trunk unmoving. She took the rest of the rope and walked back to the lip of the rock and threw her loop over the edge and into the air. The loop unraveled as it fell. Assa leaned over the cliff edge and saw that the end did not reach the bottom. It dangled in the air and swayed in the wind. The end of her rope looked like it was trying to paint a picture against the rock face way down there.

She could descend on the rope, but when she got to the end she would have to jump, and it looked like the island's sand was a very long way past the end of the rope. If she jumped, she might break something.

But, she reasoned, the ground looked soft there. If she rolled as she landed, she should be okay. She thought. She hoped.

Anyway, Hoyal could right now be finding a way to get back up here and Assa did not want to meet here again. Not here. Not anywhere, actually, but especially not up here where she could control Assa and the princesses to her whim.

She grabbed the rope and twisted it so that it wrapped around her hands once. If she pulled on the rope then, it would tighten its grip on her hand, but if she released it just a little, it gave enough for the rope to twist through her hands and allow her to slip down the length of the rope.

She also made sure the rope was between her feet and that she could put one foot over the other, clamping the rope between them and giving her body support. In this way, she felt she could alternately loosen and tighten her hands and her feet, allowing her to descend slowly and methodically down the rope and the rock face. She stood on the cliff edge and took several deep breaths, then began executing her plan.

The first step, over the rock lip, was the scariest.

The whole world seemed to tilt. The sky swooped past her head, the ground suddenly appeared a long long way down, and the rock face swung into better view. It was as though the planet pivoted around her rope and worked to make her dizzy.

Her heart began beating wildly and her hands began trembling. Assa took several more deep slow breaths. She felt almost on the verge of tears, but fought them with all her will. She loosened her grip on the rope and descended a foot or so, then tightened her grip again.

Her head was just at the level of the top of the rock. The surface spread out before her eyes like an altered world. It stretched and stretched away from her, but looked miniature, like a doll's land. She heard footsteps pounding the ground. Dawn and Dusk running in her direction. She didn't wait for them.

She descended two or three more feet rapidly, so that she could not see the top of the rock any longer. Now she was in the realm of the rock face. It was right next to her. She felt it's grit against her cheek as she held onto the rope for dear life.

Above her, Dawn and Dusk called down. Are you crazy? they said. Crazy commoner. You're going to kill yourself.

No I won't, said Assa.

What are you going to do when you get to the bottom? asked Dawn. Besides break yourself and die and become food for rats and birds.

And dragons, said Dusk.

I'll get off the island and away from you two, said Assa. She wanted to shout to them, but her words came out as whispers. Her body wanted to conserve its energy for her descent. It was more difficult than she thought it would be to just hold onto the rope. Her whole body was aching from the strain.

You should have let us help you, said Dusk.

We could have put you in a basket and lowered you down, said Dawn.

This seemed like a very reasonable approach to the problem, and Assa wondered why she hadn't thought of it, then remembered she was having a fight with the twin princesses and wouldn't have asked them for anything only an hour ago.

Now, it felt different. Maybe she should climb back to the top. She tilted her head up and looked at Dawn and Dusk. Their faces peeked over the edge of the rock like mushrooms. Their eyes were wide and they looked scared. Maybe as scared as Assa felt.

I can't come back now, said Assa. I don't have the strength. I have to go down.

Dusk clucked her tongue, as if to say she was worried about Assa. Dawn just kept staring. Assa looked away from them and returned her attention to the rope and her descent.

Dragons appeared in the sky. They descended from above and began circling near Assa.

What are they doing? she called to Dawn and Dusk.

You're doing something strange, said Dawn. They get interested in that. They want to see what you're up to.

Tell them to keep away from me, said Assa.

We'll try, but they don't listen to us much.

Assa kept to her method: a tight panicked grip with her arms and legs, alternating with a more loose grip of her arms and legs. The periodic loosening was truly an act of faith. Each time she released her grip, she felt a sick feeling in her stomach. Her fear of falling made her body do things she didn't like.

The dragons screeched at her.

Make them stop! Assa shouted. Make them stop!

We can't, said Dawn.

More dragons spilled over the lip of the rock. They flew in great spirals, following each other in great swooping paths. It was as though the entire population of dragons had decided Assa was suddenly the only interesting thing in the world.

Assa watched them out of the corner of her eye, but kept her concentration on her task. None of the dragons came close enough to touch her, but she heard the air flow over their wings, leathery sound, like what she might hear if she ran her hands over a length of cloth.

She made herself pay attention only to the rope twisting around her body. The world shrunk to insignificance. The screeching of the dragons seemed to diminish to a tiny whisper. This couldn't be so. Dragons didn't whisper. At least not the ones she had seen here. They were loud and they were anything but shy about their voices.

It didn't matter. None of it mattered. The dragons were doing their thing. She was doing her thing.

She dared to look down. The ground still seemed like an awfully long way off. Would she ever get to it?

The rock face was not sheer and flat. It had ridges and bumps and rises that she had to climb past or over. The rope snagged on some of these protrusions and Assa got worried that they might cut through the rope. This was a new worry she had not anticipated.

But she decided there wasn't much she could do about it except get down quickly so the worry would be over. Her legs were trembling, now, just as her hands did earlier. This was so much harder work than she had thought it would be.

She got to the end of her rope. Her feet tried to grab air, failed, and began flailing. She looked down past her legs to the ground. It still looked like a long way to drop.

We can still pull you up, Dusk shouted above her. Just hold on tight and we'll get you back here.

No, said Assa. I'm going to let go. She descended a few more feet, just to get closer to the ground before dropping. She took in one enormous breath, then let it out slowly. She closed her eyes and released the rope from her hands.

Her eyes flew open at that instant. Her stomach seemed to want to fly on its own. She put out her hands and watched the rock face slip past her with the speed of a swallow. It couldn't have taken very long to fall, but it seemed like at least a week passed before the ground jolted her legs and slammed against her body.

She remembered to try to roll. Wasn't that how to protect herself? But the rolling didn't work out so well. Instead of skittering across the ground in a ball, she ended up folded into a heap. Her head hurt. Had she bumped it? She must have. Her legs ached and one of her wrists stung, as though she had bent it wrong, which, she supposed, is exactly what happened. Her whole body had been bent wrong.

She was vaguely aware of clapping from some place high above her. She opened her eyes. The rock face loomed large and imposing in front of her. At the very top, Dusk and Dawn were cheering and slapping their hands together.

You did it, said Dusk. Now go find our parents.

Yeah, said Dawn. We order you to. We're the royals. You have to do our bidding. She grinned.

Assa supposed that was her try at being funny. It wasn't very funny at all. Mostly it was annoying. Didn't they know how much she hurt? Probably didn't care. They were used to having other people do thing for them and not have to thank them or even acknowledge them in any way. To them the whole world was made of servants.

Nevertheless, Assa lifted her arm with the sore wrist and waved at them. The clapping got louder.

Gradually, she noticed the dragons again. They were still flying in circles, every one of them. They had all left their roosts and were etching spirals in the sky.

Such curious creatures. Aloof, yet so vibrant in their coloring. Assa liked watching them fly. The sunlight reflected off their skins and made them into iridescent decorations, their coloring changing as they moved from blue to green to red to yellow and back again. It was so relaxing watching them. Assa could imagine them in her dreams. All she had to do was close her eyes and fall asleep. They would color her night world with delightful sprays of color. That would be nice. Much nicer than lying here on the sand of this island, with grit grinding into her hair and a chill spreading through her body.

How could it be so cold with the sun so high and warm in the sky? She put her hand up to block the sun from her eyes. The dragons screeched and hollered. They chased each other around the sun. Their noises increased in volume, then got shriller, and then they all dropped from the sky.

Every one of them.

Not all at once, but gradually. Their wings stopped flapping, folded up against each other, and their bodies became missiles aimed at the ground. The first one hit the sand with a reverberating thud that rang Assa's skull like a bell. Then another fell near her. So close she could feel the air rush past her ear as it impacted the sand.

Assa sat up. Her head hurt, and her legs still felt wobbly and weak, but she had to get out of the way of these dragons. She saw a copse of trees a short distance away and began crawling in that direction. Dragons continued to fall, now more rapidly. They were so loud when they hit the ground. Assa got to the protection of the trees and looked back at a remarkable sight: piles of dragons heaped up one on top of the other. If she took the time to count, she was sure there had to be a hundred, at least. Were they all dead? It seemed so. None of them moved once they landed.

Above her, some dragons fell on the tops of the trees. They slid along the big leaves and fell away from Assa so she was never in any danger of being hit by any of them.

Dawn and Dusk were screaming at her. What's happening? they said.

Assa raised her voice as loud as she could: I don't know.

They shouldn't be dying like this, said Dawn. Are we going to die next?

I don't know, said Assa. I don't know I don't know.

Only three or four dragons were left in the air. They broke their turning flight pattern and began flying away from the rock. Assa watched them, hoping they would get away, but they did not. Their wings began flapping more slowly. They dropped quickly, then fell into the ocean. Assa heard the splashes. She got up from her hands and feet and steadied herself against a tree trunk and got her bearings. She shifted her weight from one foot to the other, to see if she had the strength to stand on her own.

A sharp pain at her hip made itself known. She winced but decided it would be okay. She waded into the mass of dragon bodies heaped in front of her. She tried to snake a path through them on the sand, but in some places they completely obliterated the surface and she had to step over piles of dragons.

Their soft flesh yielded against her shoes and she slipped a few times, falling so that her hands had to touch dead dragon skin. It made her feel creepier than she had ever felt in her life. Their eyes didn't close. They stared up at her, or at the sand, or blankly at nothing, and wherever they looked, it made Assa feel like she was seeing something she shouldn't see.

Creatures should be at peace in their death, but these dragons didn't look at peace. They looked like they still wanted to live but couldn't.

She scrambled over them as best she could, avoiding touching them with all her intent, but failing most of the time, and eventually found herself on a beach. The ocean pounded the sand. Spray filled the air and soaked her clothes. She began shivering from the cold.

The dragons, the last few survivors, continued to fall into the ocean, a short distance away. They looked like crippled birds plummeting to their deaths. Assa felt their pain and their dismay. Or was it her own pain and dismay? She wasn't exactly sure. She knew she felt pity for the dragons. They had saved her once. Maybe they could have saved her again.

Seals from an offshore rock began barking and slipped into the water. Before long, they reached the spot where the dragons had fallen and Assa watched as the seals dragged the fallen creatures back to the rock and began gorging on them.

The sight filled her with dismay. To think this is what happens to such beautiful creatures. It was a great pity.

But she told herself she had no time for pity. Behind her she heard other noises. Vultures swooped down on the piles of dragons and began tearing off bits of dragon flesh. Before long blood was everywhere and the population of vultures increased until there were too many to count.

Assa suspected they would feed on the dragons all day. Maybe longer. She half expected to get sick from the sight, but instead she watched with fascination. The dragon meat looked quite inviting, like she would be happy to taste some of it. It reminded her of eggplant, something she rather enjoyed.

But even if she had an inclination to eat some of the dragons, she could never get near them, not with the vultures there. They looked up, occasionally, with bits of dragon stuck to them, and blood staining their heads and they were the happiest creatures Assa had ever seen.

What are you waiting for? shouted Dawn and Dusk from high above her. Go get help.

That's right. Assa came down here to help them find a way off the island. She waved at the twins and cupped her hands to her mouth. Where should I go?

Follow the path, they shouted back, and pointed behind Assa.

Assa turned around and saw a path in the sand. It looked like someone or something had dragged a large object along the sand. She had looked at the beach earlier but hadn't noticed the path. Now that it was pointed out to her, she couldn't help but see it. She began walking on the path.

She noticed the sun was beating down on her and the beach. It was going to turn the sand on the path a lighter color as it burned off some of the moisture. She looked up to try to see where the path went. It seemed to continue along the beach, then turn inland through a pile of driftwood that towered about twenty feet high and was wedged between two high rocks situated at the edge of the sand and the forest.

She picked up her speed, running despite the pain in her hip, and trotted toward the driftwood. When she got to the pile of bleached wood she saw the trail ended. Hoyal's foot peeked out from the bottom of the pile.

Assa stopped and looked back to the twins. They were out of sight, now, the rock they were on behind a bend in the beach. She licked her lips and stepped forward.

Hoyal's foot looked broken. It was bent in a completely wrong direction. She circled around the foot and saw the rest of Hoyal. She was stretched out on the sand. Blood stained her mouth and her shirt. She had crawled here from where she had fallen, leaving the trail Assa had followed.

Assa didn't have to check for a pulse to know that Hoyal was dead. There was all the blood, and she wasn't moving, and, well, Assa could just *tell*. Hoyal didn't have any kind of aura that would have indicated she was still a moving breathing being.

But Assa supposed she had to be sure. She stepped close to Hoyal and gritted her teeth and put her fingers on Hoyal's wrist and left them there for as long as she could stand it, perhaps ten or fifteen seconds.

During that time she only heard her own breath. All her senses were on high alert, trying to discern some life signs from Hoyal. She watched her chest, to see if it rose. It did not. She never felt a pulse. Assa bent her ear to Hoyal's nose and listened for breath. Again, there was none.

Assa fell back to a seating position beside Hoyal. All those dragons dead didn't come close to matching the loss she felt now that she knew Hoyal was dead. She thought she would be happy to have this knowledge, but she did not. It filled her with sadness, even though Hoyal did everything she could to make Assa's life miserable.

Assa knew she should say something. Wasn't it the thing that people did when someone died? Some kind of prayer?

Assa missed the dragons. She felt they would knew exactly what to do here. Wasn't Hoyal their master? Assa looked up at the sky. It was suddenly this amazing blue, more blue than Assa had ever seen before.

She sighed. If she had a shovel, she supposed she would have to bury Hoyal. But that could wait, couldn't it? She needed to find a way off the island. For herself and for Dusk and Dawn.

She did wonder what Hoyal was trying to do, dragging herself all this way. What was so important in this pile of driftwood?

She stepped away from Hoyal and went back to the path. She stood in front of the driftwood and looked at it, to try to discern some kind of structure or pattern that would give her a clue about Hoyal's intentions.

As she stood, with the sun beating down on the back of her head, a twinkle of light caught her eye in the deep darkness of the forest. She stepped through the driftwood pile and continued over the beach sand and past the tall trunks that rose up and supported a canopy of broad green leaves overhead, blocking out the sun and casting dark shadows on the the soft ground.

Assa stepped onto the mass of long dead leaves and moss. It was the fertile soil that the trees used for their nourishment and it supported Assa, now, in her quest to find the source of the spark of light in the distance.

A shape stuck up out of the ground ahead of her. It looked familiar, yet out of place here in the forest. It shimmered, dully, but unmistakably. As she stepped close to it, with her hands touching tree trunks as she walked, she saw that it was newly fallen dragon.

Its wings were broken and twisted. Its neck cracked and bent. The dragon's eyes stared up at the canopy. No breath or flame came from its mouth or nostrils. Not even a wisp of smoke. Assa carefully stepped around the dragon. She noted its talons, clenched tightly in death. Bits of green leaf matter clunk to the scales around its ankles.

She looked up and saw a few torn edges of broad leaves. The dragon must have fallen through them only a few minutes ago, when the rest of the dragons all died. She shook her head at the memory. The vultures wouldn't find this dragon, hidden from view. But the bugs would. They'll be crawling all over it before long. They'd eat it down to its skeleton in no time, then the skeleton would eventually rot away. Become part of the land here, she supposed.

Assa didn't want to leave the dragon. Something about its fate made her want to stay. Maybe watch it get eaten? That would be fascinating, but she didn't have the time. She knelt down and examined the skin of the dragon. It had scales. It was dry. She put her hand on it. Still warm. Sad that there was no life in the dragon anymore. Its life drained away and now it would nourish the land of this island.

She couldn't bury it, but maybe she could cover it?

She stood up and looked around. Plenty of branches strewn around the area. All she had to do was pick up a few and drag them over, and cover the dragon. Wouldn't that be a nice gesture? It would give some respect to this dragon and it would make her feel better, too.

She stepped away from the dragon and spent the next fifteen minutes or so collecting branches, twigs, moss, and leaves. She brought all this material to the dragon and laid it over its broken form. She spoke to the wind and the sun and the earth as she worked.

She spoke to the flame within the dragon. She imagined it not extinguished but eternally burning in some place she could not reach. When she was finished, the dragon rested under a canopy of forest detritus. It was not a splendid grave by any means, but it had a certain beauty that touched Assa. She spent a few silent moments with the grave, then moved on toward the spark she had seen earlier.

She had not gone more than a dozen steps before she heard a hiss and grunt that made her whole body tingle with fear. For a second she though mice were running up and down her spine. She turned around to face the source of the unnerving sounds, fully expecting to meet some creature about to devour her. Instead, she saw the pile of branches and leaves over the dragon shift slightly.

Assa rubbed her eyes vigorously, not believing what she was seeing. She took two steps—small, tentative ones—closer to the pile and waited.

Another grunt. More hissing. Some of the leaves at the top of the grave shifted, moved by some force beneath them. Assa did not move any closer. She stood very still, as though keeping the pile of branches from hearing her motions was absolutely crucial to her survival. Maybe it was. She thought to bolt in the opposite direction, but decided if the dragon was coming back to life, it could easily find and dispatch her.

Branches moved, pushed from beneath. The whole edifice she had created began to tumble to the ground, like a sand castle dissolved by waves. The dragon, now as alive as it could possibly be, poked its head up from the morass of greenery and opened its mouth and belched a long flame, that reached half way up the trunk of the trees next to it, scorching the bark and incinerating a few of the leaves. They turned into black dust.

The wings emerged next, great leathery expanses, flapping wildly, wanting to catch air and lift the dragon to the sky.

Or so Assa imagined. She had no idea what was going on. Her prayers must have resurrected the creature? But that was ridiculous. More likely, it wasn't really dead. It just needed a few minutes to gather its strength so it could rise again.

She stepped back from the dragon as it stood up on its feet. The material she had piled onto it slid off its back like water. The iridescent skin shone in the darkness of the forest. It shimmered. Assa admired the color and the brightness. It made her think of the sun. The creature *did* still have fire in its heart. It wanted to live.

It spread its wings wider and flapped them, testing, so it seemed to Assa, its strength. It rotated its head and looked around and saw Assa, staring back.

They locked eyes. Assa couldn't move if she wanted to and she wasn't sure she wanted to. The dragon stepped out of the morass of plant material that had, apparently, incubated its resurrection, and took only three steps to arrive directly in front of Assa. The dragon stood with its eyes only inches from Assa's.

Assa couldn't move. She stood completely frozen in place while the dragon breathed hot smoke all around her.

The surrounding forest breathed with the dragon. It was as though the dragon was there for the forest. The dragon had iridescent skin, of course, but it also had this weight. It had come back from the dead, didn't it? Bits of dirt and loose plant material still clung to its wings and head.

You're alive because of me, said Assa in a small voice. She wanted to speak more loudly, but could not. Her voice was diminished by the presence of the beast.

The dragon's ears moved, slightly, as though maneuvering for a position to better hear Assa's words.

I put dirt on you, said Assa. You were dead. Now you're not. Do you understand that?

The dragon held its stance. It did not move for a long time. When it finally did, by taking two steps back, Assa felt like she could relax. Her muscles loosened and her breath, which had been coming in shallow snatches of air, stretched out into great lungfuls of air. Assa thought she had been close to death, that the dragon was perhaps ready to devour her, but she had been so close to death so often in the past few days that she hardly cared anymore. Death would have come as something welcome.

The dragon turned and stepped deeper into the forest. It dropped a couple of lumps from its hind end as it walked. Assa followed the dragon, carefully stepping around its leavings, and keeping up as best she could. Now that the dragon had refused to dispatch Assa, Assa felt as though she wanted to be as close to the dragon as possible.

Its tail swung back and forth behind it. A couple of times it extended its wings as far as the surrounding foliage would allow and shook them. Did it want to fly? Maybe it couldn't fly anymore?

The dragon's steps were plodding and heavy. It broke twigs as it went, sending up a cacophony of noisy cracks, snaps, and pops. Birds in the forest rose up from their perches and scattered to the sky. Chipmunks and squirrels chattered the air and ran away from the wound of the dragon.

Assa felt safer already, as though the dragon would protect her from anything. She didn't know that was true, of course, but she felt it and decided she would accept that feeling.

The light she had seen earlier was still ahead, flitting into and out of view as the body of the dragon waddled from side to side in front of her. Assa tried to see around the thorax of the dragon, but she caught only glimpses of the light. It was bright, and looked like it was flickering. The dragon, evidently, was on its way to the light. That was perfectly fine with Assa. She would follow. If there was anything dangerous to her there, the dragon would encounter the danger first. That suited Assa just fine.

They continued like this for some time. Assa took to planting her feet in the footprints left by the dragon, reasoning that if the underlying foliage supported a beast such as the dragon, it would have no problem keeping Assa on an even keel.

There was no real path, other than the makeshift path the dragon was producing. Assa glanced behind her several times, but the forest swallowed up everything. She could hardly tell where they had been. It was as if the forest swept in behind them and filled up the space they had opened.

Have you been here before? said Assa to the back of the dragon.

The dragon did not indicate it heard anything. It just kept walking.

Is the light something you know about?

Still nothing. Just the plodding walk.

Assa didn't even know why she was trying to talk to the dragon. None of the dragons gave any indication that they understood anything spoken to them, and she certainly did not hear any of them speak for themselves. They were controlled by Hoyal in some way, that was clear, since they all died when Hoyal died.

She stopped and screamed into the air. Dawn! Dusk! Do you hear me?

She cupped her hands to her ears and turned around in the path. She let the dragon get ahead of her a little. It still crunched over the forest floor, still sent up noises, but Assa thought she would be able to hear other things. She held herself as still as possible, only the sound of her breathing breaking the air.

No return words from the twins.

She called their names several more times. As loudly as she could. No answer, but her calls produced a response from the dragon. It stopped and turned to look at her. Its long face reminded Assa of a horse. Its eyes glowed in the semi-darkness of the forest. They were the look her mother sometimes gave her when she thought Assa was misbehaving and wanted Assa to be more polite.

Assa stuck her tongue out at the dragon, who blinked several times, then turned around and continued walking.

She called out to Dawn and Dusk again. If you can hear me, you can bring the dragons back to life. Throw dirt on them. They spring right up. She said their names again and repeated her instructions.

The dragon came to a clearing in the woods, finally. The trees seemed to step back from the dragon and Assa, as though they were inviting them to this small area of cultivated space. Assa ran into the clearing, which had, at its center, a small hut with windows. In the hut a fire burned. Its glow through the window was what she had seen earlier from the driftwood pile.

The dragon walked around the hut slowly, as though reluctant to enter. The trees around the hut were pulled back. The hut was situated on a level section of ground. The grass around it had been tamped down by many feet. What feet, dragon or human or something else, Assa couldn't tell. The dragon finally stopped and looked at Assa and breathed a long flame into the air. Smoke rose from its nostrils. It gestured with its head toward the door of the hut.

Assa walked up to the hut and felt the warmth from the flame inside on the door. The heat gave her confidence that this was the place she should be. She ran her tongue over her lips and grasped the wooden handle of the door and pulled it open.

More heat rushed out and immediately touched her face. The flame inside rose to the top of the hut and almost touched the ceiling. There was a hole in the hut to release the heat and smoke safely into the air. The flame originated at the floor of the hut, fed by piles of wood.

The dragon edged past Assa and entered the hut. It had a log in its talons which it added to the pile. Orange flame wrapped itself around the log, bathing it in a semi-transparent layer. She saw the grain under the flame begin to blacken. More smoke rose into the air and went through the hole at the top of the hut.

The dragon stepped forward and put its nose into the newly created smoke and breathed deeply. The smoke shot into its lungs, as though something inside the dragon pulled at the smoke. It was like a magnet pulling at a piece of steel.

The dragon held its breath for a long time. Assa estimated it kept the smoke in its lungs for several minutes, but she couldn't be sure. Something about the encounter with this dragon gave her the creeps. Why did it lead her to this hut?

The dragon stepped around the flame. It seemed to enjoy being here. Perhaps, now that it had been brought back from the dead, even more than it might have before.

Are you trying to thank me? asked Assa. Is this what's going on here?

The dragon stepped smartly around the flame several times. An endless circle.

Because, said Assa, it's okay. I thought I was burying you, so no need to thank me. It was just dumb luck that you got raised from the dead.

As the dragon continued walking the circle around the flame, Assa heard a commotion outside, twigs snapping, and the ground vibrating. She stepped out of the hut and saw three more dragons had come to the hut. They immediately surrounded her, leaning close enough for her to touch each of their skins. They spread their wings, so that they touched each other at the tips, creating an effective cage, rather like the hut, only made of living creatures.

Stop that, said Assa. You have no reason to hold me.

The dragons' breaths sounded ragged and forced. She saw that their eyes were clouded over slightly, like they were in a daze.

Should I be afraid of you? asked Assa.

The dragons shuffled their feet in unison, so that the cage of wings moved

Assa back toward the hut. Assa pushed back, but she was completely ineffective against their power. They *wanted* her to go back to the hut.

Is it safer for me in there? she asked.

No answer came, of course. Dragons don't talk, she reminded herself. Well, that was okay. They didn't need to talk, although it made things inconvenient, to say the least, for Assa.

She looked down at the dragon feet, all arrayed in a circle around her. There was space between them. If she dropped and moved quickly, she could probably squeeze through an opening there and escape their trap. But what good would it do? She would still be on this island, and they could still move to trap her again. And she was sure that is exactly what they would choose to do. Better to keep her strength and wits about her and look for escape by another route.

The dragons moved again, as one, shuffling her even closer to the hut. Assa followed their lead and shuffled along with them. Then the two closest to the entrance separated so that the door into the hut was clear for Assa.

You want me to go back inside? asked Assa. Is that it?

No answer, just ragged breaths.

Assa sighed and entered the hut, again. The smoke began to sting her eyes. The first dragon was still stepping around the flame. Now one of the three new dragons parked itself at the entrance to the hut, effectively keeping Assa inside. The other two joined the first dragon and inhaled a great quantity of smoke, then began prancing around the flame. The three of them looked ridiculous to Assa, but were still powerful presences. They filled up the space with a heat and bulk that overwhelmed Assa.

What do you want from me? she asked them.

Dragons changed places with the guard, each one taking its turn keeping Assa inside the hut. She saw that she no longer had an opportunity to run away. There was no space between the door frame and the dragons posted there in turns. The hut was getting to be too hot. Her skin felt like it was beginning to cook. Was that possible?

She wasn't *in* the flame, but the hut felt as hot as she could bear. Any more increase in temperature and she would begin to overheat. Already her clothes felt too warm to touch. Her hair was hot against her skin. She shielded her eyes from the flame and heat, keeping her hands over them, and narrowing her eyelids to a slit.

The dragons, meanwhile, looked like they were in some kind of trance. They moaned and bellowed, as well, their sounds echoing in the small hut. Assa was trapped in the soundscape. She put her hands up to her ears to block the sound. She needed to get out of this hut. She tried to move toward the door, but the dragons stopped her. She pushed against them. Their hides felt warm to her touch, warmer than they should be. It was as though a fire inside them was about to explode through their skin. Assa did not want to be around when that happened.

She dropped to the ground on all fours and crawled toward the dragon guarding the door. It shuffled its feet and dropped its wings so that they covered the doorway like a door. There was no way out for Assa. She crawled away from the door along the wall of the hut. The structure was constructed from planks of wood that were stuck into the ground but did not go deep. In some places, it didn't go into the ground at all; the ends just floated there, supported on the sides by the surrounding planks.

She could put her hand under the plank and pull at it. She did so and felt the relatively cool air on the outside of the hut against her palm. The small relief it gave her boosted her resolve. She grabbed the plank and pulled at it. She heard popping and straining of the wood at the top of the plank as it slipped away from the load-bearing structure of the hut.

She pulled some more and the wood began to splinter. Her heart beat more rapidly. This was going to work. She put both hands on the plank end and dug in her feet and pulled with all her might. She fell back on her behind as the plank broke in two, revealing an opening just wide enough for her to slip through.

She scrambled to her hands and feet and scampered to the opening and turned herself sideways so she could slip through. Her arm was outside the hut and the cool air felt glorious all the way up to her shoulder when one of the dragons grabbed her other arm and yanked her back inside.

The dragons roared.

She screamed as the one who grabbed her raised her high. She was inches from the ceiling of the hut. Her feet, in fact, touched the ceiling. A rush of cobwebs and dust flitted by her eyes and heat seemed to wrap itself around her and begin to suffocate her just as the dragon brought her down from her heights right into the middle of the flame.

Sʜᴇ ᴇxᴘᴇᴄᴛᴇᴅ ᴛᴏ be flying, like before.

She reasoned, just before everything went black, that the doings in the hut were designed to turn her into a dragon. Why else would the dragons throw her into fire? Unless they were murderous beasts, which they did not appear to be, they would have to be some kind of keepers of a secret. The secret was how people turned into dragons.

It would be a traumatic transformation. Had to be. There were wings to sprout, obviously. And dragon skin was more leathery than human skin, so that change had to occur. None of it could be easy.

Then there was the instinct of being a dragon. So different from being human. Flying for one. And breathing fire for another. Just before Assa touched the flame in the hut, she felt certain she could be a dragon.

It felt good to think about soaring over heights and swooping down to the sea and the island. She would flap her wings and climb the thermals and find Dawn and Dusk and whisk them off the island and return them to their parents. She would salute the king and queen with a flick of her wing tip, then climb into the sky again and fly home where she would have a heart to heart with her own parents. She would explain to them that her transformation was a curse and a blessing. It was awful because it removed her from them. But it was wonderful because she was a dragon, a free and magnificent creature, able to roam the skies and rescue people in trouble. Then she would fly away.

All these things flitted through her over-heated brain as the flame in the hut came closer to her. It singed her hair. It burned her skin.

And when she woke, she was not flying.

No soaring, no gliding.

No swooping.

Instead, she was completely paralyzed. And it was dark. She tried to breath out fire, but only her own small breath leaked out. It warmed the air in front of her, but not nearly as much as an honest to goodness flame would have done.

In fact, now that she took account of her surroundings, she sensed that she was cold, very cold. And she was not in any kind of atmosphere.

A great weight pressed down on her. She had no wings and she could not move her legs or arms. Her chest barely rose as her breathing was restricted. Gradually, she came to realize that far from being in the sky, she was in the ground. Buried.

Assa could breathe, at least. That was something. But she couldn't move. Or, she could not move enough to make a difference. She was not even sure she could tell in what orientation she had been buried. Was she on her back? On her belly? Sideways? There were not clues to help her. Gravity, the sense of weight, had been taken from her. She dared not open her eyes. She didn't want to see the dirt in front of her. She sighed. The air stagnated in front of her nose. She was glad she wasn't panicking, but also didn't understand why she was not.

Sleep came a few minutes later.

She woke fighting with the dirt. Her hands plowed through the earth. Slowly, but enough that she made some progress. She pushed away clumps of it. It was like slow motion swimming and it was stifling in a way she had never experienced before.

Gradually, she began to make some progress. Clumps of dirt loosened from hard compact chunks into collections of amorphous dirt. She pushed aside handfuls of the stuff and managed to kick her legs, again in slow motion, but through the dirt, pushing it aside. Eventually, after what seemed like years, her hands broke through the dirt and touched air. The coolness of the breeze caressed her fingers and palm and wrist.

It was very cold, but Assa didn't care. It was joyous just to think that she was only a few inches away from freedom. She pushed her hand through and reached for the sky. She worked to loosen the rest of her body. It took some doing. She had to push away great chunks of earth and her energy was flagging, despite her joy.

She was just about ready to give the effort one last colossal effort when some thing grabbed her hands. It felt like other hands, grasping hers. The grasped back, not knowing who or what was grabbing her, but not caring. The warmth of a touch from some other being was all she needed to double down on her intentions and push herself out of her burial place.

With the help of her mysterious benefactors, she tilted up her torso and broke through the ground completely. Chunks of earth cascaded down her hair and arms and chest.

Are you okay? someone asked. Familiar voice. She wasn't exactly sure, but she had heard that voice before. Different now, somehow deeper? Or slower. Maybe both.

Who ever was holding her hands let go. She put her hands to her face an pushed away the dirt there.

Say something, said the voice.

In a minute, she said. Her own voice startled her. It was deeper and softer than she remembered. Like it had been crushed by her time in the ground. How long *had* it been?

Assa wiped dirt from her eyes. She felt hand on her back, brushing away dirt from her shirt. Then other hands pulling her legs up out of the ground.

She wiped her eyelids and the area around her eyes as best she could, then dared to open her lids. A blurry scene presented itself for her view. The sun was low in the sky. Dim light illuminated the scene. Two faces stared at her, both looking concerned in the shadows.

We dug you out as soon as we knew where you were, said Dawn.

You feeling okay? asked Dusk.

Only Dawn and Dusk did not look the same. They were older. A lot older.

What happened? asked Assa. She looked down at her hands. They looked bigger than she remembered. She took in her arms, front, and legs. She *was* bigger. She had hips and breasts. This was too much. How did this happen?

She looked at Dawn and Dusk.

We know, they said to her. It's all different. We're different. It's weird.

Are we still on the island? asked Assa.

Yup.

Are the dragons all still dead?

Yup. Even the ones that tossed you into the fire.

Assa put her hands to her head and shook away more dirt from her hair and ears. She put a finger into her ear and tried to scrape away some of the grit there. She could use a dip in the ocean about now. Just to get rid of all this *dirt*.

She estimated that she was ten years older than she remembered being. How could that happen? Dusk and Dawn were also older. Had she missed half her life? Where were her parents?

What's going on? she asked.

We don't know, said Dawn. She was till Dawn, still the one in charge, the one who knew stuff and tried to keep everything together.

And Dusk was still Dusk. She had this energy about her, like she wanted to be somewhere else. Anywhere else. It didn't matter. Just some place she could be having some fun because where she was now was boring. It was always boring, wherever she happened to be. Right now, she had already grown bored with the miracle of Assa's resurrection and was looking above her head to the sky. Or to the forest. Or or or. Assa didn't even know or care.

She brushed dirt from her legs and bent them up so her knees were pointed to the sky. They felt stiff, like they hadn't been used in a long time, but they seemed to work well enough.

She stood up. Dawn and Dusk, who had been kneeling on the ground, stood up with her. Assa's head began spinning. Dawn grabbed her and steadied her. This was going to take some getting used to. She felt like she was still four feet tall and here she was inhabiting a body more than five feet tall. Her feet seemed impossibly far away, like her brain couldn't find them. They existed on some other island, far out in the ocean. Her brain would have to send signals, maybe by dragon, just to get a hold of her feet and make them walk.

At least, that's what it felt like.

Walking takes some getting used to, said Dawn. But you can do it. She reached down and grabbed Assa's calf and moved it forward. Such a strange sensation. Like she was pulling some tool out of a toolbox. What was she going to do with it? Assa didn't know. Then the sensation of her leg moving came up to her brain and she saw that she had moved away from her original standing location.

Dusk grabbed her other leg and lifted it and planted it beside the first leg. Ahh, that's what it felt like to be walking.

I'm hungry, she said.

We know, said Dawn. But you have to learn to walk again. You have to learn how to use your limbs.

Fine, said Assa. But then I get to eat. Dragon steaks, if that's all there is. And a bath. I want a bath.

Sure you aren't a royal? said Dawn. I mean secretly? You sure think like a royal.

You mean having the expectation that people will do things for me just because I'm me.

Something like that, said Dawn.

We're probably all royals on some level, said Assa. We just have to find it out.

We're not royals anymore, said Dusk. At least not like we were.

She sounded wistful. She stared up at the sky as she spoke. Assa followed her gaze. There was nothing above them except sky. No birds, no dragons, not even clouds. It felt lonely and more than a little scary.

Do I want to know what happened? asked Assa.

We'll tell you what we know, said Dawn. But first, let's get you cleaned up.

That sounded good to Assa. She made her legs move and began walking with Dawn and Dusk toward the sea.

They passed the hut where she had been thrown on the flame. It was nothing but a pile of weathered wood now: gray and dry. Beyond that they walked the path she had followed the dragon on and came to the driftwood where she had found Hoyal, stretched out on the ground and dead.

The driftwood was still there, and she thought she saw some bones mixed in with them. Hoyal's bones? She wasn't sure. She bent to examine them. Dawn and Dusk stopped with her.

It takes getting used to, said Dawn. All the years you've missed.

I've missed years? said Assa.

You're older. You grew up while you were in the ground.

Assa shook her head. I don't know if I can get used to *that*.

You will, said Dusk. We did. That's not Hoyal's bones, by the way.

Assa dropped her hand from what she thought might be the skeletal remains of someone. Anyone.

Hoyal was torn apart by the surviving dragons and eaten, said Dawn. That happened a long time ago.

Fine, said Assa. They stepped onto the beach. The sand was warm and fine-grained against Assa's soles. She stood and twisted her feet so that she sunk down a couple of inches and the grains flowed in and covered her feet. She thought she could remain in place like this for many many days. Maybe weeks. The sun beat down on her head and warmed her arms and face.

Dawn and Dusk grabbed her hands and pulled her away. They all three hollered and ran to the waves breaking on the beach. The sound was booming and big. Like the drum beat of the world.

They got to the water and didn't slow their pace. They ran, splashing and laughing, finally diving forward into the coming waves. Water hit Assa like the blow of a dragon's wings. It flowed over her and pushed her back toward the shore. She got turned and tossed, then righted herself, dug in her heals and pushed forward again. The water was cold, but not unpleasantly so. It felt refreshing and cleansing, which is what she wanted.

Fish swam by her, brushing against her skin. She turned and grabbed at them, but they were too quick. They darted away before her hands made contact.

She spent ten minutes or so in the water, luxuriating in the feel of it over her skin. Dawn and Dusk got out and stood on the shore, calling to her.

It's cold, said Dawn.

Come in now, said Dusk. You're all washed off. Come on.

Assa wanted to stay longer. The water felt like her home. It wrapped her in comfort and healing. Or so she imagined.

We have food, said Dawn. Waiting for you.

Eventually Assa's hunger got the better of her. She came out of the ocean, water dripping down her arms and hair and followed Dawn and Dusk to a spacious structure that had been built just where the sand of the beach met the grassy ground of the forest, but before the trees grew thick and dark. It stood against the trees like a beacon, catching the sunlight and throwing it back at them.

Dawn and Dusk quickened their pace and Assa kept up. The sun had already dried the water from her body. She tasted salt on her lips and thanked the universe for creating the ocean.

Dawn and Dusk got to the hut and stood on either side of the door. Dawn grabbed the handle of the door and pulled it open. It swung on hinges, sending up creaks and squeaks into the air.

Our humble home, said Dawn.

Assa stepped inside. A spacious living area presented itself to her eye, furnished with several chairs and a long couch, all of which appeared to be made of driftwood. Beyond this, a kitchen area with table, chairs, and a clay cooking surface caught sunlight from a side window. A pot was set on the clay stove, with some stew bubbling on its surface. The aroma wafted up from the pot and curled itself around Assa's nostrils. Her mouth watered.

Can we eat? she said.

Dawn laughed. Of course, she said.

Dusk pulled out three bowls from a cupboard next to the stove and filled them with some of the stew and placed them on the table. Assa sat down and grabbed a spoon and dug in. Dawn put down a platter of bread. Assa picked up a slice, dipped it in the stew, and bit off a chunk.

This is so good, she said.

Dragon stew, said Dusk.

Assa raised her eyebrows. Really?

Dawn nodded. The longer you cook them, she said, the better they taste.

You must have cooked these for *years*, said Assa.

Dawn and Dusk glanced at each other.

What? said Assa. You mean you really did cook them for years?

We keep them in a pit in the ground. They age and ferment and go rotten. But in a good way.

Assa chewed and swallowed. She wasn't sure if they were serious, but she didn't care. She cleaned out the bowl and presented it to Dusk. Can I have more? she said.

Dusk grabbed her bowl and filled it from the pot again. She handed it to Assa, who thanked her.

Glad you like it, said Dawn. We get tired of it, but figured you hadn't had any, so you'd be happy to have some.

You figured right, said Assa.

She slowed her pace and ate the second bowl with more of a determination to enjoy it. The texture of the meat was intriguing. So chewy as to be just on this side of stringy. But so tender that she didn't care. The juices were sweet and had a tinge of something she couldn't identify, like a strange spice.

She came to the bottom of the bowl before Dawn and Dusk were even half way through their first bowls.

Ready for thirds? asked Dawn.

No, said Assa. I better wait till you catch up.

Don't worry about us, said Dusk. You're the one who's been out of it for so long.

Tell me the whole story, said Assa.

Dawn and Dusk looked at each other. Dawn cleared her throat. Here's the way it is, she said. After you went down the rock, we heard you calling to us. To tell us to bury the dead dragons. We didn't know what was going on. We linked up to try to see you and the dragons, but something was blocking us.

It was Hoyal, said Dusk.

She was dead, said Assa. She had nothing to do with your link ups.

Well, said Dawn, she kind of did. See, Hoyal was our cousin. She had this ability to block us and she used it. That's why she was able to capture us.

So now that she's dead, said Assa, what does that do to you?

We aren't linked anymore, said Dawn.

We're still twins, but we can't put our minds together, said Dusk.

Assa looked at Dawn, then at Dusk, and back to Dawn again. So, she said, what does that mean to you? To us?

Well, we wanted to bring the dragons back, but Hoyal, you know, she controlled the dragons. Without her, they all died.

I saw that, said Assa.

We climbed down the rope you left, said Dawn, and jumped to the ground. It was crazy, all those dragons piled up in heaps. Hoyal made them, you know. She had this magical power. She could turn fish into dragons. That's what she did. No one knows where that power came from. The dragons, because they were created from fish by her, they were completely loyal to her. They loved her. But even if they didn't, she controlled their lives. Her magic was to keep them alive. She stuffed them with fire. That gave them lift and made them strong.

We knew about Hoyal, said Dusk, when we were growing up. We knew she was different. Our mother said we should stay away from Hoyal. Everyone did. They put Hoyal in a castle away from the rest of the family. She grew up in that castle. All by herself, except for some servants who fed her and made sure she didn't escape. People said she went a little crazy. Ate only fish. Threw everything else away. Out the window or in the servants' faces. It was strange having a crazy person in the family.

After a while, said Dawn, we couldn't get anyone to look after her. She was too crazy. And violent. She wanted to take over the land. She wanted to be queen.

As they talked, clouds moved in, blocking the sun. The clouds got darker and darker until they turned almost black. Lightning shot through the sky and rumbles of thunder shook the hut. Soon fat drops of rain began spattering the roof of the hut. They pinged incessantly for several minutes, then the rain increased and began pouring out of the sky. It was as though the hut had been put into the middle of a river. Water flowed outside. The sound of it increased to a roar.

What is this? asked Assa.

Dawn blinked. Nothing, she said. Just a little storm. It'll pass.

When? asked Assa.

What does it matter? said Dusk. It's just a little water.

Assa knew about water. She lived—or used to live—on a creek. She heard water flowing all her life. It lulled her to sleep at night, but this wasn't just water. This was a deluge of epic proportions.

The rainfall increased in intensity. It came down in sheets. It was as though the rain was trying to replace the air. Assa had this tingling sensation in her stomach. It was fear, telling her that her oxygen was about to run out, and in its place there was going to be only water. Great depths of water. So much water that it would drown her.

I can't listen anymore, said Assa, gasping.

What's wrong with you? asked Dusk.

Dawn stood and put her arm around Assa, trying to comfort her. Her touch felt clammy and cold. Assa flinched and pulled away from Dawn, who stepped back. She looked concerned and worried.

Water lapped at Assa's ankles. She lifted her legs up and wedged her heels between the edge of the chair and her butt. This isn't good, she said. This isn't good.

A creek flowed through the hut now. Dawn and Dusk seemed completely oblivious. How could they not see the danger?

What is wrong with you? said Assa. Don't you see we have to protect ourselves?

Assa got up from the chair and stepped onto the table. She wasn't sure it would hold her, but she had to do something to try to protect herself.

The water kept rising. It dislodged odds and ends on the floor of the hut: a mat, a broom, some jars, a few items of clothing. They floated on the water, bumping into each other and making Assa feel as though she was on the deck of a sinking ship.

The table, which had been stable and steady, began floating in the water. Assa looked up to the ceiling. Maybe she could grab hold of something there to pull herself up and away from the water. Some beams held the roof up, but they were too wide. She could never get her hands around them.

The table shifted again. Assa bent down to grab the surface, but it moved under her and slipped away. Dawn and Dusk were treading water. They said something to her, but the roar of the water drowned out their words. They turned from Assa and swam out the window of the hut. Assa took a breath and pushed herself toward the window as well. She slipped through the opening like a fish slipping through a net too big for it.

Outside the hut the world was all water now. It rolled over her and put her under. She kept her eyes open as best she could. The water was salty, but that didn't matter. It didn't bother her. She swam easily and smoothly, putting distance behind her and the hut.

Her arms were tight against her sides. Her legs felt like they were bound together. She wiggled her body. A fin sprouted from her back. It steadied her in the water, kept her on an even keel. Water slid past her with smooth efficiency. She wanted to swim up to the surface, to get air, but her nostrils seemed to be filtering the water with no problem or effort. And they had shifted to her cheeks. And become something other than nostrils.

Above her, the raindrops splashed on the surface of the ocean. Her ocean. Assa's home. She darted through the cold water. It felt inviting to her touch. It was like she was home.

She turned down and swam toward the ocean floor, sandy and muddy many feet below her. As she neared the surface, she became aware of two other shapes near her, swimming in formation. They brushed against her and pushed water her way. The currents eddied around her, a mix of pressure and temperature gradients that wrapped her up in this new world she inhabited.

Thoughts entered her mind. She let them go. She didn't need thoughts now. Her body was perfectly shaped for this environment and she relished the feeling of being free. She manipulated her appendages, tiny but powerful, so that her speed increased. She went straight down. The water pressure all around her pressed in and compressed her, as though she was being flattened. But she knew better. She wasn't going to be crushed.

The other two fish darted ahead of her. She followed. The three of them took turns leading, the other two following and twirling behind, as though weaving some thread between them. They were a school of fish. Not individuals, but parts of a greater whole. This gave Assa comfort as well as a certain feeling of joy, something she had not felt in some time.

As they approached the bottom of the ocean, Assa felt an urge to slow her pace, but overcame it. The others did not slow down. In fact, they increased their speed, getting away from her. She, in turn, worked her fins and scales and body with as deft a technique as she could muster, new as she was to the task, and spilled water off her back and sides and flicked it from her tail until she caught up to the two leaders and saw that they were so close to the bottom that they could not stop.

In a split second she thought to put on the brakes. She *thought* to angle herself, her body, her fins, and her head so that she would *slow down*.

But that didn't happen. The split second passed. Her thoughts pushed her on. She wanted only speed.

Then she hit the ocean floor.

SHE HAD DARTED ahead of her two companions and thought that they must have slowed and veered away. Assa, because she chose not to slow down, swallowed sand as she dove into the floor.

She tasted bits of seaweed, morsels of fish feces, and tiny shells. The sensation was explosive, like her brain was ignited by her taste buds.

The material pushed past her mouth to her gullet and then to her stomach. She expected to stop now. Surely she had to stop. She couldn't just keep going through the sand. Could she?

Her eyes were scratched by the sand. They left lines and pops of light in her field of vision, as though the sand was painting on her vision.

Her tail, indeed, her entire body, worked itself hard, wriggling madly to propel her through the density of the earth.

As she continued, unaffected by the grains of sand all around her, it felt like her speed actually increased. She scarcely believed this possible, but had to accept the truth of it.

Grit raked her skin. Her eyes, so scarred by the sharp edges of the grains, became completely useless. For a short time she was able to discern some detail in the gray fog, but eventually the gray turned to black and she saw nothing.

All her sensation became kinetic. She heard nothing, smelled nothing, and saw nothing. Taste had been obliterated. The sand, the incessant grit, had torn away her skin and left her flayed and vulnerable. As she continued to burrow into whatever she had swam into, she had the sensation only of motion.

Later, perhaps a few centuries, maybe only a few seconds, she felt the thoughts of her companions again. They crowded in on her and pushed aside her own ruminations.

Remember us? they asked.

Assa remembered. They were the twins. The princesses.

Where are we? asked Assa.

Don't you know? asked Dusk and Dawn in unison.

No, said Assa. Tell me where we are. Tell me what's going on.

You're everywhere, said Dawn.

And nowhere, said Dusk.

That doesn't help, said Assa.

We just have to know, said Dawn. Are you with us?

I'm a loyal subject, said Assa. This is a phrase she learned from her parents. They told her if she was ever in trouble with the rulers of the land, she should simply repeat that phrase over and over. If she could convince them that she was, indeed, a loyal subject, they would not bring any harm to her.

Assa never quite believed that was completely true, but reasoned that in any case, it was the nearest thing she had to a defense against the excesses of the royal family. The ruled class had very little in the way of defenses against the ruling class.

This did not normally bother her as she seldom had any contact with the royal family. That is, until she began having contact with Dawn and Dusk. When was that? Assa racked her brain, trying to make sense of the memories she had of being abducted, incarcerated, and starved. She was starved, wasn't she? She couldn't be sure anymore. She knew she was ill-treated. She was sure of that. But was she beaten? That she couldn't be sure of.

We're not questioning your loyalty, said Dawn.

Yeah, said Dusk, we aren't so dreary as all that. Loyalty to us is ridiculous, anyway. We're tired of it.

Assa found that hard to believe, but didn't offer any objection.

So, we ask again, said Dusk. Are you with us?

Assa, her very being, so it seemed, in the midst of being shredded around her, could offer only one answer. Yes, she said. Yes, I'm with you.

That's what we were hoping to hear, said Dawn.

The two of them, Dawn and Dusk, now found a way to join together. Assa felt them merge in front of her. It was as though an extension of herself was out in the empty space all around her. They seemed stronger. They swam faster and with more purpose. She struggled to keep up. All the while, her perception was being shredded. Her flesh was completely gone. Her place in the world had been reduced to something she could barely comprehend. She was little more than a thought, it seemed. An inconsequential urge of the universe. Or maybe a small nudge. A gentle coax in some direction Assa could not fathom.

And her awareness was quickly growing smaller. She longed to put on a suit of flesh and bone. To become part of the world again in all its dimensions. But that was not going to happen, it seemed. She was doomed to be this notion.

Her awareness of the world slipped away. Any consciousness of the princesses seemed to be an old thing, lost in the mists of the world. Even the ground she had been traversing became a mushy ether. Then, it too, dissolved to nothing. Less than nothing.

Assa floated. This was the closest word she could come to. She didn't know what she floated on. And she wasn't even sure what *she* might be. All she knew for sure was that something she could barely identify as herself seemed to exist. Somewhere. Somehow.

Just as it appeared she was to lose everything, just as the last remnant of her self was about to disappear like smoke in the air, something jolted her back to existence.

Her parents' voices boomed at her from some distance away.

Assa? they asked. Assa, is that you?

A COUGH. WHOSE? Assa couldn't tell. It might have come from her throat. But maybe not. She struggled to find her voice. She had this feeling it was there somewhere. Just out of reach. All she had to do was twist herself around, maybe bend her being into some pretzel shape and she would find the thing, buried in the recesses of her awareness.

Assa?

Her mother's voice again. It shot into her being and made Assa see color. Spots of it floated in her field of view, isolated dots in the expanse of black. She tried to answer. No words came. She let her mind stumble back to when she first learned to talk. She pushed aside layers of meaning and soggy material, as though she was pushing aside seaweed under the ocean. She knew there was a pearl of meaning at the bottom. Maybe in an oyster shell, maybe just lying there on the ocean floor.

She made her awareness work the levers and pulleys that would more efficiently find a way through the murk. It was as though her body was made of mechanical bits and if she could learn the sequence of bends and ups and downs in all of it, she could resurrect meaning from the depths. Maybe something resembling a voice as well.

Gradually, as she worked, some of the bits came together, clicking into place and swinging material around in a manner which suggested competence. Or at least a semblance of power. The world dragged along with her newfound limbs. No longer phantom, they seemed to represent something solid and true. She manipulated a pulley here, grabbed a rope there, and swung a net along the ridge on the horizon. The net seemed impossibly far away, but it snagged something and as she continued to swing the net it grew closer and closer until it was right in front of her awareness. She reached forward with something she didn't understand. It was made of her, but had no name. Yet.

She lifted the object from the net. A pearl, indeed. Bright and shiny. She retrieved the pearl from the net and placed it in the center of her awareness. It blazed across the blackness that was her world. She studied the word. It had four letters. M. A. M. A.

At first she didn't know what they spelled. She didn't even know what words were. But eventually her awareness, swirling and yearning, coalesced around the word. The word dove into her being and activated some switch she didn't know she had. A groaning and scratching apparatus of some incomprehensible mechanism creaked and screeched to life.

Mama, she said.

Once that first word had been loosed on the world, many followed. Assa's apparatus of mechanical doings became familiar to her. She could reach into the depths without the net and find the words she wanted. She could throw them up on the black screen of her awareness, see them arrayed like stars, and read them off to the world.

Where am I?

Soon she didn't need any of the mechanisms. All she had to do was become aware of what she needed to say and the sound of her words, in some miraculous coalescence of energy and effort, became sounds in the air.

Where are Dawn and Dusk?

Child, said her father. What kind of question is that? Are you asking about night and day?

Assa laughed. Strange sound. How did it arrive in her throat? She didn't ask for it. She understood its purpose exactly, however. It was there to express amusement.

No, she said. They're friends of mine. I want to know what happened to them.

Assa. Her mother's voice again. You've been gone a long time. We found you by the mill. How did you get there? What happened.

Assa recalled her life before Hoyal. How she lived with her parents at their mill.

Did I come up the stream? asked Assa. She wanted to open her eyes. She wished she could push open the lids but they didn't want to budge. The pulleys and gears needed lubrication, she supposed. They were stuck. She wanted to *see*. Was that so much to ask?

We don't know, said her father. We found you on the bank. Assa, we were so afraid we had lost you. No word for years. The castle has been shrouded in darkness.

Darkness? said Assa.

No one knows what is happening there, said Assa's mother.

Assa tried to answer, but she was growing tired, too tired to talk. She drifted in and out of sleep for a long time. Eventually, she awoke from her slumbers and found she was no longer a fish. She had a woman's body and a human's understanding of herself and her place in the world.

She rose from her bed. Her old room seemed so small now, as though it had shrunk around her. It was night. The stars shone outside her window. No light save the light from a quarter moon angled through her window and painted the floor and one wall of her room. She stood up and felt the floor under her feet.

The ceiling appeared to be closer than was quite proper. Her room felt like ill-fitting clothes. Moonlight filled her room. The sounds of the rasping mill wheel and the creek flowing over rocks also flowed into her room. Familiar sounds, yet now they seemed beside the point of her life. She was here, but she needed to be elsewhere.

She opened the door and went out into the hall and descended the steps to the ground floor. She was hungry. That she knew for sure. A pot of some stew simmered on the wood-burning stove. She took a bowl from the cupboard and filled it with the stew. She sat at the table, being careful to fold her legs just so, keeping them from banging against the wood, and ate from the bowl.

She finished it quickly and stood up and got another helping. As she was almost through this second bowl, she heard footsteps coming from her parents' room. She turned in her chair, the operation requiring much coordination of unfamiliar muscles and bones, and saw her mother standing in the doorway.

Assa pushed her chair back and rose. She felt like she towered over her mother. Could the woman who birthed her be so small? It seemed impossible. And yet, her senses, as far as she could determine, did not deceive her.

Child, said her mother. How could you have grown so much? She displayed tears in her eyes. Assa's mother wrung her hands in front of her. Assa opened her arms and her mother stepped into her space. They held each other for some time. Assa had never felt more loved than at that moment, feeling the need of her mother to be close to her daughter.

How long has it been? said Assa over the top of her mother's head.

Seven years, said Assa's mother. You're a grown woman now.

I still feel like I'm a child, said Assa. I don't remember the years. How could I have acquired them when I don't remember them?

Assa's mother pulled away from her daughter.

Can I get you some stew? asked Assa.

Her mother shook her head. I'm not hungry.

I am, said Assa, smiling.

I made it for you, said her mother. I knew when you finally woke up you would want some food and you always liked this the best.

Still do, said Assa.

She returned to her stew and resumed eating. Her mother watched her for a few minutes, then put her hand down on the table.

What happened to you? she said. She looked frightened, as though the honest answer to her question would be the worst possible eventuality.

I don't fully understand it, said Assa. She recounted her experiences since her kidnapping, emphasizing the changes she went through, and making sure that her mother understood that she had two good friends among the royals. Assa's mother listened carefully, obviously not fully believing Assa's tale.

That sounds—strange, she said.

It is strange, said Assa. I never thought such things as happened to me were even possible. I just want everything to be back to normal now.

Things are not normal, said Assa's mother. Things are very different now, she said.

Assa nodded and swallowed. Her mother got her some bread and put it on a plate and set it down next to Assa's bowl. Assa took a hunk of it and dipped it into the stew and ate the hunk. I forgot how much I liked this part, said Assa.

Your father and I don't know what's coming, said her mother. No one has been in or out of the palace for years. It's guarded by dragons.

Assa's eyebrows lifted. Dragons? she said.

They came soon after you were taken from us. They surrounded the palace and breathed fire for days, burning everything around it. Smoke rose from the fires and draped over the palace. But they never dissipated. The palace has been buried under black smoke for so long and no one can come close to it or they choke to death and no one has come out of it because—well, no one knows why. They might all be dead inside, the entire royal family and the court. Or they might be asleep. Or they might simply be trapped. But that's not all. The land is sick. It doesn't support crops like it used to. We have not had a good harvest in a long time. The mill hardly has anything to grind. Your father and I want to move on, to some other place.

This surprised Assa. Move on? she said. To where?

It doesn't matter, said her mother. If we stay here we will wither away. At least if we move on we might have a chance at a life. We only waited, because we hoped you might return and you would need familiar surroundings to get your bearings.

Assa listened carefully to everything her mother told her. Dragons keeping the palace hostage. It sounded just as dire as her mother believed.

I know the daughters of the king and queen, said Assa.

Yes, said her mother, but they are just as much victims of this as anyone. They are helpless against the dragons.

Maybe not, said Assa. Just before we parted ways, I felt something from them. It was a message. I couldn't quite understand it, but it was important.

A sound came from her parents' room. Assa's father shuffled into the kitchen.

You're up! he said with what sounded to Assa like false cheerfulness. He shuffled over to his daughter and kissed the top of her head.

Assa took his hand and held it tightly. She could not keep tears from welling up in her eyes. Her father was slow-moving and seemed defeated. His chest looked caved in on itself, and his face was drawn and sad. It was startling to see him so different from what she remembered.

He had not been a lively man before, not by any means. She had always remembered him as slow and steady. But this wasn't like that. This was someone who had been slowed down by life, not because that was the way things were.

Assa looked at her mother, who seemed to offer some sympathy to her daughter, as if acknowledging what Assa saw in her father.

We were so worried about you, said Assa's father. But you came back to us. He smiled crookedly and released Assa's hand. He got himself a bowl of stew and sat at the table with his daughter and wife. He ate quietly, almost daintily.

I heard the mill last night, said Assa. The turning. It woke me up. The mill brought me back to life.

That's good, said her father.

Mom and I were talking about how we could bring the palace out of the smoke. How we could bring the land back.

Bah, said Assa's father. The land is dead. The mill grinds dust now. We need to find a new home. Or maybe we need to die. He smiled again, but it was not genuine. He made his mouth assume the shape of a smile. It gave the impression of a child trying on a new word. Assa glanced away, unable to look at him. She had no idea he had become so demoralized.

Mom mentioned that, said Assa. But where would you go?

Assa's father slurped more stew. He dipped a hunk of bread in the bowl before answering his daughter. No one knows where we will go. There are others. We all feel the same way. Any place would be better than this place.

That's not true, said Assa. I lived in the ground for a long time. It's not better than here.

Her father didn't answer. He dipped his spoon in the broth and brought the contents up to his mouth. He did this several times, in silence.

Finally, he spoke. You have had adventures. That's good for a young person. You will have more. You are still young. We are not. We have to find some place where we can grow old and die in peace.

Such strange words from her father. Did the end of the mill spell doom for them all? Assa stood up. I'm going to contact the princesses, she said.

Her father chuckled. Princesses, now? You are friends with princesses? My daughter is rubbing shoulders with royalty. Be careful, now. You don't want to catch royal diseases. And you don't want to inhale the smoke that smothers the royals. They can't help us anymore, you know. They have lost the land.

He finished his stew and pushed it forward on the table. He leaned back in his chair, a sour expression on his face.

Assa thought she had to get the land back, if only to bring her father back from this strange state of being.

She rose and excused herself from the table and went outside. The air was clear and cool, just what she needed after the stifling atmosphere in the house. Was it always like this? Was the house she grew up in always so suffocating? She could not go back inside. Not now. Maybe later. The very thought of reentering the house filled her with nausea.

She ran from the house to the forest on the banks of the creek. It was familiar, but different. The years she had been away took growth from the trees and the bushes. They were shorter and narrower. Leaves did not billow off branches with the same vigor. They did not reach as high for the sky. She entered the woods and stepped on less springy undergrowth. A burning sensation rose up in her throat and a sour taste invaded her mouth.

Was this how her parents felt now? This sense of disgust with the world? She set her teeth firmly against each other and pressed on into the woods. The mill, indeed, seemed to be grinding only dust. It chewed grit between its gears. It was as though the smoke enshrouding the palace had drifted over, sending clouds of particles to the mechanism that once turned grain into flour and now simply created an annoying reminder of their diminished prospects.

She emerged on the beach side of the woods and turned south toward the rocks overlooking the strait. She liked the feel of the sand beneath her feet. It, at least, felt real and normal. Nothing more normal in life than walking a sandy beach.

The ocean sent waves in their eternal procession to crash on the shore. The beach gave way to a rocky surface that rose from sea level. Assa did not slow her pace. She began climbing the rock and before long stood at the apex. She had been purposely keeping herself from looking toward the palace, but now she turned her gaze inland.

What she saw shocked her.

A massive cloud of black smoke enshrouded the hill that supported the palace. The cloud roiled and writhed. Strands of thick dark smoke curled up and twirled into thunderclouds that sat over the hill. The smoke was like a creature gobbling up the air around it and turning it into a monster. At the base of the smoke, she saw a circle of dragons, all turned inward and breathing flame into the cloud. Indeed, the were clearly producing the cloud from the combined accumulation of their flaming breaths. Assa estimated there were at least fifty dragons. Maybe more. They were tiny dots in the distance, but their iridescent skin was a dead giveaway to their identity.

Awful, isn't it? came a voice in her head.

She spun around, as though she expected to find someone else up here on the rock with her. No one was there. She was completely alone. The voice in her head was familiar.

Dawn, she said. Where are you?

You're looking at me.

In the palace?

Yup. Me and Dusk and my parents and some of the court. Those that survived.

I see dragons, said Assa. All around the palace, belching smoke.

We are surrounded by smoke, said Dawn. It's our cage. We can't run through it without choking to death. We can't put it out because the dragons are too strong. We are running out of food. The royal stores are low. We are rationing what's left.

Why are there dragons at all? I thought they all died when Hoyal died.

A few survived. They were immune to whatever killed the others when Hoyal died. They multiplied and now here we are.

You have to run out of there, thought Assa. You'll die if you stay.

Assa, said Dusk, we can't leave. We're trapped. Come get us. Kill the dragons if you have to.

Assa didn't know how to do that. There were too many dragons. They must have been multiplying with enormous energy.

As she looked at the palace, shrouded in smoke, she saw some of the dragons spiraling up into the air. Their calls screeched across the sky. Some of them flew out to the ocean and dove into the water and came back up with fish in their talons. The fish writhed in their death throes as the dragons took them back to the other dragons, encircling the palace and belching flame and smoke. The fish were seized upon and eaten in a great frenzy of chewing and flailing of wings and limbs.

Assa had not noticed previously that this procession of dragons fishing in the ocean proceeded without pause, dragons coming and going and dragons eating constantly. She saw that once a dragon had eaten its fish, it returned to the circle of dragons and belched its smoke anew. Assa recalled that when she was on the island with Hoyal and the dragons, the creatures then belched white smoke. They must be able to change their smoke as the need arises. The black smoke they were putting out now completely shrouded the palace from view.

There are many many dragons, thought Assa to the princesses.

You must find a way to defeat them, came Dusk's voice. We're counting on you.

We'll reward you, said Dawn. My parents will shower you with riches. You will be wealthy and adored for bringing back the palace.

Also, said Dusk, the land will return.

Assa had been paying so much attention on the smoke surrounding the palace that she had scarcely noticed the land surrounding the palace. She surveyed it now, and saw that the princess was right.

Dried and withered trees were everywhere. In the place of acres and acres of greenery, she saw only brown. In some places black streaks criss-crossed the land, as though the earth had been scorched. As indeed, it may have been:

perhaps dragons swooped down on the land, frolic or malice their motive, and breathed fire as they flew, leaving trails on the ground.

Houses of her neighbors still dotted the countryside, but some were burned up, and others looked dilapidated, as though they were no longer inhabited. Her land was dying. That much was clear.

I know nothing of dragons, thought Assa to the princesses.

You have to find out, they said to her. And soon.

Why do they want to do us harm? thought Assa.

She heard Dawn and Dusk groan. We don't know! We're trapped.

Don't you have a naturalist or a wizard trapped with you? Can't you ask?

We have no wizard, said Dawn. You commoners always think there are wizards in palaces. There is no such thing as a wizard.

And naturalists? asked Dusk. What's a naturalist?

Someone, said Assa, who knows about animals and plants. They might know something of dragons.

Dragons are not animals or plants, said Dusk. They are curses.

Assa had no response to this. She saw that the dragons were as industrious as ants. They were strong as lions. And they were as determined as tigers. They were filled up with fierceness and a singularity of purpose. Nothing was going to stop them from choking out the royal family.

And with the royals would go the land. Once the palace fell completely, the rest of the land would follow. The dragons would leave the palace as a cinder and turn their attention to the rest of the structures of the land. They would make short work of the little houses and huts where the people lived. Assa saw it all. It was so clear to her what was happening.

She closed off her connection with Dusk and Dawn. No reason to listen to them any longer. They might as well be dead. Maybe they were dead already. She might be hearing thoughts that were just swirling around in the air.

Assa descended the rocky point and began walking back to the house of her parents. There was much to do to get ready to leave the land and she wanted to help them all get out of here as soon as they could.

WHAT ABOUT THIS? asked Assa. She held up a box that held bracelets and necklaces, her mother's precious decorations.

No, said her mother. I don't need that. Leave it. We need to travel light.

Assa tossed the box into the trash pile in the middle of the living room. The pile was high and growing higher. She and her parents had decided they would take only what they absolutely needed to survive. Jewelry did not fit that description. Mostly they packed clothing, food, blankets, and a few other necessities. They each allowed themselves one or two sentimental tokens of their time spent here. Assa kept an acorn that she had found when she was a little girl and had kept all these years. Her mother retained the ring her husband had given her when they married, and her father kept a bracelet Assa had made for him out of reeds she had found on the banks of the creek.

Assa's father wanted to take the mill. This was obvious to Assa, but, of course that was impossible. The mill wheel was too large and too heavy. Impossible to put it on their cart, and certainly impossible to drag it.

Assa wanted to take something that would remind her of her friendship with Dawn and Dusk, but she had nothing. This actually made it easier to live with the decision she had made to let the royals in the palace perish. She told her parents nothing of her decision. When she returned from her conversation with the princesses, she embarked on a push to get her parents to leave the land. They had to if they were to survive.

Assa pulled out a map of the land that her father had stored away in a cabinet. She spread it out on the table. Her father had drawn it many years ago. It showed the mill at the center. It looked surprisingly fresh and alive, not like it felt to actually be here. Assa's mother dragged her husband over to look at the map.

Assa spread it out flat with the palm of her hand. Next to the mill was a long line: the creek. It ran to the edge of the page where another long line, crossing it, indicated the shore of the ocean. Beyond the edges of the map, Assa imagined a vast land, spread out as far as her mind could dream.

Which way should we go? she asked her parents.

We've never been far, said her mother. We're not sure.

Well, said Assa, what's up north?

Forest, said her father.

Good, said Assa. We could live in a forest, couldn't we?

Maybe, said her father. I've heard it is very wet. Too wet to grow anything. The crops get waterlogged and moldy.

Huh, said Assa. She had not ever heard such a thing. How about south, then, she said.

Assa's mother shook her head. No, she said. That's desert. Too dry for anything. Even for people. It's all snakes and cactus.

Assa drew in a deep breath. Inland? she asked.

That might work, said Assa's father. But there are mountains. They are high and they get cold. We could freeze to death.

So you're telling me this spot, right here, is the only place we are able to survive. Anywhere else is too dangerous.

Assa's parents looked at one another. We've never really thought about it, said her mother. We never thought we would have to leave where we are now. This was our home. She sighed and looked defeated.

This is crazy! said Assa. We have to pick a direction and go. We have to take the chance. Because if we stay here we'll die for sure. Where are other people going?

Some are going to the sea, said Assa's father.

A twist in her belly made Assa go a little weak at her father's words. Not the sea, she said.

Why not? said her mother. They have boats. They can sail away and find something better.

We're not sailors, said Assa. We don't have the knowledge to navigate.

No, no, said Assa's father. Your mother is right. The ocean is probably the best way to go. We can drift for months and months if we have to. Eventually we'll find some place that we can survive in.

To Assa it seemed like a crazy idea, and it brought back terrible memories of the time she spent on the island in the middle of the ocean. Dragons lived there. Nasty things.

But then, she reasoned quickly, dragons lived here as well. And they were suffocating the land.

She let her eye scan the map again. The ocean was a narrow band on the edge of the paper. It looked so quiet and inviting. So tame. But the map was wildly inaccurate. The ocean extended for uncounted miles, thousands and thousands. If they were to be set adrift on it, they could end up anywhere. Or nowhere. They could be lost until they died.

I don't even know if we would get seasick or not, said Assa.

I've heard you get over it, said her father.

Okay, said Assa. Let's find us a boat.

Her parents smiled at her.

That's the way, Assa, said her father. Don't despair. We can find our way out of this if we just stick together.

Assa nodded. The voices of Dusk and Dawn were much subdued in her head, but she could still feel them there: tiny and wispy, like spider silk, floating on the periphery of her perception. She felt a sour taste on the back of her tongue. She wanted to forget the princesses. If she thought about them now, if she tried to tell them anything, if she even *listened* to anything they had to whisper, she might change her mind.

That's right, said Assa. We just have to stick together.

THEY PARED THEIR possessions down to the barest minimum they thought they might need. Then they loaded those up on makeshift wagons, and began walking toward the bay, pulling their wagons behind them.

The palace, still shrouded in black smoke, marred the land like a sore on a body. It was behind them most of their route, but sometimes, when they went around a bend, the sight of it startled Assa anew. It still seemed impossible that such a thing could be there. Assa looked away when the image presented itself, preferring to gaze at the ground in front of her or at the faces of her parents. They seemed to have acquired a new determination once they were on the path to the bay.

They journey took several hours. By the time they arrived, it was late afternoon. The sun was only a short distance above the horizon. It would touch the water soon, then they would be in darkness. Around them, many people from the village were crowded on the shore. Assa recognized some of them, but most were strangers. She nodded to the people she knew. They nodded back, but seemed wary of her.

A few boats were moored to the docks. Fishing boats, mostly. Assa was shocked at how small they were. Could families really board these and live on them for extended periods of time?

Assa's parents were in conversation with their neighbors. Assa heard voices all around her. A cacophony of questions and answers. The captains of the boats were arguing with people. They said they could only take a few. But the people on shore weren't accepting this judgement. They *needed* to get on board the boats. They *needed* to survive.

I built this boat, said one of the captains. It's going to save me, not you. If you want a boat, build one yourself.

Assa thought this was a terrible thing to say. How could people condemn others to being left behind like this?

She walked up to the captain and grabbed him by the lapels. The captain, startled, moved to push Assa away, then, when he saw she was a young woman, relaxed a little and endured her uncivil manner.

We're your people, said Assa. You can't refuse us.

Bah! said the captain. It's not me that refuses you. It's the boat. It isn't big enough. If everyone who wants to get on one does, it would sink. How about that? Is that what you want your escape to be? A grave in the ocean?

Assa held his lapels as long as she could. Her hands began trembling. The captain put his hands on Assa's wrists and gently moved them from him down to her sides.

People are going over the mountains, he said. You might want to think about that.

Assa looked down at the ground. We can't, she said. We would die. Can't you let us on? Just the three of us? Please?

She looked up, but the captain was already gone, melted into the crowd.

I don't know if this is going to work, said Assa's mother. No one wants us on their boats.

I know, said Assa. How long would it take to build one?

Assa's father laughed. We can't build a boat, he said. We don't know how.

We're going to have to learn, said Assa.

She brushed past her father, who looked puzzled, and walked toward the woods on the edge of the clearing. Some people were already there, testing the limbs of the trees. Assa stood beside them and surveyed the trees.

We have to cut them down, she said, and lash them together and make a raft.

The man and woman immediately beside her nodded. It's not going to be easy, said the woman.

The man looked from the trees to the water. Can it even work? he asked. There's too much water. The waves would swamp the raft, wouldn't they?

Don't have to worry about that, said Assa. The wood floats. You can have all the waves you want crashing over your raft, it won't sink.

The man looked doubtful. Assa pushed by him and found a tree that looked small enough to cut down and big enough to provide some support.

From her pack she pulled out a saw and applied the blade to the tree and began sawing. She worked for several minutes before her mother and father came and stood beside her.

We can't go on the ocean in a raft, said her mother. Assa, we have to find some other way.

Assa didn't stop. She sawed and sawed. A small pile of pale yellow sawdust began accumulating at the base of the tree. She was making progress, but it would take a while. All she had to do was apply herself and not let herself get tired. Getting tired was the worst thing that could happen. Behind her, she heard cheers as one of the boats launched into the water. It was probably filled to capacity with townspeople eager to leave, eager to find sanctuary somewhere else.

Assa wanted that sanctuary as well. She doubled her efforts, pulling and pushing on the saw blade with all her strength. Sweat began popping out on her forehead. It ran down to her eyes, stinging them and making her close her eyelids to keep out the biting saltiness. She paused her sawing motions only long enough to release her hands and wipe her eyes. Then she resumed her efforts with wet hands, slick from her sweat. The saw slipped out of her palm. She grabbed the handle once more. Only a few trees. That's all it would take. A few trees lashed together. It would not be the best transportation, but it would be enough to get them somewhere, anywhere.

Food would be a problem, but they could catch fish from the ocean. The ocean was filled with fish, wasn't it? They wouldn't have to cook fish. They could just eat it raw. Assa knew people did that. They could cook food again when they got to some place away from here.

Her vision, still blurry from the sweat, was not keeping her from her task. She was determined.

A hand wrapped itself around her hand. She stopped. Her father put his other hand around her shoulder.

This won't work, Assa, he said. We have to find another way.

Assa drew in a deep breath. She wanted to keep sawing. She had only one purpose now, to build a raft for her family. If she focused only on that task, she wouldn't have to address the voices in her head. Dawn and Dusk. They were still there. Small, but insistent. They kept asking her what she was doing. They kept asking for help. But Assa couldn't help them. She couldn't defeat the dragons. No one could.

We have an idea, said Assa's mother.

No one has any ideas, said Assa. Ideas don't matter anymore. Only survival is important.

Child, said her mother, listen to us. Assa's mother put her hands on Assa's cheek. She held her daughter for a few seconds, then kissed her forehead. Assa's heart melted. The collapsed into her mother's arms and began weeping.

There, there, said her mother. You're such a brave girl. You're such a strong person.

Those words only made Assa weep even more.

Assa's mother let her cry. The tears covered her cheeks. Assa wiped them away, but they continued to fall.

Here's what we're going to do, said Assa's mother. We'll go back to the mill. The mill is made of wood. We can take it apart and build a boat from the pieces, then float it down the creek to the sea. How does that sound to you?

Assa pulled away from her mother and blinked several times. Why didn't I think of that? she said.

You may be the smart one in the family, said her mother, but you don't know everything. Come on.

Assa's father put his hand on her shoulder and the three of them began walking back to their house.

We've wasted precious time, said Assa.

We know, said Assa's father. We should have thought of this before.

None of us is used to this, said Assa's mother. It's scary. That makes our brains scattered.

Yes, thought Assa, but she should have been smarter. Her parents were old and their brains were slower. She was younger. She should have figured out the mill thing.

Do you have plans? asked Assa of her father. You built the mill, do you know how you'll unbuild it, then make a boat out of it?

I have some ideas, said her father. He explained to Assa how the struts of the mill wheel could be dismantled, then lashed together to make the sides of the boat. They had some tar pitch that they could put into the spaces between the wood to make the boat watertight. There was still some piles of wood in the back of the house, left over pieces that could be used to make the keel and pull the ends of the wooden pieces together.

It sounded like they could do it. It would be much better than the raft Assa had planned.

I have some cloth we can use as a covering, said Assa's mother. To keep the rain and sun off of us when we're on the water.

It sounded like it made sense, but it also sounded so difficult. Could they truly build a boat and put it on the water and survive?

The road back to their house was more melancholy than the same road had been when they left their house. There had been something exciting about leaving the dead land. Now, retracing their path, there was something depressing about passing the same terrain. The trees seemed a little more dead, the land just that little bit more barren.

Assa tried to keep her eye on the path, maintaining a rapid pace and urging her parents to keep up. But even with the best of intentions, she could not help peering out of the corner of her eye at the desolate landscape all around her. The limbs of the trees were still and vaguely menacing, like they might strike Assa at any moment. The grass was dry and crackling. Wind went over the blades and made rasping noises in the air, and sent shivers up and down Assa's back.

A few crows circled above, the only bit of brightness. Assa loved the sound of crows, cawing in the wind. It made her think of better times, when the land was alive and fresh.

But the crows flew off to attend to their own interests, whatever those might be. Assa watched them with wistful interest. If only she and her family could fly. She flew, once, when she was a dragon. But that ability wasn't coming back to her.

She clapped her hands together, imagining wings on her back. Wings flapping, holding and releasing air. Then shook herself out of her reverie. They had work to do. She and her parents. Assa needed to focus.

They trudged grimly on, no one saying anything. Their packs of belongings seemed to grow ever more heavy as they went. Assa wanted to drop them by the side of the path. She felt her parents probably thought the same thoughts. Who wouldn't, after all this walking? They came to a curve in the path, familiar to Assa. They were very close to their house.

As they neared it, the sound of the creek seemed strange. It flowed, as always, but it had a different pitch.

Do you hear that? asked Assa.

I don't hear anything, said Assa's mother, a deep and sad weariness in her voice.

The creek, said Assa, it's different.

Don't be ridiculous, said Assa's father.

She wasn't being ridiculous. There was something different. She put her hands up to her ears to listen better and in a rush of perception the truth of the noise came to her. That wasn't the creek. Or, at least, it wasn't just the creek. There were other sounds.

Assa dropped her pack on the path and ran with all her might toward her house. When she got there, her worst fears were realized. Dragons, dozens of them, were swarming over her house.

Their talons gripped shingles on the roof, broke them off, and carried them aloft in the direction of the cloud-shrouded castle. Other dragons were busy dismantling the mill. They had already inserted their talons in the seams between components of the wheel and had wrenched them apart.

The wheel, what was left of it, lay in heaps of broken lengths of wood. The dragons breathed fire on the longer pieces, burning them into smaller pieces that they then picked up and carried toward the castle. The dragons worked with dour efficiency, not wasting a motion or a gesture. All their energy was directed to taking apart Assa's house. Except for the noise. Their work was punctuated with screeches and calls, letting the world know they were doing the work they were meant to do.

Assa hesitated for only an instant, then she picked up a length of wood, felt its heft in her hands, raised it above her head and ran toward the house and the dragons, swinging the wood like it was a weapon. She caught some of the dragons by surprise and managed to hit two or three of them in mid air. They screeched even louder. One of them plummeted to the ground, its wings a tangle of leather. Another was merely deflected momentarily by Assa's club. It veered away, dropped its load of wood, and righted itself and returned to the house as though nothing had happened.

The dragon on the ground breathed fire into the air, but the flame was weak and dull. Assa stepped up to the dragon and brought her club down on its head several times until the skull cracked open and blood poured onto the ground. The flame was completely extinguished.

She looked up and saw the rest of the dragons still working industriously on her house and the mill wheel. There wasn't much left of the house: a few fragments of wall and some loose pieces of wood scattered about. The mill wheel was almost completely gone: a few sections lying here and there. Some pieces were floating down the creek.

Behind her, Assa felt her parents huffing and puffing along the trail. She wanted them gone, now. She didn't need them here anymore. They would just get in the way of her killing.

Assa waded into the remnants of her home and began swinging the club around her in a great circle. There were only a few dragons left. Now that most of the house had been carried away, there was no reason for them to remain. Those that did were able to dodge the club with ease. They lifted themselves into the air and screeched at Assa and spit long flames. Assa felt the heat of their breaths on her skin. The smelled burnt hair. Must be her own, melting and warping on her head.

She swung the club some more, knowing it was futile, but unable to stop. Eventually she felt a hand on hers. Familiar and strong. She looked up. Her mother looked at her. A smile was on her face. Pity seemed to color the smile. Assa wanted her feet to keep going, but they wouldn't. They stopped. Her knees felt weak. As she fell to the ground, her mother caught her.

WHEN ASSA REGAINED her senses again, she saw both her parents looking down on her.

This is getting tiresome, said Assa.

Shhhh, said her father. You need some rest.

Where am I? asked Assa.

You're safe, said her mother. For now. Get some sleep and we'll figure something out.

That didn't sound good. Assa let her mind wander until she encountered those voices again. The twins. The princesses. She was sure she had been rid of them. What good did they do her? They were just impediments to what she needed to do.

How's the dragon hunting going? asked Dawn.

None of your business, said Assa.

How's the whole deserting your friends thing going? asked Dusk.

You aren't my friends, said Assa. You're royals. We can never be friends. You'll always be able to order me around.

We trusted you, said Dawn.

And I trusted you and what did it get me? A dying land.

That's not our fault, said Dusk.

Maybe not, said Assa, but you haven't done anything to fix it.

The dragons, said Dawn, as though beginning a thought. When she didn't complete it, Assa moved to distance herself from the voices again. She looked up at the dragons in the sky. A row of them, carrying various pieces of her house, flew toward the castle. Assa imagined they were going to throw the bits onto the fire ringing the royal household and shrouding it in smoke. The sight of them made her want to send Dawn and Dusk back to the recesses of her mind. Or better yet, to have them extracted from her consciousness completely.

She turned to her parents.

What do we do now? she asked them.

They, too, looked to the sky, watching the dragons flying lazily toward the castle.

What connection do you have with the dragons? asked her mother.

What? said Assa. No connection. I don't know anything about the dragons.

They came when you came, said her father.

Yes, but that has nothing to do with me. I don't know anything about dragons.

Assa's father regarded her with slightly hooded eyes. Assa felt frightened of what he might be thinking. This was a completely new sensation to her and she mentally stepped back from him, as though she could retreat into the alternate reality world that had cocooned her for those years before she got here. She turned to her mother, who looked bewildered. And who wouldn't be? Everything was strange and dire now. None of them knew what to do.

Well, said her father. What about it? What's up with the dragons?

Assa stammered something incoherent, unable to form words. She took two steps back from her father, stepping on chunks of wood from her house, which tilted her balance so she had to throw out her arms to keep herself from falling.

None of us knew what a dragon was, said her father. They were just strange creatures from stories. Fantasy. Nothing that could possibly harm us or the land. Then you disappear and the dragons swoop down on us. Doesn't that seem strange to you?

Stop it, said her mother. You can't accuse our daughter like this.

I'm not accusing, said Assa's father. I'm just asking questions.

He brushed past his wife and went to the one fallen dragon. He kicked it in the body. This is what I think of your dragons, he said. Then he raised his foot and brought it down on the dragon's head. Assa heard the skull crack. Blood spurted onto the ground. The dragon's eyes stared up blankly at the sky, reflecting gray clouds in a milky luminescence.

What do you say? he asked his wife and daughter. Aren't you going to join me? He continued to stomp on the head until the eyes exploded, sending a yellowy viscous fluid dribbling out of the tears in the eyeball. The skull eventually flattened completely under his heel and he moved onto the rest of the dragon, crushing its rib cage and shredding its wings until only ribbons remained.

The mud under the dragon worked its way up, or the dragon's body worked its way down into the mud, Assa wasn't sure which, but eventually it was difficult to tell where the dragon began and the ground ended. She and her mother watched with mounting horror as Assa's father seemed possessed by something Assa could not understand. Where was this impulse of his coming from?

Stop it! said Assa.

Why? asked her father. He did stop and looked at Assa with an expression Assa could only interpret as accusatory.

Is this one of your friends? Am I hurting a friend of yours? Do you want to give it a proper burial?

Dragons don't have burials, said Assa. They get burned up. The other dragons eat their ashes.

Assa's father stopped. Is that right? he asked.

Yes, said Assa. She had no idea where that information had come from. The twins didn't tell her. Hoyal never told her.

So the other dragons are going to come and roast this dead critter, then eat it?

Assa looked wildly from her father's face to her mother and then at the broken dragon body mashed into the ground.

Something like that, said Assa.

So, said her mother, you do know something about dragons.

Her father stepped off the dragon's body. Assa felt only pity for him. But also pity for the dragon that she had killed and that had been treated with such disrespect. She stepped forward and took her father's hand and pulled him off the shredded wings.

He moved slowly and quietly, as though he needed to hold some kind of reverence for the fallen creature. Suddenly.

They aren't bad, said Assa.

You don't understand what's been happening, said her father, if you think they aren't bad.

They just do what their instinct tells them to do. They're no different than dogs that way.

Dogs don't destroy houses. They don't hold the castle hostage under smoke.

If that's what they were created to do, then they would. The dragons need a leader. They had one. A royal. But she died.

So now they keep us all hostage?

Something like that, said Assa. They're looking for a leader. They need a human to guide them.

Assa's father looked calm again, his usual self. It was as though his mutilation of the dragon's body was something done by another person, someone who merely looked like her father. A little.

Are you that human? he asked his daughter.

Assa looked at the smoke shrouding the castle. The dragons that had picked apart her house were no longer visible as separate creatures: They had merged with the rabble of dragons circling the smoke and belching fire.

She saw some of the dragons tearing into the wood. Fuel for their flames. The smoke seemed to get bigger and blacker. It felt like it could not get any bigger. It already filled the sky. It send up a column of smoke that rose higher than the clouds, then spread out in the upper atmosphere, casting everything under a ghastly shadow.

If this continues, she said, we'll all be dead. No sunlight will come through and we'll wither, just like the trees. We'll all be picked over by the dragons. Our bones will end up in the fire and we'll turn to ash.

No one said anything after that. Assa's parents were not the capable people Assa had thought them to be. They did not rise to the challenge of the awful things happening in their own land. She wanted to scream, but even that felt futile.

You can go, said her father.

What? said Assa.

You got away from this world once, he said. By flying, wasn't it? Or turning into a fish or something? Isn't that how it went?

Something like that, said Assa, but I can't leave you to die.

We'll all die if you stay, said her mother.

Yes, yes, said her father. We all will. If you go, at least one of us will be alive.

That's what you want? said Assa.

That's not what any of us want, said her mother. It's what has to be.

Assa didn't know how to turn into a fish or fly. That just happened to her. How could she explain that to her parents?

She stepped over to the dragon and nudged its lifeless body with her toe. Even crumpled on the ground like this, its body mashed into pulp and its wings tattered, torn, and shriveling, it had a certain majesty. The luminescence of its skin was marred by mud and looked as though it was beginning to fade, but she still found grandeur in its presence. It would be something to be able to fly, as she once did.

I don't know how to do it again, she said.

You were a fish, said her father. Weren't you?

I think so.

Then slip into the creek, transform yourself, and swim away. Swim to the ocean. You'll be free.

I don't know how, said Assa.

We'll help you, said her father. Come on.

He put out his hand and Assa took it. Her mother took her other hand and the three of them walked to the bank of the creek, next to where the mill once turned. The water was swift and dark, almost black. Assa knew fish swam through this water. She saw them, sometimes, flitting by. Their silvery skins flashed light like sparkling gems. They swam through the water. It must be like flying through air. You could go up and down. The freedom would be magnificent.

Assa's father sat on the bank and dipped his feet into the creek. The water flowed around his legs. Her mother did the same. They sat beside each other, holding hands and leaning close, their shoulders touching. Assa stood to one side, watching them. Were they ready to die in this broken land, and let their daughter leave?

I don't know how to do it, she said.

Just sit with us, said her mother. Let your feet dangle in the water. At least do that. Come on. It feels good. We never did this enough.

We never did it at all, said Assa.

Maybe you didn't, said her father, but we used to come here all the time. Especially when it was hot. We'd take dips in the creek.

Assa blinked. She had never seen her parents do such a thing. She had never seen her parents like this: hanging on each other, looking at each other with dewy eyes.

She took off her shoes and socks and sat beside them, but not too close. She dipped her feet into the rushing water. She moved closer to the water and let her calves and knees get wet as well. It did feel refreshing, the water wrapping her limbs in cold. It was a cleansing.

I spent a lot of time in the water when I was building the mill wheel, said her father.

I helped, said her mother. We got wet a lot of the time. We were soaked for days. I still remember it. We had nothing, but we loved being in the creek.

I love the creek, too, said Assa. But that doesn't mean I can be a fish. Can you be a fish?

Of course not, said her mother, but you're different, aren't you? You've had all these adventures. You've been transformed.

Assa kicked at the water. She listened to dragons screeching far off in the distance, like they were trying to seep into her brain, change her thinking.

Hoyal did it all, she said. She made us change. The dragons were—something else. They aren't real.

Oh ho, said her father. Now we're getting somewhere. If they aren't real, what are they?

They're something else, said Assa, trying to be dragons. I think. Assa's mind reached for some meaning, as though she could find it in the water. Flashes of silver flitted by her.

Up the creek, far off in the distance, she saw dragons collecting into a column and diving, one by one, into the creek. They emerged with fish in their talons and flew to the castle. The dragons were not only destroying the land, they were eating all the food as well. It was so strange. Dragons were not part of the land, had never been here, but now they were going to be the end of them all.

She looked at her parents. They were gesturing toward the water. Her mother nodded toward the opposite bank. Her father put his hands together and moved them forward, like he was diving. Fake diving. He wasn't going to plunge into the water, he was just trying to get Assa to immerse herself completely in the creek.

They seemed so interested in saving her. Why weren't they trying to save themselves?

Assa moved off the bank and slipped into the creek. Her feet touched the muddy bottom. The water reached up to her waist. Two more steps and she would be in the creek completely.

She turned to face her parents. They blew kisses at her. They looked like they were crying. Or were they? Maybe it just a trick of the light here. Were they really ready to let her go?

The royal twins were there in her head again.

What took you so long? said Dusk.

What do you mean? said Assa.

This is the answer to all your problems, said Dawn, but you refused to believe it.

I don't think this is solving anything, said Assa. I'm doing this because my parents want me to.

Your parents are smart, said Dusk. Just dunk yourself in the water.

It's so cold, said Assa.

Just do it! said Dusk.

Assa slipped further into the water and submerged her head. The creek closed over her completely. She was in a dream world. The sound was muffled, yet somehow magnified. She heard pings and tiny impacts of something: stones? She couldn't tell. She pushed off the bank and swam with the current.

Is this what you wanted? she asked the twins.

That's it, said Dawn. You were really going to leave us to die in the smoke.

You aren't going to die in the smoke, said Assa.

How do you know?

You've been in the smoke for weeks. If you were going to die, you'd be dead by now.

Oh, said Dusk. The commoner knows so much. We should listen to her wisdom, shouldn't we?

You must need me for something, said Assa. You keep contacting me.

How's that swimming going? said Dawn.

I'm going to have go up for air, said Assa.

No! said Dusk. That's the one thing you must not do.

I have to breathe, said Assa in as reasonable a voice as she could manage.

No you don't, said Dawn. Take a look at your arms.

Assa turned her gaze to her hands and forearms. A faint iridescence seemed to float up from her skin. A long time ago, such a sight would have alarmed her. Now, it just seemed like another day in her life when something miraculous occurred. It was remarkable, but not enough to matter anymore. If she couldn't save her family, what did any of it matter?

Do you see it? asked Dusk.

I'm glowing? said Assa.

She heard laughter from both Dawn and Dusk, then more excited words from them.

You're turning into a dragon, said Dusk.

Not a fish? asked Assa.

Hmmm, said Dawn. Maybe. Maybe a fish first, but then a dragon. Definitely a dragon.

Assa's body began to shape shift. Her arms contracted, her legs, clamped against each other, began to merge. Her feet spread out to a fish tail. It all proceeded in a stately and unremarkable manner, but it *was* remarkable.

Her shoulder blades, somehow, lengthened and broadened, all at the same time. They burst out of her back and stretched out in the murky water, pushing against the current.

What's going on? asked Assa. My legs are stuck together. Shouldn't I have talons?

It's the fish stage first, said Dusk.

But I have wings already! said Assa. She moved her wings so that they pushed against the water. The current grabbed her wings like they were ship keels and swayed her in one direction, then the other. Her tail was not helping her. It wanted to wriggle her body in a direction opposite to where her wings wanted to take her. The creek felt like home, but it was fighting her. It knew she wasn't right. To top it all off, she needed to breathe. She couldn't remain under water much longer.

Your stages are getting mixed up, said Dusk. Breathe in water.

No, said Assa. I can't. I'll drown.

Do it! said Dawn. Do what we say. We won't let you die.

Assa tried to pull herself up out of the water toward the surface of the creek. But her tail was an impediment. It had powerful muscles buried under the skin and it fought to push her down.

She reached, desperately, for the air above her, but her wings wouldn't quite obey. It was as though they knew better. Or thought they knew better. In the end, it no longer mattered if she was going to drown or not. She couldn't hold her breath any longer. She closed her eyes and determined to do what had to be done. She steeled herself, and drew in a long deep breath of water.

At first panic engulfed her as the unfamiliar sensation of water entering her lungs made adrenaline surge through her system. She flapped her wings spasmodically and flicked her tail from side to side. She expected blackness. Welcomed it.

But that didn't happen. Instead, the water flowed out of her nostrils, then she took in more of it. The ruckus in her body subsided. She began to breath in and out normally, taking in water like it was air, stripping out the oxygen from it, and breathing out the water into the creek. She had gills? It appeared so. They adorned the sides of her face, just above her cheek bones.

Now what? she asked the twins.

Now you come save us, they answered in unison.

Save you? said Assa.

Come quickly, they said. The dragons have been working to melt the walls of the castle, and they are getting closer all the time. The castle walls are hot. We have barricaded ourselves, but they will break through in several places soon.

But what can I do? asked Assa.

You're a dragon now, said Dusk.

No, said Assa. I'm not. I'm part dragon and part fish. I have a tail. I can't pick things up. I'm not even sure I can fly. And what about breathing? I'm breathing water now, not air. I can't leave the creek.

Assa heard muffled cries in response.

They're in! said Dawn in a scream.

She heard another scream. Dusk? Had to be.

I don't know what to do, said Assa to the ether.

She didn't get a response. Only the flow of water, silently rushing by her, seemed to offer any sensation she could possibly understand. But she didn't understand. Not really. Water was supposed to be for drinking, not breathing. She looked up, through the depths, to the dark sky above her.

SHE WASN'T SURE how long she spent trying to see something in the sky. She wasn't even sure what she wanted to see. Some sign, perhaps. Something to tell her she was on the right track and the princesses weren't steering her in the wrong direction. There were places in the world that she could not enter, surely. Wasn't that the lesson of life: know your place? Without place, you were nothing. Without the land, you were lost. Most likely dead.

But now she wasn't even on land. She was a water creature. The liquid passed over her body in a shiver. She wriggled through the current like it was her home. How can a substance be her home after only a few moments of contact?

She turned and rose to the surface, trying to see through the water. A sheet of reflective surface spread over her. Assa worked her arms, which felt different because they were fins, so that she remained in place. The effort made her reconfigure her entire being, making her use muscles and impulses she did not know she had.

Through the surface of the creek she was able to see her parents, some short distance away, as though they did not want to leave the confines of the creek. It must have felt like some kind of sanctuary to them. Off to the side, a short distance away, she saw a pile of wood, burning. The wood looked like it was pieces of their house, the house that the dragons had dismantled and left as junk.

Above the pile, her father, or her mother, or perhaps both, had built a spit. On the spit were pieces of a dragon, roasting in the flame and smoke. Assa laughed when she saw this. It had to be the dragon that her father had pummeled on the ground. She liked that her parents had the ingenuity to take that creature and turn it into sustenance.

She slipped back down to the depths of the creek and followed the current toward the ocean, not really thinking about it for a moment, then realizing that the ocean was nothing but an escape for her. If she got to the ocean, it would mean she was free of the land. She would be able to swim anywhere she wanted, consort with any other creature out there. Eat her fill of the plants and animals in the salty realm. Dodge predators intent on eating her.

She would roam the wild depths to her heart's content, perhaps, at some point, lay eggs that would produce descendants. In short, she would have a life of freedom and perhaps even ease. All these things were owed to her as a creature of the world, as they were owed to anyone born. Or hatched.

The lure was fantastic. No attempt at burning things would touch any creature in the ocean. It could not. No smoke would choke her breath. No dragon could touch her.

And yet.

Assa slowed her pace. The water, still urging her forward, began to push against her, instead of sliding up next to her and journeying with her, as a companion. Already, as a fish, she understood the duality of her world. She could go with the flow, choosing ease and contentment. Or, she could turn her body against the flow, and work hard to counter the motion of the creek. She could, in other words, work herself to ruin, if that's what it took, to return to the source.

She spread her fins. The water pushed against her. Like a whispering friend, it urged her forward. If she closed her eyes, she could imagine the voice of that friend. It would be a loyal friend. Not necessarily wise or smart, but buoyed by a belief in Assa, in her innate ability to be tough and resilient. Cheering her on.

Assa resisted. She opened her fins further.

The current groaned around her. It had to readjust its flow over her body. Her pace slowed. She felt the current whipping at her tail. She tried to bat it away with her tail, which still felt like her legs, wrapped by some binding material, so she had to get used to her two legs acting as one, but not having the instinct to do so. Instead, she felt like she was tugging at the binding at inopportune moments. Even so, she used her meager skills to turn herself around. The worked her fins as best she could to push her body against the current of the creek.

It was a strong current. The same current that turned the mill wheel that ground wheat for the people of the her land. It had power, and she was fighting that power.

Water streamed over her body. It flowed past her eyes. She felt the current over her eyeballs. Nothing like this had ever happened to her before. She was going to go to the source of the creek. She felt an electric thrill do through her body. Not down her spine, though. That was not a fish's way, apparently. Fish did not entertain the possibility of thrills.

No matter. The creek, she knew, extended up into the mountains. Before it got there, it passed through the castle. Right under the smoke and fire that the dragons had made. She pushed against the current. It parted before her. She had to keep up her motions. If she dawdled for even a second, the current pushed her back and she would have to work minutes again to make up the loss.

She passed strands of plant material as she went. Other fish swam past her, going in both directions. How could they do it so easily, when she had to work at it every minute. Every second?

No matter, no matter. She had her work to do. She was going to do it.

After a while she saw that perhaps she shouldn't be working in the middle of the creek. The current was much stronger here. Maybe too strong.

Some of the other fish found eddies and little areas of quiet current on the edges of the creek, near the banks. She slid over to one such eddy herself and the relief was immediate. The current did not push her forward, neither did it drag her down. Instead, she found some peace and calm. A certain ease filled her being.

She breathed in the water and breathed it out with an unhurried pace. The light above was beginning to fade: The sun was setting. Soon she would be in darkness and did not know how she was going to fare in a world that did not light her way. Would she have to find her own illumination? The prospect did nothing for her state of mind, which was filled with trepidation at her new state of being. Not to mention the feeling that she had some mission to accomplish now.

She searched for the voices of the twins. They seemed to have disappeared. Or, at least, gone to sleep, as though they needed to retreat from the world.

Assa understood. She had the exact same feeling. It would be paradise to retreat from the world. Let the world go on without her.

She called to the twins. Are you still there? What's happening in the palace?

She let her mind float out of her fish body and into the water and up into the air. Or imagined she did so. It was difficult to tell if it was actually happening or if it was just her imagination.

She once heard her father say that imagination was all anyone needed to survive, even thrive. With it anything was possible. Without it, nothing ever happened. Assa never understood such pronouncements from her father. They seemed like the sort of thing that made sense to old people but did not have anything of interest to someone her age. Now she thought she understood some of it.

Did fish sleep? She wasn't sure, but she knew she felt sleepy. That didn't mean much because she wasn't a real fish. Not like the creatures swimming with her who had been created by other fish. They were fish from the beginning. Before the beginning. What was she? Not a real fish, surely, since she was born human and was now something made from—what? Her imagination?

Her musings did nothing to prevent the sun from setting. Her world became nothing but water. No light from anywhere. Perhaps if the moon would come out, but it was in its quarter phase and would not rise for some hours. She had only starlight above her, and precious little of that, since clouds had obscured the sky.

As she waited for morning, Assa felt other creatures in her vicinity. Some of them brushed against her. Other fish, no doubt. Maybe snakes? She had seen snakes in the water on other occasions. Not often, but sometimes. Enough to know that they were out there.

The contact unnerved her. She jumped, as though startled out of her skin. Her bones felt like they were infused with electricity and her entire body was alive to the possibilities of being damaged by her unfamiliar environment. Or of being eaten. Isn't that what nature was: eat or be eaten?

She tried to push these thoughts away, and called out to Dawn and Dusk again. Still no answer. Were they still alive? Maybe they had been suffocated in the black smoke?

She moved her fins tentatively and edged out of the eddy and back into the current of the creek. It pushed against her, but her rest seemed to have rejuvenated her, at least a little. She pushed back against the current and eased herself forward. She found she was able to sense the extent of the creek. The banks were *there* on the edges of her perception.

The floor of the creek, sandy, with rocks and gravel strewn everywhere in some kind of pattern, were also there. She found that her senses were sufficient to steer her clear of the banks and the bottom. She was able to navigate a path that took her between those extremes. She still had to fight the current, but after a while it felt like a familiar friend. She used the current to aim herself. She headed in the direction that the current seemed to be coming from. It was a perfectly efficient navigation technique.

She worked in this way for some hours. Occasionally she steered toward an eddy and rested for a while. Each time she came out of an eddy, she was stronger and more sure of herself.

As she swam, she began to fear the touches of others less and less. At some point, she realized that she needed to eat and that some of those things touching her were probably food. She opened her mouth and gulped down worms, bits of vegetation, and some other creatures she did not recognize. It didn't matter: They all were nutrition for her and she ate with gusto, feeling the food in her stomach and feeling the juices there go to work on the morsels: breaking them down and filtering the nutrients throughout her body. Her blood pulsed with life, her skin felt glowing, as though she could cast her own light. She wanted to cast her own light. She wanted to be as alive as she could be.

Eventually, after what seemed like days and days, but which could only have been a few hours, the water above her began to lighten. Not much, but enough to notice.

The sun was coming up.

A new day, and her fish senses discovered something else on the edge of her awareness. There were flying creatures everywhere. They were mostly perched, but they had energy, fierce energy.

Those must be the dragons.

And something else touched her senses. She wasn't sure what it was at first, it seemed too large and too solid. It was as though something from another world was trying to edge her consciousness out. It took her a long time to understand what was happening, but eventually, the truth came to her. She stopped swimming. She had reached the end of her journey: She was next to the castle.

WHEN SHE WAS a young girl, Assa would imagine going to the castle. She glimpsed it on the horizon, and its mystery always intrigued her. She would think about who lived there, how they spent their days and how their lives affected her life and the life of the land.

She wanted to be a princess. She thought such a life would be the most grand thing she could imagine. She would live in a marvelous house made of stone, she would have the power to tell others what to do, and she would wear the finest clothes and have the best parties. She would invite all her friends and they would eat the finest food and give the best presents.

These thoughts of the grand life consumed her thoughts for weeks at a time. Her parents indulged her fantasies, but eventually told her that the castle was the sort of place that affected everything. The royals who made it their home had the power of imagination. Their thoughts would emanate from the castle and bring life to the land. The point was to let Assa know that it wasn't all grand balls and fun in the castle. The royal family had important work to do for the life of their people.

Assa doubted that such things could be real, but she never told her parents. As she grew, the castle became part of her world, just as the ocean, and the creek and the rocks on the beach were part of her world. And, as when anything becomes too familiar, it loses its magic, just a little.

Eventually she saw that the castle was not much more than a bump in the land and that the building itself had nothing to do with the health of the land, not really. What brought the land to life was the people who lived in it. And the plants and animals that populated it. The royals, who lived in the castle, were just regular people who happened to have a lot of wealth.

Assa's life went on as it did for all of her life. She worked at the mill with her father. The mill ground grain into flour, which they then sold to the people of their town, and that's how they lived. The royals faded from her thinking.

They lived as they lived, doing what they needed to do to survive, just like everyone else.

Periodically, some of the enforcers from the castle came to the land and made sure the people paid their taxes so the castle and its inhabitants could keep going. Assa always resented when they came. It was not right that they were allowed to run roughshod over the people of the land. What right did they have?

Assa asked her parents just that question, but they told her some things were not to be questioned. The royals did things a certain way, and had done them that way for generations. It was not for the likes of Assa or her parents to question those ways, much less to defy them.

This satisfied Assa. She understood things being the way they needed to be. It was the same as with the mill. If it did not turn, then it did not do its work. In fact, the turning *was* its work and nothing she did could change that. So it was with the castle and the royals. They did their work, as they needed to do and nothing she could do would ever change that.

But there was still some tiny part of her that wanted to see the castle and experience some of its glory, if only for a short time. One fall night, soon after her tenth birthday, when she was sure her parents were asleep, she slipped out of bed, put on warm clothing, and creeped out of the house and into the cool night. The moon was full, as she knew it would be be, and she followed its light toward the castle.

The woods were close around her and the branches brushed against her skin, leaving scratch marks on her face and hands. Assa didn't care about the marks. Except that her mother would see them later and know that she had been out of the house. She didn't want to think about what her parents would have to say about that.

She knew she was doing something she shouldn't. But her spirit was alive with the thrill of being outside of her house, especially in these circumstances, when the world was dark and the castle was there, on the horizon.

As she walked through the forest, birds called to her. She heard their screeches. Some of her friends told her that dragons lived in the forest and they ate anyone who dared walk there. Assa didn't believe those stories at all. Not for a second. Dragons were made up things, she was sure of it.

It took her at least four hours to get close to the castle. That was two hours longer than she thought it would take, and this worried her. It meant she would not get back until after the sun rose, which meant after her parents woke up. She approached the castle, therefore, with the thought that she was going to have to explain to them what she was doing here. She did not look forward to that at all.

The castle wall was milky in the moonlight. She walked up to it over marshy ground. Her shoes were covered in mud. Her hair was snagged with leaves and twigs. She knew she looked a mess but she didn't care. On the other side of this wall were the king and queen and the princesses. She knew the princesses were named Dawn and Dusk. She had heard about them.

Assa looked up at the wall. It went higher than her eye could follow. Above the castle, some bright stars, brighter than the moon, twinkled like jewels on velvet. Now that she was here, she didn't know exactly what to do. Did touching the wall of the castle mean anything? Could she tell people she had been to the castle?

She leaned her back against the castle. The stones that made the castle wall were smooth and cold. She shivered against them. Her mind drifted. She heard sounds on the other side. She pressed her ear against the wall to listen more carefully. There were scratching noises. The stones seemed to call to her. Was the whole world alive except for her corner of it? How could the castle be talking to her?

As she held very still and attempted to take in more of what the wall had to say to her, she turned to the air and opened herself to more of the castle surroundings. She noticed birds flying overhead. They called to her. Crows, mostly, but other birds as well. Their voices crawled into her brain and lodged there, looking for comfort, she supposed. She took her ear from the wall and wondered where she was getting such ideas. Was the air around the castle saturated with voices? How could that be?

Assa walked along the foundation. The ground was lumpy and dry. Dried grass covered the lumps and made crackling noises as she walked. She came to a large wooden door. It was more a structure in itself than a door. It was big enough that two carriages could ride through the doorway side by side. It had a handle made of metal. It was so big, Assa could not have moved it.

Above the bridge she heard voices, several of them. Men were talking to each other. They mentioned something about the queen and king, how they were not very nice people. Assa was shocked to hear this. Everyone in the land thought the king and queen were the best people. They took care of everyone living in the land. They made sure the land was strong and fertile. How could anyone not like them?

That king, said one of the voices, he's so fat I could use him for a sofa.

You think the queen sits on him? asked the other voice.

She wouldn't dare. If he moved wrong he'd crush her.

Laughter at that comment. Then: It wouldn't take much to kill them both. Then we'd have the castle for us.

What us? What do you mean?

I mean the servants. The regular people. We'd have the castle for us. Wouldn't you want to have the castle?

A pause.

Then the other voice spoke up. It would be okay, I guess. We wouldn't have to do whatever that fatty and that ugly told us to do.

Assa dared not move as the talk went on. They continued in light tones, as though they were discussing what they might have to eat for dinner that night. All the while, as they were talking, they walked back and forth on the top of the wall.

They were on the lookout for anyone that might try to invade the castle, she supposed. They were on the lookout for people like her, who shouldn't be there. If she was another kind of person, one with weapons and bad intentions, she might be dangerous to the castle and the royals who lived in it. Why didn't the men above the door see her?

She pressed herself against the door and edged sideways to the other end of the door, intending to get to the other side and finish circling the castle. As she moved, she heard hoofbeats. They were distant, but they rapidly approached her. Three or four horses were coming in her direction. The door behind her began to swing open. It pushed against Assa, so she had to step forward to keep from being toppled to the ground.

She could get away from the door by running forward and veering off to one side. She could slip down in the dried grass, hold still, and be invisible and safe. Then, when the horses went by and through the doorway, she could wait a few minutes and return to her house.

But that's not what she did.

Instead of doing the safe thing, she slipped around the door and into the castle. She looked wildly around, knowing she had to find a hiding place quickly. In the darkness, she was able to make out a courtyard of sorts: an open area with steps leading up to higher floors. There were also doors, smaller ones, arranged in a circle around her. She found a dark corner to one side and slipped into it. She was pretty sure no one could see her. A few dark figures walked across the courtyard. They were dressed in what looked like rags. People in the castle wore rags? This shocked her, but she did not have time to think about it. The hoofbeats came thundering into the castle. Four people on horseback, flying through the doorway, which closed behind them quickly.

The horses were reigned in by their riders and the courtyard was filled with the panting and snorting of the animals. She smelled their sweat and the riders dismounted. More people in rags came to take the horses away. The four people stood in a group, laughing. She saw two short people in the shadows. Short as herself. They looked like young girls. Were they the princesses?

Assa's instinct was to keep in the shadows and watch the group, but she decided she would do a bold thing for once in her life. She stepped away from her hiding place and began walking to the group.

Hello there, she said, in as casual a voice as she could manage, though she was distressed to hear a quaver in it, like she was scared. She *wasn't* scared. Not really. Nervous, maybe. Unsure of her place, perhaps. But not scared.

The four riders turned and looked in her direction.

Who is that? said one of the girls. I don't know that voice.

Assa heard the sound of a sword being pulled from its sheath. She saw the sword raised above the head of one of the taller figures. Identify yourself immediately, said an older female voice.

My name is Assa.

Assa? said the girl's voice. We know no Assa.

I live by the creek. My father is the miller.

Laughter from the group. Is that so? And how did you find yourself in the castle? Did you, perhaps, scale the walls and overpower the guards?

Assa laughed with them. No, she said, I waited for the doors to open and sneaked inside.

Now they laughed even more, uproariously, as though they were going to fall on the ground in convulsions.

So, said the girl's voice, our defenses are shattered by a peasant girl. A *commoner*. Leave now, commoner, and nothing will happen to you. If you stay, we cannot guarantee your safety.

Assa listened as the doors began to swing shut.

Go on, said the girl's voice, you have only a couple of seconds.

Assa's legs wanted to move and take her out of the castle and back home, but she made them stay in place. The royal family would not hurt her, surely. They would not harm anyone they were charged with protecting. Assa was sure of that. It would be like a mother bear harming her cub. Wouldn't it?

The door slammed shut. Someone stepped forward and latched the door. A silence fell on the scene. They all stood quite still. Apparently all of them, including Assa, didn't know what to do next.

A couple of people from the riding party stepped toward Assa. Assa's legs, which she had willed to remain still, suddenly could not move quickly enough. She turned from the shadowy figures and ran along the interior wall away from the riding party. The horses, startled by her movements, neighed and began to step smartly. Several of the party worked to quell their movements, but the two smaller people, the two girls, ran after Assa.

Assa knew she was at a disadvantage: She didn't know the castle at all, and she was only one against the two. Also, soon there would be many in the castle, perhaps everyone who lived here, pursuing her. She was an intruder, after all. They could not tolerate such a thing. She was a disturbance to their world.

Assa passed several openings as she ran. Some had doors, some did not. She chose one of these openings, essentially at random, pulled the door open and ran into the passageway that opened up before her. It was dark and narrow, but she had committed herself. The pursuing girls did not let up their pace. Their footsteps were rapid and strong. Assa increased her speed as much as she dared. She passed other doors, and other openings. The castle was a labyrinth. She had not expected that.

She came to some stairs and went up them. She tripped once and bruised her shin, but quickly righted herself and kept going. The stairs wound up in a spiral and emptied out onto the top of the castle.

Moonlight streamed down around her. It seemed as bright as daylight after being in the darkness of the passageway. The stars were also as bright as ever. She stopped. The land below her was spread out like a frosted cake, the trees and grass fields bathed in the soft sugary moonlight. In the distance, the ocean sent threads of surf to the beaches. The creek cut a meandering line of gleaming white through the scene. She had never seen such a breathtaking sight. The beauty of where she lived was suddenly not something she had to imagine or make herself believe. It was all there, spread out before her, a perfect vision of grandeur.

A hand grabbed her shoulder. Another pair of hands wrapped around her and pulled her to the stone floor. The girls had caught up to her, as they would have to have done, she knew. The three of them lay in a tangle on the rocks. Assa was prepared to accept whatever punishment might now fall upon her. One of the girls held her arms to the floor. The other straddled her and worked to keep her legs still. Assa tried to kick and flail. She attempted to roll over. All to no avail. The girls were stronger than she was and they were determined to hold her.

Now stay still, said the one holding her hands.

What are you going to do with me? asked Assa.

In a couple of minutes the guards are going to be here. They'll do what they want to do with you. Probably throw you in jail with the rats and let you die.

Assa didn't believe this. Ha! she said. You're lying.

The girl straddling her grinned. Assa saw her lips in the moonlight. They looked like worms. Glowing worms. Assa laughed once, then began snorting and laughed more. Soon she was hysterical with laughter.

What's wrong with you? asked one of the girls.

You are princesses, said Assa, but you don't look like princesses.

They didn't answer her at first, merely looked at each other. What makes you think we're princesses? they asked.

Assa stopped laughing. You mean you're not?

Our mother is Hoyal, said one of them.

Who's that?

Don't you know anything?

How could I? I live in the village. I've never been here.

And why did you come here today?

I wanted to see the castle.

You've seen it. Was it worth it? It's a pile of rocks.

I thought I would meet the princesses.

Now it was the girls' turn to laugh. They did not hold back. After they finished they each slapped Assa on the cheek. Not enough to cause any damage, but enough that she felt the sting. Then they stood up and stepped away. Assa scrambled to her feet, but did not run from the girls.

They each grabbed an arm and began walking rapidly along the top of the wall. Assa was dragged along. They soon stopped in front of a stairway that led down to some place that looked awfully dark. Assa expected to be taken to the depths of the castle where she would be meeting rats in a tiny cell. Would they feed her? Would she be cold? She didn't know.

This is your way out, said one of the girls. Go down the steps as far as they will take you, then follow that tunnel. It will go a long way but if you keep going you'll find a way out of here. They each put a hand on Assa's back and pushed her hard. Assa stumbled forward, almost fell, but caught herself and began walking down the stairs. Soon it was too dark to see anything at all, and she navigated by keeping her hands out and on the walls. Behind her she heard voices. The girls explained that the intruder got away. Other voices, adult voices, questioned the girls about the intruder, but they said she was too fast. Assa just kept going down. Soon the voices were lost above her. She was alone and cold and frightened. All she knew to do was to keep walking.

Assa remembered that time with some fondness. Her great adventure. Now, years later, she was at the gates of the castle again. She remembered the girls that helped her. Back then, she didn't know they were the princesses, but now, she was sure they could not have been anything else. The princesses were the children of the castle. They were allowed to run all over the grounds. They were allowed to ride their horses out into the land. They were, of course, accompanied by guards who were there to protect them, but they still had enormous power and freedom.

Assa envied them for a long time. She wanted to run free as well. But her parents and the mill needed her at home most of the time. She was allowed to go to the beach and spend time at the ocean, but that was all, and it didn't last long. Enough time to wade into the surf and collect a few shells, perhaps. Maybe sit on the sand and watch the sea birds playing with the waves. It was a taste of freedom she loved, but it was always so short-lived that she sometimes wondered if she had really left the house at all. Was the beach and the ocean some kind of illusion?

Now, here she was, immersed in water. Where was it? Water surrounded her and flowed through her. Water was her entire world, but she didn't feel any of it. She was so at home in it that it disappeared from her perception, the same way she didn't feel air when she walked through the forest or on the beach. She saw a fly above her, hovering on the other side of the water's surface. Some instinct in her jerked her body forward and she leaped up, broke the surface tension and gulped the fly.

It buzzed briefly against the inside of her mouth, but quickly stilled itself and she swallowed it down. For the briefest instant she felt the tiny bulge of its body, but that sensation disappeared. The fly was in her stomach. She flipped her tail with delight. That was *good*. She looked up at the surface again, searching for more food. Who would ever have thought that she would be looking forward to eating flies?

A few more buzzed around the surface. She ate them down. They were good, but she saw that if she was going to remain a fish for very long, it was going to be a time-consuming job to keep up her strength. Flies were tiny. Each one took work to capture and swallow. To make the equivalent of a good hardy meal she would have to work for a long time.

A sense of dread began to fill her mind. Her body looked for more nutrition. She tried to quell that yearning. She expended more energy going after a fly than she could possibly obtain by swallowing the fly.

Her thoughts were spiraling down so that she didn't want to move at all. She stopped her fins from moving. She stilled her tail. The only motion she allowed was water flowing through her gills. It sustained her. Water wasn't enough, of course, but it was at least refreshing and free. She did not need to exert herself to receive the oxygen she needed.

Hey, came a voice to her brain. Dusk's voice. What's this? You giving up?

Not giving up, she thought, just taking care of myself.

You have people to rescue. Dawn's voice. Come do what you have to do.

I'm a fish, thought Assa. What can I do?

Haven't you learned? Dusk again. Nothing you are is permanent, she said. What is wrong with commoners that they don't ever *get* that?

Sister, came Dawn's voice, I ask myself the same thing all the time.

What are you saying? asked Assa. That I can become something other than a fish?

Weren't you something other than a fish yesterday?

Yes, but—

Not buts! said Dusk. We want you to be a dragon.

Assa felt her head nod, but her fishness did not nod with her. Instead she wriggled in the water, her whole body writhing. She had the remnants of her human body inside her and still wanted to use it the way she had grown up with it. That didn't work, but she saw that there were equivalent extensions of her perception in her new fishness.

You want me to be a dragon, she said to Dusk and Dawn.

Yes, a dragon. What else? How else are you going to help us?

Assa thought about dragons. She recalled the shape of their bodies and wings and the texture of their skin. She focused on their screechy sounds. The way their talons gripped the air. How their eyes seemed like smoky jewels. She took in all that she had observed of dragons since her adventures began.

That's good, said Dusk. Visualize like crazy. That's what'll get you there.

Assa imagined her fins stretching and bones snaking through them, like spider webs made of steel. She wanted her wings to have strength, after all. S he saw her tail morph into a dragon behind: wide and fanned to catch air and guide it around her. Legs sprouted out of her belly. She seized the image of them. Attached sharp talons to the ends of her toes. She was a sculptor working in flesh and blood and bone.

Her mind worked feverishly to keep all the images in place. Her snout elongated and her heart beat like crazy to push oxygen into her lungs, which were, themselves made of fireproof material and they *burned* on the inside. The heat was so strong that it turned the moisture in her system to steam, which escaped out of her nostrils.

Suddenly, she felt buoyant. She rose in the water until she broke the surface. Some tiny part of her wanted to dive back in. She wanted the security of the embracing and enveloping water, but that could not happen anymore.

Fire and water did not mix. She rose out of the water, dripping rivulets from her hide and wings. She belched fire. It sprung from her throat in a long flame. Assa spread her wings and stepped out onto the shore of the creek. She flapped her wings and saw that she was not on the outside of the castle.

She had transformed herself from an outsider to an insider. The creek flowed through the castle, which was a wonderment. She did not know such a thing was part of the castle. The water that turned the mill wheel at her house came from the castle. The creek originated here.

She screeched as loud as she could. Her eyes saw only dimly in the darkened environment. The smoke from outside streamed up around the castle, blocking out any sunlight. She turned to take in the walls and the stones everywhere.

It so dark that she began to feel like she would die of depression. No one could live long this way.

Cries of desperation came from behind her. She turned. Shadows moved in the darkness. Several figures moved like smoke through the darkened air. They each held swords or spears and they were running full bore toward her.

Assa spread her wings and flapped quickly to grab air and rose slightly off the ground, but not quickly enough. A spear caught her wing and ripped through the skin. It clattered behind her on the stone floor.

Her flight, which had only just started, was abruptly stopped and she flapped to the ground, broken. She tried to raise herself up again, but it was no use. Her disabled wing precluded any possibility of flight.

The figures advanced on her. She heard shouts and cries. Someone came right up to her with a sword held in front. The tip looked as though it was going to cut through her throat. Assa ducked as low as she could go and scampered along the floor with what she hoped was decisive speed, but there was no escaping the onslaught.

The army of armed, and, as it seemed to her, crazed, individuals, were on her in an instant. She felt the strength of their bloodlust. They wanted her shredded and bleeding on the stones. The press of their animosity did nothing to quell her fears and Assa prepared to meet the darkness of death.

But just as their blades were about to make new contact with her flesh, a call pierced the air above her. The group of attackers looked up.

Enough! came the voice from above. Spare this one.

They all looked around at each other, as though they needed more direction from the voice. Or was it from the air itself? Were they looking for something to tell them what they needed to do?

Slowly the tension in the group relaxed. Assa felt slightly less imperiled as she watched the blades lower and the heads of the figures droop. Blood poured out of her wing wound. It pooled on the stones and crawled along the groves in thin rivulets. She tried to move her hand to cover the wound and stop the bleeding, but her hand was a wing and it flailed uselessly.

How did dragons ever survive wounds in the wild? It puzzled her, now, as her life leaked out of her. The thought of how to survive occupied her mind completely and she opened her mouth to beg for help, but the sound was not words, only screeches.

That was a mistake. Her vocalizations prompted the ire of the group again. They turned to her and she saw fire in their eyes.

Which reminded her of her most important defense.

Assa opened her mouth wide and belched flame. She swung her head around as best she could so that she sprayed heat in a circle surrounding herself.

The figures jumped back. The effort at fire breathing exhausted Assa immediately. She felt weak and small, but she had established some territory for herself.

She panted, gasping for air. Her wing sent pain signals to her brain. She turned her attention to the tear and without thinking, relying wholly on an instinct completely foreign to her, yet completely embodied in her, she breathed fire onto the wound.

Her skin seared and blackened. There was pain: sharp and cutting, as though something was chopping her to bits. But the wound closed up. She looked at it and marveled at her own ability to weld flaps of her own skin together. Could anything be more wondrous?

On the periphery of her vision, she noticed the army had begun to move closer to her again. She stood up on her feet, spread her wings wide, to make herself as large as possible and flapped them to try to grab air.

But the wounded wing was still weak and could not support her. This did not trouble her too much. She could still breathe fire, though it was taking more effort than when she first tried. She released a thin flame. Not enough to do a great deal of damage, but sufficient to let them know she was not beaten: She still had strength in her and was willing to fight.

Behind her, the door to the outside was her escape. She needed only to sidle up to it, burn through the bolts holding it closed, and make her escape. She no longer thought about her mission to the castle. That was already nothing but ancient history. All her instincts were invoked, now, to make good her escape from this place. To return to her home and her original form and let the castle be.

She took tiny steps toward the door. The group, encircling her like the petals around a flower, moved with her.

Its heading to the door, someone shouted.

Don't let it escape!

Again, from on high, the voice of salvation: Do not harm this one!

Why not harm it? said one of her surrounders. It looks tasty to me. I like nothing better than roasted dragon!

Two figures, murky in the darkness, came sprinting toward Assa. She recognized their gait. When they arrived at the surrounding group, they pushed two of the warriors aside and stepped up close to Assa. They were unarmed and without malice. They bent down on their knees and got so close to Assa that she could smell their breaths: stale and rotten.

Assa, said Dusk. Is it you? Tell us it's you.

Dawn blinked and smiled at her. Assa made no sound. Instead, she nodded her head and blinked back at them. Dusk and Dawn wrapped their arms around Assa's neck. Assa opened her heart to their love. Or their neediness. She wasn't sure which it was, and at that moment did not care.

We knew you would come, they said. We have a place for you.

A murmur of discontent pulsed through the warriors.

What's this? asked one of them. You protect *dragons*?

You have done well, said Dawn. You have done your duty. Not let us do ours, as princesses and keepers of the castle.

Dusk remained close to Assa. She leaned her head even closer and whispered in her ear: Everything is okay. We'll protect you from the mob.

They moved slowly across the courtyard. The warriors were confused and unsure of how to proceed. One of their own, it seemed, was helping the enemy. They stood in disarray, no longer a coherent fighting group, but a ragtag bunch of tired people trying to hold up heavy weapons and not doing a good job of it. The tips of their swords clattered against the stone floor. A few of them sat down with their head in their hands.

Meanwhile Assa, with Dawn and Dusk as her escorts, moved quickly to a door in the wall, almost exactly opposite from the door that marked the entrance to the castle. Dawn pulled on the heavy handle and the door swung open. They entered a narrow hallway and shut the door behind them. Then they kept walking, but this time, due to the confines of the space, in single file: Dawn leading, Assa next, and Dusk trailing.

What took you so long to get here? asked Dawn in Assa's head.

What do you mean? asked Assa.

We've been calling you ever since the dragons surrounded us.

Assa thought back, trying to remember if she heard their calls. Her previous life seemed like it took place on another world. And maybe it did.

I didn't know you wanted me here, she said.

It's not like the castle is inconspicuous, what with its armor of smoke and its army of dragons.

Of course, said Assa, but I had no idea I was supposed to help you. I still don't know what I'm supposed to do.

Don't worry about that right now, said Dawn. Just follow us.

I'm following you, said Assa with irritation. Can't you see I'm following you?

Don't get so touchy, said Dusk. We just saved your life.

I don't see it that way, said Assa.

Silence from the twins. Assa listened to their footsteps in the hall. Her wing tips, too extended to close in completely, scraped against the walls as they walked. Assa felt her blood begin to flow through the wounds that the walls opened up. She didn't care. She wanted out of this dragon suit. She felt like if she could unbutton it from around her, she could step out of it and get back to her own life. Her real life.

And how, exactly, do you see it? asked Dawn. There was ice in her voice. It gave Assa shivers. Something in the deepest part of her brain clicked in an urge to burn the air around her, just for the heat, but she quelled that urge, although she noted its power. She wasn't sure, in other circumstances, that she could do so. This exhilarated and frightened her. She had powers that she didn't even know she could harness. She only hoped those powers would not come back to haunt or harm her.

I'm a peasant girl, said Assa. No matter how you dress me up as a friend of princesses or some powerful dragon or the savior of the castle, I'm not any of those things. You don't see that. You both think I can be something else.

The passageway wound in a long, and, what seemed to Assa, *pointless* spiral or circle. They seemed to be going up, but she wasn't sure. Sometimes the slope of the floor indicated a downward direction, but then it would right itself and go up again.

Thing is, said Dusk, you *are* something else than you think you are.

Shhhh, said Dawn. We don't tell her yet.

Why not? asked Dusk.

It isn't time.

It'll never be time, according to you, but we've kept it from her long enough. We need to tell her.

Tell me what? asked Assa.

Neither of the twins said anything. The silence in Assa's head was frightening. She wanted them to talk. Right now, it felt like she *needed* them to talk. If only to keep her from going crazy.

Assa stopped walking. Dusk ran into her from behind. Hey! she said. Warn me before you stop.

Dawn kept walking. Just keep following me, she said. I'll tell you what you need to know when you need to know it.

Enough! said Assa with words, punctuating them with screeches from her throat that echoed in the close quarters of the walls of the passageway. She also belched a short flame, completely unexpectedly. It scorched the stones above them, blackening them and coating them with a layer of black soot.

Dawn stopped and turned around. Well, well, she said. Our sister has bite.

Ha! said Dusk. Finally the truth.

Assa heard her talons scrape against the floor as she turned her body and looked at Dawn, then at Dusk, then back to Dawn again. She heard her breathing, felt the heat of her expelled air fill the space between them.

Sister? she asked.

Well, said Dawn, I guess it's out of the bag now. Yes. You are our sister.

No, said Assa. That's impossible.

Dusk stepped closer and put her hand on Assa's back. We know it's a shock, she said, and we'll give you some time to get used to it, but it is true.

I'm a royal? asked Assa. She felt disgust through her entire body. She couldn't be royal. It was not even remotely possible. Royals were born from royals. They lived separate lives from the commoners. Everyone liked that arrangement. If she was a royal, then that meant her parents had to be royals as well. But that meant her parents were the parents of Dawn and Dusk. But that meant—

No. None of it was true. None of it *could* be true.

How are you doing with this? asked Dawn. You wrapping your reptilian brain around it.

Dawn! said Dusk. Be nice.

I didn't mean it in a bad way, said Dawn. She's a reptile, you know. At least for now.

Whatever, said Dusk. She turned her attention to Assa. What our sister is trying to say, in her inept fashion, is that we're concerned for your welfare. We hope you are doing okay. Are you?

Assa's wing tips hurt. Also, the cut in her wing was making her itch and causing her considerable pain, despite its being closed up and, presumably, healing. Her talons had been catching on the stone of the castle floor, and it was *cold*. Not to mention the revelation of her being a royal, which was turning her brain inside out. So, taken all together, she was not having exactly the time of her life. Not according to any concept of comfort or pleasure.

I've had better days, she said.

Dusk lightly punched her on the shoulder. Or, rather, where her wing met her back. Was that called a shoulder on a dragon?

But this is a *great* day, said Dusk. You're one of us. Isn't that fantastic?

If I'm one of you, why did my parents and me live in a crummy house on the creek for all those years? Why are they still living there?

Okay, said Dawn. Here's the first thing. Those aren't your parents.

What?

Not your biological parents. They adopted you.

No, said Assa. No no no.

Yes, said Dusk. Don't make this difficult. You need to accept what we're telling you so you can accept the next step.

Next step? What was the next step?

My parents love me, said Assa.

Well of course they do. Why wouldn't they? Adoptive parents care about their adopted children.

I'm not adopted. I can't be.

Dawn sighed. We'll let that go for now, she said. You're obviously in shock. Or Denial. Something. She turned to Dusk with a what-do-we-do-now expression.

Let's keep walking, said Dusk.

I've had enough of walking, said Assa.

Dusk pushed her forward. No you haven't, she said.

Assa stumbled and nearly fell on her face, but righted herself in time and kept going. Where they had been going up, they now began descending. As they walked, they passed small openings in the wall. Assa looked through the openings and saw only black smoke streaming up in thick columns. The smoke did not enter the castle. It must have been some kind of magic from the dragons.

Where are we going? said Assa. I'm tired.

You'll find out soon enough, said Dusk.

They came to some stairs and went down them. Assa and the twins splashed through shallow puddles of water. This only made Assa even colder. She noticed Dawn and Dusk were shivering in the cold.

Assa, without thinking, opened her mouth and belched a long hot flame against the wall. Dawn and Dusk ducked down to the floor to get away from the heat.

Hey! said Dusk. Watch that.

Dawn rose and grabbed Assa by the throat and slapped her on the snout, hard enough to cause her some pain, all before Assa even registered what was going on.

Don't ever do that again, said Dawn. You could have killed us.

Assa tried to move her hand to rub the spot where Dawn hit her, but couldn't. Her arm had turned into a wing, after all, and lacked the dexterity necessary to do what she wanted it to do.

Her frustration got the better of her and she kicked the wall, bruising her toes as she did so, but not caring one bit. She spread her wings. They scraped against the walls. Dawn and Dusk backed away from her. They could see Assa was getting out of hand and would not be contained. Assa's dragon brain roiled under her human consciousness. She felt like she was trapped in a suit not of her making.

She wanted to break free.

Flame shot out of her mouth. She tossed her head from side to side. It felt good to release all this energy, though somewhere else in her mind, tucked in a far corner, she knew that she was going to regret it. Her flailing became more violent and her original wound opened up again, leaking blood onto the passageway floor. Her feet slipped on the slick pool and she fell on her backside, trapping a wing underneath. She heard bones snap. Pain shot through her. The wings must be useless now. This fact entered her consciousness like a gonging bell.

She was broken. She was no longer human, and now was not even a good enough non-human. Finally, after depleting her fuel, or so she imagined, she could no longer belch flame. Her teeth were scorched and felt rough as tree bark. She could do nothing more than cry. Tears welled up in her dragon eyes and fell to the floor. Her chest rose and fell with her breath, the only motion she could muster.

Dawn and Dusk, who had retreated to a safe distance, now approached her and stood above her with their hands on their hips.

Why are you being this way? asked Dawn.

If we could be dragons, said Dusk, you wouldn't see us being so pathetic.

Leave me alone, said Assa. I don't want to be a dragon anymore. I want my old life back.

Dusk bent down on one knee and ran her hand along Assa's wing. You've broken yourself, she said. How could you do that? How are you going to save us now?

Assa spent the next several hours on the cold floor of the passageway while Dawn and Dusk tried to get her back into shape. They did what they could to try to fix her wings, but they were pretty mangled up.

Dragon bones heal quickly, said Dusk.

How do you know that? asked Assa. And don't say it's because you're royals. I'm over believing that sort of thing.

It's because we've seen the injured dragons heal themselves, said Dawn. When they first wrapped us up in the the smoke. Some of them would fall and break things, but they would put themselves back together again and fly off. It was amazing.

I'm not really a dragon, said Assa.

You were when you were born, said Dawn.

Assa looked at her. What?

Okay, said Dawn. Not exactly. You were born kind of strange. Your arms were wider than they should have been. And you had this terrible breath. Everyone that was there talked about it. But the worst thing was that you had this strange scaly skin. It was ugly. They were going to kill you. The experts in the court said you wouldn't live long and it would be the kind thing to do. We didn't know it at the time, but you were a shapeshifter and that sort of thing makes everyone kind of squeamish. There have been other shapeshifters born in the royal family. Long time ago. All of them were killed.

Assa could scarcely believe what her sisters were telling. If they were her sisters.

If we were old enough, we would have fought for you. We would. But we were only kids ourselves. Not even three. All we knew was that we were going to have a sister or brother, but then we didn't.

What happened? said Assa.

The guy who delivered flour said the miller and his wife couldn't have children. He said that they would take you.

They never told me, said Assa.

They didn't want to open up the story of how you were born.

But this is crazy, said Assa. I'm not a royal. I don't feel like a royal.

That's only because you weren't raised as one, said Dawn. You're one of us, all right. And now you have to save us. Isn't it fantastic?

Assa didn't think it was fantastic at all. They were going to *kill* her, but when they get in trouble they want her to *save* them?

I don't know how to save you, she said. I'm not even sure I want to.

We heard that! said Dawn and Dusk in unison.

I don't care, said Assa more clearly. I don't want to do anything to help you.

Come on, said Dawn. We were only kids.

When did you know about me, that you had a sister?

Not until Hoyal took us to that island.

She was a crazy woman, said Assa.

Our parents and the court kept you a complete secret from us. We swear.

Assa didn't know if she could believe them. She didn't know if anyone should believe anything any royal ever said. They didn't care about anything except themselves.

Are my parents royals too? asked Assa.

No, said Dawn. They're just— Well. They don't have royal blood, but they're fine people. The salt of the Earth.

Spare me, said Assa.

Oh come on, said Dusk. Don't be that way.

What way? asked Assa.

You know. All hurt and pretending like you think we're awful.

I'm not pretending. You are awful. All of you.

We're the ones in trouble, said Dusk. We can't get out of the castle because of the dragon smoke. We're dying in here. Some in the court have already died.

And what do you want me to do? asked Assa.

Dusk put salve on Assa's wing, the one with the cut. She petted Assa's skin and massaged her legs. Assa found the contact repulsive.

She shuffled away from her sister. Dusk sighed and stopped. A great distance seemed to have opened up between them. Assa remembered a time when the three of them were at least civil to each other. Even a time or two when they had fun. But learning the full extent of her history made her very wary of Dusk and Dawn.

I still don't know what you want me to do, said Assa.

In your dragon form, said Dusk, you can meet up with the other dragons and convince them that this castle is not worth their time. Get them to stop belching smoke and choking us out. Get them to fly away.

I'll think about it, said Assa.

She watched Dawn and Dusk carefully, to see their responses. Both of them were silent for several seconds, as though trying to come up with other reasons for Assa to help them.

Assa felt like she had to understand her past better before she could agree to any kind of work for the castle. After all, the people in the castle had only wanted to kill her. Kill her! The very thought made her want to melt through the walls and escape. Could she do that? *Could* she melt through the walls? Maybe. She never knew she could be a dragon, and now this. She had a dragon life. A dragon body and dragon thoughts. Dragon breath.

Can we ask one thing? said Dawn.

Seems to me you've asked the biggest thing possible, said Assa.

We just want you to come with us to see the king and queen. Once you meet them, you'll change your mind.

I don't think so, said Assa.

Pu-leeze! they both said together.

Assa was almost amused, but mostly she was annoyed. Royals were such hypocrites. They were truly awful people and she wanted nothing to do with them.

No, said Assa. Just show me the way out.

Nothing of the sort happened. While they were discussing life and its woes in the passageway, guards descended upon them from both ends.

We tried, said Dawn. We tried to get you to cooperate. But you wouldn't. Now they're going to do it their way.

The guards pushed Dawn and Dusk aside, more roughly than Assa would have thought appropriate for princesses. Then they displayed a net and advanced on Assa and dropped the net upon her.

Assa tried to break free, but it was no use. Two or three of the guards cinched the net closed. Assa's wings were trapped against her body. Pain ripped through her as the broken bones were newly irritated by the rigors of her confinement.

She tried belching fire, but with her wings constrained, it appeared she did not have that power. All she could do was cough roughly. Not flames came out of her mouth.

She finally relaxed and accepted that her scales and skin were going to be damaged as she was dragged along the stone floor.

Dawn and Dusk called to her in her mind. Just let them do what they want, they told Assa. If you don't fight it, it won't hurt so much.

Why didn't you tell me? said Assa. Why didn't you say they were coming to get me?

It was obvious! said Dawn.

Not to me, said Assa.

Oh, Assa, said Dusk, we're so sorry. We don't know how to get you to do what you needed to do.

Assa didn't understand how they could communicate so badly for so long and still be alive and thriving. The princesses had no idea of how to interact with other people. Maybe none of the royals did. Maybe that's why they got rid of Assa when she was little. Sent them to her parents. Who, she now realized were not her parents at all, but just a couple from the village that wanted to raise a baby from the royal family. She would have to talk to them about that at some point. If she ever got out of *this* predicament.

At least they didn't kill her. That was something.

The guards, it seemed to her, were not going to be quite so accommodating. She felt like if she happened to die while they did their dragging, it would not be seen by them as especially tragic. Or even noteworthy.

The fibers of the net afforded her some protection from friction with the rocks, but not a lot. Standing up on her feet was completely out of the question. She would be knocked back down in an instant.

That left trying to keep her skin from getting burned off by attempting to keep herself situated on the knots of the net. She could do so for only a few seconds, then the bumping over the rocks would jostle her off the knots, and she would feel the roughness of the stones against her scales.

She tried to exhale fire again but she was completely depleted: she had nothing to burn. She wished she was not cursed with the wings. She wanted arms and hands again so she could take some control of her life.

The journey, bumping over the rocky floor of the castle, through passageways and banging against the walls, finally ended when her draggers stopped. They opened a clanking door and tossed her inside.

They pulled on the net and she tumbled out the other side, sprawled over the wet floor. Rats scurried away from her into the dark corners. She immediately stood up on her feet, and turned to confront her jailers, but they were already gone, on the other side of the door, which swung shut with a bang. She heard a key in the keyhole and the latch lock into place.

It was dark in the room. She called to Dusk and Dawn, but they did not answer in her head. The rats, quickly accustomed to her presence, came out from the dark recesses of Assa's cell and lifted their little heads up to her. She could step on them and kill each one. She wanted to, but decided she would wait. They might be her only company for who knew how long. And it was just possible that dragons liked rats and rats like dragons. They might end up being good friends, and Assa felt like a good friend about now was something to work for. Something to even hope for.

On one wall, a narrow slit extended a couple of feet through the rocks to the outside. It appeared to be a window. She saw no light through the slit. Or, at best, a very dim light. Mostly what she saw was a wall of smoke. It undulated and rippled through the window.

Assa walked to the window. Rat feet scampered over the floor as she moved. That was going to get irritating after a while, she thought.

At the window she peered through the opening. The smoke was hot. She felt waves of heat emanating from it. She opened her wings and warmed them on the thermals rising from the smoke, even as she winced at the pain lacing through her wing bones.

There was something fascinating about the smoke encasing the castle. She was in the center of it. What was she supposed to do now? Heal? Maybe she could escape by starving herself. If she didn't eat for several weeks she would get skinnier and skinnier.

Maybe then she could slip through the window and fly out of the castle. It was much too narrow to allow her escape right now. Her dragon belly was too bulky. Her wings could slip through. She tried it now. She put one wing into the opening. It touched the smoke on the other side and the warmth ran through her wing. It immediately soothed the pain in her bones. That felt good.

She put her other wing through the opening, standing with her back to the window. Her wings liked the feeling of the smoke enveloping them. She stood for several minutes, allowing the healing energy of the smoke to do its work.

Before long she felt an urge to belch smoke again. She opened her mouth and released a long and hot flame into the cell. It burned the air and heated the walls. She instantly felt better, cozier. The rats, perhaps ten of them, all stood up on their hind legs and twitched their noses at her flame. They appeared to like the heat and light.

The smoke had healing properties? Was that possible?

She turned around and tried to put her nose through the window slit. It was too narrow. She was able only to get a very short distance.

She noted the pain in her wings was gone. She stepped away from the window and looked at them carefully. She ran her snout over their surface and did not feel any breaks. The smoke seemed to have healed the bones completely.

Huh, she said out loud. Things are very strange in this castle.

She called to the princesses once more, attempting to find some connection beyond the cell, which now appeared to be her home. At least for the foreseeable future. Still no answer. She hoped they weren't going to get into trouble for helping her.

Sleep called to her. It snaked into her being through her ears and swirled around her dragon sensibilities. Sleep meant important things to dragons. It meant they couldn't fly. It meant they could stoke their fires and build up flames. It meant many things and Assa wanted sleep now more than anything else, but she fought it as long as she could.

Her eyes drooped. She shook her head to try to shake the sleep away from her. The rats, sensing her imminent loss of consciousness, dared to walk forward and some of them began chewing on her wings.

This would not do. She *couldn't* go to sleep if the rats were going to devour her. She pounced on one and stepped on it with all the might in her leg. Its life was crushed out. She felt its bones break under her feet.

She dispatched more of them in the same way. Their squishy little bodies were flattened and fluids oozed out of them. She grabbed them up in her teeth and went to the narrow window and tossed them into the smoke. The process took a full hour to complete. The first few were easy to stalk and kill, but the cleverer ones were harder to kill. In fact, a very clever one managed to hide from her in dark corners for a long time. She used her wings to brush it out. She screeched at it. She felt completely puffed up with power as she killed the last one and disposed of it using the narrow window.

At last, after exercising her hunting powers, she was exhausted and felt as though she might be able to sleep in peace. She curled up against a wall, using the stones as comfort for her back.

Her feet remembered the squealing of the rats. Not a pleasant sensation by any means. She stared at the window until her eyes closed. She wanted to shapeshift again. Turn into a bird and fly away from the castle, but she had not powers any longer. Could not transform a single cell of her body.

Instead, she welcomed the transformation of sleep. To go into the dark world and live there for a time. The comfort she would find there, and the rejuvenation, might be enough to make her want to see this world again. Maybe.

AFTER ONLY A couple of hours, she woke from a deep slumber with her nerves alive and electric. She heard crashing sounds above her.

Her first thought was that the castle was under siege by some enemy bent on destruction. Her blood, laced with energy, made her wings tremble. She had the urge to fly away, but was still confined in the little cell where she had killed all the rats. There was no way out, just as there had been no way out before she went to sleep.

She knew better than to attempt flight. She *knew* it. But it didn't matter. Her dragon instincts were too strong and she spread her wings and began flapping them in a futile attempt to catch air. She noted, with some satisfaction, that her bones appeared to have healed. That was good. But her attempts at flight were bringing them a new danger.

More crashing sounds, as if rocks were being hurled at the castle. Or maybe the castle was crumbling. Her wings flapped uselessly. She reigned in her urges as best she could so that the wings weren't extended all the way. They still pulsed and trembled. She still snorted, even sending a weak flame every now and then, but she was keeping her motions as small and quiet as possible.

The shaking was unnerving. The walls vibrated as though an earthquake was moving them. The mortar between the rocks began crumbling, sending little dust clouds into the air. A giant crack appeared at the bottom of the window. It angled away from the opening in a zig zag pattern like lightning. Assa put her wing tip there, to see if it went all the way to the outside. The thick leathery skin of her wing went in about six inches or so, then stopped. That was disappointing.

Still, if the walls were this weak, maybe she could help them along. She pressed her back to the crack, braced her feet on the floor. Took in a deep breath, held it, and pushed against the wall for all she was worth.

It didn't budge.

She braced herself again and took an even bigger breath and held it, feeling the power there in her belly, and pushed against the floor with her feet. Her back felt like it was going to ooze into the crack, but the wall did not move.

She opened her mouth, frustrated at the futility of her confinement, and breathed a long hot flame that scorched the wooden door, leaving a blackened stripe down the center.

So. It seemed frustration would bring up the fire. What little there was left. She felt depleted and vowed to keep her flame to herself from now on for as along as possible.

She listened to the castle, hoping to learn more about what was happening. The crashing seemed to have subsided considerably. Assa put her wing through the window of her cell and felt for something in the air. There was only black smoke, the eternal smoke that shrouded the castle and would not subside. Would not recede.

The door clanged open. Several guards stood on the other side, holding a net like the one that confined her yesterday.

We've got to get you out of here, they said. Don't fight us. We're trying to help you.

Assa moved to the side, an attempt to evade capture, but knew it was no good. There was nowhere to go in this cell. She stopped and faced them. She folded her wings against her body and squatted on the floor. The guards tossed their net over her. She did not fight them. They cinched it shut and she stepped forward before they even pulled at her.

They continued down the corridor. Rocks were strewn everywhere. She and the guards had to step around them. Chunks of the walls and ceiling were missing.

The guards spoke between themselves and Assa listened.

The east tower has fallen, said one of them.

I don't think the old man can help us, said another.

We have to stick together. The castle is all we have.

All we have is surrounded by black dragon smoke and we're stuck inside. We're in trouble.

Why did the tower fall?

The smoke is weakening the castle. The whole thing is going to fall if we don't get the dragons to go.

And the old man thinks this one will help.

It's all we have.

I'm telling you. If we don't start making progress soon, I'm sneaking out of here.

Oh, please! There is no out of here. You'd choke on the smoke. Or the dragons would eat you. Don't talk nonsense.

It's nonsense to stay here. We're sitting ducks waiting for our shelter to crash in on us.

They didn't seem interested in Assa. She was nothing more than a sack of bones they had to transport somewhere. To another cell, perhaps.

Her mind roiled with possibilities. She wanted to take all of them out, but she knew she couldn't do that. There were too many of them and they had weapons. Even if she belched flame, she could only, probably, disable one or two of them before the rest would cut her to pieces.

Still.

Her dragon instincts worked overtime in an attempt to construct a plan. She could surreptitiously cut through the netting and flip free. Then run in the opposite direction from the guards, maybe find a bigger window than the one that was in her cell and slip through that and fly away. It would be a dicy endeavor. She would have to fly through the black smoke, blind. She wouldn't know where she was going and might end up running into something, like a mountain or a tree that she didn't want to have to encounter.

Meanwhile, where were the twins? They had abandoned her and she was not happy about that. Didn't they say they were her friends? Didn't they keep trying to be friendly with her?

Not for a while.

They clanked up some stairs. Assa's body banged against the rocks pretty hard. She felt bruising and pain in her bones. It was like the broken wing bones got broken all over again and she didn't like it one bit.

She tried to make herself into a ball, but that didn't seem to be working. She moved her wings to protect her head as best she could. The guards were completely oblivious to her pain and suffering.

She ended up at the top of the stairs in a large cavern of a room. The ceiling had fallen in. Piles of rock were strewn around the space and black smoke covered the opening above her. If the smoke wasn't there, it would have been sky.

The guards pulled her across the floor and when she was approximately in the middle of the space, they dropped her and stood in a circle around her. One of them put a boot up on her shoulder, keeping her down with a casual air of fake boredom.

Assa tried squirming away from him, but he laughed and kicked at her. Not too hard. Not enough to cause damage, but enough to let her know he was still in charge.

She stopped squirming and relaxed. He eased back on his boot, just a bit, to let her know he was willing to be a little nicer if she was willing to cooperate.

Assa's belly smoldered with resentment and anger. If she had the fuel, she could have unleashed a yards-long flame into this area. She could burn them all.

But she had no fuel. Nothing. So she waited.

Presently some heavy footsteps clumped up the stairs that she had been dragged over. The guards all turned to the top of the stairs, waiting. Assa heard a puffing, labored breathing and she knew who was coming. The king. The fat king was about to enter the broken room.

All the guards dropped their heads so their chins rested on their chests. The king waddled into the room and walked directly to Assa and stopped. He looked own at her. This is the one? he asked no one in particular.

Yes, said one of the guards.

The king wheezed. Air got into his lungs, as far as Assa could tell, but it was not a pretty process. It was as though the air had to be dragged into the king's body kicking and screaming. She wanted to help him. Her dragon self wanted to burn the passageways free of obstruction for him. But that urge passed quickly. She needed more than his urging to continue this. She wanted him to let her go. She roared.

Or tried to. Instead of a monumental expelling of air, she managed only a whimper.

Pathetic, said the king. Is he really able to help us.

I don't know, sir, said the guard who spoke earlier. We can only do as your majesty requests.

Yes, said the king, only. Even as you're plotting to leave the castle.

I beg your majesty's pardon, said the guard.

Don't pretend, said the king. It's what *I* would do in your situation. It's what anyone with any sense would do. You have a plan of escape don't you? You've thought one through?

The guard stammered. I. I. Your majesty, it is forbidden to—

Yes, yes, said the king. Forbidden. I understand. Can this creature speak?

I think not, said the guard.

But it can understand.

That is our information, said the guard.

The king prodded Assa with his foot. She snarled at him and moved to try to bite his toe off. The king hastily pulled back and chuckled, while the guard yanked hard on the netting, cinching Assa more tightly in its bounds.

She's got some spirit still, said the king. My daughters seem to like that.

Yes, your majesty, said the guard.

The others stood silent, watching. Assa sensed that they were frightened, but was not sure what they were frightened of: the king, the guard who was speaking, or her. She wanted to think they were frightened of her. That thought, merely letting it play about her being, gave her a kind of power. It made her want to be in the world again. Fill it up. Or let the world fill her. She wasn't sure which.

They talk to her, said the king. In their minds.

Yes, your majesty.

You don't believe me, said the king.

I have no reason to doubt your majesty, said the guard.

The king was silent for a second. Then he spoke to the guard. Release her, he said.

All the guards stirred. None jumped to do as they were instructed. Assa held her breath and waited.

Did you not hear me? asked the king. I said release her.

Begging your majesty's pardon, said the main guard, but you're telling us you want her freed?

Yes, yes. Freed. Now.

But we—you—have worked hard to hold her. Now you want to let her go for no reason? We don't understand.

Have I lost my regal standing? Are my orders to be questioned? Is my massive girth now cause to doubt my instructions?

The guard stammered. I—I—merely was *suggesting* the possibility that your majesty *may* have acted a bit—oh—*quickly*.

The king stamped his foot and raised his voice. Release this dragon from her net. Immediately!

They waited another split second, then sprung into action. The guards, all of them, fell upon the net and began working it.

They attempted to untangle Assa from its hold, but found themselves working at cross purposes. When one got a section loose, another managed to re-tangle it all over again.

Assa thought of helping them, but figured she would only make matters worse. The rope that made up the net had frayed in some places, clumped up in others. Some of the fibers connected up with other fibers and made lumps of netting that were impossible to untangle. She remained on the floor, as immobile as possible while the guards worked. Soon she began to realize that the guards were not attempting to carry out the king's orders. In fact, they were working to thwart those orders. They were making only a show of untangling her, when in reality they were working the fibers to encase her even more tightly.

Assa wondered how long it would take the king to realize this. She watched as he circled the guards slowly, pacing with deliberate waddles. His arms crossed over his chest and his lips pushed forward in a pucker. She saw he was getting redder and redder, the rage building up in him. Assa recognized this rage. It was the same anger that she felt when her dragon instincts wanted to lift flame from her belly and shoot it out into the world.

Enough! said the king. You all take me for a fool. I will not have it.

The guards stopped their activities. They stood and made certain that they did not look at the king. They did not want to catch his eyes.

My power is slipping away from me, I know that, said the king. But this. This is truly no good to you or me. We must work together now if any of us are to survive.

Begging your majesty's pardon, said one of the guards. We are completely loyal to your majesties, both you and the queen.

Quite so, said another guard. It is simply that we are clumsy with our fingers. They all held up their hands and wiggled their fingers.

Do any of you have knives? asked the king.

Murmurs of denial. No knives. No blades whatsoever.

And what, said the king, do you call those things hanging at your waists.

Ah, said one of the guards. Our swords. Yes. Well. That *could* work. I suppose.

Give me a sword, said the king.

None of the guards moved. The king walked up to one of them and struck him on the face. The guards did not move.

Give me your sword, said the king.

When the guard did not move, the king struck him again, twice. Then he reached toward the handle of his sword. The guard did not stop him. Assa thought he would. She thought all of the guards would now rise up and attack the king. Slay him with their swords.

But none did. Instead, as the king, obviously unskilled in the use of a large blade, clumsily took the sword from the guard's sheath and let it fall to the stone floor in an awkward clatter, the guards all receded toward the walls of the room. They stood in a circle and watched as the king, puffing with the exertion, bent down and picked up the sword by the handle. He turned and aimed it at Assa. She scrambled to move away, but could could hardly budge.

Don't fear me, said the king in a trembling voice. I am here to assist you.

He put the tip of the blade on Assa's hide. It did not draw blood, but it did poke her. She flinched.

She could not see the king's face now, but she heard his labored breaths. He worked the tip along her skin until he contacted the fiber of the netting and began sawing motions to try to sever the fibers. It did not work. Assa heard the guards smirking. The king doubled down on his efforts and began sawing more vigorously, but it was no use. The blade was too long. He could not bring any pressure to bear on the tip. He needed a knife, just as he had asked for in the first place.

Now a curious kind of standoff occurred. The king did not want to admit defeat, so he did not stop his attempts at cutting the netting. He also, obviously, no longer had influence on the guards, who defied him with open contempt. Assa did not know what this meant for the castle, the land, or the twins, for that matter, but she did know what it meant for her: she was to remain trapped. At least for the foreseeable future.

The king, completely disgusted, threw the sword to the floor. He whirled on the company of guards and screamed at them. You *must* do as I say.

None of the guards spoke for several seconds. Then one of them, in a calm and quiet voice, said: No, your majesty, we don't.

The room went completely silent. The only thing Assa heard was her own breathing, uncomfortable in the confines of the netting.

The king turned from her. She heard his feet shuffle. He faced the guard who had been doing most of the talking. I have never executed one of my subjects, said the king.

The guard nodded.

But if you do not obey me, now, I will be forced to do exactly that.

I do not wish to incur your majesty's wrath, said the guard, but with all due respect to your bloodline and your power, not to mention your inflated ego and your ridiculous sense of yourself, I must tell you that I will not obey an order to release this creature. She is an important dragon. She will seal our fate. Was it not you who asked us to capture her in the first place? Was it not you who told us, all of us trapped in this castle, that she would bring the dragons upon us?

The king put his head in his hands. Yes, he said. Yes, it's true.

Then you understand our reluctance to comply, said the guard. Assa noted a certain pity in the guard's voice. It replaced the tone of defiance. How could these people switch so easily from defiance to soothing? From anger to compassion? It was a miracle of emotion twisting on a par with her miracle of shapeshifting.

The king began weeping. Discomfort laced through the group of guards. She felt a sadness in the air. Her own dragon eyes began to well up with tears. She tasted the salt of them as they flowed over her mouth and she licked at them.

The guard approached the king and put his arm around his shoulder. It's not the end of the world, said the guard. Not yet, anyway.

Some of the guards chuckled at this comment.

I'm so lost, said the king.

We all are, said the guard. We're all under a great strain.

My daughters wanted me to release the dragon. They are so upset.

Girls get that way, said the guard. You can't control it.

Girls get that way? thought Assa. What did that mean?

Fire is an elemental thing, said the guard. It's important to use it properly. Dragons are the repository of fire. We need to handle them very very carefully.

For example, we've taken away this dragon's fuel. It can't belch fire anymore. But if we released it, it would find fuel and most likely continue the siege we are under. Perhaps make it worse.

You should be one of my advisors, said the king.

The guard dropped to one knee and bowed his head.

I would be honored, he said.

But I can't, said the king.

The guard hesitated. Assa saw his head tremble, as though trying to decide if he should lift it or not. I beg your majesty's pardon, he managed to stammer out.

You openly defied me in front of the others. I can't reward that. In fact—he glanced at each of the other guards in turn—I will need to lock you up, just like the dragon. The other guards advanced on the first guard, who shot straight up and pulled his sword and held it up in front of him for defense.

It was no use, however. The other guards moved as one unit and surrounded him. Hands reached out and grasped his arm and made him drop the sword. Two other guards restrained him and hustled him away out the door.

It was a quick and decisive turn of events. The king had reestablished his dominance, and regained the loyalty of his guards. Three of them remained behind with the king. They stood near him, silent sentries, obviously ready to do his bidding.

The king turned back to Assa and put his hand on the netting over her wing. I'm sorry for this, he said to Assa, in a tone of voice reserved for injured and pitiable animals. Is that what she was? Nothing but a lame dog for others to coo over?

Assa opened her mouth, wanting to release flame, but only a small growl came out, hardly enough to impact anyone's ears. She reached for the princesses, but nothing was there. Where had they gone?

Above her the smoke, still streaming in ropey segments, seemed to flow over them all, the same way the net held her tightly.

The guard is right, said the king. I shouldn't release you. You are too dangerous. But what are we to do with you, then?

One of the remaining guards cleared his throat rather noisily.

Yes, said the king. You have something to suggest.

I don't resume to know anything, said the guard.

Yes? said the king. Spit it out.

But perhaps it would be prudent to slay the beast?

Assa's heart suddenly began to beat wildly. Her blood felt hot, as if her skin was on fire. The king wasn't going to have her killed, was he?

You speak with understated eloquence, said the king.

Thank you, your majesty.

I would have this beast dispatched in an instant, he said. But for my daughters. They would be distraught. They speak to it. They say it is actually human. Can you imagine? The fantasies of children, especially girl children. It is a burden on anyone, much less a king.

That sounded better, thought Assa. He wasn't going to kill her, was he.

On the other hand, said the king.

No! thought Assa. No other hand. Only the first hand.

Yes? said the guard, with his sword ready, raised high.

They do get over things quickly, said the king. In a few days they would be onto some other fantasy. Maybe they would build a toy house and play with that.

Did the king realize his daughters weren't little girls anymore? Could anyone, even a dimwitted king, be so ignorant?

Still, said the king. I wish I could make a decision. You see the beast's eyes?

The guards, wary of the king's demeanor and his power, did not move. They remained as still as possible, waiting. Assa felt the power in their swords. It was not a true power, it did not come from their hearts. It did not go through their arms and inhabit the swords. Instead, all the power was in the steel and it was out of their control. Even if they had the skill to wield the sword properly, they did not have the heart to use it wisely.

The guards, all of them, were like children. Or, more accurately, like cats. They appeared to be independent, but that was not the case. They were completely dependent on the king, just as a cat, for all its pretensions to independence, completely relied on the humans that housed it.

The king, for his part, seemed completely out of his element. Some people should not be trusted with power. It was a weak system indeed that allowed such a man as the king to gain power. Assa resolved, right then and there, to abolish the system if she ever had the opportunity to do so.

Absurd! When would she ever have the opportunity? Not in her lifetime. Her life was not destined for power. She was the daughter of a miller.

Of course, the king did not know that. The king thought she was a dragon.

Finally, after much consideration, the king motioned for the guards to drop their swords. They all lowered their weapons.

Assa breathed a sigh which quickly turned into a growl, which she had not expected. She was not one to growl. Not now, especially. Not when she was still captive. How would it help her to pretend to be aggressive?

The king laughed. You're a fierce one, aren't you?

Assa held her breath.

But timid! said the king. A most charming combination. What should I do with you? You are trouble. As troublesome as all the other dragons. The king waddled around Assa, moving a slow circle as though surveying a piece of land he wanted to acquire. Did all kings think they owned everything? Or were destined to own everything? Or were owed the world? Probably. It must be why so many of them went to war against each other, fighting over pieces of land.

Which made no sense. The land could not be given to anyone. It remained where it was. People had to move. Much better to own people, than land. With people you could order them around. Was that what kings really wanted to do?

Assa's head swirled with thoughts that were doing nothing to assure her survival. They were merely irrelevant secretions of her brain. She was too frightened of the reality of her situation, which was that she could be dispatched at any moment.

I've locked my daughters up, said the king. Did you know that?

Assa couldn't tell if he was addressing her or the guards. Maybe both. The guards shifted their weights from foot to foot in nervous anticipation of what the king might do or say next. Assa felt the uncertainty as well. The king was a completely unpredictable agent. She had no idea what he might do or say next.

One of the guards cleared his throat. We had heard rumors, he said.

Rumors! said the king. Of course. The blood of the castle, hmmm? You all feed off the energy of rumors. You all want rumors to be true. Or at least juicy. I don't blame you. Who doesn't love a good story, after all.

The princesses, said the guard, are they in danger?

Well of course they are, said the king. We're all in danger. Haven't you noticed? The king waved at the smoke outside the crumbled walls. Or he waved at the crumbled walls. Either way, the implication was clear. Things were not in good shape for any of them.

I need to assemble a team to rebuild these walls, said the king. I need to try to fight back this cursed enemy. But no one has the heart for it anymore. We're all so tired. Haven't you noticed?

The guards said nothing. The king was acting strangely and none of them knew how to respond. Assa certainly did not. It was unnerving to see the extent of the disarray and the lack of direction.

My daughters, said the king, they were dangerous to themselves. I had to lock them away. The queen thinks I am inhumane. She could be right. She would release them in an instant. Which is why I had her locked up as well. In a separate enclosure.

The king's voice seemed to drift away on the air. It was as though he had disembodied himself from his own flesh and blood. His words felt as though they did not come from him, but were dictated by the air. He was a puppet of forces unseen and, perhaps, unseeable.

The princesses love to talk to things, said the king. They send their voices in the air and fancy that other voices in the air answer them. Have you heard of anything so absurd? Even for females?

The guards did not answer. Assa grunted. Tried to say something. Anything. She cursed her lack of adequate vocal chords.

They also say they can help other people shapeshift into creatures. The king raised his hands to the sky. Such ridiculous antics from my daughters. Such— insane—ravings. I had to lock them up. *Had* to. Let no god judge me harshly. Let no fate knock me off my pedestal. For I used my power for good. For *their* good. I found wisdom in some of the old books. They said to put the insane into a room of their own and line the room with cloth that had been worn by a queen. That would stop the thoughts roaming. Can you imagine? I think those who wrote those old books were crazy in their way. As crazy as anyone.

The king walked around Assa several more times, huffing and puffing all the while. He sounded like a dragon himself, belching air the way Assa belched fire. Sometimes. When the circumstances were right.

The king stopped. I wish I could fly. That would be— He hesitated. Well, he said, no point in wishing for something that cannot happen. Even a king has limitations.

The king stepped toward a guard. Give me your blade, he said.

The guard surrendered his sword.

The king took the sword and began cutting the netting holding Assa in place. He worked quickly and surprisingly efficiently. Assa felt the bonds loosening and her muscles relaxing. The guards who had been surrounding her, suddenly felt the need to be somewhere else. They bolted for the door.

The king looked up, momentarily, as if he wanted to order them back, but then seemed to think better of it and chose to let them go. The room was empty except for Assa and the king.

Assa's wings, which had been bound and held tightly, loosened and slipped to the ground. The king worked quickly and soon most of the netting was in tatters, splayed around Assa like water droplets after a wave has broken on the beach.

Assa rolled over on her side and groaned at the effort and the pain in her wings and body. She was sure that the netting which had bound her must have broken something, but she got up on her feet and tested her wings. They spread wide and seemed to hold together well. No strange bends or breaks were evident.

She thrust up her head and looked at the black smoke streaming over her. The tips of her wings tasted air and twitched almost uncontrollably. She opened her mouth, wanting to belch smoke, but nothing came out, again. It was as if her throat was completely dried out and would not admit of anything coming through it. She was so hungry she could barely stand it.

Well, said the king. You're free. Do you know what you want to do with your freedom?

Assa wanted food. She needed to eat something. Anything. Her nose twitched, just as her wings had done. There was food present. She smelled it. Her dragon brain identified it and wanted to get some of it. Was it the rats? She walked, a little unsteadily, toward a dark corner of the room where piles of stones and bricks and mortar were strewn in an unorganized heap. She kicked at some of the rubble.

The king, behind her, laughed. Some spirit left in you, I see, he said.

Yes, Assa had spirit, but she needed nutrition. Something to keep her going. No rats under the rubble.

She turned to the king. Her nose twitched again. The food was apparently royal. Her brain told her to leap forward and kill the round creature in front of her. He would provide her with all the sustenance she needed, at least for the moment. At least until she could join her flock.

Assa blinked. Her flock? Is that what the other dragons were? She wanted to be part of them?

Assa took two steps toward the king, then waited for his move.

The king raised his chin and stared at Assa. His eyes held some fear, but not enough. He thought he could be friends with Assa. He knew so little.

Assa took three more steps. Small ones, but direct. She wanted him to know that she had the power. She could control the next few minutes. And would.

The king looked resigned to his fate, whatever that might be. He wanted to step back. Assa could see that. His leg moved, slightly, and his weight shifted, as though he was getting ready to back away. But he didn't. He stood his ground. Assa's dragon brain took in that information and turned it over a few times, processing it into something she could use: a plan of attack.

It was clear within a few seconds. There would be nothing to it. All she had to do was keep going forward. The king might try to escape, but her wings, spread wide, would keep him in the room, with the rubble strewn on the floor and the smoke covering them above.

I know what you're thinking, said the king. But I released you. Don't forget that. I gave you your freedom. I deserve some consideration for that.

He was unsure of himself. Not used to being the one in peril. He usually put others in peril. Or, at least, made people think that he could put them in peril. It was a reversal of the usual power balance and he didn't know how to react.

We're all hungry, said the king. Not just you. We haven't brought in any food for a long time. The dragons won't let us. They have closed off the castle.

Everyone thought you were dangerous, but I decided you're not. You could talk to the other dragons. Make them go away. How about it?

Assa listened to the words and wanted to pay them their due, but the hunger that dominated her being could not be pushed away. She felt her tongue pucker, anticipating the taste of the king's flesh. She imagined gnawing on his bones and it felt better than anything she had ever thought about before. She had never been this hungry.

Here's the thing, said the king. If you fly away and make the other dragons give up this ridiculous siege, you will have our eternal gratitude. You will be our hero. You and your family will never want for anything.

Assa understood the words, but she doubted them. Wouldn't anyone say almost anything to keep themselves safe? There was no reason to suppose that the king meant what he said. It was all just a way to save himself.

Assa got close to the king. The king stood his ground, not backing off even an inch. She was towering over him. All she had to do was bend her neck down, open her jaws, slam them shut, and the king's head would be in her stomach.

Her dragon brain commenced the process necessary to put those events into motion. She felt her jaws separate. The king continued to stare at her, defiant to the end. She dipped her head down. The king did not flinch from her hot breath. Did not betray any fear at all.

Her dragon brain was about to send the signal to snap her jaws shut, but it never did. Instead, her Assa self put a halt to the proceedings. She backed away from the king, who looked up at her with a strangely pitying expression. Why did the king feel sorry for her?

He stepped back and waved his hands in the air. Go, he said. Fly. What's what you do. What are you waiting for?

Assa put her wings out as far as they would go. As the extremities of her skin touched air and felt heat and movement, her dragon brain kicked into its flight mode and her wings moved up and down, as though on their own. They felt like events happening to someone else, but they were happening to her.

She directed her attention to the air. It hung over her, shrouded in black smoke, but it was there, beckoning. Her wings grabbed air and with a jerk and a lurch, she was airborne. The king clapped his hands wildly, as if he was applauding a dramatic performance. And maybe he was.

The smoke approached Assa with dizzying speed. She rose above the rubble of the broken room and plunged into the thick blackness with rapidity that kept her from being prepared. She had to hold her breath to keep from inhaling the smoke.

Her wings hesitated and hiccuped a little. Her body felt like it was going to fall back to the stone floor, but she overrode her instincts and redoubled her efforts and flapped more rapidly and strongly. She captured smoke under her wing, thicker than air, but it served the same purpose: it was support for her being.

She was flying again. As before, it felt both strange and normal. She had to fight to keep her eyes from closing. The smoke stung them and, in any case, she couldn't see anything. She relied on her sense of motion to tell her up from down, and she kept going up for a while, until she was sure she had cleared the top of the castle, then altered her course to go parallel to the ground.

In a few seconds she broke through the smoke and gulped air. The environs of the castle spread out below her like a quilt. The sky was a deep blue, fleeced with just a few clouds here and there. She hovered in the air, her wings doing things she hardly believed them capable of. They trembled, cupping air underneath them.

She hung over the earth, in wonderment. There was the shore of the ocean off to her side. There was the thin thread of the creek. She traced its path with her eye and stopped at her home, the mill wheel dipped in the water of the creek like a ditched carriage wheel. The rest of her village looked like a child's toy. And what of the smoke behind her?

She turned in the air, her dragon brain executing the maneuver with ease and grace. She tipped her body forward, ever so slightly, and shot down from the heights toward the base of the smoke. She landed near the castle and waddled up to the smoke.

As she got close, she saw the smoke emanated from the mouths of dozens upon dozens of dragons, arrayed at the base of the castle like a long row of gargoyles. They sat in a crouched position with their mouths angled up.

Flames shot out of their mouths, but the flames were relatively short: no more than a foot or two. Most of what came out of their mouths was smoke. It billowed from the flames and rose up in a curtain.

Each dragon would stop, periodically, to catch their breath, then resume belching fire and smoke. There were so many dragons, however, that the effect on the smoke curtain was negligible. It appeared to be a constant emanation of smoke with no breaks or clear areas.

Join us, sister, came a voice in her dragon brain.

Assa looked around. Who said that?

All of us say it. Come be a part of the incubation.

Such a strange sensation, to feel the voices of the dragons. They were not like the voices of the princesses. The dragons had a coarser profile. It was as though the words had been hewn from some rough block of stone. They scraped at her brain, made her itch and sent shivers down her spine and through her whole body. Her talons trembled.

She gathered her thoughts and observed her dragon brain taking those thoughts and turning them into the same sort of jagged words and then they were launched into the void.

Where do I go? she asked.

The dragons answered her with puzzlement. You don't know?

Assa sensed an error on her part. She should not have asked the question. It made her seem like a creature not of this group.

I have been disoriented, said Assa.

Words from the dragons appeared in her head: No matter. Join us now. You'll remember.

Assa stepped forward and wedged herself between two shimmery green dragons. She tilted her head back and tried to belch flame and smoke.

Nothing came out.

Sister, what is the problem?

I have not eaten fuel in a long time, said Assa.

The dragons on either side of her pushed her toward the castle. She tumbled backward and rolled down a sharp incline and stopped when she landed next to the stone wall. Other dragons pulled her toward an opening.

She was on the other side of the smoke again. The castle felt cold and claustrophobic after she had been flying. An opening at the base of the castle loomed up and the dragons pushed her through it.

She went willingly, and found herself in a cavernous room, damp and cold.

It was well below the level of the ground. Puddles of water had collected here and there throughout the room. In the center of the room a pile of wood, as tall as five dragons standing on top of each other. It was as though some mad firewood chopper had been loosed on an expansive forest and told to do her worst to the trees.

Assa's dragon brain shifted into high alert. It sent hunger pangs through her body and pierced her tongue with appetite-whetting juices. She pounced on the wood and began devouring.

Her teeth chomped through the wood with frightening efficiency. She had no idea her teeth could lacerate wood so completely and she felt puffed up by the knowledge. She kept finding new abilities and it was wonderful.

She mashed up big bits of the wood and swallowed the pulp. Her stomach—she could feel it!—fairly leaped upon the mash and worked quickly to turn it into fuel. Her dragon brain wanted to ignite the wood and belch a pillar of smoke, but her dragon brain also quelled the urge.

Assa observed the little battle of wills in herself and was amused by it. Were all dragons constantly dealing with the challenges of life in this way? Did all dragons have to contend with competing urges all the time?

She let her brain and stomach do their little tug of war, while she continued to chew on the wood. Presently, other dragons waddled into the room. She glanced at them. They looked tired and even old, their scales were all wrinkled and looked like they might fall off.

Each of them glanced at Assa and nodded at her. Assa, a chunk of wood in her hands, and splinters of wood in her teeth, nodded back and grinned. Or, at least, her Assa self grinned. Her dragon body did not have the muscles or features to grin, so she imagined her snout wrinkling a little.

The other dragons looked away from her and fell upon the pile of wood, the same way she had. They *loved* the wood. It was evident in the gusto with which they consumed it. The sound of crunching wood and mashed bark echoed in the room. Her dragon brain adored that sound. It was as if she was home.

Easy there, sister.

The voice she had heard when she first flew out of the castle was in her dragon brain again. She turned to see one of the dragons looking at her.

We don't want to eat it all now, said the voice. Leave some for the others, eh?

Assa dropped the remnant of wood she had been devouring.

I didn't know how much I should eat, she said.

No matter said the dragon. We just have to be careful of this pile. The people in the castle cut this wood for their fires. But we get to eat it. Nice, isn't it?

Assa acknowledged the beauty of the situation.

When it runs out, we'll have to deal with that. But for now, we're in heaven. All good for the eggs.

Yes, said Assa, not knowing the least thing about what the dragon was saying.

Come on now, said the dragon. It advanced toward Assa and put out its wing to help her along. They walked around the wood pile to the other side of the room and out the doorway. More corridors. Whoever designed this castle was clearly in love with hallways and passageways. They were everywhere. Assa held her wings close to her body to keep them from being scraped on the walls.

Keep walking, said her escort, a few feet in front of her. We're almost to your station. Where did you come from?

I'm from out of town, said Assa.

I can see that, said the dragon. But where?

On the other side of the ocean, said Assa. An island.

Huh, said the dragon. I've never heard of dragons leaving their islands. How did you hear about this castle?

Unsure how to answer, Assa reached for the nearest words and plucked them from her dragon brain. I saw the smoke and came over, she said. I thought I could help.

Well good for you, said the dragon. We appreciate it. The more smoke, the better for the eggs, hmmmm?

Exactly, said Assa. It's all about the eggs!

Don't you know it.

As they walked, Assa felt the immensity of the castle around and above her. The weight of all that rock seemed impossible. How could humans assemble such an immensity? And how could they allow the dragons to take it over?

She saw a light at the end of the corridor. It bobbed as they walked, peaking out from either side of her dragon escort. It was not a blazingly bright light, but it did indicate the end of the corridor, possibly, and loomed larger as they approached it. Her escort seemed excited by it and stopped conversing with Assa, which she was glad for. She did not have much to add and was not sure she could continue to come up with convincing lies.

They arrived at the arched opening and the dragon quickened its pace. Assa did the same.

The dragon paused at the doorway and opened its mouth and breathed out a mighty flame.

Assa, completely controlled by her dragon brain for the moment, could not help herself from stepping beside her escort and doing exactly the same. Flame shot from her throat and a corresponding cascade of black smoke accompanied it. The smoke rose up and joined the smoke of a hundred other dragons. They were arrayed along the walls of the castle, exactly as she had seen them on the other side.

There's a spot for you there, said the escort.

It pointed with its wing along the row of dragons. Assa saw a gap, like a missing tooth and walked over to it. She settled into her gargoyle pose and opened her mouth and let her dragon brain take over. It did so with efficiency and joy. It shot a slow burning flame, barely visible into the air.

The flame was not the important aspect, though. It was the smoke, and her dragon brain knew exactly what to do, exactly how to ensure that she belched enormous amounts of smoke.

Her mind wandered a little, looking for something to attach itself to. She was aware of all the other dragons. They were all engaged in a mighty task and she was part of it. Nothing like this had ever entered her being before. To be a part of something so big.

No other dragon offered to speak with her, however. They were silent and resolute. Their task was their life.

Assa, conscious that the king had released her with the intention of having her subvert this process, was not at a loss as to how to do so. She let her consciousness return to her dragon brain. It seemed she was meant to do this.

Nothing else mattered. Nothing else came close to mattering. Not in any real sense. Dragons were designed to belch flame and smoke.

She did exactly that for the next four hours.

Just before she was about to deplete her fuel, the dragon she first met approached Assa and gestured for her to go back to the wood pile.

Assa had been belching smoke for a long time at that point and she was tired. Her throat felt dry and rough. Her neck was sore from bending backwards, and her jaws were stiff with fatigue. She wobbled forward, her dragon brain telling her it was best to do as this other dragon suggested. Or was it ordered? She wasn't sure how to take its ways.

Her dragon brain seemed to know what to do. She wanted to warp it back into her Assa brain, but, alas, that seemed impossible at this time. She longed to shapeshift back into her old shape, but that, too, seemed an unreachable goal right now. She was here to bathe the eggs in smoke. Isn't that what the dragon had told her?

The only thing was, she never saw any eggs. All she saw were other dragons, belching smoke as she had done.

You need to stop before you get too close to running out, said the dragon to Assa. And I can't be the one to tell you what to do all the time. You need to take control of the situation for yourself. Do you understand?

Assa nodded.

Speak up! said the dragon. You have an inner voice for a reason.

Assa allowed some words to be subvocalized for the benefit of the irritated dragon. I understand, she said. This is all new to me.

New? New? How ridiculous. What should newness matter? You have a task and a stage upon which to perform that task. What more could you want? What more could anyone want?

A life that wasn't going to bore her to death would be nice, thought Assa.

What? asked the dragon.

How long does it take to incubate dragon eggs? asked Assa.

What? How long? What a crazy question. Don't you know anything?

Assa elected not to answer. Whenever she said anything, it seemed to cast suspicion on her and she didn't need that.

They arrived at the wood pile room.

You've got an hour, said the dragon. Get some rest if you need it. But make sure you eat enough to combust for four. Got it?

Got it, said Assa.

The dragon left the room, running off to who knew where. Not that Assa cared. She just wanted to be left alone for a while.

She stretched her wings and flexed her muscles. She was starting to get some circulation back into them and the stiffness was beginning to recede. She noticed a dark corner off to one side of the wood pile where dragons were devouring the fibers and bark like it was going to disappear any minute.

She felt hungry, that was true. But not enough to care. She was much more interested in getting some rest.

She ambled to the dark corner. It wasn't exactly warm, but it was out of any draft, and the body heat of the dragons eating seemed to give a little bit of coziness to the place. She folded up her wings, tucked her head into her shoulder and crouched down to what she hoped was a spot out of sight of all the other dragons.

Her eyelids drooped. They felt heavier than lead.

Hardly had she begun to experience weird dragon dreams about giant waves crashing onto flaming trees when she felt a kick in her side. She opened her eyes and grunted at the air. Three dragons stood around her. One of them, slighter bigger than the other two, stared at her and growled.

What do you want? asked Assa.

You've been conked out here for hours. What's going on?

Hours? said Assa.

The three of them nodded. Their teeth were black, scorched from the smoke they had been exhaling for what Assa had to assume was hours.

Are you here to help us or are you here to sleep?

The dragons weren't exactly menacing, but they also did not offer her any kind of kindness. I'm here to do what needs to be done, said Assa.

Then get up, said one of the dragons. She wasn't sure which one. Probably the bigger one, but when there were a group of them like this, there was no way for her to tell. The voices did not come from any particular direction, they just appeared in her head.

I can't do this nonstop, said Assa. I need some rest. Why don't you all need rest too?

Rest is for the undedicated. Are you not dedicated?

The three of them flexed their wings and opened their jaws slightly, revealing tongues as blackened as their teeth. A subtle shift in energy occurred as they did so. It was as though they had moved the air around them. She was now beginning to think she was in some danger.

Assa moved her wings so they were out of the way and she struggled to get up, but she was too close to the wall and the three dragons were too close to her and she had very little room in which to maneuver.

The three of them stepped closer, making her task even more difficult.

Is there a problem? asked Assa.

We think maybe *you* are the problem, said the first dragon. Its voice seemed to intensify in belligerence. It was as though the dragon had decided Assa was an enemy and it was going to intimidate her.

Assa had a few reserves of flame left. Her dragon brain kicked in at that moment and she opened her jaws and belched a flame as big as she could muster. It was not exceptionally long, only a couple of feet, but it seemed to do the trick. The dragons moved back, allowing her room to stand up and face them.

I don't like your attitude, she said, hardly believing her own words.

The three dragons spread their wings so that Assa was still surrounded by them. She had no fire left in her, and she guessed that they knew this. Her dragon brain clicked and whirred. Or maybe it hummed and sang. Hard to tell. In any case, it came up with a plan, right there, on the spot.

I think I know what you're doing here, said one of the dragons. You don't act like a dragon and you don't think like one. You're more like a human. Anyone ever tell you that?

Assa's dragon brain was no help to her now. She needed her former brain, the one that was the engine of Assa, to help her now. She reached down as far as she could go, down into the center of her being and found the nugget of gnarled up desires, hopes, fears, and instincts that was an eighteen-year-old human female. It was a strange thing to think of herself that way, but that is what she found. The dragon part of her was merely a coat she had put on over the young woman.

Dragons had fury, it was true. Assa knew that from having spent the last few days in a dragon's body, consulting a dragon's brain, but it was limited. Now she found her human center and it felt as unlimited as possible.

She moved her dragon limbs in ways it was not meant to do. She ducked under the surrounding dragons, skittered across the floor between two of them, and ended up on the other side of them. The dragons, completely caught off-guard, whirled on her, but she was too fast for them.

She deployed her wings, grabbed air, and rose above them, then proceeded to kick them with her feet and talons. As she did so, the dragons cowered and shrunk down on themselves, actually making themselves look smaller. Maybe they shrunk. Assa wasn't sure, exactly, but she moved her self higher into the air.

The dragons, three of them, finally coming out of their confusion, found the wit to band together. They put their heads next to each other and exhaled a ferocious column of flame. It shot across the room and splashed on the opposite wall.

Assa had anticipated this move and flew out of its path immediately by going up even higher. She hung in the air near the ceiling of the room and looked down on the three dragons. Other dragons, who had entered the room in search of wood to eat, saw her and heard her: she began mewling and crying in a dragon sound she didn't know she had, but which was right there when she needed it.

The entering dragons, touched by her sounds, which were distress signals, nervous signals, and warning signals all wrapped up into one cry, saw that the three other dragons had banded together to, at the very least, intimidate Assa, and they quickly moved, as one, to surround the three and force them into a corner.

The three put their heads together again, as if they were going to shoot a combined flame again, but the surrounding dragons—there were seven of them—raised their heads in unison and motioned to the three with thrusts of their snouts that they should reconsider their plans. Wisps of smoke drifted up from their nostrils, a most effective warning against any possible action they might have contemplated.

The three backed down, with whimpers of their own. A cacophony of voices now entered Assa's brain.

What are you doing to that poor dragon?

She's not a dragon.

We should burn you to dust.

Listen to us listen to us.

She's not a dragon.

She's something else.

Assa tried to separate out the voices and identify which dragon belonged to which voice, but it soon became impossible to even attempt it. There was a tension in the room which she could not dispel. She knew this, and she was not against letting it play out, but she needed something more. She needed protection, and the situation was too precarious for her safety. The three dragons might very well convince the seven that *she* was the one at fault who needed to be vanquished or done away with.

One of the seven peeled off the rest of the group and flew up and approached Assa, who hovered over the scene, still unsure what her next move should be.

Through the tumult of voices and alarmed feelings, one dragon voice entered her dragon brain.

Are you okay?

Something tingled in Assa's brain. She was disconcerted by the question, but even more disconcerted by the voice. It sounded like Dawn. Dawn was trapped in a dragon, just as she was?

She remained cautious, however. She did not want to tip her hand in case she was imagining things.

I'm okay, she said.

Looks like those dragons are bullies, came Dawn's voice.

Looks like, said Assa.

Silence between them. Assa tried to see humanness in the dragon eyes in front of her, but she could not. Was she imagining things? How could Dawn be in a dragon? She laughed at herself. The same way *she*, Assa, could be in a dragon. She thought to risk her safety, just a tiny bit.

How are things in the palace? she said. How are things with your sister?

The dragon blinked, then her eyes went wide and her lids quivered. That didn't look good to Assa.

Are you a real dragon? asked the dragon.

Stupid stupid stupid, thought Assa. This wasn't Dawn. She was foolish to think it might be. Assa dropped her head a little and tried to feign fatigue and fear. Or something. Anything to distract this inquisitive dragon.

I'm just scared, she said. I'm scared of those three bullies. I'm so confused.

Confused?

Yes, I don't know who I am anymore. Why am I here?

Well that's simple, said the dragon. We're here to incubate the eggs. To hatch out the next generation. You really aren't okay, are you?

If that's why we're all here, then why did those ones try to hurt me?

There are some who don't believe in what we're doing.

Can't they just fly away? asked Assa. They don't have to stay.

Some have. But some have stayed behind to sabotage the effort.

This was news to Assa, and not very welcome news at that. She wondered if she had been singled out as one of the saboteurs. In fact, wasn't that what the king wanted from her?

Don't worry, said the dragon. We don't think you're one of those.

Really? Asked Assa.

We think you just don't understand the whole picture. Those three who were bullying you, well, dragons have a way of doing that sometimes. It's not very attractive, but there it is. Every creature lives a messy life, don't you think?

Assa wasn't sure how to respond to that. It did seem like most living things had issues with the rest of living things. They were always battling each other or trying to get out of the way of some predator, or trying to kill something else that was living. She saw it in nature. She saw it in people. They were never willing to just be with each other and get along.

Well, what wasn't exactly true. She got along with her parents. Except they didn't tell her the whole story of her life, did they? It was a little like they were battling her. Or, at least, the truth of her.

Tell me more, said Assa.

I think I need to take you to the incubation chamber, said the dragon.

It flew through the window and disappeared up the castle wall. Assa angled her wings and her body to follow. They rose high. They moved in the space between the castle walls and the wall of smoke. There was just enough room there for the two of them.

Assa's wings flapped majestically. She liked flying and she liked being the one who was asked to fly with this dragon that mysteriously seemed to know so much more than her. So much more than any of the other dragons as well.

They passed the crumbled room, which Assa thought had been at the top of the castle, but which she now saw was only at the top of an outcropping of the castle. There was more castle above that.

They rose to the very pinnacle of the castle. There, topped by a pointed roof, a smallish room, surrounded by four open windows. Her dragon guide lighted on the ledge of one of the window openings. Assa followed by lighting on the one opposite. The smoke here was not as thick as below. Obviously, it had dissipated and was now more of a thick haze than full blown roiling smoke.

Look inside, said the dragon.

Assa turned in her window and peered into the room. It was filled with dozens and dozens of oblong greenish objects. The green was of various shades and some of the eggs had lightning bolt lines on them. The light in the room was not the best, but she saw they were stacked into one large pile. So many eggs!

Where did all these eggs come from? asked Assa.

They were brought here by all the dragons. They have been buried in the ground but did not hatch. Some are very old. Centuries old. Others were laid only last year. But all of them never hatched the way they were meant to.

Assa wanted to reach in and touch the eggs, but she sensed that would be an unwelcome action so she refrained.

I never knew there were eggs everywhere in the ground, said Assa.

You're young, said the dragon. You haven't laid any eggs yet, have you?

No, said Assa.

Well, said the dragon. You'll see. Once your body and instincts take over, you'll dig a hole and deposit an egg or two into it.

Assa searched her dragon brain for this urge or intention. It was no where she could sense. Maybe the urge to lay an egg was obliterated by her human brain intruding?

So why are they all here? she asked.

Our legends tell us that unhatched dragon eggs require bathing in smoke from the combined breaths of many dragons.

But why don't the mothers just do that? asked Assa.

The dragon paused. Assa though maybe she had gone too far with her questions. Had she betrayed her origins as a non-dragon?

You are an odd one, said the dragon.

Assa agreed. I'm not exactly a bright one, she said. My mother, uh, she always said I was going to die of stupidity.

More silence. Huh, said the dragon. Well, that might explain a few things. I think.

Assa held her breath, waiting for the dragon to accuse her of being an imposter.

Eventually, the dragon seemed to turn more kind toward Assa. Well, it said, you don't have to worry about any of that here. We think you're just like the rest of us: a dragon embarked on a grand plan. We're going to hatch out all these dragons and we'll be a force to reckon with in the world.

A force to reckon with? Assa didn't like the sound of that.

What would we do with all that power? asked Assa.

The dragon was looking at the eggs piled in the room with rapture and a certain expression that Assa could only describe as goofy. It was like she was made drunk by the sight of the eggs.

Assa studied the dragon carefully. She was tense, as though she was ready to spring away from the window at any moment. Assa, unaccustomed to dragon behavior, did not know how to interpret this. Was the dragon preparing to fly away from this task? Or was she simply feeling the authentic feelings of a normal dragon?

Assa was bewildered by the life in all these eggs. Her dragon brain, however, she now realized, was not bewildered at all. She saw the eggs and she wanted to belch smoke at them. She felt an overwhelming urge to do so, but she knew she could not. She had not ingested any fuel.

The humans, said the dragon, they have the wrong idea about us. They think we try to protect *their* females. They have legends about us. But that's ridiculous. Why would we care about human females? Does it make sense on any level?

Assa admitted that to her it seemed somewhat ridiculous.

You'll find, as you get older, that humans don't have a lot of sense.

Assa didn't offer her opinion on the subject. Whatever she said now might make it clear to this dragon that she had more than a passing acquaintance with humans. Her dragon brain kicked in and told her that human females were never in need of protecting. That human myths and misconceptions accounted for a certain kind of lie that humans promulgated against dragons.

It could be that some of them find our eggs, said the dragon to Assa. They find these green eggs when they dig up the earth for their houses or when they plant their crops and they think they know what these eggs are for. They think they're strange gems, maybe, or the droppings of something they can't understand. So they make up stories.

Assa, again, chose not to respond to these speculations. She had never heard of anyone finding a dragon egg. And why did the dragons just bury their eggs? Didn't they want to make sure they hatched and that the dragon babies were okay?

Assa's dragon brain rose up at the thought. It recoiled and startled her enough that her eyes went very wide and her head cocked back and her neck snapped. Whoah, she thought. Had she violated some dragon tradition by thinking it might be better to nurture a newborn dragon rather than let it fend for itself underground?

Assa knew that other creatures left their eggs in the ground. Turtles, especially, seemed to find it expedient to deposit their eggs and then leave them. Assa had seen some of the babies emerge from the sand near the ocean. The turtles would crawl toward the water. Some of them would make it. Others would get snatched up by passing birds to be eaten.

The successes did not rouse the parents to fits of pride and the the failures did not bring them down to the depths of misery or despair for the simple reason that they were gone and did not witness either the triumphs or the defeats. Were dragons the same way? It would seem they would have to be. But then why this sudden interest in hatching out the buried eggs?

You don't have a lot to say, sister, said the dragon. Are you awestruck? Bored?

Assa's dragon brain scrambled to find an answer. The green is so beautiful, she said.

The dragon hesitated. I suppose so, it said. That's all you see in front of you? A pretty color?

Isn't that enough? asked Assa. Isn't beauty something we can all adore and appreciate?

That's not a very dragon's-eye view of things, sister.

Assa was aware of that. Her dragon brain was recoiling at her own words. They felt like they came from some place other than where she was. Another planet, maybe? Another universe?

She didn't even understand how she had become a dragon in the first place, and now she was navigating the tricky course of being a dragon and not letting on that she wasn't a dragon. It was enough to scramble her brain. Her brains.

Anyway, said the dragon, enough of this tour. I only wanted you to see what you were working for. Once the babies hatch out, we'll double our population. We'll be more secure in the world. Ever since Hoyal died, it's been difficult for our kind.

Hoyal? The mere mention of the name brought back a flood of memories, culminating in the image of Hoyal falling to her death.

Ah, said the dragon, I see a glimmer of recognition. You know about Hoyal, don't you?

Assa admitted that she had some knowledge of the person.

She held us together. With her, we didn't need more dragons. It was safe to leave the eggs in the ground. But now that she's gone, the humans have turned on us. They want to hunt us down. Slaughter us. Eat us. You must have noticed.

Assa nodded.

So we need greater numbers.

Of course, said Assa.

You understand, said the dragon. I can see it.

What is not to understand? said Assa. We all have a duty. Let's get back to it.

Assa half-expected the dragon to clap her on the back, then remembered dragons don't have hands and turned from the eggs and went out the exit from the incubation room. The dragon followed, then passed her in the narrow passageway so that Assa was following her again.

How long will it take for the eggs to hatch? asked Assa.

Oh, not more than fifty years, said the dragon.

Assa blinked. That couldn't be right. I don't think you heard me, she said. I was asking how long the eggs would take to hatch.

Oh, said the dragon, you've got me there. Fifty years is much too optimistic. I'd say it will take about a century.

A century? One hundred years?

Yes, said the dragon. It takes a long time to hatch a dragon. It's a good thing we live so long.

I don't think I can belch smoke for that long, said Assa.

You must, said the dragon. You must be a loyal sister.

But one hundred years, said Assa. All the humans will be dead by then.

That's no matter, said the dragon. They would have died anyway.

Assa's human brain turned over the years, thinking about all those months and seasons, piling on one another. Did all these dragons know what they were getting into?

This sort of thing happens now and then, said the dragon. Every few thousand years, like clockwork. All the eggs get gathered up and we stream smoke over them and they hatch. Don't you know *anything* about dragon history? Don't you know *anything* about our world?

She was learning, that was for sure.

They continued on in silence until they found themselves back at the wood pile. The dragon stepped into the room and addressed the dragons that were there for their dose of wood.

Now listen to me, it said. You've all been picking on the newcomer. I want it to stop now, got it? We're all working together to hatch these eggs. It's important work and we can't have us fighting each other. Fighting the humans is distracting enough. The dragon paused and looked around. The other dragons looked up at her.

Thin trials of smoke rose from their nostrils, like the smoke from dying embers in a fireplace. The room had the feeling of deadness, as if a corpse had been laid out where the wood was. Were they afraid of this dragon? Assa couldn't tell. Maybe they were plotting the dragon's demise. She couldn't tell that either. Or maybe they were just bored and wanted the dragon to stop talking.

A dragon sneezed, then made slurping noises to contain the slobber and keep it from dripping down its chin. Assa laughed. She couldn't help herself. The laugh was clear in her human brain, but it came out different in her dragon self. Her jaws opened and closed, the teeth clicking against each other and her nose snorted a dart of flame. She was surprised, thinking she had depleted her fuel and no flame was possible.

The dragon who had been addressing the rest of the dragons turned to her with a look of disbelief on her face. Assa recognized it immediately, even though she was not particularly familiar with the facial expressions of dragons. Their scaly skin prevented her from seeing what they were thinking.

Most of the time.

This time, however, it was different. A kind of shock registered in the dragon's eyes. A strained look creased its features. It was a mixture of bewilderment and anger. The power of the feeling was there in the face, but she felt it in the air, too. All her senses were suddenly on alert and ready to bring in the stimuli to her brain.

Who are you? said the dragon very quietly.

The words registered in Assa's dragon brain and she knew the charade was up. In the next instant, she spread her wings, grabbed air, and rose to the ceiling.

The rest of the dragons were slow to respond even though the dragon that had been chaperoning her around and had been her champion only seconds before, had taken to screaming at the others. Stop her! Stop her!

Confusion reigned. The dragons were slow to realize that their leader had changed its mind about Assa. Some may have thought this was theater of a kind. Or the leader had perhaps gone batty. Who could say? Assa was not inclined to examine the situation. Instead, she darted for the entrance, gliding with all due speed down in an arc that razed the tops of dragon heads, and missed the wood pile by mere fractions of an inch.

She heard wing beats and foot steps behind her, but did not stop. She shot through the passageway. A dragon, bedraggled and forlorn, was in front of her, making its way to the room with the wood pile. It looked up as Assa approached and cowered against the wall, allowing her to pass.

Dragons had finally scrambled and deployed from the room and were in hot pursuit. Assa shot out of the hall and broke into the open air.

The wall of black smoke rippled in front of her. She rose up in the space between the castle walls and the smoke, riding the thermal current for all she was worth.

Her dragon brain had taken over and was working her wings with a fevered energy, as if she was made of adrenalin. Her ears picked up the sounds of other dragon wings and she knew several were following her. The castle wall ran out in a short time, and she continued rising, through the smoke that gathered above the castle.

She was blind for a second or two, her eyes burned from the ash and smoke, then she was in clean cool air, lit by the sun, and decorated with fleecy clouds above her. Her dragon brain exalted in the view and the room—so much air—and she poured on the speed, heading west toward the ocean.

The dragons behind her were not interested in letting her go. They matched her speed and trajectory. Assa dared to glance back and saw seven dragons, in formation, stubbornly keeping up. Assa knew she could not outpace all of them. At least not for very long. She crossed the beach and was over open ocean as she considered her options.

Her dragon brain kept up her wing beats. It also provided her with images of what might happen if the dragons caught up with her. They would fly over top of her and under her, to confine her actions. Then they would use their talons, in mid flight, the tear her wings to ribbons, which would send her plummeting to the water. Without workable wings, she would just be a lizard with encumbrances stuck to her back. She would have no way of swimming and would drown.

Assa at first was not sure if these images were prophecy or fear. Or dragon brain flights of fancy triggered by the pulse of excitement roaring through her body, but she didn't have to know. The dragons were pursuing her and they were determined. Did she really have to know anything else?

She attempted some evasive maneuvering, dipping down and then up, veering to one side then another, but there was no cover. Nothing to hide her from the dragons. And they had been dragons longer than she had been. They knew exactly what their bodies could and could not do, and therefore were well aware of all her capabilities as well. It was not a good situation.

On top of it all, there was a roaring in her ears. She had tried to ignore it, but it could not *be* ignored. It was as though someone had been standing next to her ears and was shouting as loud as they possibly could, over and over, filling her head with palpable sound.

Assa tried to banish it from her mind. Both her dragon brain and her human brain were unnerved by the volume. She wanted to jettison the sound, but could not figure out how.

She veered away from the pursuing dragons, or tried to. They veered right along with her and they were gaining air on her.

She angled her wings so that she went up. She was determined to keep going as long as she could. Surely they would not follow her to the heights of the atmosphere.

Assa set her teeth grimly and kept flying up. The air grew thinner. The seconds ticked by. Her skin felt the cold of her surroundings. She dared not look back. Ice began forming on her extremities. Even her wings became frosted with a white sheen. It was drawing heat from her skin and muscles.

She felt her strength begin to wane, but she was driven by survival and strength was not all there was to her survival right now. She listened for the flap of dragon wings behind her. Clouds flitted by her. She tried to dodge them, instinctively, but some could not be dodged and she flew through them. Ice particles peppered her with pain. She cried out, tried to force a length of flame over her tongue, but she could not manage it. Her fire was almost completely out.

Behind her, the flapping wings had abated. She kept climbing until her own wings, unable to catch enough air, began to falter. Her breathing grew labored. She tried to take deep long intakes, but they were more like eternal tries at getting something, anything, into her lungs and they were failing.

She was almost completely depleted of heat and energy by the time her wings could no longer grab anything. She stopped flapping and held her altitude for the briefest instant before gravity asserted itself and she began to descend.

That was when she angled her neck and head so her eyes looked down. She saw no dragons. This filled her with delight and a profound sense of triumph. It was the first battle she had won against the dragons. The expansive blue sea was spread out below her. Far in the distance she saw a line, the coastline of her former home, where she had lived as a girl with her parents. Where the creek flowed past and the mill ground grain and the plants pushed up greenery to try to reach for the sky.

The sound of the dragons were no longer in her head. This was an immense relief to her. She shivered from the cold. That was not a terrible thing. It was important to feel the world around her, even if it meant being uncomfortable for a short time.

Her mind was not completely blank, however. Two voices were still there, pushing against her consciousness like cats trying to get through a door. Scratching, mewling.

Assa! Where are you? What's going on? Are you okay?

Dawn and Dusk.

I'm flying, said Assa.

We know *that*, they said. Come back and save us.

I can't, said Assa. Her wings were extended as far as they would go. She kept them open and let the air flow under them. She circled in lazy spirals, letting the ocean come up to meet her.

She didn't much care how long that would take or what would happen then. All she cared about was the feel of the cold wind over her body and the whistle of the air over her ears. Flying was a revelation. Everyone should have the opportunity.

Assa! Did you hear us? We are in trouble.

I was in trouble, said Assa. I took care of it. Maybe you should do the same thing.

No answer.

Ha! thought Assa to herself. I told them.

You don't understand, said Dawn. The dragons have set fire to the castle.

Assa knew that statement was designed to alarm her to the point of being their knight in shining armor. She was supposed to drop everything she was doing or had a mind to do and race back to the castle and rescue the princesses.

That was the way it was with dragons and princesses, wasn't it? At least in some of the legends she had heard when she was a child and her parents used to tell her stories about things that didn't exist. Because they thought that's what little girls liked to hear. They thought that make-believe was more real to little girls than what was really real.

I don't believe you, said Assa.

Again, no answer from the princesses.

Assa knew the king had kept them from communicating with her. So they had found a way around that. Good for them. But they didn't have to lie to get her attention. The dragons did *not* set fire to the castle. She knew that. If they did, the eggs would burn up. Generations of dragons would be turned to ash.

You are a wicked commoner, said Dusk.

Assa laughed. Not as wicked as liars like you.

Below her, Assa saw dots of green, brown, and white. These were islands peppering the blue sea. She angled her body so that her spiral spun in the general direction of one of these islands.

The more modulated voice of Dawn came through into her brain. My sister, she said, did not mean what she said.

I think you are mistaken, said Assa. She meant exactly what she said. You both think I'm nothing, don't you? Just because I wasn't born from a king and queen.

You're not nothing, but you're so stupid, said Dawn. You *were* born from a king and queen.

What? said Assa. More lies? You never stop, do you?

This is not a lie, said Dawn.

It isn't, said Dusk.

Their tone seemed solemn and true. Assa listened to the stream of air whistling over her wings and talons. The sea spun around under her, matching her spiral perfectly. It was as though she had slipped into some predetermined path, laid out just for her benefit.

What are you talking about? said Assa.

You are my sister, said Dawn.

And mine, said Dusk.

Liars? said Assa. I don't believe that adoption story you told me.

Listen to us, said Dawn. It's complicated. When you were born, the castle became invaded by dragons. They were everywhere. They roosted on all the ledges, and they got into the pantries, and flew everywhere. The people in the castle tried to keep them out, but dragons are strong. And smart. They either broke all the locks on the doors and windows, or just ripped off the doors and windows and got inside. It was like they wanted to invade and take over. The castle became their home. Their giant nest.

Yup, said Dusk. That's just how it was. The advisors to Mom and Dad, they said that you were the problem.

Me?

It happens, said Dawn. You have to understand that with royal people marriages and babies and, well, life in general, is different. They can't live just for themselves or even for their families. They have to live for their people and the land.

The land? said Assa.

Stop asking inane questions, said Dusk. Yes, the land. Hoyal was their most trusted advisor and she told them we had to get rid of you.

And they agreed?

Of course, said Dawn. They had to.

No, said Assa. No parent would do that.

You still don't *understand*, said Dusk. Will you ever? Will you ever just realize that your little life is unimportant?

Assa was starting to get an inkling of that. Her life was easily thrown away, it seemed.

Here's the thing, said Dawn. Hoyal wanted you sent far away. She probably actually wanted you dead, but Mom and Dad drew a line there.

Whew, said Assa.

Don't be bitter, said Dawn. You're still alive, aren't you?

Barely, said Assa.

Commoners are always complaining, said Dusk. If they stopped complaining so much, they would have a better life. I don't know why they don't see that.

I'm not a commoner, said Assa. You just told me that.

No, but you live like one, said Dawn. You act like one. You ask stupid questions like one. You might as well be one.

Fine, said Assa. So instead of having me roasted alive, you threw me to the miller couple. My mother and father.

Who said anything about roasting alive? said Dawn. At the most they would have given you too much of a sleeping herb and you would have gone peacefully from sleep to death.

We're not uncivilized, said Dusk.

Good to hear, said Assa.

The air streaming over her wings felt thick, like molasses. She was losing her strength and could not find any way to lift her again. The ocean was coming up fast to meet her. Other dragons were circling around her, as though they sensed her imminent demise and would be on hand to devour her. They kept their distance. Were they afraid of her? It hardly seemed possible. She spread her wings out as far as they would go, trying to capture as much air as possible.

You had a good life, said Dawn. They found parents who wanted you. Who loved you and raised you. I understand that's very much a thing commoners crave.

I think anyone would want that, said Assa.

She's right, said Dusk.

What do I do now? said Assa. The dragons are coming for me. I think they want to kill me. Maybe eat me.

Dragons don't eat dragons, said Dawn.

But they kill them, said Assa. Don't they?

Go to the island, said Dawn. Where we buried Hoyal.

I don't know where it is, said Assa.

Use your dragon brain, stupid, said Dawn.

Her dragon brain. Assa pushed away the sounds of Dawn and Dusk. They struggled against her will, but eventually they retreated to some distant corner of her mind. There they seemed to sit, tiny and quiet, like mice behind a wall.

Next, she grabbed her own stream of thought, as if it was a rope, and tied it up and tossed it aside. It tangled up in the corner next to the princesses.

Assa, with her mind thus cleared, looked around the world. The sky was wide and distant, covering her like an inverted bowl. The water below her was a cold and forbidding expanse, featureless except for a few dots here and there. Distant and mysterious.

Other dots circled in the sky but they were insignificant now. They would have no effect on her own flight. She knew she was a dot, of sorts, to them. They would look down on her and see her erratic and aimless flight. They would be frightened of her.

With such aimless wandering, the mind behind it could be disturbed. Even dangerous. The dots receded. Caution on the wing. Ah, so that was the answer. Assa increased the erratic nature of her flight. She dodged here and zig-zagged there. All the while the dots in the sky receded further and further away. The dots on the water, however, did not mimic that motion. They came closer and closer. It was as if she was flying into a constellation.

The dots resolved themselves into tiny land masses. Islands. She searched for landmarks that would tell her which one was Hoyal's graveyard, and eventually she saw the castle where she and Dawn and Dusk had been held captive.

She angled her wings toward that island. Wind streamed over her eyes, stinging them with their intense speed and pressure. She saw lights in her field of vision. Flashes of lights. It was as though they erupted from the ether. She fought the urge to close her eyes. She wanted to remain fully conscious as she slammed into the rampart.

It was with some surprise that Assa eventually found that she was not going to smash her dragon self on the walls of the castle on the island.

Her dragon brain took over just near the end, angled her wings to create a stall, which slowed her way down, and allowed her feet to drop onto the stones where she ended up standing proud, her breaths coming in ragged bursts and her feet feeling like they needed the comfort of the stones, which were cold, but not unpleasant.

The cooling moved up from her talons, through her knees, and into her body. Nothing felt more like being a dragon. She had the impulse to release a long flame, just to feel the pleasure of it, but she was still depleted. No fuel for any flame.

Her eyes, which she had fought to keep open, now drooped in a preparatory nod to sleep. She fought that urge and looked around.

The place was empty of everything, even the rats she remembered from before. There were no dragons. She couldn't see any and her dragon brain made it clear to her that there were not any in the structure. She felt no presence of any of them. They had all, apparently, migrated to the castle on the mainland. And why not? That's where the eggs were.

So why am I here? she asked Dawn and Dusk.

No answer.

Assa sighed. Her sisters had a selective way of communicating with her: sometimes ready to talk non-stop. Other times unable to reach her at all. Or unwilling to. She wasn't sure which.

She went to the window and looked up at the sky. Where were her pursuers? She searched for many minutes but could not see any of them in the sky. So she had outsmarted them. That felt good.

She withdrew from the window. Now that she was no longer being chased, she felt able to let go of her fear and manic energy. She had depleted herself in so many ways and needed rest.

The corner looked inviting. She walked to it and let herself plop down on the stone floor and curled herself up against the wall. The simple strength of the stones felt reassuring on her back.

She folded up her wings so that they trapped some of her body heat and she began to sink into sleep. She knew she would have thrown flame on the corner if she had the ability. That would have warmed up the space and made it more inviting. But she had no flame left. This troubled her. Was she a true dragon if she couldn't belch fire? It did not feel like she was.

A fleeting thought that she might have to defend herself from attack flitted over her dragon brain. She would be vulnerable in sleep.

She elected to leave one eye open. She found she was able to do that and still sleep. Her dragon brain, taking in her will to be safe, activated the proper channels to make this happen.

Assa was proud of her dragon brain. It was like an elaborate toy she could order at will. It often did exactly what she wanted. Not always, since she sometimes wanted things that dragons could not do, but often enough that she didn't think she ever wanted to give up her dragon self.

Her final thought before sleep was of her parents. The last time she saw them they were eating a dragon. Roasting it. What would they think of her being a dragon for the rest of her life?

Did they miss her? She didn't care that they weren't her real parents. She had no love for royals. Certainly not the king and queen, who were inconvenienced by her and elected to throw her out with the trash.

A tiny rage welled up in her, but not enough to disturb her sleep. She entered the dark kingdom, and had no flying dreams.

THE SUN WAS already high in the sky when it rose above the bottom ledge of the window and filled the room with binding yellow light. Assa's one open eye cringed from the burning heat and closed her eyelid, which disturbed Assa's reverie and her wings unfurled with a jolt, pushing her over and rolling her to one side.

From there she rose up with fear coursing through her body. It was as though someone or something had injected fire into her veins. Her entire body was alive and electric.

She stood, taking in great gulps of breath. When no danger made itself apparent, she relaxed, and let her wings droop. Her talons scraped against the floor. Her ragged breaths clawed at the air in the room. The sun was welcoming. Its heat warmed her and made her feel safe. She went to the window and looked in the direction of the sun. She closed her eyes and let its heat roll over her skin.

She had the urge to fly, but her dragon brain said she was too weak. She might not be able to grab enough air with her depleted energy. Her wings would flail and she would plummet.

This intrigued Assa. Her dragon brain knew when she was too weak to fly. Fascinating.

She would have to take the stairs. She retreated to the interior of the castle, which was damp and cold, and began plodding down the steps. She estimated she was a good two hundred feet or more above the ground, so she had a few steps to traverse.

The stairway was enclosed by close walls. They pressed against her as she descended. So many castle passageways she had been walking through lately. All of them were made for people, not dragons. All of them made her feel out of place and wrong.

For her, now, the only real place was the sky. The only real feeling was flapping her wings and dancing with air, grabbing it, shaping it, letting it guide her. Well, that and belching flame. It felt good to shoot out a good stream of fire.

As she got to the lower levels of the castle, she saw that water was everywhere. About two-thirds of the way down, she saw that if she kept going, she would enter a pool of water and drown herself. She stopped.

Her talons were in water. Cold water. She shivered and stepped back up the steps. A feeling of doom descended upon her. How could she find a way out now that her castle was flooded?

She sat on the steps and hung her head down. Her heart felt heavy in her chest, as though it was going to drop through her rib cage and fall into the water.

She was so hungry. She tried to remember the last time she had eaten. It was some of the wood. Her body had used up that energy a long time ago. She felt like she was running on hope and nothing more. She looked up. The stairs appeared to go on forever. She lost them in the shadows above her. She needed to go up and reconsider her position, but it looked too far to even attempt. She had no strength left.

She reached out to her sisters.

Dawn? she said. Dusk? Are you there? I need help.

She listened to the ether. Seconds ticked by.

The called again.

As she waited, her dragon brain clicked and hummed. The connections flared up with heat and dissipated into the ether. It was as though her persona was being reconstructed into something other than herself. She pushed her thoughts to one side. They slipped out of her head and plopped to the water below.

Or, at least, that was how it seemed to Assa. She looked down at the splashes. Tiny fish leaped out of the water and fell back in. She dropped her head down and scooped up a couple of them in her mouth.

They wriggled and fought against her tongue and cheek, but she clamped her teeth onto them, squirting liquid on her gums and the back of her throat. Then she swallowed.

That wasn't bad at all. She searched for more of the little creatures. A few broke the surface. She dispatched them to her stomach with all due speed.

This wasn't going to relight her flame, but it would give her much needed sustenance. She plunged her entire head into the water.

It was dark and slightly warm, but it was sufficiently nurturing, apparently, to sustain a multitude of fish. Only a few of them broke the surface of the water. Many more remained underneath, hidden from view, but not form Assa's jaws.

She scooped dozens of them into her mouth and chewed them up and swallowed. She felt a few of them, which had escaped her teeth, in her stomach. They moved about, no doubt confused by their surroundings, but soon they stopped, no doubt felled by her stomach juices.

Assa could not stop eating. She scooped up fish after fish. Soon her belly was full and she felt strong enough to climb the stairs back up to the top of the castle.

She turned around and faced the flight of stairs in the narrow passageway. They led up, through the darkness, to something resembling light and freedom.

Or was it?

She paused. The water below her looked a lot more inviting all of a sudden. She remembered how she got to the castle on the mainland. She had been a fish. Why not become one again?

Assa held her pose for some time while her dragon brain clicked over the possibilities. She could climb back up and fly. That had its attractions. Or, she could descend into the murky water below. Become one of the fish.

All the salt water she had ingested in the last few minutes might have settled the question. She wasn't sure, but, in any case, decided it didn't really matter. She was no longer going to resist the pull of the sea.

She exhaled her breath until her lungs were empty. Then she plunged down into the water. She followed the steps down even further. Her glided through the water like she was born to the environment.

Her scales, lavishly washed by the water, seemed to shrink and press in on her.

Her wings shrunk to fins.

Her lungs strained against the impossible task of keeping up with her body, which moved quickly through the water. Her dragon brain, reaching for something familiar, latched onto her wings and tried to flap them.

But her wings were no longer wide and thin. They were ticker, and smaller, They hugged her body and moved under the control of her fish brain with subtle motions that steered her body through the water. Where her wings were always trying to catch air, her fins now continuously attempted to steer water. It was similar but different. Her dragon brain was telling her to breathe breathe breathe. She resisted, until her fish brain asserted itself with insistent agreement.

Breathe breathe breathe.

Assa's panic response tried to kick in and keep her holding her breath, but it was impossible to sustain. She had to breathe in. She released her stop on the process and sea water flooded over her gills.

She had gills? Yes, they had sprouted in the last few seconds.

Her dragon brain, resigned to insignificance, receded to the shadowy corners of her fish brain, which snapped and sparked and sizzled and hopped. It was as though her fish brain had never known freedom and now it had a taste of real freedom. Freedom that meant it was able to steer Assa in any direction.

She bumped up against the walls of the passageway, and scraped along the steps. She followed the stairs down down down. It kept going down. Assa realized that for a while she had been below sea level. That she had missed the exit from the castle, if, indeed there was an exit. Maybe the whole point of this structure was this underground cavern she was now entering.

The steps gave way to emptiness. She shot out into a vast cavern. Some of the rocks in the cavern walls were luminous, casting light on her and her surroundings so she could see much more clearly than before.

What she saw surprised and shocked her.

Hundreds of green oblong shapes were stored in every nook and cranny of the cavern.

She had found a dragon nursery.

ASSA SWAM IN circles around the cavern. She had never been in such a large enclosure. It was massive in scale. She swam down, looking for the bottom, but gave up after a while. It was dark. She could see that the water went down for a long long distance. Maybe farther than she could actually swim.

Her fish brain, duller than her dragon brain, concluded that it must be the end of the world down there, but Assa fought against that conclusion. There was no end of the world. She would have to be careful of her fish brain. It could cause her great difficulties with inaccurate information.

Assa though the problem through. The castle was built on a cavern, obviously. It was flooded with sea water, which meant it was below sea level, which meant the island had been built around the cavern. She recalled that the island had little in the way of sand or soft soil. It was mostly rock. Where did rock come from? Volcanoes.

A tingle went through Assa's fish body. Volcanoes push up material from deep in the earth and make land. They make islands. This island in particular.

So she was swimming in the mouth of a volcano. That thought thrilled Assa. More accurately, it thrilled her fish brain, which found the prospect novel and exciting.

Assa swam next to some of the green dragon eggs. They looked exactly like the eggs in the castle on the mainland. The dragons, it seemed, liked to lay their eggs, then leave them. Sometimes in dirt, sometimes in water.

Assa's fish brain told her to jump out of this cave, but she didn't know how. She swam in circles, searching for an exit, but finally stopped using her eyes and let her fins and scales feel the current around her.

There was a complex swirl of motion cradling her form. It was as though the water was doing a dance on her skin, and it was pushing her, gently, this way, then that way. She swayed in the water and the water pushed her up and then down, but there was an underlying current beneath the bustle.

It pointed her in one direction.

She followed the current and it got stronger. The dance slowed considerably and the current pushed her with an urgency she could not deny. Ahead, the rush of water made a sliding motion and she went along for the ride and found herself going down a dark rivulet of flowing water that cut through the rest of the water. An artery of motion in the midst of the ocean.

It took her past craggy outcroppings. Some of them scraped against her skin. Her eyes bulged and led her on.

She tried to smell what was before her, tried to taste it as she glided past, but the sea was giving her nothing and her eyes were taking in darkness as if it was a syrupy molasses. It invaded her head and slogged down her fish brain. The darkness creeped into her bloodstream and coursed through her heart. It washed over her consciousness. There was no luminescence in this trail through the cavern.

Eventually the current reached its peak and pushed her through a hole in the side of the cave and out into the great wide ocean.

Still dark. The current had mostly dissipated. Some small remnant of it still remained, but it was now just a slightly lower water temperature compared to the rest of the sea.

Her fish brain gloried in the crunchy saltiness of it. She wanted to bite down on the sea water, but that was her Assa brain trying to assert itself. No use here. Nothing to bite down on, only the other fishes swimming past her and declining to acknowledge her.

There were no individuals in her species. They all existed for the school and she was without one.

She disliked the darkness here. She pushed away from the cone of the volcano and worked her fins and body so she began climbing. It was like climbing through air, but not exactly. There was more resistance, for one thing, but also the feeling that there was a limit. The top of the ocean was as far as a fish could go. For a dragon, though there was a theoretical top to the atmosphere, it didn't feel that way. It felt like the air went on forever.

If a dragon was determined enough, it could fly right up to the moon. Even past it. After all, the moon was just a spot in the sky. It was there to be visited and maybe even plucked out and strung on a chain and hung around one's neck.

As Assa rose through the water, light began to filter down to her. Sunlight.

She worked her tail with renewed energy. It would be glorious to be drenched in light again after so much time spent in blackness. The dragon eggs were hatched in blackness. Is that why the grown up dragons liked to make black smoke? Did it remind them of the coziness of the ocean and the Earth?

Assa turned the question over in her mind, as though she was getting close to something important about dragon existence. But her fish brain was no longer conversant with the ways of dragons. That realm seemed so far off that it could have happened to someone else. Was she ever a dragon? Was it even possible?

For that matter, was she now a fish? More than that, was she now a fish determined to climb through the sea and reach the surface?

If this was a dream, she was willing to keep it going.

Her fish brain seemed to have taken over. She was climbing at a relentless pace, pushing her self for all she was worth, pouring on the speed until she was going at such a pace that she could not imagine herself stopping.

The surface undulated above her. She saw points of sparkling light in a constellation of surpassing beauty.

Her Assa brain remembered stars.

Her dragon brain, diminished, but still present, thought of mountain ranges.

Her Assa brain discerned a subtle danger. Shadows moving over the top of the surface. She began to put the brakes on her progress, but not in time. Though she slowed her pace considerably, momentum drove her body forward and she breached the surface of the water.

Her mouth popped into the air, followed by her gills and half her body. She began descending, but not in time. One of the shadows, gliding over the water, belonged to a dragon.

The dragon knew where Assa was going to breach and had been waiting here for her. As Assa appeared out of the water, the dragon swooped down, extended its talons, and wrapped them around Assa's body. Assa was powerless to resist. She realized that her fish form was ideally suited to watery life, but had no use for defending herself against such an eventuality as she had to deal with now.

She writhed and twitched, trying to release her self from the dragon's grip. The dragon hardly noticed. It flapped its wings and rose on the air. Assa watched as the sea receded away from her. She gasped for breath, but there was no water here. Only air. Useless oxygen that was not dissolved in water. Who could live on this thin soup?

She did, once. Twice. But not now. Her gills strained for sustenance. She looked up at the belly of the dragon. It undulated and seemed to have its own waves.

Its talons, moreover, had ripped through Assa's skin and was now digging into her guts. A most unpleasant feeling.

Her fish brain was preparing to retreat, but Assa would not let it. You must remain here, with me, she told her fish brain, which declined to answer. Assa remained insistent. Don't you leave me! she shouted. The dragon seemed to hear her. It tilted its head down to look at Assa. Assa tried grinning at it. Let me go! she said.

The dragon looked briefly puzzled, then looked away. Its wings, hinged and leathery, still flapped lazily and Assa already envied the creature for its ability. *She* had been flapping her wings only a short time ago and now she was prey.

This couldn't be the end, could it?

She tried to turn in the dragon's grip. She flipped her tail so that it slapped agains the belly of the dragon. Her gills fought for oxygen. It needed water, where was the water? It seemed to be asking the sky. No water here. Except for clouds. Assa screamed, her fish brain straining at any action that might bring her relief.

But nothing came to assist her. No voices came to her. No instructions, no change in course, no mercy, no reprieve.

Instead, the sky began to blacken. As it did, she flapped her tail even more violently. It felt like the end of something, she wasn't sure what. The blackness began to creep into everything. The air turned dark. The skin of the dragon darkened. Even her own flesh felt like it was blackening. Her senses were turned inside out. Her head felt like it might explode from the strain of trying to take in air.

Then, finally, the dragon seemed to think the whole enterprise not worth the trouble. It released Assa to the void and belched a column of flame, and flapped loudly as it flew away.

Assa began a plummet to the water with an exultant heart. She had made the creature release her. Surely that was a triumph.

Then, as she saw how far she had to fall, she began to worry. If she hit the water at the wrong angle, she would surely injure herself, perhaps beyond repair. She had to attend to the wounds in her side, the puncture holes where the dragon's talons had dug into her. If they did not heal, she would bleed to death, wouldn't she? It seemed probable, but she couldn't be sure.

She did not know enough about fish to know if they might lose all their blood or not. Assa grabbed air with her fins and tried to orient herself in the atmosphere. She fought the urge to sleep. It was strong and it was scrambling her senses and her instincts, but she knew it was from lack of oxygen, nothing more.

She worked to orient herself tail first, reasoning that a small entry profile would help her slip into the water unscathed. Or, at least, not further harmed.

In the event, nothing of the sort happened. She had very little effect on her orientation, which turned into a rotating tumble, completely against her wishes. She did not hit the water tail first. The ocean rushed up to her with terrifying speed and slapped against her flank.

A mighty splash erupted around her body. Cold water gripped and cradled her with a loving embrace. She was stunned and shocked by the gesture. The sea was really her benefactor, wasn't it? The sea would care for her and hold her and keep her intact. The wonder of it filled her mind, even as her lungs, finally, drew in great rivers of water. They flowed into her gills and seemed to course through her entire body.

But even with the benefaction of the ocean, she felt depleted and wounded. Her strength had diminished and the punctures in her skin were painful and weakening.

She tried to swim, to move her body for its own benefit, but there was nothing there. No strength. Her fish body was ideally suited to life in the ocean. It had sleek skin and was nine-tenths muscle, plenty of strength to power her way through the deep, but it wasn't working now. Not like it had been. Assa began sinking toward the bottom. Her descent was going to take a while, but she chose not to fight it. Not now, at any rate. Maybe later, after she had gathered some strength, she might do so.

Instead of fighting, she elected to sleep. The water cradled and held her. As she fell, slowly, she felt like the currents were rocking her to sleep. Such a reassuring motion. So much like the rocking of a cradle.

Assa?

A voice in the wilderness, but whose?

Assa! Where are you?

She felt mud on her fins. Where did mud come from? Her eyes beheld a deep blackness. Obviously, she was not made for this environment. The sun did not penetrate so deep. She had no eyes that would function well here. Mud tickled her flank. Soft granules. She wanted to burrow into them. She sensed a certain comfort there.

Assa, where are you? Answer us now!

She wasn't going to get any sleep with that racket clanging around in her head. Dawn and Dusk. The two extremes of the day, always there. No escape from their incessant chatter.

She could choose not to answer them. Would serve them right. Where were they when she needed them?

We know you're out there, Assa. We know you're still a commoner doing common things. Don't you think we know? Don't you think we could find you if we had to?

No you couldn't, thought Assa without broadcasting her thoughts. You're stuck in a castle guarded by demented dragons who want to hatch their clutch of eggs. They aren't going to let you do anything.

Come on, Assa. You must know something by now. You must have learned something that will help us.

Ha! said Assa. This time she let it go out of her head and into the world. It must have travelled though the murky depths of the ocean, must have breached the surface of the water, and then must have flown to the castle and smacked into the heads of the princesses, because a short time later an answer entered her consciousness.

So, the twins said in unison, you *are* alive. We were worried.

I don't believe you, said Assa. You don't worry about anyone but yourself.

You are cruel, said Dawn, to think that of us. We have always cared about you.

Then come save me, said Assa. I'm stuck at the bottom of the ocean. I can't move. I'm about to burrow into the mud and drown myself.

Don't be so dramatic, said Dusk. We know you better than that. You're a survivor.

I have survived, said Assa. But not the way I wanted to. I never wanted to be a dragon or a fish and that's all I'm allowed to be now.

You could stop feeling sorry for yourself and do what anyone would do, said Dawn.

And what is that? asked Assa.

Swim! said Dusk.

Assa considered the option. It didn't appeal to her. The mud felt much more inviting.

Swimming is for fish, said Assa.

But that's what you are! said Dawn.

Assa didn't agree with that statement. Certainly she had the form of a fish, but she wasn't a fish, not in any real sense. She possessed a fish brain, it was right up there, lodged in her fish skull, but that wasn't her identity. She yearned to have arms and legs.

In fact, she still thought she had arms and legs. Her human brain tried to move them all the time. It was an involuntary action, stymied only by her current form. Every ounce of her being was convinced that she was a young woman. Nothing in her experience or her processing of the world indicated that she was anything but a person wearing a fish costume for some unfathomable reason.

I'm not a fish, said Assa.

You could have fooled me, said Dawn. You've got all the signs of fishiness. You probably smell like one.

I don't smell like anything, said Assa.

If you died now, said Dawn, you'd rot and the fish smell would be awful. Overpowering. People would puke from the smell of you.

What are you talking about? asked Assa.

It's true, said Dusk. Don't deny it. You've smelled fish. You know what I'm talking about. They are nasty. If you lie there in the mud like you're doing, you'll turn into a smelly rotten old fish.

Assa's fish brain was serene and joyful. She liked the feeling of the mud below her and the water above and around her. It was cozy and right. But her human brain was beginning to boil. She wanted to shut Dawn and Dusk out of her mind.

What about you? asked Assa.

What about us? said Dawn.

Are you just smelly things waiting to die?

We're not waiting to die, said Dusk. We're waiting for *you* to come *rescue* us. Now get to it.

You don't deserve rescuing, said Assa.

She heard them both sigh. They laughed in unison and Assa heard that too. They had nothing more to say to her, it seemed.

All you have to do is go upstairs in your stupid castle and break all the eggs. Once you do that, the dragons will fly away and leave you and the land in peace.

You don't know what you're talking about, said Dawn. We can't just break the eggs.

Yeah, said Dusk. It doesn't work that way.

Let me tell you something, said Assa. I'm your sister, or at least that's what you think. I don't know if it's really true or not.

It's true, Dawn and Dusk both chimed in quickly. It's true.

Well, then, said Assa. Would your sister steer you wrong?

It's possible, said Dawn.

Sure, said Dusk. Sisters can be mean.

Oh really? said Assa.

Not that we mean to be, said Dawn. It's just the way sisters are made. There's something in the sister gene. At least, that's what our parents tell us. When they tell us anything.

What's a gene? said Assa.

Never mind, said Dawn. The plan was for you to become a dragon and break the eggs. Not us.

No one told me that, said Assa.

It was completely *obvious*! they both said. Loudly.

Assa wanted to put her hands over her ears, only she didn't have any hands. They were gone. Or they never existed. Something. She tried to find a thread of sanity through her recent changes, but it was difficult. Like trying to isolate a single strand from a head of hair. They all looked the same, and they tangled up and disappeared in the melding of all the other hairs. That's what her brain felt like. Her self was lost in the tangle of all the other beings in there.

It was like walking through a marsh where the roots grabbed at her feet and ankles. They were trying to pull her down. Just like the thoughts tangled up and pulling her down in her head.

Assa, said Dawn. None of it matters right now. Just get yourself up from the mud and start swimming. We'll guide you.

I don't need your guidance, said Assa. I'm going to stay a fish.

No! said Dawn.

No! said Dusk.

We're done, said Assa. I don't want to hear you or talk to you anymore.

She closed the connection between them and immediately felt relieved. The castle was so far away from her now. It was not only in another world, it *was* another world. A world she didn't have to be a part of anymore. She had her simple world now, surrounded and supported by water. Her shapeshifting abilities were just a prelude to this existence. Was anything simpler or more satisfying than the elements of living?

The cares of the world fell away from her. The mud of the ocean floor grew increasingly more open to her. She wriggled her body down so that mud covered her. Only her head, with its eyes protruding slightly, poked out of the mud.

She felt like this was the best place to be. No place could ever be better. Above her, creatures of the sea swam back and forth. Some circled and others hovered. They were all looking for food. A few of the smaller fishes got eaten by some of the bigger fishes.

Assa observed the drama with indifference. She was safe. She didn't have to worry about getting eaten. Though she *did* have to consider the possibility that she would have to get something to eat. Did she know how to hunt? She searched her fish brain. Not exactly. She found no template for chasing food and capturing and eating it.

Well.

How was she supposed to survive? She let her awareness drift over her fish brain, prepared to snag any bit of information she could use. It was like flying over a complicated garden overrun with brambles and vines. The tangle of plants made a matted and forbidding clump, as if it was trying to capture air and keep it.

She dipped her awareness into the tangle of her fish brain and was immediately caught. Her fish brain seized on her awareness and tried to swallow it whole. She felt prickles of pain and, panicked, pulled back until she was hovering over her awareness again.

She moved in slow and lazy circles. She was disembodied, surely, but not separate from her world. She had multiple awarenesses and needed to integrate them into something that would help her become a creature with purpose and weight. She needed to survive. Wasn't that the prime purpose of creatures?

She allowed her awareness to rise above the tangle of her fish brain, and immediately felt relief. It was as though she had been bound and someone had come along and released the ropes holding her in place. She floated up, out of her fish body, so that her awareness was now a thing without the confines of flesh and bone.

She saw her fish body below her. Buried and frightened. Could anything look so pathetic? It was hard to imagine.

She climbed up, past falling bits of fish waste, through the bodies of schools of fish. Up and up. The light from the sun began to warm and illuminate the water around her. The surface of the ocean undulated above her, flashing sparks like strings of stars against the sky.

Just as she was about to break through the surface to the air above, she stopped herself. She hovered there, just on one side of the barrier between air and water, the undulating dividing line. Her most recent bodily incarnation lay below her.

Was it being eaten at this very moment? Possibly. Nothing remained still and alive for long. Not in the ocean. Hungry mouths populated the deep more densely than grains of sand littered the shorelines of the world. So if Assa left her fish body unattended, what would happen to her?

The question scarcely meant anything anymore because she didn't even know who she was. She couldn't be this tiny bit of awareness, could she?

A large form flowed over her. She was lost in the intricate workings of its insides for a split second, red and warm, gurgling with squishy life, tubes everywhere, blood flowing like water through pipes. Then it was gone. A large fish. Maybe a shark. Maybe a dolphin. She couldn't tell. Really, in some sense, it was all the same. She had been one of those, once. Had been one of several of those: a body with a will and material clumped around that will, like clay clumped up on a house.

She could keep going.

The sky was there for the taking.

In the end, it was the heat of the sun that turned her will. That warmth was too inviting to resist. She made her decision and did not hesitate. She shot straight up and broke through the surface of the ocean and gasped for air, forgetting that she didn't need air. She was a disembodied—something. Not sure exactly what. That knowledge could come later.

Dragons circled around her. They were intent on the spot on the ocean that she had just jumped out of. They angled their necks and heads so they could see it.

Assa felt suddenly as if she was vulnerable to attack. Could they see her? Were the dragons able to discern disembodied wills?

Not need to wait for an answer. She darted away from her location, picking a route at random. It took her away from the mainland, but she didn't care. Not then. She needed to put some distance between herself and the dragons.

But the dragons were not so easily fooled. They moved in the same direction. They seemed to know she was there.

Assa considered dropping back into the water, but the thought frightened her. The water was cold and uninviting. Dark. She wanted to be out here, in the freedom that air brought. She moved as quickly as she could, skimming above the water with great speed.

Here was an advantage over having a body. She was able to outpace the pursuing dragons. They slowly fell back despite the fact that they were going at full speed. Full *dragon* speed. Which was not enough to catch her.

This filled her with elation. She whooped and added movement to her flight, altering the path with wriggles and flourishes. The very air itself seemed to support her happiness.

Which was the way it should be.

Once the dragons were safely behind her and out of sight, Assa executed a giant curve and began a flight back toward the mainland.

Well, said Dusk, aren't you the happy one.

Yup, said Assa. You going to try to bring me down now?

I wouldn't dream of it, said Dusk.

I would, said Dawn.

Of course, said Assa. You've never seen happiness you didn't want to destroy.

Now where did that come from? asked Dawn.

Just a little something I've noticed over the months of our friendship.

We're not *friends*, said Dusk. Why do you keep forgetting that? We're sisters.

Even worse, then, said Assa. Sisters should support each other. You don't do that. At least not with me.

You're right, said Dawn. Sisters do support each other. Which is why you should support us. Now.

Assa groaned.

You know it's the right thing, said Dusk.

I'm free, said Assa. Do you know what it's like to be this free? I can fly anywhere I want. As high or as low as I want.

You have to get into a body, said Dawn.

Why?

If you don't, you can't help us, said Dusk.

I think, said Assa, that I'm okay with that. I don't want to help you.

No answer from either of them. Assa felt a deep satisfaction, knowing that she had shut the twins up for once.

While they, she supposed, contemplated her refusal of assistance, Assa elected to angle her flight high. She rose above the waves, riding the air like it wasn't there. The blue water receded below her and she saw dots of islands littering the seascape. All of it, though was dwarfed by the mainland off in the distance. It was a line of darkness on the horizon. As soon as Assa saw it, her heart, or what stood in for her heart, melted. Her entire life, until a short time ago, had been lived on that bit of land. Her parents were there, her woods, her house, her land.

She didn't even notice the thick column of black smoke coming up from the line of darkness. It rose high above the ground and seemed to come to a barrier in the clouds, where it spread out in all directions, creating a dark canopy of smoke over everything. She had not noticed how deliberately awful this was until this very moment. Until this climactic moment, when the elation of pure flight was at its peak in her being.

You have to help us, said Dawn. Her voice was weak and unconvincing. Assa thought of it as a pathetic attempt at convincing her of the truth of their situation. But Assa didn't need Dawn's voice to tell her. For the first time, she noticed that the air around her was flecked with dark particles. Tiny, but definitely there. How could she have been so blind to it? The fire the dragons had been maintaining was filling her world with darkness.

Please, said Dusk. You have the power. You need to use it for good.

For good? asked Assa. Do you even know what that means?

At least as much as you do, said Dawn. You're no different from us. You want the same things we do.

And what is that? asked Assa.

She let the air bob her up and down. She didn't have to do this. She could have existed independently of the atmosphere, but she chose not to do that. Instead, she embraced the ups and downs of the atmosphere, making her being match the being of the air. It was as though she wanted to become air, wanted to make the air become her. Such thoughts were foreign to Assa, at least until now.

She had sometimes talked about being one with her surroundings, as when she was in the woods, or on the banks of the creek. But this time, here and now, it was different. She was little more than ephemera, now, and she was being tossed about by the winds in the atmosphere. She was the wind in the atmosphere. This was liberating and limiting, all at the same time. Liberating to be in such a different state of being than she had ever experienced before. Limiting in that she had little power to move the world or anything in it.

And Dawn and Dusk. Would they ever leave her alone? If she had known having sisters would be so annoying, she would have declined the opportunity from the beginning. Much better to think of the twin princesses as members of the royal family that had nothing to do with her. They had their lives, which involved royal balls and high tea and such. Or so she imagined.

And Assa had *her* life, which involved her woods and her family and the royals were these strange creatures that lived in a big castle, like bees in a hive. Or dragon eggs in an incubator? Who knew what she would have thought about them eventually. Maybe they would become the comical figures of her later life. Crazy royals with their strange customs. Who knew what they were or who they wanted to be?

Assa's thoughts wandered, literally. She let them wander. All she wanted from them was to cohere and they weren't doing so. Suddenly, she felt a whoosh of something nearby: a force pushing the ether against her. Was this what she wanted from herself? Did she know how much the world was against her at this moment?

Such thoughts did nothing to quell her trepidation in the present moment. The world was nothing. Nothing to it at all. This frightened Assa. There had to be something more than her disembodied self.

Suddenly she wanted the connection, however tenuous, with Dusk and Dawn. They would be her anchor, wouldn't they? Or they could be. All was bearable if there were people around you to support you.

She called out to them. Dawn? Dusk? Are you still there?

She felt tendrils of herself snake thorough the air, slinking in between oxygen molecules. They laid out a labyrinthian path.

Thus engaged with the world, she didn't notice the forces massing against her. The dragons had discerned a disturbance in their field. Knew there was something amiss. Or, at least, not that things were not as they normally should be. They coalesced into a flame above the spot where Assa, oblivious to the energies conspiring against her, hovered. By the time Assa sensed something different about to reach a crescendo, it was too late. Dragons swooped down over her, trying to snag her essence with their bodies.

Dawn, she called. Dusk. I need help. They've found me.

But no answer from her sisters. The connection between them was maddeningly erratic. How could this mode of communication be worth anything if there was this constant breakdown in communication?

More dragons swooped over her. Assa exerted all her efforts to keep from being snagged in the tangle of sinew, muscle, bone, and blood that coursed over her being. She succeeded completely three or four times.

On fifth occurrence, however, she was dragged along the ether, smeared just a bit. She knew, in some sense vital to her survival, that it was the beginning of the end. More dragons swooped over her, engulfing her spirit momentarily. She emerged from the encounter, mostly whole, but more slowly each successive time. Eventually, she was more caught than escaped.

By the time the dozenth dragon flew over her, she was done. The creature's backbone was too much for her. She lodged up into it and did not escape. She was trapped as surely as a fish gets trapped in a net.

The dragon flew at a breakneck speed. It made Assa dizzy and she fought to keep her equilibrium, but found herself bounced around inside the dragon, falling through organs and muscle tissue. The hinged wings beat with great power. She felt their swinging reverberate through the entire body of the dragon. And she was stuck inside it.

She still retained a little autonomy. She exercised it and moved around the interior of the dragon.

Here was the creature's stomach, filled with chewed wood.

Here were the lungs, inflating and deflating with frightening efficiency. The blood, thudding and booming, pumped blood through the arteries. She retreated from it. It was too much. Too big and powerful.

If she got too close she would be pulled into the flow and end up in the bloodstream. That seemed awful. She would be elongated and stretched along the arteries. What chance would she have, then, of getting back to her true self.

The darkness was overwhelming. No light penetrated the hide of the dragon, which existed as a tough canopy, holding her inside. She put her presence up to the smooth interior of the hide. It was soft, but also unyielding. There was no crossing that boundary. She had no power to do so. All she could do was go along for the ride.

Or could she? Surely she had some influence on the dragon. She existed, after all. She knew that much about herself.

She moved up past the lungs to the throat and eased herself along the path it defined. She pushed herself through the constriction there and emerged on the other side in the creature's tongue. Strange place. It flapped in the wind and smacked against teeth. It was scorched from the belching flame. She thought she could smell the singed flesh, but, of course, that was impossible without a nose. Or was it?

She paused a moment and tried to savor the aroma. It certainly felt real.

No matter. No time to stop and investigate. She had a plan. She retreated from the body of the tongue and slipped into the chin, then around the jaw and up into the skull. Protective armor. Solid. And beneath it? The source of the dragon's—everything. She dropped through the thick bone and gummy interior lining of the skull and flopped onto the soft density of the brain of the dragon.

Here was a mishmash of gooey clumps and conduits. So many connections. They invaded her own being and the notion of a net came even stronger to her.

She moved slowly, taking in the spectacle. Flashes of light everywhere. Corridors going in every direction, as if she was in a maze. Which way to go? She hovered in one place and turned her being around in every direction possible.

Corridors everywhere, like the corridors of the castle. Far down the corridors, more flashes of light, as if flames were burning, illuminating the dark interior of the dragon's brain.

Assa paused at the threshold to the dragon's brain. She had a dragon's brain herself and wished it was as open to the elements as this one was. She was able to walk through it without any hindrance.

She stepped on neurons and synapses. The sparks around her sizzled the air. It singed her being. She was a thought in the dragon's brain now, wasn't she? It seemed like the correct characterization. The path before her was illuminated by the sparks. The twisting tunnels of material was not the sort of thing she would have thought would be inviting, but it was all there, waiting for her to enter it and make it her own.

She crawled through the muck. Fibers of the dragon's brain clogged her own interior. The filaments seemed to want to interact with her. She did not fight it. Why fight anything at this point? She could have tried to crawl out of the dragon's brain, but she chose not to. Instead, she was going to plunge into the world that was presented to her. She was going to see where it would take her.

The dragon, meanwhile, was hesitating in its flight. It stopped and hovered, then flew a few more lengths, then stopped again and twisted in the air. It flipped its head from side to side.

Assa knew all this because she felt herself being pulled this way and that with rapid force and snapping emphasis, as though the dragon was trying to evict her from its skull. And why not? Wouldn't she want an alien invader out of her head?

It didn't matter, though. She had become so entangled with the dragon's brain that it would have taken much too much force to pop her out. For what it was worth and for all that it mattered, she and the dragon brain were now so entangled that it would take some supreme power to pull their separate strands apart.

The dragon, however, did not want to accept this. It kept flapping its head from side to side. It kept twisting its neck. It tried a certain maneuver many times in succession: It would turn its head twice on its neck so that it was facing forward, but its neck was twisted. Then it would quickly untwist itself so its head spun around and its neck instantly returned to its normal configuration. This spun Assa around in one spot.

Her instinct was to hang on to her surroundings, so she clutched at the stringy clop of the dragon's brain to keep herself from spinning away. Nothing, however, could dislodge her. She heard muffled screams through the skull of the dragon. It was so distressed that it was calling out in pain. Or horror. Assa wasn't sure which.

It swooped down rapidly and splashed into the sea. Was it trying to see if the ocean would swallow up whatever was in its head? Assa could only guess at what was going on.

The dragon emerged from the water and belched flame. Assa could hear it sizzling on the other side of the skull. A whole world out there. Water and fire. Air.

But a whole world in here as well. All those elements were swallowed up in the tissue of this dragon brain. It held the riches of the world.

Assa waited for the dragon to tire. She knew it had to happen. The thing couldn't keep exerting energy to no purpose. Its wings would get tired. It would use up its power.

She did notice its rate of speed had diminished greatly from when she had first entered the brain. It was as though she was a hindrance to its operation.

Eventually she heard voices. Muffled ones that she barely recognized.

Assa? they called to her. Someone here knew her name? How odd.

Assa, talk to us. Where are you?

Ah, thought Assa. Dawn and Dusk. Always there. Two ends of annoyance that never seemed to leave her alone.

I'm in a dragon's brain, said Assa.

No answer. Assa liked that. She had surprised them.

No, said Dawn. Really. Where are you?

I told you. I left the fish that I was in, floated up to the top of the ocean, and a dragon snagged me in its brain. Maybe on purpose, maybe not. I'm not sure.

Well, said Dawn.

Well, said Dusk.

Yes, said Assa. Well.

I didn't know anyone could do that, said Dawn.

Neither did I, said Assa.

But that's good, said Dusk. It means you can come rescue us now. Kill the eggs.

It doesn't mean anything of the kind, said Assa. All it means is that I'm stuck in a dragon's brain. I don't know if I'll ever get out.

You can *control* the dragon. Make it do things you want. You're in its *brain*.

Oh, right, said Assa. I can just move this clump of brain here, work that lever over there, turn that crank next to it and that'll make the dragon move exactly the way I want it to.

Well, said Dawn. Yes. That's exactly how it works.

Assa laughed. It's all just a mess here. A jumble of icky guts.

It's not guts, said Dusk. Guts are in the stomach.

Assa laughed. Okay, not guts. It just looks like guts. Like the stuff you pull out of an animal after you slaughter it. The parts you throw away.

I've eaten brains, said Dusk. I know what it looks like.

You haven't seen brains the way I'm seeing brains, said Assa. It's up close. It's not the same as seeing the whole thing. I'm seeing all the tiny strands buried in the depths of the brain up close.

That means it's like a machine, said Dusk. You can work the strings of the machine.

Or a puppet! said Dawn.

Dusk sounded excited. Yes, yes! she said. Like a puppet. Do you know what a puppet is?

I know puppets, said Assa, but I'm not a puppeteer.

Well, said Dusk, you're going to have to learn. Why don't you grab a string and pull on it? See what happens.

Assa moved through the dragon brain. The dragon, for its part, was still intent on shaking her loose, or so it seemed to Assa. It flew in erratic paths, flopped its head back and forth, and called out to whatever spirits it might believe in. The sound of its calls was piercing. Assa felt pain in her heart from it. She was concerned that she might break into pieces.

She watched the sparks course up and down the jelly of the dragon brain. In and out. Around and through. The light did a dance and put on a show. The individual points spiraled up, then down. At first they seemed to be random, but as Assa watched she thought she was able to determine some pattern to the flashing and movement. When the dragon bobbed to the left, a pulse of sparks coursed through a pathway *here*. And when it bobbed to the right, the pulse coursed *there*. Assa felt a thrill of excitement and discovery. This was good. This was something she could use.

How's it going? asked Dusk.

I'm learning, said Assa.

Don't take too long learning, said Dawn.

Okay? asked Assa.

Our parents are sick, said Dawn. The smoke is getting to them. They're coughing and having a hard time breathing.

Assa didn't know that. Are they dying? she asked.

What difference does it make? said Dusk. Maybe they are and maybe they aren't. You should still get on this task you've been given and get it right. Get it done *now*.

Easy for her to say, thought Assa.

Yes it is, said Dusk.

What, said Assa, you can read my thoughts? Even the ones I don't want to broadcast?

Call it a gift, said Dawn. We can all do it.

I can't, said Assa.

Yes you can, said Dusk. You've just never tried.

I don't think I want to, said Assa.

You should do it with the dragon, said Dusk.

Yes, thought Assa. The dragon. The dragon she was riding in. She was frightened half out of her mind with the thought that what she did here could affect everyone in the castle.

I'm the king of the castle, said Assa.

What? said Dawn.

I remembered that sound. From when I was a kid. I'm the king of the castle, and you're the dirty rascal. That's me, right? The dirty rascal?

Don't go loopy on us, said Dusk. We need you to do this job. Get that dragon out here to smash those eggs.

Dragons don't want to smash their eggs, said Assa.

Are you already out of it? said Dusk. Are you in another world right now?

Assa laughed at the thought that Dusk and Dawn, and everyone else in the castle were waiting for her to work her skills. Skills she wasn't sure she even had. Her parents were part of the group, too. Her *real* parents, she had to believe now. If Dawn and Dusk were actually telling the truth. Were they? Who knew?

She pushed against the dragon brain, just to see what would happen. The dragon's flight path altered a little. A frightened squeak came from the depths of the dragon's throat. Well, said Assa to herself, that made a difference. What if I did *this*—and she kicked with all her might in the direction of the center of the dragon brain. This time the dragon fell out of the sky and plummeted with incredible speed toward the ocean's surface. The dragon was completely out of control. It tumbled in the air. Its wings flapped spasmodically. It shot flames from its mouth in all directions, like a pinwheel. Assa tumbled around inside the skull of the dragon. She had to fight to get her bearings.

What's happening? came the voices of Dawn and Dusk in unison, calling to her.

The interior surface of the skull made her think of the insides of eggs. Was she going to hatch out of this dragon skull?

No, no, that wasn't what this was about. It wasn't about her rebirth. It was about saving the castle by killing dragons.

Assa moved something in the ether which gave her the sensation of setting her jaw. She dove into the center of the dragon brain and spread her arms and legs. They caught on the jelly like a fish caught in a net. The dragon seized up in mid-flight. No more spastic flailing about. Instead, the dragon curled up on itself so that it was a round ball. It kept falling.

That wasn't quite what Assa had in mind.

The dragon was doing a fine imitation of a rock plummeting to the water.

Assa moved her arms and legs. The dragon responded by moving its limbs. Assa kept working her limbs and fingers and toes. She got the dragon to unfurl its wings. It caught air. Assa recognized the sensation from when she had shapeshifted into a dragon. The feel of good solid air under her leathery wings felt not only good, but *right*.

She straightened up her body and the dragon followed a split second later. She flapped her arms. The dragon's wings flapped with strong beats. They soared above the clouds so Assa could get a better look. There were other dragons in the sky. They looked at Assa's dragon and rolled their eyes, evidently believing that Assa's dragon was being some kind of jokester, making strange flight paths and behaving in a clownish manner. If it meant they would leave Assa and her dragon alone, that was okay with Assa.

She angled away from the flame and headed to the mainland. The clouds flew by. Some surrounded her momentarily and she was greeted with the wonder of a completely white world for a second or two.

Then she would burst out on the other side and be surrounded by only blue. Lots of it.

She learned to speed up the dragon's pace. She got to the point where she was pushing it to go so fast that she began to hear the air whistling over the scales of the dragon. She remembered hearing such sounds when she was a girl. She thought, then, that the high-pitched moaning had to be some kind of geological phenomenon. She never dreamed it was the sound of a dragon flying.

Nevertheless, Assa piled on the speed. She didn't know how fast they were going, but she knew she had never travelled so rapidly in her life. The air rushed by her, blocking out all other noise. She could sense Dawn and Dusk trying to contact her, but the rush of the air muffled their calls.

Just as well. Assa wasn't interested in them.

She rode on the dragon's path in complete contentment until, a few minutes later, the dragon coughed. Its whole body shuddered. She heard its heart skip a beat, then another. The blood coursing through its veins slowed down a little and the heat of the dragon's body seemed to dissipate into the air. It was getting colder. More than that, it was beginning to falter. She kept the wings beating as best she could, but they were beginning to not respond. The dragon needed more energy. Probably needed more food. They were still a long way from the mainland. She didn't think the creature could make it. Useless thing! It should be better than this.

Disgusted, she searched the ocean for land. Any land. An island here or there. It didn't matter. Just somewhere this creature could get some rest.

She scanned the waves. White caps rose up everywhere. The voices of Dawn and Dusk rang in her head. She didn't like that. She had grown disgusted with them. Their need was not her need. Wasn't that so? Didn't they have their own problems, just as she had her problems? Shouldn't they find a way to fix things on their own?

Assa, you have to keep that dragon going, said Dusk.

Don't let it fall into the water, said Dawn. It'll drown.

Dragons don't drown, said Assa. They can swim, just like any animal can.

No, said Dusk. Not this dragon. These dragons. Their wings are too big. They get tangled up in water. They panic and they don't know what to do.

Please stop talking to me, said Assa. You're just chattering. You have nothing to say.

We're trying to help, said Dawn.

You can help by letting me be. I've got enough going on with this dragon losing power.

She angled the creature on a gliding flight path that lost as little altitude as possible. She spotted an island that looked like it was covered with trees. It had an emerald quality of lushness. Lots of wood there, she was sure. Enough for this stupid dragon to gain some strength and a little endurance.

She tilted the dragon's head down. It responded with a drop in altitude. She half powered, half rode the dragon down. It mostly flew on its own, but she was also able to do some things to help it. The island grew in size as they descended, but not much. It was a small enough piece of land that she could have walked its perimeter in less than ten minutes. She also saw that some of the green was due to moss on the rocks that seemed to make up most of its surface. No matter. Even though it was not covered with trees, she did see a good outcropping near the eastern shore of the island, which was somewhat protected from the elements by a cliff that rose above the beach. The cliff offered an imposing façade as they drew closer. They circled the island at least three times until Assa found what looked to her like a good landing spot. She and the dragon glided in and lighted on the beach with admirable aplomb. They ended up standing, with the dragon's wings fluttering and then folding in on itself.

At which point, the dragon promptly tipped over on its side, exhausted.

No no no, said Assa. You can't go to sleep now.

But there was no stopping the creature.

Its brain began slowing down. The flashes of light grew dimmer and less numerous. It was as though someone was slowly snuffing out all the lights. She tried to walk the network, hoping to seize the dragon's will and bend it to her notions of what needed to be done, but it was no good. The dragon was not to be budged. Its brain settled into a holding pattern of lights. Its body twitched and waves of muscle spasms rolled over its bulk. It tucked its head into its shoulder, closed its eyes, and welcomed the darkness of sleep.

Assa had nowhere to go and nothing to do.

She fended off the voices of Dusk and Dawn, who were intent on breaking into her reverie. Nothing could move her, though. She found herself mimicking the dragon: moving into a rest phase. Her energy dissipated and her view of the world was dark. No light came from anywhere. She knew it would return when the dragon opened its eyes. Dawn and Dusk were there, on the edges. They would have to wait.

ASSA WAS SHAKEN awake with a dreadful lurch. The dragon seemed to jump out of the sand and reach for the sky. But it wasn't flying.

It opened its eyes and Assa saw what was happening immediately: Several other dragons, much bigger than her dragon, were attacking her dragon. There were three of them. They surrounded her dragon and were taking turns approaching her host and beating on it. Scratching it. Landing blows on its body and head.

Assa was rattled inside the dragon's skull. She tried to get her bearings and her footings, but to no avail. Every time she righted herself, or thought she had a grip on stability, a new blow would land on her host. It tried to fight back, but feebly. All it could do was raise its wings to try to protect itself, but the attacking dragons simply ripped its wings to shreds.

Which meant this dragon was not going to be her ticket off the island. It bellowed and roared. Or tried to.

Its voice was so weak, however, that it could barely emit a low pitched growl before falling over and receiving more body blows. Assa read the signs quickly. This dragon was either going to die soon, or be so incapacitated that it would do her no good. She needed a new host, quickly.

She watched each of the three assailants, evaluating them for size and strength. They seemed quite capable of looking after themselves. They also looked like they had eaten and were strong enough to fly to the mainland easily. They looked like they were also very determined creatures who knew exactly what they wanted. That might be a challenge, but she though she would be up to it.

The attacking dragons were relentless in their quest to pummel her host into submission. Soon, her dragon was not putting up even a token fight.

It flipped over on its back. Its breathing was ragged and it was full of pain where cuts and blows had weakened it. It was waiting to die.

One of the attacking dragons, the biggest one, advanced on her host's throat and bent down with its jaws open wide. Assa maneuvered herself to a position from which she could make the leap.

She slipped down out of the dragon's brain and into its throat and down even further to the creatures lungs where great dry howling gusts of air assaulted her. It was like moving through sandpaper. She felt parched and broken. The strain was like having herself dragged through rocks and flayed open.

In any case, she had gone too far. She needed to stop at the throat. A shudder went through her dragon. The heart momentarily increased its rate of beating, then subsided and finally stopped.

The body was tossed from side to side as the other dragons fell upon it and began devouring. She moved back up to the throat and waited for a set of jaws to return to the kill. When they did, she felt the contact and leaped from the dead dragon into the jaw of one of the other dragons.

The pathways were familiar, yet subtly different. This creature's body was vibrant and full of life. Must be from having all this wood around. It was well fed.

She journeyed up the jaw and through the muscles and tendons there. The nerves were another pathway. She had her pick. Soon she was in the brain of the dragon and wasted no time moving to work the conduits and synapses there. She had learned from the other dragon, the one that was now food for this dragon. She moved to pull this dragon away.

It disgusted her that dragons ate other dragons. Cannibalism was beyond the pale and she would not stand for it.

Her new dragon fought her. It raised its wings and flapped vigorously, as if to shake Assa's presence loose. But Assa was not about to be shaken out. She held fast as this new dragon tossed its head from side to side. It screeched and belched long columns of flame.

Assa noted the flame was thick and robust. It was as though this dragon had a fire pit in its stomach and needed to release it or it would overheat. That was fine with Assa. It meant that the dragon had power. She let it flail about for a few minutes. She reasoned that once it got all that out of its system, it would be more pliable to her will.

It didn't work out that way. The dragon wanted more of the kill. The other two attackers were gorging on the dead dragon's flesh. Assa's dragon wanted to join them and it pulled against Assa's will, agains the presence in its own brain. Assa wanted to scold the thing, but that wouldn't work. She didn't know what to tell a dragon to make it do what she wanted to do. She pulled the stings but the puppet wasn't responding.

You think you know everything because you're a commoner, said Dusk.

Not now, said Assa.

You think you live in a dragon's brain, said Dawn. You think everything is real.

Everything *is* real, said Assa.

We'll see, said Dawn.

What are you talking about? said Assa.

Make this one fly, said Dawn. Go ahead. You made the other one fly, now do it with this one.

I'm working on that, said Assa.

Not very well, said Dawn. You 're getting pushed to a corner of the brain.

Dawn was right. While she had been talking to Dawn and Dusk, the dragon had found ways to shunt Assa aside. The jelly of the brain nudged her this way and that. At first it felt random, but soon she saw there was a method to the pushing. It was as though she was a bit of dust and the dragon had a broom sweeping her first in this direction then in another direction, and so on. She ended up going in a zigzag pattern to the bottom of the skull, lodged in a little grotto there.

How could the dragon know? Dragons were stupid creatures. Weren't they?

With Assa more or less tucked away for the moment, the dragon returned to the carcass of its dead cousin.

It tore off one of the wings and tossed it aside to the beach where blood ran from its tear and stained the sand. It plunged its teeth into the leg of the dragon and pulled away a great hunk of flesh. It was warm and dripping with blood. The blood ran down the dragon's chin and over its scales.

Assa struggled to work the control of the dragon brain. If she couldn't get it away from this kill, she wasn't going to be able to get it back to the mainland to smash all the eggs. The eggs were going to hatch and all these mindless flying furnaces were going to wreck havoc on the land. Maybe the planet.

Her dragon chewed on the dead dragon's flesh and extended its wings in ecstasy. Assa grabbed at bits of the dragon's brain in an attempt to sway it to her will. Nothing worked. It felt like nothing was going to work. The thing fell upon the carcass again and gnawed on the bones of the dead dragon.

The other two attackers appeared to be sated. They stopped eating, although not before they had consumed a great deal of dragon flesh. It was as though these three had not eaten in a long time. Maybe they hadn't. Maybe they got tired of eating wood all the time and wanted something soft and warm.

Maybe she could jump into one of the other dragons. They did not seem so single-minded. She felt as though her new dragon would spend the rest of its life on this one carcass.

Birds began circling the sky. Vultures, mostly, but also other scavengers. Some seagulls and a few crows. They jostled for position in the sky, then a few bolder ones dropped down and landed near the carcass.

The dragon shot a flame out at them and they scattered. But even as they did so, others came down to join them. It was soon thick with birds. The dragon shot flames, but the tactic was at best a temporary thing. It didn't deter the birds to any significant degree.

More and more came. Some of them landed on Assa's dragon and began pecking at it. The dragon covered itself with its wings in an attempt, Assa supposed, to protect itself from the pecks of the birds.

Because the birds were no longer only interested in the dead dragon. They had moved on to Assa's dragon. They swarmed over it. Assa tried to help the dragon by pushing away the birds, but they were persistent and Assa was not able to work the dragon well enough to take care of itself. She did not know how to keep the birds away.

They were unerring in their strategy. They went after the dragon's eyes, pecking at them with all due haste and energy. The dragon lowered its lids as best it could, trying to keep out the beaks, but its lids were at best only a short term solution. They had scales on them, it was true, and they were tough, but the birds pecked and pecked, eventually breaking through the lids and getting at the eyes themselves.

Pinpricks of pain emanated in waves from the eyeballs. The sensation coursed through the dragon's body, added to all the rest of the pain from all the other beak jabs along the length of the creature.

Assa, bewildered, fought to control the pain. She knew if she could find the proper levers in the brain, she could nullify the pain that was going through the dragon and causing it no end of suffering. It writhed on the ground, trapping its wings under its body and wrenching the limbs and breaking bones.

It was now a useless dragon for her purposes. She wanted to ride it to the mainland and destroy the eggs, but she had not anticipated the attack of all these birds. Were they waiting, all this time, for the dragon to become incapacitated? Were they such consummate and patient opportunists that they could wait for the lifetime of this dragon before attacking it?

The scales which protected her dragon were wearing away. Some chipped off, others were torn off. Assa was at the center of a storm of beaks, all working together to bring an end to this dragon.

Assa, desperate for some way out, worked the dragon's legs. Stand up! she shouted to herself as much as to the dragon. Some response from its body came through to her. It tried to right itself, but the barrage of attacks were proving to be too much.

It now seemed to Assa as if every single scale had a bird assigned to it, and each bird was filled with the power of revenge. Or the lust for blood. Something.

Frenzied chirps of birds rose up into the air. They entered the dragon's ears and went into the dragon's brain, where Assa took them up in her own brain and did not know what to do with them. They were a cacophony of sound, a symphony of pain. She longed for the cool calming sound of the creek at her house, its waters flowing past in a kind of reverie that always calmed her.

Nothing here was calming. She had been responsible for the death of one dragon, and now, it seemed, she was going to be instrumental in the death of another. The dragons were, as a group, a nuisance and dangerous, but that did not mean she needed to see to it that they all died.

Assa felt under barrage herself, just as the dragon was being assaulted by the birds.

The dragon pushed out a meager flame. It scorched the air only a little. Some of the sand near its mouth got singed. Birds had broken through the skin of the dragon here and there. They began pulling up pieces of the dragon's flesh.

What is going on here? asked Dawn.

What are you doing to these dragons? asked Dusk.

Not now, said Assa. I'm dying here. Or it feels like it.

You're not dying, said Dawn. Just get out of there. The dragon's dying, but you're not.

I don't know how to get out, said Assa. I'm trapped.

You're not trapped. You're just a silly commoner in over her head. But we can help you.

You can't help me, said Assa. You're just two stupid princesses who don't know anything outside of your castle. You don't know what it's like to be me.

And you don't know what it's like to be us, said Dawn.

I've got this dragon's brain all around me, said Assa. It's like I'm in a forest of slime. I step one way, but the slime pulls me down into the depths. I step another way and the slime grabs me.

It's not slime, said Dawn. It's just your own brain.

Assa looked at the dragon's brain. It was as intricate and tightly woven as anything she had ever seen. It was as if someone had taken all the fibers in the world and twisted them into one dense blanket, then thrown it into the air where it trapped the entire population of living things.

Assa couldn't see beyond the dragon's brain. She couldn't even imagine anything beyond it. Not now.

The light dimmed. It didn't go completely out, but it was close enough to extinguishing itself that she had to make her visual sense more sensitive. She somehow turned up the sensitivity to light that was in her. She didn't know where the switch was to do this, but it was there, in her depths.

That's not you! said Dawn.

What are you talking about? said Assa.

The light going away, said Dusk, is the dragon dying. Have you noticed its heart is slowing down?

Assa listened for the heart beat. It was there, but faint. Yes, she said.

We feel it too, said Dawn.

How could you? asked Assa.

It's because of the birds, said Dusk. They came from the castle. They have become haters of dragons.

Well, said Assa, that may be so, but it doesn't help me. They killed the creature who I could have used to save the castle.

Such a pessimist, said Dawn.

Maybe so, said Assa. But what do I do now?

She saw that the birds had turned on the other two dragons. They had been lulled into keeping their guard down by the fact of the first dead dragon's remains. They were so intent on consuming it that they did not see the danger swirling out of the air to the attack.

They were rolling in the sand, now, covered in seagulls and crows. Their screams were difficult to listen to. Assa tried to block them out, but she had nothing to cover her senses, especially her ears. She did not even know where her ears were.

One of the other dragons managed to lift itself off the ground. It grabbed air and rose. Erratically, and slowly, but it did rise, with scores of attacking birds hanging onto it.

Assa watched it go up and over the ocean in a meandering flight. She was sure it didn't know where it was going. It just wanted to get away and thought that getting into the air would help.

But it didn't. More birds swooped onto it. They clung to it and grabbed at its wings and tore extended ragged rips into it. Before long the wings were in tatters and the dragon which had fought so hard to get airborne, fell back into the ocean. The birds fell with it, doggedly clinging to its hide. The splash was a pathetic little blip in the water. The dragon sunk out of sight within seconds. The birds that had been tormenting it dispersed and rose into the air and then came back to the island, presumably to finish off the remaining living dragon, who was thrashing about in the sand in its last throes before death.

Assa was plainly shocked. Birds and dragons fighting each other? The sky was a big place. Couldn't they all share?

Well, said Dawn, that was something to see.

It was awful, said Assa.

Not so awful as all that, said Dusk. Three more dragons gone. That can't be all bad.

Assa understood the sentiment, but didn't share it. Dragons, like all creatures, were just trying to do what came naturally. They were simply trying to survive and be themselves. Was that so bad?

I detect some commoner sentimentality, said Dawn.

I'm not, said Assa. I just think there must be a better way to run the world.

Ha! said Dusk. The world runs itself. We have nothing to do with it. All we do is live and, sometimes, let live.

Dawn and Dusk both laughed uproariously.

I'm glad you're amused, said Assa. But I'm still stuck in this dragon's brain. And let me tell you, it's no fun.

Don't worry about it, said Dawn. Everything will take care of itself.

Assa didn't know what she meant by that. The world was not going to take care of her. The world was trying to kill her.

I think, said Assa, that you are both loony. Being cooped up in that castle has made you that way.

You are so right, said Dawn and Dusk in unison. But that doesn't mean we're not right. Just you see.

Assa was mystified by their talk. When would they become real and true human beings? Was that even possible.

Her host dragon gave no more signs of life. It had completely expired. There was no life in it, but there was some movement. Little twitches along the length of its body, which meant the birds were not finished with it yet. As she endured the pecking of the birds, Assa heard the cracking of bone around her. The birds had gotten to the skull, and they were breaking in!

Snaps and crunches. Beaks grinding against bone. Light coming from the outside, streaming in through the cracks in the dragon's skull.

Assa didn't want this. She tried to move away from the sounds. She slid down into the jaw of the dragon, but there was resistance. So little flesh there now, after the birds had eaten away most of it. There was mostly only bone fragments left, and she couldn't move through them. She had to remain in the brain tissue.

But the birds were eating away at the brain. Their beaks invaded the jelly and scooped up hunks of it. Assa wanted to cry.

Boo hoo! said Dawn.

Big cry baby, said Dusk.

Assa didn't even try to answer them. They were terrible people, really. The worst. They had no sympathy for anyone except themselves. And maybe their parents. Maybe.

Have your cry, said Dawn.

Let it out, said Dusk. It'll do you good.

Assa held firm. She wasn't going to give them the satisfaction. She shrunk herself as small as she possibly could, and tried to fit into a corner of what was left of the dragon's skull. It worked, but only for a while. She was small, but not small enough. Beak points pursued her. Not on purpose, but just because she was there where the dragon brain was. The birds were going to scoop her up eventually.

Here's the question, said Dusk. Do you want to be eaten up whole, or in bits?

The beak points were everywhere, now, at least a dozen of them, each beak hungry for bits of the dragon brain. They ate pieces of it, diminishing Dawn's safe zone with each bite.

Make a decision, said Dawn. Now. You can be whole, or you can be in pieces.

It's your choice, said Dusk.

Assa had her back to the skull. There was maybe an inch or so of brain remaining between her and the beaks. If she didn't move, all the beaks were going to scoop up a piece of her each and she would be in the bellies of all these different birds. What would she be then? What could she do then?

Being in a seagull. Yuck.

A crow? Assa thought that wouldn't be so bad.

She watched the beak points for several seconds, then made her move when a black beak dipped into the brain. She moved as rapidly as possible to the beak and let it swallow her along with a piece of dragon brain.

Immediately she was in a confined space. The crow had a lot more savvy about things in its brain than the dragons did. She was buffeted and tossed around in the crow's cranium, much like the dragons were buffeted and tossed around by the winds blowing over the ocean. She didn't get much of a chance to look out and see where she was going, either. The crow seemed to know she was there and had pushed her into a corner of its skull. It was just as cozy as being in a warm bed. Assa enjoyed the sensation, but she missed the feeling of power she had with the dragons.

There was also no possibility of affecting the flight path of the crow. It did not allow her to mess around with its neurons or its connections or its synapses. She tried, extending one tendril of motion toward the clump of brain tissue enclosed in the skull, but it did no good. The crow cawed at the sky. It flapped its wings and it glided with tremendous grace and assurance in its power and strength. Already Assa admired the crow, but they were not partners in any way. The crow did not try to eject Assa out of its brain, but neither did it try to make friends with Assa. She was simply a slight annoyance. Maybe less than that.

So, said Dusk, you're coming home.

Maybe, said Assa. I don't know what this crow plans to do.

No one knows, said Dawn. But it's a good guess that it will come back to the mainland.

It just took a little trip to the island to get some dragon food, said Assa.

Something like that, said Dawn.

Listen, said Dusk, when you get here there's some things you will need to do.

Assa groaned.

Stop that! said Dusk. Listen to us. Do you want the land overrun with dragons? Once they hatch, there's not much we can do about them.

Seems to me we could get all the birds to go after them, said Assa. They took care of the dragons on the island pretty good.

Those were grown up dragons, said Dawn.

Yeah, said Assa. So?

Grown up dragons are slow and stupid, said Dawn. They're like old people, only they get old really quick.

Okay, said Assa.

The thing is, they don't hatch that way, said Dusk. When dragons come out of their eggs, they are like demons. They are fierce and smart. They'll fight anything, and they'll win. No birds would have a chance with them. If all the eggs hatch in the castle, well, you can say goodbye to any possibility of a good life.

How do you know so much about dragons? asked Assa.

We have storytellers, said Dawn. And books. Do you read books?

Assa was beyond feeling insulted by the princess twins. They liked to make it seem like Assa was a dumb commoner. If that made them feel better, she supposed it was no loss to her.

I've read a book or two in my life, said Assa.

Well, we have these books, said Dusk. In the castle. They're really really old and they tell all about dragons. And other things too.

Yes, said Dawn. Like how the land was in the olden days.

How was it? said Assa.

We'll let you read the book, said Dusk. When you save us.

That's another thing, said Assa. How come I'm the one to save everyone? I don't know anything about being a hero.

That's just it, dummy, said Dusk. Heroes don't come from royalty. The hero that saves the land is *always always* a commoner. Like you.

Except I'm not a commoner, said Assa. I'm your sister.

Except, said Dawn. You were raised a commoner. Big difference.

Assa tried to see what the difference was, but the distinction escaped her. Did blood matter, or didn't it? It seemed to depend on the situation.

I still don't know what I'm supposed to *do*, said Assa.

It's actually easier now than it was before, said Dawn. Before you had to work a dragon's brain to make it smash dragon eggs. *Now*, you can work a crows brain to make it kill dragon eggs.

I saw those eggs, said Assa. They were thick. You think a crow can smash them?

Crows smashed through dragon skulls, said Dawn.

A *lot* of them, said Assa.

Don't worry so much, said Dusk. Just enjoy the ride. You'll be at the castle soon.

You hope, said Assa.

We hope, said Dusk and Dawn together. We always have hope.

THE CROW WAS in no hurry to get anywhere. Night fell. Assa could feel it rather than see it. It took in starlight and filtered it through the network of its interior. The dark sky filled the crows skull with a feeling of solidarity and family, as though the blackness of the night was a companion, or a relative. The crow's feathers ruffled in the cool evening air. It glided over the water and caught patches of warm air that lifted it with a minimum of effort. Assa tried a couple of times to force her way up through the brain to the eyes. She wanted to see what was happening out there, but the crow kept her tamped down. Assa was confined to such a small space that she herself grew smaller and smaller, like she might disappear.

This did not alarm her. In fact, she welcomed the thought and played around with the possibility for a few moments. To disappear would not be so awful. Not at all. It might allow her to finally find some rest. And keep her from being the one who was supposed to save the land. How was she to direct the crows when the crows would not allow her the power to direct anything?

Dawn and Dusk were no help. It was as though they were playing some kind of elaborate game which had not rules. Or, at least, no rules that Assa could discern.

She knew that crows often travelled in threes. Was that why she was in a crow now? Was she part of a triplet with Dawn and Dusk? Then they must be somewhere in crows around her? Isn't that what should happen now? All this getting into and out of creatures brains, it had to have some purpose to it, didn't it?

Assa crawled up into the eyes of the crow. She wanted to see what the crow saw, but there were complications with that. The pathways were not apparent to her. She went down one route and ended up at a place she did not recognize.

Which was not strange at all, since she had never been in a crow before. The crow had its territorial instinct, that was certain. It denied Assa access to anything that would help her navigate the strange world she had been thrust into. She saw glimpses of light, a little. It made her think of starlight, dim, but definitely there, like a pinprick pattern of lights off in the distance. The far distance. The crow was black, like the night. Even its beak was black and its eyes, its legs and feet. Everything about it was black. Even the interior. Blackness all around. Assa felt as though she was a blind person groping around in a room she did not understand. Who would build a space in which there was no possibility of knowing what was going on?

You still there, commoner? Dawn's voice. Or Dusk's. Assa could hardly tell the difference anymore.

I'm still here, said Assa. Stuck in a crow. You know what we should do next?

Our Dad is in trouble now. Just like our Mom. Breathing trouble. It's getting crazy in the castle. Everyone wheezing and gasping for air. Not much time left, commoner, for you to do what needs to be done.

I still don't know what that is, said Assa.

You still don't know? Their voices in unison, now, like they wanted to join together for emphasis. How long does it take to learn something with you?

How long does it take to explain something to me? asked Assa.

We thought commoners were more tuned in with the natural world.

Why would you think that?

You grovel in the dirt. Make stuff from wood. You know. It's all about the squishy and the icky. You hunt, don't you?

The castle has hunters, too, said Assa.

But we never see that, said Dusk. Or Dawn. They melded now. The two of them. They felt like two voices in one body. Or two beings in one body. It was difficult to tell which. Assa only wanted something to tell her what to *do*.

No one can tell you what to do, said Dawn.

You can, said Assa. The king can. The queen can. All of you can. That's what you're *for* isn't it?

Dusk spoke softly in Assa's head. She picked her next words carefully, a little too carefully for Assa's taste. It was as though she was afraid of Assa. Concerned that Assa might lose it. Explode with rage? Was that it? Was that what she sensed in Dusk's words?

You have to dig into yourself, said Dusk, and then you have to dig a little further. You absorbed the world outside the castle, didn't you? The mill, the creek, all of that? You walked the seashore. You waded in the ocean. You had a garden. You planted seeds. You weeded the rows of crops. Didn't you? You spent time in the flowers. Probably laid there for hours sometimes, just letting the breeze blow over your face. You pulled water from the creek and drank it. You fished. You hunted. You did all those things. You know what to do next.

Assa had done all those things. Dawn and Dusk didn't? Is that what they were trying to tell her? The poor royals with their awful lives, so full of opulence and riches and privilege. They yearned for the terrible life, the one that Assa had lived. It was more real to them. Was that it? They lived a fantasy life and yearned for something more gritty?

Assa was tired of being in the brain of the crow. She pushed against the skull of the crow. There was some resistance, but not a great deal. The skull was thin, after all. All bird bones were thin. They had to be, or else the bird would be too heavy to fly. Her father taught her that. He showed her bird bones after the birds had died and fell on their land. Assa remembered how she had held the bones in her hand back then, how they seemed lighter than air. How could this structure hold a bird together at all? How could it connect to other bones and make a whole? It seemed impossible.

She kept the bone and put it under her pillow at night. She slept with it there for several months. It gave her dreams, or so she thought. She dreamed of flying back then, of plunging into clouds and putting miles of air between herself and the ground. She thought, back then, that dragons were imaginary. People had mentioned them to her, but she understood them to be parts of stories that were completely made up. Nothing real about them.

And yet.

Her dreams did not have all the answers, did they? Dragons lived. Their eggs littered the landscape.

Such a revelation when it came to her. Such a strange thing to suddenly realize that her world was inhabited by creatures that she had thought to be mythical. She hoped she never ran into such a revelation again. It was more disconcerting than anything she had ever encountered.

She slipped through the skull of the crow. It was not paper thin, the skull, but not much thicker. She diffused through the veins of the feathers on its head, then crawled about on the tips of the feathers, letting her essence filter though all the feathers there. Eventually, she was in each feather, letting the structure of it define her essence.

The crow seemed to understand something strange was happening. It altered its flight path so that it wove through the air. It was as though it wanted to shake the bits of Assa off of its wings. It ruffled its feathers. It shook its wings. Assa hung on.

It was like the time she pulled a fish out of the mill wheel. It had gotten caught as the wheel turned in the water and was flopping in the wheel. It was a ghastly sight. Assa watched the fish twitch and flop, trying to escape the wheel, but it was not good. The wheel had the fish in its grip and would not let go.

Assa watched it go in circles over and over again, fascinated by the sight and at the same time appalled by what she was seeing. She eventually went inside the mill wheel room and disengaged the wheel so that it stopped turning. She went back outside and climbed up on the wheel until she got to the fish. Its gills pulsed with determination, as though it could grab oxygen from the air with enough effort, but it was no good. It wasn't going to work. The fish was going to die if Assa didn't do something for it.

She grabbed its slick flopping body and gently tried to pull it away from the wheel. It wouldn't go at first, so she worked hard, risking hurting the thing until it finally squirmed out of its trap. She held it for a brief couple of seconds, feeling the strength of the muscles along its flank, the determination to live that gave it strength and standing in the world. There was so much power in that small form. Assa absorbed the lesson.

Never give up. There was always a chance, no matter how small, that determination and the will to survive would get you through.

She extended her hands and flopped the fish back into the creek. It made a great splash in the water, then held its position under the splash for maybe half a second, then darted away.

Assa remained on the wheel for some time, looking up at the sky, and feeling the strength of the air around her. A breeze flowed over her face. If also filled her ears with a sound like the buzzing of insects. It was the kind of sound that she would have wanted to expel if she had the power. But she had no power to do so, so instead she thought to let the sound enter her ears and fill her with a gentle buzzing.

She remained on the wheel for some time. It creaked slightly. It made cracking and twisting noises, as though it would collapse under the weight, even though her weight was negligible. She had saved a live and that felt good and right. It didn't matter that tomorrow she might catch that fish and kill and gut it, and have it for her dinner. That didn't matter in the least, because that was in the future. It had nothing to do with now.

In any case, she did not owe the fish anything. She did not have to spend the rest of her life saving its life. She did that once. Wasn't it enough? Assa thought that it was enough. More than enough.

Besides, if the fish was a great beast, equipped with teeth and claws, and if it was hungry, and if Assa was in close proximity to it in its fierce incarnation, it would have had no qualms about devouring Assa even if she had saved its life previously. Assa understood this. It was nature, and it was the way things were. Beings all worked to consume other beings. There could be nothing simpler in the universe and nothing more right.

Assa wondered what would happen if she leaped from the feather tips right now? Would she fall? Would she, indeed, be taken up by the wind?

Nothing of the sort, said Dusk.

Enough of this memory nonsense, said Dawn. Did you think you could simply forget your responsibilities?

What responsibilities? asked Assa.

To us. To your people. To your land.

To your castle, you mean, said Assa. All you want is for me to save your castle.

We need you to smash the eggs.

I don't know how.

You guide the birds, said Dawn. The crows. That's how.

I don't think so, said Assa.

She moved a fraction of an inch into the air around the crow. It buffeted her and caressed her, all at the same time. It was glorious to feel the wind there. She remembered the fish, how it grabbed at the air, even though the air did it no good whatsoever. She wanted that feeling, now, that impulse for hope in the face of all adversity. That fish had nothing but its will.

Assa stretched herself just a little further. She had only a tenuous grip on the tips of the crow's feathers. Nothing was going to hold her there now.

Nothing.

Don't do this, said Dawn. Or dusk. What did it matter?

Don't, Assa, don't, said the other one. Their voices melded into one.

Assa laughed at them and let herself go.

She rose from the crow, which angled away from her, as though glad to be free of her presence. Maybe it was. Assa didn't care. Her numerous bits of consciousness floated in the air like dust motes. Each one the merest hint of nothing. It was as though she had turned into a dust cloud. Could she do anything as a dust cloud? It appeared so.

She was able to angle her flock of nothings so that they added up to a slightly more significant nothing. She caught the wind and moved toward the island.

The castle awaited her.

Assa drifted in on a cool breeze. Her various modes were subtly connected, enough that she thought of herself as a cloud rather than individual bits.

She approached land and saw the shoreline, a sandy strip of tan lashed by waves. The creek that extended from it came to a small house with a mill wheel. Assa saw all this, and recognized it, but she did not feel an emotional attachment to it. It was as though she was watching a painting of some forgotten aspects of her life. It made her think that she was not part of the world any longer.

A boat was on the river. In the boat were three figures: her mother, her father, and—her. Assa. She was watching her own self.

The boat rowed up the river toward the house. She was in the boat. Assa flipped in the air. All her bits swirled around as though they had been pushed by a great hand that swooped down from the sky. Her senses scrambled and rescrambled themselves. Her vision blurred, her sense of hearing collapsed.

None of it mattered. She had a mission.

She increased her speed toward the castle. Dozens of dragons pushed smoke into the air, shrouding the castle in a black curtain. Before any of the creatures could possibly object, or even notice, all her bits slammed into the dragons, lodging in each brain.

She knew what she had to do. The dragons must smash their own eggs. It was the way things had to be.

Each of her bits crawled along the pathways of the various dragons. Each dragon was awakened from its trance. Each dragon lifted its head and belched flames. The orange mixed with the black. The fierce energy of the dragons shook the ground and rumbled the air. It was as though the whole world had made way for the dragons and Assa was guiding them.

They all converged on the egg room, still stacked high with green spheroids. Assa made them belch more smoke. They didn't want to, but they had no choice, now that Assa was in their brains. She had filled them up with the urge to destroy.

Now wasn't that something? Wasn't that power?

The vision of smashed eggs filled Assa's brain, and with it, it filled the dragon's brain. She also had another vision: scorched eggs. She saw blackened spheroids. They were ugly and crusted over. There were hints of broken bones inside, the dead baby dragons, unhatched, but still deceased. The paradox of it: death before birth. And yet, the banality of it. Just so much wet material. That's all people were, weren't they? All any creature was.

Assa marshaled her energies and directed it toward the dragons. They were her proxies. She was the puppet master. She seized their will and bent it to her own.

A terrible strength rose up from her and infused the dragons.

They flew as one entity and sat in front of the eggs, relishing what was to come next.

THERE WASN'T MUCH left of Assa after the operation had been completed. The smoke had cleared and the eggs were absent from their room. The dragons were gone from the mainland. The land was peaceful and everyone—the royals and the commoners—were contented again. Assa wasn't sure she had done the right thing. Wasn't sure anyone could even know what the right thing was, but it was done. No way to change it now. The dragons flew and flew and flew. They had their own lives.

Assa dropped out of their brains.

She caught the air as it whistled past her, but it was no use. She had no strength left. Her consciousness, fractured beyond recognition, slipped into a turmoil of twisty nothingness. She tried, feebly, to collect her disparate parts, but they would not coalesce. It was as though she had let her essence become too diffuse, too relentlessly divided. The molecules of air were bigger than her. They swallowed her up. There came a point where she could not tell where she was and where the air was. Then she knew only movement. The swift movement of wind with no intelligence, or, at least, no intelligence she could understand.

With her last wisp of awareness, she wished for her own salvation.

The palace was a labyrinthine affair. Assa had never encountered anything like it. She understood her house: straight forward and every pice of wood in its place. The roof rose to the sky, was walls held the roof up. The rooms were little things, but big enough, like the belly of a dragon, they did what they needed to do. There was fire in them, and the warmth of family. You could see from one side to the other.

Here, stumbling along close hallways, the stones scraping on her shoulders and head as she passed, she felt stifled and suffocated. The guards, one in front, leading, the other behind, trailing, were encased in mail and the metal jangled and clanged, sending sound waves to the rock walls, where they echoed with disconcerting reverberations.

At each intersection, two or three choices of halls awaited. If she had been given a piece of paper with instructions as to where she should go, she was sure she would have gotten hopelessly lost. Fortunately, the guards knew exactly where to turn and which path to take. They turned smartly at each crossing and Assa followed.

Her way was lit from above. Long tubes apparently went up to the roof of the palace, from where they let in shafts of sunlight. Did no one travel these corridors at night? It must be so. How could they find their way without light?

After walking for what seemed half an hour, but could have been longer or shorter, they stopped in front of a heavy and large wooden door. The corridor widened considerably so that the three of them stood side by side instead of in a line.

Are you ready? asked one of the guards.

What? said Assa. The Queen is here?

In the room on the other side of this door. She is waiting for you. Don't disappoint her.

How would I do that? asked Assa, suddenly desperate for more information. She suddenly realized that though she had wanted this audience, she did not know how to behave, not really. The queen held the power of life and death in her breath. One word from her, and a subject would be dispatched in an instant. No reliable stories had ever circulated indicating that the queen exercised this power, but the mere fact that she had it was enough to make Assa's knees weak. She prayed that she would behave in a manner both humble enough to please the queen and bold enough to persuade her of the truth of what Assa had to say.

The guard pushed the door. It was so heavy that he had to lean into it and exert considerable force. Assa wondered why such a door was necessary. Did the queen require such constant protection that an impenetrable door was necessary to her well-being?

As the door swung on its hinges, it opened up a long line of light along its side. The line thickened and brightened. Assa blinked. She put her hand up to her eyes. A hand, unseen by Assa, grabbed her arm and a voice came in her ear. Let me do the talking at first. The queen will tell you when she wants to hear from you. The arm urged her forward and she began walking. Her eyes began to adjust themselves to the light and she saw she was in a vast room. The ceiling was at least thirty feet above her, and they consisted mostly of large squares of glass through which sunlight entered and bathed the room in light.

It was a welcome change from the awful claustrophobic confines of the corridors she had just walked through.

A woman sat on an ornately decorated chair some distance in front of Assa. The person walking beside her was silent now and Assa simply followed her lead. Her shoes made loud reverberating clicking noises on the stone floor. The sound filled the room like spirits filling a church.

When we stop, said the person with her, you need to bow. Do you know how?

Assa nodded.

Have you practiced?

Assa shook her head.

No matter, said the woman. The queen is interested in you. She will not be too harsh with your ignorance if your bowing is less than optimal.

Less than optimal? Assa did not even consider that bowing would be an important part of this meeting. She tried to imagine herself bending at her waist, but the adrenaline coursing through her system only made her want to flee. Her mind could not hold any image: They all flitted away.

Another thing, said her companion. You do not speak to the queen until I give you the signal.

What signal? asked Assa.

I will elbow you in the ribs.

It seemed a decidedly unregal way of conducting business, but Assa had no call to contradict her escort.

Assa did notice that the woman on the chair was not looking at them as they walked. She was leaning to one side and conferring with a man. The man nodded several times and murmured something Assa could not hear.

Finally, she stopped. The echos of her footsteps rang through the room for two or three seconds, then went silent.

Now, said her companion, who put out his arm to one side, then brought it close to his belly as he folded his body and dipped his head forward. Assa tried to do the same, but was very aware that her attempt was not nearly so graceful. She kept her head down for a couple of beats, then stood straight up. Her face felt full, as though the blood had all rushed to her cheeks and nose and forehead. Dizziness threatened to topple her, but she braced herself against a fall and managed to hold herself upright.

My queen, said her walking companion, may I present Assa.

The queen looked at Assa. And what does this Assa wish from me?

Assa remembered the elbow signal and did not say a word.

Assa wishes to inform the queen of a decidedly dangerous situation affecting the royal family.

Indeed? said the queen. Pray do recount to me this dire tale.

Assa felt a strong jab in her side.

I had a dream, said Assa.

A dream? said the queen. Indeed? And why would you trouble me with your dream?

It concerned your royal highness, said Assa.

I don't believe in dreams, said the queen. They are tiresome things. Everyone has them and none of them make sense.

Assa hesitated. As she gathered her wits to say something useful, she noticed two girls, about her age, enter and sit beside the queen. They looked a little bit like Assa. She smiled at them. They smiled back.

We are getting ready to leave the castle, said the queen. We have much to do. Why have I given you audience?

Assa tried to catch the eyes of the two girls. They would not look at her. Or, rather, they looked *at* her in a way that she sensed they did not see her. She was just a commoner to them.

Your majesty, said Assa, I think that I may have had something to do with the dragons leaving the castle.

Indeed? said the queen. You are, then, our hero?

I believe so. I convinced the dragons to take their eggs away from the castle.

The queen laughed. That was you, was it?

Yes, said Assa.

The queen looked at Assa with penetrating eyes. People said she knew everything. Assa did not believe this. After all, she had come to this land without knowing exactly what she was getting into, and now she was leaving.

I expected that our savior would have the wits to destroy the eggs, said the queen.

That is what I thought would happen as well, said Assa. But instead, the dragons took them away to a far island. I made that happen.

The queen appeared to think this over.

Who brought you here?

My parents. They were worried about me. I have been telling them about the dreams for many days now. They think I may be senseless. They wanted me to see you and asked for audience. You granted it.

Well, said the queen. Not exactly. My assistants granted you audience.

Assa herd the feet of the guard next to her shuffle from side to side.

Well, said the queen. You have my attention. What would you like from me?

A ship, said Assa.

The queen laughed. A ship? Truly?

Yes, said Assa. I wish to sail on it.

And a crew, said the queen. Would you like a crew as well? Might I interested you in a fine one?

No crew, your majesty. Just a simple ship. Me and my parents would like to take a trip.

To visit a dragon nursery, no doubt, sad the queen.

Something like that, said Assa.

The queen pulled her ear lobe and tilted her head at Assa. Assa looked back at her without breaking her expression or letting herself back down in the slightest.

Very well, said the queen. You have a boat. What do I care? We're leaving this place, my daughters and I.

Assa bowed several times. Thank you, your majesty, thank you thank you.

Enough thank yous, said the queen.

The guard grabbed Assa by the shoulders and hustled her out of the room and back into the hallway.

You are most fortunate, he said.

I wanted to tell her more, said Assa.

You have nothing more to say, said the guard.

Yes, I do, said Assa. I wanted to thank her daughters.

Never mind about her daughters, said Assa. Take your trip to the dragons. Find what you need there. Then come back to the land. Will yo do that?

Assa looked at the guard. He was so big, so round. Did he really want her back?

Why should I come back here? asked Assa.

Because I'm the king, he said. And I command it.

Assa wasn't sure she cared if this man was king. But she decided it might not be a bad idea to return.

Once she had seen the dragons hatch.

Other books by Emen:
The Institute • Thieves

About the author:
Emen not like other people here, that much obvious. He is maybe more of a foreign person, okay? Come from other country where he grow from boy to man. Emen spent lots time reading books in old days, when he was in school. But not in school long! Emen have to drop out and make money. Money more important than storytelling. But now Emen use writing to make money. Wow! Is good deal. Is activity with endless possibility. Emen no live in land of his native anymore. Now live in America.

9 781949 644548